THORNYDEVILS

Other books by TW Lawless

HOMECOUNTRY

THORNYDEVILS

TW LAWLESS

Published by TW Lawless
www.twlawless.com

First published 2014

National Library of Australia
Cataloguing-in-Publication entry:
    ISBN: 978 1 925 11283 2 (pbk)
    978 1 925 11284 9 (ebk–ePub)
    978 1 925 11285 6 (ebk–mobi)

Cover design by Greg Alex-Vasey
Edited by Christine Nagel Literary Services
Designed, typeset and printed by Palmer Higgs Pty Ltd
palmerhiggs.com.au

Distributed by Palmer Higgs Books
phbooks.com.au

THE PUPPY FARM

1

Melbourne. Winter 1989

Peter was thinking of a Beatles' song as he ran along King Street; the one that had been written about Melbourne when they had toured here in 1964. *Rain.* It was the B-side to *Paperback Writer.*

The rain had just started pissing down. Peter loved Melbourne but hated its rain. It wasn't anything like the warm downpours of Townsville. It was always cold and chilling, like rain you would equate with being lost on the Yorkshire Moors, and always unexpected. Five minutes ago it was sunny. No, Melbourne's rain was more like a mother-in-law's kiss: unwanted, unnerving and unpredictable.

Now, he was running down King Street with a sodden footy magazine held over his head, as the sudden deluge pelted down. He stepped onto the pedestrian crossing as a car swept around the corner, nearly knocking him over and spraying him with water. Peter swore at the car as he righted himself, then continued running across the street, saturated and humiliated. The rain, impatient drivers and the thought of having to leave the comfort of a warm bed and a willing lover were all running through Peter's head when he reached the sanctuary of *The Truth* office's front door. He pushed it open gratefully and stepped inside.

Shazza's head was hanging in her hands like a broken limb from a tree. She didn't raise it as Peter peered over the counter, but moaned a painful greeting.

'What happened this time?' Peter said cheerfully. He wanted to bang the front door bell but he suspected that Shazza might throw her typewriter at him.

'Can't remember,' she grunted without looking up. 'Only meant to go to the club for a couple of quiet drinks. I reckon someone spiked me drink.' Shazza managed to raise her head slowly.

Poor Shazza, Peter thought. Her face was a nightshade of death, and two bloodshot eyes hung from her head like a pair of clots. Her head dropped into her hands again.

'I'm gonna give up the piss. For sure this time. Honest. I'm done with this,' she said with conviction. 'Care to join me?'

'I only get pissed on the weekend. You know that,' Peter retorted.

'And what about the rest of the time, Mister Clancy? You drink milk?'

'A nightcap every night never hurt anybody. It helps me sleep like a baby.'

'How's that? You wake up with a wet bed?' Shazza managed a hoarse laugh. 'What's the bet, I can give up the piss before you. You want to lay some money on the table?'

'I don't need to, Shazz. I am the master of my drinking habits,' Peter grinned.

'Jeez, you're deluded. Don't come crying to me when your liver has kicked the bucket and you've turned yellow.'

Peter skilfully turned the conversation towards work. 'Any messages?'

'Talking about delusions. Message from one of your colourful sources.'

'Which one?'

'How do I say this? He, or should I say, she? What was her name?'

'Have you ever thought of writing down information? In your current condition I wouldn't rely on that memory anymore.'

'Written down. Just before me memory cells packed it in,' Shazza said as she handed Peter a screwed up piece of paper. 'That's right. *Concheetah*, she called herself.'

'I haven't heard from her for a while,' Peter pondered as he slipped the note into his trouser pocket.

'So, what the hell is it? Boy or girl, or both?'

'A Les Girl.'

'One of those,' Shazza observed. 'You keep odd company.'

Peter left Shazza in her death throes and made his way to his desk, past an assortment of cubicles left and right, each containing one of an odd collection of characters who had listed their occupation as journalist. A motley, moth-eaten, maggot-ridden bunch.

One of them was Kyle, the cadet journalist. Doe-eyed, naïve and riddled with acne vulgaris. Peter enjoyed torturing Kyle. Nothing too cruel, just a few life-lessons designed to keep him in check. A kind of journalistic hazing, a tradition passed down the generations. The obligatory cigarette hung limply from Kyle's mouth, and the requisite steaming coffee sat on his desk. He looked up at Peter, admiration in his eyes. He still had a lot to learn.

'What was that thing again? The introverted pyramid?' Kyle asked.

Too early to think. 'Inverted pyramid, Kyle,' Peter muttered as he stumbled past. *Coffee. I need a coffee.*

'The coffee machine's working?' Peter asked of nobody. 'I could really do with a coffee.'

There was no reply. The air hung heavy with male odour and smoke. *This place could do with some female influence,* Peter thought, but what female in their right mind would ever want to work here? Besides, female journalists weren't all that common. Not at *The Truth*, at any rate. *Why do people become journalists, anyway? We all start out acting like war correspondents, but we eventually have to concede to being lowly paid. Then we become cynical after dealing with broken marriages, affairs with the grog and thwarted ambitions. Most of us will be dead in our fifties, if we're lucky, or we'll get a second wind writing racy thriller novels or become an old hack. Where do journos go when they die? Wherever it is, it has to have hot coffee and plenty of booze.*

Mad Dog was having a loud argument with the coffee percolator as Peter approached the kitchen.

'Anything wrong?' Peter asked hesitantly.

Mad Dog spun around and looked like he might go into a combat stance but instead he threw a cautious, wild-eyed stare at Peter. Mad Dog, as he had designated himself, was the most notable of the staff photographers. No one knew his real name. It had to be Mad Dog and nothing else. Not Dog. And certainly not Mad. Peter had once heard a vague rumour that it may have been Neville or Quentin, but only Bob knew his real name and he wasn't confessing.

Mad Dog had cut his teeth—and most probably altered his brain waves—as a war photographer in Vietnam. He had had the reputation of getting close to the action, into the core of battle. Now he was, according to the Mad Dog, confined to outing the morally rancid of society. Apparently, Mad Dog had once crawled into a Viet Cong tunnel and got a photograph of a surprised medical team operating on a wounded brother-in-arms. Peter had long wondered why Mad Dog was here and not residing in a comfortable mental health facility.

'Useless as tits on a boar pig,' Mad Dog replied as he twiddled the buttons on the machine. Peter recalled when Bob had bought it for the office, all of four, long years ago.

'The coffee's too cold,' he complained, as if on the verge of tears. Peter was ready to throw a sympathetic arm around the battle-weary photographer, when he remembered it was Mad Dog. Mad Dog had a bite. Instead, Peter had a fiddle with the machine and then thumped it with his fist. A red light flashed it into life. *A promising indicator of a successful coffee machine resuscitation.*

'That might work,' Peter suggested. 'Leave it for a half hour.'

At that, Mad Dog seemed to relax. Peter was the undesignated office coffee machine mechanic in his department, which was a heavy burden in a place full of hard-core caffeine addicts. *Why couldn't it have been Kyle?* Kyle was young enough to understand the inner workings of appliances. Coffee was to journalists like a blood transfusion to a road trauma victim. If the machine broke down completely (and he suspected it wasn't far away), God help him. Peter wouldn't be able to stem the tide of rebellion. And it would be he that would be the object of the mob violence. He would be chased up Bourke Street by a rabid, baying pack of journos.

'Can you ask Bob to buy another machine? This one's about to shit itself,' Mad Dog asked through gritted teeth as he flipped an empty cup in his hand and shoved his face closer to Peter's.

'I asked him last week. Like I did the week before and the week before that,' Peter replied defensively, feeling as if he had been pushed against a wall and now had a bright light pressed into his face.

'Ask the fat cunt harder.'

'I'll mention it to him again today.'

'You know this place runs on coffee. We have to have our coffee. We can't function without coffee.' Mad Dog was addressing the rebellious crowd at the Bastille with his political manifesto. His declaration was so loud, in fact, that some of the journos managed to look up from their work long enough to clap. One even held a clenched fist in the air. *Put it down, Kyle,* Peter thought. *You're a cadet. You have no rights.*

'See?' Mad Dog beamed as he looked around the office.

'All right, all right, don't hang me yet.'

'You need me today? Whose life are we ruining today?' Mad Dog asked gleefully.

'I'll let you know. I've got to ring a source,' Peter replied as he inched away from Mad Dog's clutches.

'When you're ready, I'm ready for action.'

Peter always wondered why a war photographer would want to hang out of trees or lie under a garbage lid to take photos of bare-breasted women or clandestine lovers. Maybe Mad Dog thought he was still at war? At war with the public.

Peter retreated into the sanctuary of his cubicle, leaving Mad Dog hovering impatiently over the coffee machine. He placed his tie-dyed, knotted Indian sling bag on top of a mountain of manila folders. His battered briefcase, a hangover from university, had managed to fall apart as he was walking along King Street one morning. Its contents of papers and photographs of the latest page three girls had spewed across the street. *Embarrassing.* The sling bag was a quick replacement but it had subjected him to office ribbing like, *going hippie?* and the like. He had developed a fondness for the bag. It appealed to his sense of the bohemian.

Peter had the reputation of having the messiest desk in the office, followed closely by Reg Whitlock. Reg's desk lurked somewhere under bales of racing guides, tied up with tatty string, photographs of horses and jockeys and betting chits. He lived his passion. As *The Truth's* racing columnist, Reg was usually at the tracks getting the certs, running tight with the racing fraternity and the lowlifes; you didn't see him much. Not much time to tidy up his desk. When Reg was around, he always liked to inform you his racing column was the moneymaker for *The Truth. Shake your moneymaker, Reg.*

It was a close contest, but Peter's desk had been judged and awarded the Brown Turd by Bob over Reg's. Third year in a row. Piles of tumbling folders and press releases, a collection of takeaway coffee cups that Peter had stacked into a pyramid at one side of the desk. It was going to rival Giza, one of his colleagues once teased. Even the drawers were jammed with files. Yet he could still locate any file he wanted. It was a gift. Like finding a clean handkerchief at a rubbish dump. In the detritus somewhere was his beloved word processor, his collection of blue biros and paper clips. A journalist's rule: you can't do your job without paperclips or pens. The other rule: no cartoon strips, personal pictures or motivational sayings stuck on the cubicle wall. How would you ever be taken seriously as a Seeker of Truth if you did that?

He was always going to clean his desk. *Promise.* It had become something like an alcoholic declaring they were never going to drink again. And there were always the excuses that Peter trotted out: *I'm too busy. I'm hung over. I'm expecting a phone call. I need a coffee. I'm expecting a headache* et cetera, to the point that even Shazza had offered to clean the shit pile, as she had termed it, but Peter had balked when she had wanted a bottle of Jim Beam out of it. But there was work to be done.

He sat down and gently shifted a pile of papers to one side, placing the cup in a familiar area of the desk, already marked by numerous coffee cup circles. Then he realised he didn't have a cup of coffee. *I really need a cup of coffee.* He looked lovingly at the coffee machine. Mad Dog was still hovering. Could he wait until Mad Dog had made his?

Concheetah. She was a great source of information about what was happening on the glittering streets of St Kilda—Melbourne's version of Soho—where high-heeled drag queens rubbed shoulders with Mohawked punks, elderly ladies with their shopping jeeps, and rat-infested druggies. Concheetah and Peter had had a relationship, dating back to the early 1980s. In those days, drag queens could be arrested for wearing women's wigs and underwear on the streets. Peter had campaigned through articles in *The Truth* for the repeal of such draconian laws. When the laws were changed, Peter had become something of a folk hero to the drag queen community. Free admission to the Vegas showgirl-style extravaganzas at the Duke of Cambridge, the Ritz Hotel in Fitzroy and Bojangles were some of the perks of notoriety that Peter took up, on occasion. The shows were packed every night with voyeuristic patrons. At the centre of the shows was the lusty, sultry Concheetah doing her imitations of Ethel Merman and Judy Garland, or Ava Gardner in death-defying stilettos. Peter hadn't taken up any of the frequent invites to the backstage parties. Seeing drag queens naked was his greatest fear.

Peter unscrewed the paper Shazza had given him and read the message: *Meet me at the Duke of Cambridge in thirty minutes. Very important information. Very, very important information. Love C.* What a drama queen, Peter thought as he threw the note in the wastebasket. He'd go. But not before he had had his coffee. He tossed a hopeful glance at the coffee machine again. Mad Dog was gone. Peter wondered whether he should take the crazy photographer to his rendezvous, but decided against it. Concheetah's recent tattle-tales had been trivial gossip, and a little bit of Mad Dog went a long way. He'd go alone. But not before he had had his coffee.

Peter's trusty car, a metallic red hardtop 1975 V8 Triumph Stag (nicknamed the *Shag* by Peter when it operated at full capacity, or the *Snag* when it wasn't, which was often), was parked in a laneway a block away from the office. Peter had won the Shag three years earlier in a bet with a Carlton supporter friend. The friend hadn't seemed too upset to be handing over the car. In fact, he had looked relieved. Peter had felt like James Bond when the Stag had been delivered to him. That was until it had roared to a shuddering stop in busy traffic on Park Drive five days later. Since then, there had been numerous visits to *Tony Andretti's Mechanics* on Johnston Street for another *Fix It Again, Tony* plea. Peter always wondered how much longer his lowly salary could support the Snag. After all, it was eating into his expansive drinking budget.

But there were endearing factors to the old beast, he thought fondly as he opened the door, jumped in and pushed the keys into the ignition. It was a place to deposit old newspapers, coffee cups and takeaway packaging. He looked at the passenger side footwell but couldn't see the floor for litter. Peter usually only cleaned out the car when he had a date. *Had it been that long?* Peter sighed as he cast a critical eye over the burgeoning mound of rubbish. The Stag was a home away from home. On occasion, Peter slept in the car, usually when he had had too much to drink or he was casing a place for a story, or the time when he locked himself out of his flat. The Stag was a haven, a sanctuary from the pressures of the office, the editor, the client, the deadline and *what the hell is that smell? Is there is a small decomposing animal in this car? Ha, ha, I've found Jimmy Hoffa!* Peter picked carefully through the litter until he found the rotting half-hamburger. *Eaten when? Can't bloody remember.* Peter wrapped a newspaper around the slimy mess and opened the driver's window to throw it into a nearby bin.

He was going to clean the car for certain. He surveyed the mess again. *Maybe if I ask Shazza nicely. Maybe she'll do it for a bottle of vodka.* Peter flicked over the ignition. The car, as expected, didn't explode lustily into life with a throaty roar like an Aston Martin. It was more a series of syncopated farts and groans that transmuted into that Triumph Stag racing roar. *Success.* Peter breathed a sigh of relief as he slipped the gear stick into first. *Situation stable, not as shit as expected,* Peter thought as he pressed down the accelerator.

2

Concheetah was rehearsing a show tune with her band, the Erotics, and a backing troupe comprised of three drag queens when Peter and his first VB beer of the day entered the darkened expanse of the empty Velour Lounge. Peter grabbed a table and chair near the stage. This was no mime-to-a-tune show like the other drag clubs—this was the real deal. The whole ensemble was dressed in mufti today, as you would expect, but on show night they would be attired in their full regalia: the band in silver lederhosen and oiled bare chests and the backing girls in sequins with ample cleavage and two-storey wigs. It was not only the best drag revue in Melbourne, it was the best show in Melbourne. Rehearsal or not, Concheetah, as always, was in full ensemble, and, as always, giving her best performance. She was old Hollywood. A Star. Dietrich. Garland. Gardner. *I'm ready for my close-up, Mister DeMille.*

Concheetah blew Peter a kiss as she wrapped up the song and handed the microphone to her personal assistant and live-in lover, Ted, affectionately known as Tapping Ted. Ted was an ex-thespian who had reached the dizzy heights of compering a children's show in the early 1970s called *Captain Capers,* dressed as a sea captain. He and Concheetah lived together in a high-rise flat nearby, but Concheetah was known to have had a string of lovers during their time together, some famous, some infamous, some gay, some straight. *Poor suffering Ted.* He overdosed every so often, after his inflamed jealousy couldn't tolerate any more. Once he was revived, Concheetah would rush to his bedside full of guilt and then came the romantic reconciliation.

Of course, Concheetah still slept around, but she tried to be more discreet. It was a truly beautiful Hollywood love story: Bogie and Bacall, Burton and Taylor.

Peter smiled as Concheetah sashayed across the ballroom floor towards him, wriggling her hips, full lips in a pout, followed obediently by the tentative, Tapping Ted dressed in tight shorts and singlet. Tapping? Tapping because he always wore conspicuous, tap-dancing shoes in the club. Was Ted going to rip up the stage as a mincing Irish dancer or maybe perform a Gene Kelly routine or the Swan Lake ballet in taps? It was terrible to imagine. Peter bit his lip at that thought, hoping he wouldn't burst into howls of laughter. He had noted after coming to several shows, that Ted usually stood at the side of the stage ready with a drink of champagne and an encouraging word and a dry towel to mop Her Highness's face. And he always cried during the show's finale, Abba's *Dancing Queen. Poor Tapping Ted.*

And then there was the Diva Concheetah, herself. Peter knew the truth even if it hadn't come from the rouged lips of Her Highness: In another incarnation, Concheetah was once Colin, a humble carpenter from country New South Wales. Apparently he had even fathered children. Maybe life looked too short to play it straight.

'Darling, darling Peter,' Concheetah breathed with a wild flourish of arms. Peter stood politely, as he would have done for any lady, to be smothered in a tight embrace and French perfume. Yes, she did look like Ava Gardner but the real Ava hadn't been nearly six feet tall with large masculine hands and a prominent Adam's apple. Concheetah finished off any remnant of Peter's restraint by planting a kiss on each of his cheeks. As he fell back, blushing, into his chair, and Concheetah eased herself into hers, a tight-lipped Ted lit a cigarette, attached it to a long-stemmed holder and handed it reverently to his mistress. Peter felt his face still burning. Was he ever going to stop feeling embarrassed in front of the diva? You could take the boy out of outback Queensland but you couldn't take the Queensland out of the boy. He took a drink while Concheetah took a deep puff of her cigarette.

'Teddles,' Concheetah ordered without looking at her companion, 'Champagne. Glasses. Presto.'

Ted trotted and tapped across the ballroom, arms flapping as if his life depended on it, towards the direction of the bar.

'Your voice sounds croaky,' Peter remarked bravely. 'Straining the vocal cords?'

'Too many frogs in my throat,' Concheetah winked, 'not enough princes.' She broke into a gale of laughter and took hold of Peter's hand. *Why did I ask? Why did I bloody ask*, he thought.

'And how is my Prince Peter?' Concheetah removed her hand from Peter's to adjust the cigarette.

'I'm fine,' he replied vaguely. 'Still chasing the dogs. Still searching for the answers.'

'And you're looking so ruggedly handsome,' she cooed back, fluttering her false eyelashes in his direction. 'Like Dennis Quaid. Definitely, darling. That man could park his boots under my bed anytime.' Concheetah took several deep draughts from her cigarette holder.

'Is that a compliment?' Peter grinned as he drained the remainder of his beer. 'I get mistaken for Rob Lowe constantly.'

'Rob Lowe!' she barked loud enough to distract Ted, who was gathering up the glasses and champagne onto a tray at the bar.

'He definitely looks too faggy, my dear.' She smiled quickly at Peter than turned to the direction of the bar. 'What are you doing over there, Teddles?' Concheetah demanded in a masculine voice. 'Making the fucking stuff?'

'So sorry, my dear,' Ted answered defensively, 'I'm having trouble popping the cork.'

'I know about *that*. Okay. Just bring the bloody thing here,' she commanded . 'You're not butch enough to pop a cork.'

'Yes, dear,' Ted blustered as he walked gingerly towards them bearing the refreshments, his tap shoes making gentle clicks on the floor. Concheetah leaned in closer to Peter.

'He was once my ageing Svengali and I was his Trilby. We were the couple. Now look at us. I'm the star and he's the decrepit old poof. What am I going to do with him? He hasn't popped my cork for ages, darling.' Concheetah looked longingly at Peter who was doing his best not to provide any non-verbal clues that he was in agreement. He tried to fix his stare beyond her Hollywood Highness, to the bandstand where the band members were packing up their instruments or flirting with each other. Concheetah removed her cigarette from the holder and stubbed it out. Ted slapped the drinks tray down on the table, nearly dislodging the glasses and the champagne bottle. His tapping shoes crashed down in unison, as if he were standing to attention, and making his arrival more dramatic.

'It looks like I'm no longer required,' Ted said angrily, glaring at Peter. 'I'll be rehearsing my piece for the show.' He added a flick of his head, and marched off towards the bandstand, shoes machine-gunning across the floor.

Concheetah pushed the tray towards Peter.

'You do the honours, Peter dear,' she cooed, turning towards Ted so he could hear. 'It looks like Teddles thinks it beneath him to entertain our friends.' Ted's only response was to arch his neck and toss his head, accompanied by a double click of his shoes.

'That silly old man. He'll be the death of me. I need a drink,' Concheetah moaned as she turned back to Peter. Peter grasped the champagne bottle by its neck, placed it between his legs, ripped off the wrapper and started grappling with the cork. It took several attempts before it popped, gushing a fountain of champagne over his jacket.

'Bloody hell,' he complained, as he tipped the overflow into a glass for Concheetah first, and then for himself. 'My best suit,' he grumbled. He grabbed a handkerchief from his pocket. 'Cheers,' he lifted his glass and took a sip.

Concheetah reciprocated, draining her glass in one motion. 'It looks like you sleep in that suit, darling. It's positively organic,' she sniffed as she pushed her empty glass in Peter's direction.

'What else can a poor journalist wear? It would eat into my drinking budget.' Peter blushed as he poured Her Highness a refill and continued to sip the contents of his glass.

'I'm sure I could find a suitable replacement that's affordable and definitely more stylish. You need a woman's input, my dear,' she winked, squeezing Peter's hand once more. 'I'd love to take care of that wardrobe of yours. You need a total makeover.'

Peter's eyes were diverted to Ted, now wearing a glittering bowler hat. He was taking his position on stage and instructing a guitarist who was holding an acoustic guitar. His gaze then drifted back to Concheetah, who was staring into his face. 'I'll think about it,' he mumbled, pulling his hand away slowly. He reached into his jacket pocket to retrieve a pen and notepad. *Yes. Time for a change of subject. Quickly.* He pushed away his glass even though it was only half empty. 'You said in your message that you had important information for me?' He lowered his voice in order to sound more professional.

Concheetah took a sip from her glass. 'We've been invaded by the police, Peter.'

'Why are they hassling you? Is it is the drag show?'

'No, of course not. Those days are gone. Off duty cops come here all the time.' She leaned in again. 'I know of some who are gay and others who like to cross dress,' she laughed. 'Can you imagine it? An officer flatfoot dressed in a lovely sequinned gown. *You're under arrest. I'm going to handcuff you.*' Concheetah flapped her hand at Peter.

He nodded. 'Hard to imagine. I thought only pollies liked doing that,' he commented vaguely, wondering where the conversation was headed. He knew the champagne was already headed to his brain. He wondered for a moment whether the champagne might be going to Concheetah's head as well. It was mother's milk to her. She could handle this stuff. VB, on the other hand, was harmless compared to this.

Concheetah poured herself another glass and continued. 'They came in here the other night. Two detectives from St Kilda. The senior one had nice wavy hair, a moustache and blue eyes. Looked a bit like Tom Selleck, if you ask me. Can't remember the other one. You can always pick a pig. Big macho cocks in ill-fitting, cheap suits. They sat and watched the show with their guests.'

Peter could hear the guitarist playing on the stage. It sounded like a dramatic Spanish Flamenco tune right up until it was interrupted by the sound of soft tapping. Ted was rehearsing his *piece de annoyance.*

'Not too loud, Teddles,' Concheetah roared, 'I have an important meeting going on here.'

The guitar and the tapping softened.

'That man,' she whispered, 'He tells me after he woke up from his last overdose that he feels like a neglected artist. *You get all the attention,* he says. *I was once a star of television.* He's so deluded. Anyhow, I suppose Ted wants his time in the spotlight.' Concheetah shook her head and rolled her eyes in one motion then threw the reminder of her champagne down her throat. 'It's going to look tragic. Hopefully the audience will toss rotten tomatoes at him. Why did I agree? Why?'

'You said two detectives came in here the other night?' Peter asked, returning to the subject.

'And guests,' she added curtly. 'Didn't you want to know who they were? Isn't it your job to ask the questions?'

'Okay. Who?'

'That Italian guy you did the story on recently.' Concheetah crossed her legs in Peter's direction and whispered, 'I recognised him from the paper. You know. He was caught in a pool with a starlet from that soap show. By the look of the photos he was giving her swimming lessons: breaststroke.'

'Him,' Peter laughed. 'Tony Donarto.'

'All of them were very chummy.'

'He's Deputy Mayor of Melbourne and a successful businessman. Though I think he will soon be the former Deputy Mayor of Melbourne. I'm sure he mixes in wide circles.'

'Aren't you going to ask me what happened next?'

'Okay. What happened?' Peter sighed. He was losing interest.

'I went over to greet them in my usual hostess style. You know. Be friendly and get them drinking more,' she began slowly, tears welling in her eyes. 'As I was standing there saying my spiel that slime Donarto…' She stopped to wipe the tears away with a tissue pulled from inside her bra.

'He hit you?' Peter attempted to guess.

'No,' Concheetah cried. 'He grabbed my crotch! The bastard! I wanted to hit him but with two cops there…'

'Did he hurt you?' Peter's eyes widened.

'No. He couldn't grab hold,' she murmured. 'I'm strapped into the cockpit, darling.'

'Yes. Of course.' Peter blushed. 'I should have known. What happened then?'

'I pulled away. I think I said something like you *wouldn't be able to handle it.*

'And? Any other developments? He'd tried having sex with you?'

Concheetah shook her head.

Peter nodded, closed his notebook and put his pen on the table. Interview terminated.

'Did you find my tale of woe boring, my dear?' Concheetah sounded miffed. She poured another glass of champagne. In the background Ted was still tapping as the guitar droned away.

'Look, Concheetah,' Peter sighed, 'I don't know if I can make a story out of this. This is St Kilda. I'm sure patrons attempt this all the time.'

'But these are men of authority,' she said tearfully. 'I thought you could help me. This is police harassment, Peter.'

'I want to help you, but the cops didn't do it.' He found himself patting her shoulder sympathetically. 'There isn't enough to work on at this stage.'

'The cop bastards were laughing. I was humiliated,' she paused. 'Oh dear. I have to put this beautiful body of mine on the line so you'll have your scoop. *Rape me please, Mister Donarto.* Fuck you, Peter Clancy.'

Concheetah flicked a finger at Peter, stood up and started to drift towards the stage. Peter followed, feeling uncomfortable that he had hurt the diva. Ted was holding a walking stick with one hand, waving the other in the air and dancing around it as if it was a maypole, like a possessed Morris dancer. The guitarist strummed a series of chords in a flurry of unbridled passion. The guitar stopped and Ted fell dramatically to the ground like Torvill minus Dean. It was an operatic tragedy without the opera.

'Come on, Concheetah,' Peter retorted defensively above the music. 'My editor won't even touch it.' Ted lay motionless. Peter looked him over with a small element of concern, hoping the old dear hadn't carked it on stage. Then again, that could be turned into a story.

'Use your creative licence. Your rag is renowned for that.'

'It's not enough. If they'd taken it…'

'When I'm lying on a hospital trolley at the Alfred, raped beyond recognition, I'll remember that.' Concheetah stood at the stage with arms akimbo, watching Ted rise slowly to his feet. *Interview terminated.* Peter decided it was an appropriate moment to exit this melodrama. He slowly tiptoed towards the door just as an argument erupted between Concheetah and Ted. He stopped at the doorway to watch the unfolding fracas.

'Ted, all I said was it's not your best. It needs a lot of work,' she screeched.

'You give me no praise,' Ted shrieked back, throwing his glittering hat like a Frisbee. It curved high into the air and fell heavily onto a table, sending a bottle crashing to the floor. If Ted could do that every night, Peter thought, then maybe he'd have something.

'You treat me like I'm a common whore. You'd be nothing without me. I should never have left Captain Capers to further your career.' The walking stick clattered to the stage and Ted stormed off, his tap shoes sounding like small explosions with every step.

'Ted, come back,' Concheetah pleaded. 'Stop being so bloody sensitive.'

Poor Ted, Peter thought, poor Concheetah. *It looks like another overdose waiting in the wings.* A modern day Romeo and Juliet. Concheetah turned and glared at Peter.

'Got your story now? Famous drag queen in lover's tiff. Lover threatens suicide.'

Peter thought it over back in the Shag. It was tempting to use the argument as a story. He should have taken Mad Dog. Deadline was tomorrow and still he had no story. Well, there was that lead he had been given about the Collingwood player and a politician's wife. That was sinking low. He did have some ethics. *Never betray your footy team.* That was like betraying your family. He was glad Bob understood, especially since Bob sat on the Collingwood committee.

When Peter returned a little before eleven o'clock, Shazza was not at her desk and the other journalists were out. Maybe she had crawled off to some darkened corner to die like a poisoned dingo. The others were probably trawling through Melbourne's dirty knickers to find that titillating story that *The Truth* was renowned for. Reg Whitlock would probably be at Moonee Valley today. The rest of them would be scouring the pubs, clubs, brothels and gutters, mostly based on titbits of information supplied to them by Joe and Joan Public. In Peter's experience, that information was usually unreliable and largely distorted by whatever mental illness Joe or Joan had been most recently diagnosed with.

Peter rarely dealt with the great unwashed these days: he had his own sources, or *puppies,* as he liked to call them. He had painstakingly built up his puppy farm over the years. When he first met them, some of them smelt and only a few were housetrained, but they were his puppies. When you had reached the top of your game you had your own sources, all carefully cultivated, manicured, fed and watered, and lovingly paid for out of his expense account. Listed as postage and sundries on the company accounts. No more said.

Over the years, puppies had come and gone. Where once he had had a virtual lost dog shelter full of them, over recent years, it had reduced to a mere handful as they had been progressively murdered, found a conscience or retired. Or began dogging to more lucrative media outlets. At the peak, Peter had a puppy at Russell Street police headquarters, another at Parliament House and a third who was a madam at a prominent St Kilda brothel. *Kitty.* Kitty had been a great source until she had discovered religion and taken up a missionary position somewhere in Africa. *And then there's the frigging commercial television stations!* They paid far more than Peter could ever afford. TV had cornered the market and made sleaze stories ever harder to get for the paper. Headlines like *S&M Dungeon Discovered at Celebrity Singer's House* or *Mass Orgy Weekend Planned in Boy's Boarding School* were drying up. *The Truth* was peddling more petty suburban tattletales, neighbourhood disputes and alien abductions these days, although why they always happened to folk in rural Healesville instead of toffy Toorak remained a mystery. The puppies were finding greener pastures to frolic in.

Peter fell into his chair and mustered all his energies towards generating a lead story. The argument between Concheetah and Tapping Ted would have made a great front cover story, something *The Truth* readers expected: *Celebrity Drag Queen and Boyfriend in Violent Confrontation.* Pity he hadn't taken Mad Dog to capture the action. Concheetah would never speak to him again but that's journalism: headlines before emotions. Concheetah was becoming an unreliable puppy anyway. It would be no loss. He would just have to avoid that end of town for a while, in case he got attacked by a stiletto or a flying handbag. *Then again.*

The deadline was the event that all journalists lived by and were controlled by. They didn't live from day to day—*not tonight, darl, I'm having a deadline*—they lived from deadline to deadline, and each one of them had his or her own way of dealing with the impending event. Some faced it down like an enemy assault, while others tried to distract themselves with idle chatter with colleagues, or cups of coffee and chain smoking. Like death and taxes, a deadline was a certainty. There was no escaping it.

How did Peter Clancy deal with a deadline? Face it down, meet it head on, but only after having another cup of strong coffee, shuffling through files, talking to colleagues, having another cup of coffee and listening to Bob yelling from his office: *You'd better pull your finger out, Clancy!* It always worked. That's what great editors were. Part martinets, part psychologists. Forget girlfriends, best friends, parents, lovers; the greatest relationship a journo would have ever have would be with a great editor. Robert Damien Xavier Connolly was such an editor.

Peter was dealing with those thoughts and just mapping out his story on the word processor when the door of Bob's office flew open and a familiar rasping bellow blasted out of it like a sand blasting machine scouring rusted metal.

'Peter!' Bob stood in the doorway, or rather blocked it with his ample girth: 'Get your arse in here.'

'What the?' Peter retorted. 'I'm on a deadline. I'm working my arse off here.'

'This won't take long.'

Peter stood up and noticed that Bob was wearing a tie. Bob wearing a tie only meant one thing: he had had a meeting with the owner of the paper. *The office rumours were true.* He was walking slowly towards Bob's office when a chill suddenly came over him. *The wind of change.*

He should have been filled with trepidation when he entered Bob's office but he and Bob had a good relationship. They had never had a cross word—strong differences of opinion occasionally, but never a full-on argument. They had a matey banter with each other that had developed out of mutual respect. It was a marriage made in journalistic heaven.

Bob had a cigarette in his mouth and another lit in an overflowing ashtray when Peter entered the smoky office. He squashed into his chair, a ream of documents on the desk in front of him. He loosened his tie but Peter still felt nervous. The Owner was a faceless man who seemed to reside on another planet. You never saw him but his presence was always at the paper. He only thought of the circulation figures, the advertising, not the stories or the people who wrote them. Peter had noted that Bob had been to more meetings of late than normal. From office rumour, he knew that circulation and advertising had dropped off.

'You look nervous,' Bob observed as he watched Peter shuffling his feet.

'You've been to another Owner's meeting. Should we be worried?' Peter smiled weakly.

'Why don't you take a seat,' Bob replied. 'You're making me as nervous as a nun in a brothel.'

Peter eased himself into a rickety chair and sat with his arms folded across his chest.

'Will you relax?' Bob guffawed, grabbing a Jameson's whiskey bottle from a desk drawer and two glasses. He poured out the whiskey until it nearly reached the brim of the glasses and handed one to Peter.

'*Slainte*,' Bob held up his glass and threw back most of the whiskey. Soon after which his bloated face turned a deep crimson.

Peter unfolded his arms. '*Slainte.*' He followed suit, although he raised his glass carefully and took a slow sip. *Champagne and whiskey.* He didn't want to be too hammered before he hit the Tote after work and became reacquainted with his bed companion.

'It's cause for a celebration, mate.' Bob smiled as he polished off the contents of the glass. He poured himself a refill then waved the bottle over Peter's glass. Peter covered the glass with his hand.

'But the Owner?' he mumbled. 'Aren't we in the shit at the moment?'

'Not really. Business has been a little slow lately,' Bob explained. 'The paper just needs revamping.'

'So we're not shutting down?'

'Where did you get that idea from?' Bob laughed. '*The Truth* will never close its doors while I'm the editor.'

'That's good.' Peter relaxed into his chair and took another drink. 'I couldn't envisage working for another paper. Also, nowhere else would have me.'

'You're a big part of the revamp.'

'Come again?' Peter leaned forward.

'Columnist Peter Clancy, Crime Investigator: A Finger on the Pulse of the Crime Capital of Australia. How's that sound? It could be called *The Pulse.*'

'You're joking, aren't you?' Peter sputtered just as he was pouring the remnants of the Jameson's from the glass down his throat. It splashed onto his shirt. He made no attempt to clean it up.

'The public wants more substance in their papers. They're getting sick of looking at page three girls and reading about local celebrities who can't control their sexual desires.'

'I thought we were doing all right with tits and genitals. It's been our winning formula for years.' He grabbed the bottle off the desk and poured himself another drink.

'Our circulation has been dropping over the years, as you know,' Bob rejoined. 'These days, people want to know why's there so much crime in Melbourne: the Hoddle Street massacre, the Russell Street bombing, Walsh Street. They're scared. People think that the great city of Melbourne has been taken over by crims and psychopaths. They want a voice with reason. Someone with his feet on the ground, not some toff from *The Age* who knows the police minister and nothing else. They need someone who can make sense of it all. Someone who will keep them informed and get them through this. I'm giving them Peter Clancy. The Pulse.' He raised his hands and clapped.

'I'm not a body counter,' Peter retorted. 'I did Madgies Court when I was a cub reporter in Brisbane. I hated it. Listening to the scum of the earth and pontificating magistrates who thought they were High Court judges just wasn't my cup of tea. I don't want to hang around courts and police stations.' He hesitated. 'By the look on your face I don't have a choice, do I?'

'Of course you don't.'

'Apart from that, how will I get the info? Will someone send it to me? I know for sure who's fucking who but not who's killing who. I'm not sure about crime.'

'You were my first choice.' Bob took a last puff on his cigarette before stubbing it out and then lighting another. 'Especially after what happened to you up at Clarkes Flat.'

'What's in it for me?' Peter asked. He was losing momentum. 'I might do it on certain conditions.'

'How's five thousand words weekly and a five per cent pay increase sound?'

'Two thousand words and a ten per cent increase sounds better. I could buy a new car.' Peter smiled.

'Done. Everyone's a winner.' Bob shuffled papers. 'You have those great sources of yours that you can utilise. The puppies, as you call them.'

'A few of them are in the cemetery, but I still have a handful of good ones.' He could feel himself lying. In reality, he only had a handful of unreliable sources and after tomorrow's edition he would definitely be able to take Concheetah off that list. Peter finished off the whiskey and resisted the urge to pour himself another. *Maybe a splash more.*

'You know informers in the police force?' Bob asked.

'Yeah. Sure. An inspector at St Kilda,' Peter lied. The reality was he knew a constable who did traffic.

'Good,' Bob replied. 'What about at Parliament House?'

'I know someone in the thick of it.' He once knew a girl who worked in the parliamentary canteen. Should he tell Bob the truth? The offer was simply too good to pass on and, besides, he was only stretching the facts a little. He knew he'd find the sources. He'd have to.

'You'll need one of these,' Bob reached into a drawer and retrieved a box. He handed it to Peter.

'What's this?'

'A scanner,' Bob replied, shaking his head. 'You can listen into the police channels.'

'I've never used one.' Peter took the scanner out of the box, examined it briefly then returned it to its container.

'It's essential if you want to know what the coppers are up to. You'll be able to be one of the first on the scene. Keep it with you at all times.'

'I'll put it on my utility belt,' Peter joked.

Bob ignored the comment. 'I'm putting a lot of faith in you and this project, Peter, so don't you let me down.'

'I won't. You have my word on that.' Peter finished off the whiskey and pushed the glass away. *Enough.*

'I have one big request, though,' Bob added as Peter stood to leave.

'What's that?'

'Two words. Stafford Ellison. You have to get rid of those mangy, stinking suits. You can't wear them if you're going to write a column. You have status now. Put it on the newspaper's account.'

'That's the second time I've heard that today,' he replied sadly. 'And I thought I looked good in this.'

'A derro might, but not a professional journalist. I want you in a new suit, as soon as you come back from up north. You can start the column then.'

'Shit, I almost forgot!' Peter darted forward in the chair. 'When was that again?'

'It's tomorrow,' Bob shook his head. 'You've done yourself more damage than I thought. How could you forget you're giving evidence in the Hillard trial? And you'll be writing a story about it. Not under your name. It'll be The Pulse's first outing. All right?'

'Why the hell do I have to go up there again? I wish I'd never got involved.' He hung his head in his hands. 'I hate it up there. Frigging Brownsville! Can you at least put me up in a hotel near the sea?'

'It's all arranged. Consider it like a holiday. You'll be able to catch up with old friends, eat off the land, lynch people, the usual thing. Or maybe, this time, they'll lynch you,' Bob laughed. Peter could still hear him laughing when he returned to his desk and the dreaded deadline.

3

Peter was feeling pretty chipper by the time he entered the welcoming doors of the Tote at five-thirty. The smoky interior, the smell of stale beer, the rumbling conversations of the patrons and the muffled rock music were a loving hug to him. He pulled out a stool at his favourite end of the bar and perched himself on it. The story was written; he had a new, better paying, infinitely more challenging job. He was a pig in shit. But what about the downside? Sources had to be worked on. With a bigger expense account he could get better leads. He would have to get used to seeing dead bodies again. The last one was in Clarkes Flat. Peter shuddered as the image of her lying dead on the bed became stronger, only to be jolted back into reality by Irmgard appearing out of the smoky mist like a Valkyrie.

'How are you? I was starting to miss you,' she remarked from the other side of the bar, pouring a VB from the tap and handing it to Peter. He had become so accustomed to her thick, German accent that it rarely posed a challenge for him these days.

'I've been waiting all day to see you. You're a vision.' He winked and took a sip of his beer. Irmgard had come from Munich and was here on a backpacking holiday of Australia. She had been working at the Tote as a barmaid for three weeks and had been fucking Peter for about one. Irmgard said that she loved Aussie men. *The best in the world.* She loved their earthiness and sense of humour. She would know. She had confessed to Peter one night that she'd slept with about twenty Aussie men, as part of her research when travelling around the country. Irmgard thought he was the best lover she had had thus far in Australia. He had affectionately nicknamed her Boom-Boom in response.

'When do you finish?' Peter asked.

'Nine. Do you think you can hang around until then? I want you at full strength.'

'Of course. For you, I'll be firing on all eight cylinders.' He was beaming with excitement. Irmgard smiled and moved away to serve another customer. She had been staying at his place every night and he had been getting very little sleep. He was exhilarated but utterly exhausted and running on two cylinders. He could feel aching muscles where he thought muscles didn't exist. Irmgard was a hungry German-Amazonian beast. Was there a pill for utter exhaustion? Ginseng wasn't working. He might have taken Boom-Boom out on a date except that he had baulked at cleaning out the Shag.

Besides, Boom-Boom made a pleasant change after two months of celibacy. He had finally broken off with his on-and-off girlfriend, Suzi Night, once again. She was the leather-clad, mercurial vocalist of Hangman's Noose. She had a voice that could make you cry in one song and pierce your eardrums in another. The band had a regular spot on Wednesday and Saturday night at the Tote, but they were currently touring Australia as support act for a major Australian group. Suzi and Peter had met about a year ago, a few days after Michelle had left, but they had broken up three times during that period. Usually it was about the same issue. Suzi was going to be a big, big rock star and she didn't have time for love. Hangman's Noose was going to conquer the world. Peter, well, he couldn't commit to buying a newspaper. This time it was final.

Peter watched Irmgard move around the bar. *What a body*, he thought, *and she'll be in my bed tonight. That's if she allows us to get past the couch or the bathroom.* A warm gust of lust coursed through his body. He took a final drink and was about to call for Irmgard, when he felt a sharp thump in his back. Peter stiffened to counter the impending onslaught. Who had he upset this time? A familiar voice made him relax and turn in his chair.

'Slugger. What do you want?' Peter sighed and rolled his eyes. Slugger Douglas was standing behind him, shuffling and nervously jabbing short punches at an imaginary boxing bag. Slugger had never really left the boxing ring. In fact, twenty years earlier he had left a large part of his frontal lobe on the ropes at Festival Hall when he had been knocked out cold by the American Jimmy Malone. Slugger hadn't been expected to live. He lay in a coma for six months and Jimmy Malone was so distraught thinking that he'd killed Slugger, that he had become a pastor in his hometown of Chicago. When Slugger had awoken from his coma, Jimmy declared it a miracle. Miracle or not, it probably would have been better if Slugger hadn't lived. In his heyday, Slugger had been rated the best Australian boxer never to win a world title.

He now survived on a disability pension, lived in the public housing high-rise apartments nearby and hung out at the Tote, regaling any poor unsuspecting patron with tales of past boxing glories, interspersed with hallucinations about flying elephants and snakes. Slugger always liked to boast that he had been a *fixer* for the Painters and Dockers after his boxing career and he still knew what went on in the underworld. Maybe there was a measure of truth in his claims, but you would have had to sieve through all the delusions first.

Poor old Slugger. FITH syndrome. That's what Peter's former nurse girlfriend before Michelle—Bridget—would have diagnosed him with. *Fucked in the head.* Punch drunk and a pain in the arse, especially when he hadn't taken his psych medications, which was often. And, strangely, one of Peter's sources. Most recently it was the Tony Donarto story. Slugger was taking his medications and relatively lucid when he'd given him that tip-off. It had turned out to be a good story once Peter had checked it out, analysed and cross-examined Slugger's claims.

He'd sent Mad Dog on a clandestine special ops mission to obtain photographic evidence. Mad Dog loved that, although dressing like a ninja had been slightly over the top. Slugger gave the address where and when the affair was being conducted and, from his perch in a tree, Mad Dog caught the couple in a juicy embrace at the pool. It was a sensational story. Donarto was going to have to resign his seat on the council, the soap star had suddenly left for Hollywood *to pursue her career* and Donarto had threatened to beat Peter up if he ever saw him in Lygon Street again. That was where Donarto liked to hold court. How Slugger knew Donarto and how he had knowledge of his private life, Slugger wouldn't disclose. He would only say that he knew people. What Slugger's motivation was, Peter could only guess.

Then Slugger stopped taking his medications. After that, it was back to flying elephants and snakes.

'Look here, Jack,' Slugger snuffled through a nose that was spread across his face like a scoop of mashed potatoes. 'Jack' was Slugger's nickname for Peter. He thought that Peter had a resemblance to Jack Dempsey, the former heavyweight champion. He bore no resemblance to Dempsey whatsoever but Slugger saw things that others couldn't.

'What is it, Slugger?' Peter said abruptly. 'I'm trying to have a quiet drink. Can we talk a bit later?' He turned his back on Slugger and took a sip of his beer.

'Need to talk, Jack. Need to talk.' Slugger did a boxing shuffle and then flopped himself onto the stool next to Peter.

'I'll buy you a beer, all right, if you leave me alone after that.' Peter relented. 'But no crazy talk about the flipping zoo you have in your flat.' He motioned to Irmgard. 'Light beer for Slugger.'

'I want a full strength,' Slugger yelled, waving his hands at Irmgard who was about to fill his glass.

'How many have you conned out of people today?' Peter asked.

'Just the one,' he replied. Irmgard was listening in and held up two fingers.

'I'm thinking of your health.' Slugger gazed at Peter, wide-eyed. 'Okay. Have a full strength, then. Don't come crying to me when you fall arse over head.'

Irmgard poured Slugger's beer and placed it on the bar. They were all part of a conspiracy to limit his beer consumption, as he had a habit of falling over on the footpath when he had too much and the regular patrons and staff had got tired of picking him up.

'Thanks, Jack,' Slugger slapped Peter's back. 'I'll give you a scoop for the paper.'

'Sure you will,' Peter smirked. 'Know anyone in the underworld? Can you introduce me?'

'I'm taking my medications again,' he announced.

'Sure you are.'

'Swear,' Slugger crossed his chest. 'A nurse comes around every day and gives them to me. They said if I refused they'd put me back in the psych ward.'

'Tell me, then.'

'I don't know if I should,' he hesitated. 'You just do sexy stories. I should talk to someone at *The Herald*.'

'I'm a crime reporter as from today,' Peter replied. 'You can run it by me.'

'You know I was in the Druids Hotel the day that Paddy Shannon got shot. I was sitting at the bar,' he whispered. 'I saw who did it. Plain as bloody day.'

'Who was it, then?'

'Can't say,' Slugger replied after taking a slow sip on his beer.

'Why are you telling me?'

'I was leaving that until later. For when you write a book on my life. A tell-all biography, Jack.'

'I'm going to do that?' Peter laughed. 'You've put a lot of trust in me.'

'Who else do I bloody know that writes for a living? No one. I know where the bodies are buried, if you want to know.'

'Can you remember?' Peter said dismissively.

'I'm not joking, Jack,' Slugger thumped the bar with his fist. Irmgard heard it and walked over.

'What's wrong, Slugger?' she asked.

'Jack doesn't believe me. He thinks I'm nuts,' he grumbled.

'Slugger's fine. No crazy talk at all,' Irmgard acknowledged. 'He was just telling me about one of his fights in great detail. The one he had with Mohammed Ali in America.'

'Okay?'

'See?' Slugger drained his glass and handed it to Irmgard. 'You can buy me another beer as an apology.' She replenished his glass and stood with them.

'All right,' Peter conceded. 'So the lights are on. Just a little dim, I think.'

'I know what's going on down at the wharves.' Slugger leaned in closer to Peter. 'I have the rundown on what they're doing.' He looked back at Irmgard. 'Sorry love, but this is top secret stuff.' She smiled and moved away to serve a customer.

'She'd be a top sheila in the sack, that German sheila,' Slugger commented as he watched her retreat.

'She's not bad,' Peter grinned. 'She doesn't usually like doing it in the sack, though.' Slugger broke into a laugh.

'Lucky bastard. Can't set me with up anyone, can you? I've been feeling like a bit of skirt since I've gone back on the meds.'

'If you give me good information I'll set you up with one of Irmgard's friends. She'd probably even sleep with an old bloke like you.'

'Okay, sounds good to me,' Slugger beamed and rubbed his hands together. 'Here it is, Jack. Between you and me.' He glanced around the bar. 'They're bringing the stuff in on the boats.'

'And?'

'You know. The stuff,' Slugger repeated tersely.

'What stuff?'

'The heroin,' he whispered, 'the smack.'

'I thought it was nearly impossible to get it through the docks. You've got Customs, Federal Police everywhere.'

'Not the way they do it. '

'How does whoever they are bring it in?' Peter tapped his fingers on the bar.

'On Navy ships.'

'Navy ships?' Peter repeated as his eyebrows rose.

'You know warships, that sort of stuff. The ones with bloody guns and missiles and blokes in silly hats. Get my drift?'

'The Navy would be bloody strict about personnel carrying heroin. Wouldn't you think?'

'Not all of them do it,' Slugger replied. 'It's what they call a rogue element, you see.'

'You haven't been taking your meds have you, Slugger? Is the admiral involved, too?' Peter chuckled.

'Don't be a smartarse, Jack.' Slugger grabbed him by the arm. 'I'm telling you something serious.'

Slugger released Peter's shoulder and continued. 'The Navy blokes buy up in Asia, store it on board and hand it over at the other end to someone on the docks. The Customs mob don't go on the Navy ships, do they? Easy bloody peasey.'

'What I don't get,' Peter responded after a long silence, 'is that Navy ships don't come here often and there would have to be a few of them involved to ensure a regular supply. Melbourne's got a lot of junkies. There's no large naval base here like Garden Island in Sydney.'

'I'm telling you, Jack,' Slugger shouted. 'I got it from the horse's mouth.'

'Someone on the wharves?' He asked with increasing disbelief.

'Maybe,' Slugger hesitated. 'Too risky to tell you.'

'You're not going to say?' Peter shook his head.

'You don't believe me, so I'm not going to say anymore. Bugger ya.'

'Fine,' Peter replied. 'Go home and take your medication. Talk to me when the lights are brighter, all right?' There was a brief silence. Peter watched as Slugger looked around the bar, his eyes following Irmgard.

'Are you still going to set me up with the German friend?'

'She's sitting on the other side of the bar,' Peter replied pointing to a masculine looking girl with purple hair. 'Go and introduce yourself. Say you're a friend of mine.'

Slugger turned his eyes towards the girl. 'You're joking, Jack. She looks like she belongs in a bloody circus. She's not a clown is she?'

'You wanted some skirt,' Peter retorted. 'I didn't say she was a model. She looks hot when she takes all the crap off.'

'I guess I'm no oil painting.' Slugger felt his nose. He rose hesitantly from his stool rubbing his hands with anticipation. 'I tell you what, it's been a while, Jack. I can't be too choosy these days. It used to be showgirls once.'

'Go,' Peter implored with a wave of his hand. 'Leave me alone. Please.'

4

Peter could hear the faint tone of an alarm clock. In his semi-consciousness he wondered why it sounded muffled, like it was under water. He moved his head slightly. The alarm clock was now drilling through his head, as per normal. He realised he had moved his head from the protection and comfort of Irmgard's ample breasts, which had acted like twin ear muffs, smothering the noise. She was lying face down on top of him, snoring loudly. Peter now realised he couldn't breathe properly. He took a deep breath and managed to roll from underneath her in a single motion, and switch off the alarm clock. *Shit!* He had to be at the airport in forty minutes. *Shit! What happened last night?* Peter spun to the side of the bed looking for something, anything, to wear. It was obvious what he and Irmgard had been up to, but as to the events that had transpired before that, not a bloody clue. He found a pair of underpants hanging on the bedside lamp and slipped them on. Irmgard kept snoring. He rolled alongside his German vixen and stroked her hair. He was about to kiss her neck.

'Cup of coffee, Jack?'

Peter spun around to be confronted by Slugger Douglas, wearing a pair of torn grey Y-fronts, holding two cups of coffee and a devilish grin. He started to walk towards Peter who was now sitting bolt upright, propped against the bedhead.

'Don't come any further. I don't want those jocks coming too close to me. I don't want to catch anything,' Peter waved frantically. 'How the hell did you get in here?' he stammered.

'I stayed here last night. You invited me,' Slugger beamed.

'I let you stay with me?' he responded nervously, 'You came home with me and Irmgard?'

'Yeah. After the pub shut,' Slugger replied.

'What did you hear? What did you see?'

'After I got Helga on the couch,' he grinned, 'I didn't hear or see anything else except her naked body and her cries...'

'You and Helga?' Peter interrupted, looking Slugger up and down. He didn't look in too bad nick for a man in his fifties, except for the decomposing underpants. But...

'What a lovely girl,' Slugger continued. 'Can I put these coffees down? They're getting hot.'

'Sure,' Peter replied. Slugger moved towards the bed and carefully put one down on the bedside table next to him. Peter took a quick sip.

'You make an all right coffee, Slugger.' Peter looked around the room for more articles of clothing. He grabbed a pair of pants that were lying on the floor. He stood up and slipped them on.

'Good night,' Slugger smiled. 'Best I've had in ages. I reckon I owe you one for setting me up with Helga.'

Peter didn't reply. He jumped off the bed, opened a battered wardrobe and rummaged around. He pulled out two shirts and a pair of jeans, threw them on the bed and looked back in the wardrobe. Moments later a pair of shoes and a duffel bag were on the bed.

'Are you going somewhere, Jack?' Slugger asked with a quick scratch of his groin. Irmgard's sonorous snores punched holes in the air.

'Going to Townsville to cover a trial,' Peter blurted as he reached into the bedside table drawer and pulled out a crumpled collection of underpants and a wad of loose socks. He zipped up the bag and slipped on a shirt and a pair of shoes in a flurry of motion. He took another drink of his coffee.

'Townsville,' Slugger said finally. 'You poor bastard. I remember going through there once with Jimmy Sharman. What a hole.'

'Exactly,' Peter responded breathlessly. 'Hate the place. The arse end of the world.'

'How long are you going for?'

'About three days,' he replied as he did up the buttons on his shirt.

'I'll look after things while you're gone.'

'There won't be much to look after.' Peter looked at Irmgard. 'Tell

Irmgard I'll ring her tonight. Got to go.' He snatched the duffel bag and headed out of the bedroom.

'There's something big happening on the wharves, Jack,' Slugger called out, as Peter brushed past him.

'So you said last night.'

'I may have mixed things up a bit,' Slugger admitted. 'Not all there yet.'

'Well, you'll be back to your old self by the time I get back. Firing on all cylinders.' He checked his watch. 'Got to go.'

'I know people on the docks,' Slugger followed him through the lounge. 'I used to work there.'

'We'll talk when I get back,' Peter returned. 'Just take the tablets.'

He was out of the door before Slugger could reply. Slugger stood in the stairway watching Peter run down the stairs towards Johnston Street and a taxi blowing its horn repeatedly. Slugger adjusted his underpants and went back inside.

The taxi was nearly at Melbourne Airport and Peter was still wishing he could relax. He had a lot to think about. New job, Irmgard, sleep deprivation, Slugger, Townsville and the next deadline. Always the next deadline. It could feel like a gathering storm when there were too many events happening. Maybe Townsville would be a good location to wind down, if he could just get past his dislike for the northern city. Imagine it was Cairns? Or Cannes? Then Peter thought of Concheetah and smiled. Would he do almost anything for a story? Most times, but today…the front page of *The Truth* would be:

Former Captain Capers Star Unveils his Dance Act at The Velour Lounge.

BROWNSVILLE REVISITED

5

Townsville

Peter lay naked on the bed watching the overhead fan beating lazily. It wobbled and hummed as the blades turned. He suspected the fan was going to detach itself from the ceiling any minute now and fall on him. It might injure him, but the blades would never cut him. They were moving so slowly that he could see that they were covered in a black crust. *In the heart of darkness.* Martin Sheen's opening scene in *Apocalypse Now.* The only difference, Peter hadn't smashed the mirror. Not yet.

Peter wanted to smash the whole room but drunkenness had been his only deterrent. Bob had certainly booked him into a motel on The Strand. The Bayview Motel, as its name suggested, was near the sea but as far away from modernity as a motel in Haiti would have been. Obviously, 1966 had been a big year for motel expansion in Townsville.

Peter had started off at the neighbouring Seaview Pub when he first arrived from the airport, then he trotted off to the Bayview, took one look at his room, laughed with shock and immediately decided to get hammered. Yes, Peter Clancy had fallen off the wagon and straight into his version of hell. He had done well to last a year without going on an all-out bender, but the Motel Hellside had been too much. Now, he was stretched out in a non-air-conditioned room that felt like it was the backdrop for depressed people to check themselves out, with the police finding their bodies in a sea of pills and bottles of booze three days later. He was lying on sheets already wet with humidity, perspiration and spilt alcohol. The heat was sleep depriving. It should have been a pleasant change after the biting chill of Melbourne. Peter had opened the windows earlier in a vain search for a relieving sea breeze, only to be attacked by a swarm of rapacious mosquitoes. It was a motel in Haiti located near a dengue-ridden swamp. The only thing missing was the gunfire—though he could hear drunken voices fighting in the park across the road. *I'll get you back, Bob. I fucking promise.*

The mini bar was empty. It had been empty since nine o'clock when he had skulled a mini bottle of Johnny Walker Red. It was now eleven-thirty. There had been only six bottles in the mini bar but Peter had dug out all reserves to get drunk on so little. Getting more kilometres per litre. This was going to be the only way to get a semblance of sleep.

Peter thought he might have achieved a heavy state of inebriation at the Seaview but he had almost been rescued by a blonde angel-faced nurse called Cherie—weren't all nurses like her?—who had nearly pulled him away from his beer to her room at the nurses' quarters. He might have gone willingly had he not intended on getting wasted and remaining faithful to Irmgard.

A new development. He had recently decided to embark on a bold experiment: practising fidelity. He'd tried celibacy, monogamy and polygamy, but fidelity? Irmgard was going to be different. So Cherie had left disappointed and Peter had returned to his cell-like room to wallow in alcohol and self-pity. Now he regretted his decision. A beautiful woman in your bed was a far better option than clutching an empty mini bottle and watching a rerun of *Prisoner* on television. Finally, Peter fell asleep around midnight, after covering himself in a moist sheet in the hope that the mosquitoes wouldn't devour him.

He managed to appear at the Bayview Motel restaurant for breakfast at eight, feeling itchy all over—the sheet hadn't worked— and suffering a top ten hangover. He passed on the tropical fruit, which came out of a can, the gravelly cereal and the leathery bacon and eggs, opting instead for two pieces of toast. He found a single table in the corner and carefully scraped a large wad of butter and Vegemite onto the toast. Even that level of exertion made his head throb. All this suffering could be rectified by a good cup of coffee. He noticed a hovering waitress carrying a jug.

'Double espresso,' Peter called in a parched voice, 'extra strong.'

'What?' the waitress asked.

'Espresso,' Peter shook his head, 'you know. Coffee. The drink that isn't tea.'

'We don't have that sort,' she replied as she approached Peter with the coffee jug. 'No one asks for that here. You're from down south aren't you?'

'Maybe I am. That shouldn't matter. Have you ever thought that tourists come here or do you tell them to go to Cairns?' Peter rasped back at her, watching the girl's eyes glaze over. 'Okay, just give me what you have.'

The waitress poured the coffee quickly and left. Peter took a sip then banged the cup back on the saucer.

'It's frigging cold!' He cried in frustration, 'I ask for a cup of coffee and its cold! I just want a cup of coffee. Please.' He felt like he was going to do a Mad Dog. The other guests, all three of them, looked up from their meals. The waitress strode back to Peter's table. He had his head in his hands, feeling utterly broken. He looked up just as the waitress was putting a finger into the cup.

'What the hell are you doing?' he asked with disbelief. He could feel his mouth drop open.

'It feels hot enough to me,' she announced as she removed her finger from the cup, shook it like a thermometer and wiped it on her apron, adding, 'Are you sure?'

'Believe me, I know what a cold cup of coffee tastes like. I know what a bad cup of coffee tastes like, and this ticks both boxes.' He looked up at the waitress, pleading. 'Why do you think I moved from Queensland to Melbourne a long time ago? To get a good cup of coffee. That's why.'

'Well,' she snapped. 'There's no reason to get angry. No one else has complained.'

Peter took several deep, slow breaths. Either loss of temper or complete insanity would be first past the post. He and the waitress traded stares, each waiting for the other to crack. Peter finally concluded that you can't argue with dumb. *Dumb and brick walls. Forget it.*

'Forget it,' Peter stood up quickly. 'I'll find a coffee shop in town… I hope.'

This wasn't hell on earth, he thought as he left the restaurant, this was really hell. *In hell the coffee is always cold.*

Peter wished he had brought his cunning kit with him as he approached the Townsville courthouse, a bunker-like complex among tropical palms. He could have arrived dressed as a rabbi-with-a-false-beard or a grey-old-man, and the Max Hillard group gathered at the courthouse entrance would not have been any the wiser. There were about thirty of them. Some were holding placards saying *Release Our Hero*, *Trial by Southern Media*, and *Leave Our Town Alone*. Peter stiffened, dropped his head and increased his pace as he drew nearer. He could see the masculine features of Mrs Daphne Hillard out of the corner of his eye and saw her propel her large frame at him with fists flying. One punch just missed Peter's nose. He ducked and ran up the stairs.

'Traitor mongrel,' Mrs Hillard screeched repeatedly, with the group providing a chorus of insults. He stopped when he reached the top of the stairs. Mrs Hillard remained at the bottom, continuing to hurl invective up at him. The police constable who was supposed to be providing security sauntered up to the group and looked up at Peter and grinned. Yes, Peter was in the heart of darkness.

Peter hadn't entered a courtroom since his time at a Queensland newspaper. He knew the process *ad infinitum, ad nauseam*. Barristers, wigs, juries, gowns and judges parading like peacocks. The drama of the court unfolding. It always appeared far more exciting on television. Even *Rumpole of the Bailey* had made it look sexy: the accused sweating bullets, shitting bricks, looking dishevelled, angry, lost. The reality was mostly like watching a boring test match with the occasional boundary or dismissal. Peter recalled a case where a young court reporter was so bored and so hungover that he had fallen asleep during proceedings. Peter had been unceremoniously woken and removed from the court when his snoring had distracted the judge. This time Peter wasn't a spectator. He was going in to bat. He was going to be called as a witness, and, he hoped, not a nervous one.

He was directed to a crowded waiting area and was pleased to see Dave Tindall looking dapper in a suit and tie, sitting by himself.

'You look like a groom, mate,' he laughed as he shook Dave's hand. 'Where's the bride, or has she run off?'

'And you look the same,' Dave grinned. 'Like you've just got out of bed with the latest hangover.' They both laughed.

'What have you been up to?' he asked as he sat down. Dave followed suit, loosening his tie.

'Got out of the police force. Thank God,' Dave smiled. 'Only a few months ago. Got a good payout and now I'm looking for another career.'

'How about you join the Victoria Police?' Peter suggested. 'They could do with a man of your calibre and intellect. They're a little short on those qualities at the moment.'

'I never want to be a copper again,' Dave declared, hanging his head. 'After what I've been through.' He paused. 'I have given serious thought to becoming a private investigator. I even did a course for it. I could start up my own company with my payout.'

'You're frigging joking.' Peter shook his head. 'A professional pervert? You've been watching too much *Magnum P.I.* It's not like what you see on television.'

'And you can talk. Professional pervert.'

'I've been promoted. I'm now a crime writer with my own weekly column.'

'I'm impressed. From naked bodies to dead bodies. That's a step up. Better get used to the smell.'

Peter swiftly changed subject. 'How's your mum?' he asked.

'Not well,' Dave replied, 'She's in a nursing home. She wanted to be here, but she had a stroke a week ago.'

'Real shame,' Peter responded. He'd always liked Lorna Tindall. 'She's the real one who deserves to see justice been done.'

'Do you think that's going to happen here today, Peter?'

'Well, we've wasted our time if it isn't.'

'Look around you,' Dave lowered his voice. Peter looked at the faces in the room. There were about twenty people who had been called as witnesses.

'How many people here do you think are the prosecutor's witnesses?' Dave asked.

'If it is just us I'm going to start worrying.'

'There's not many,' Dave replied. 'Most of them are character witnesses for Max and Doug.'

'Hardly anyone came forward?' Peter asked, sounding defeated. 'I should have known.'

'The local media are on their side. It's the usual thing: *The southern media are picking on us* stuff.'

'I wonder who's putting out that message?' Peter smiled. 'I had a frosty reception out front. Ma Hillard threw a left hook at me. Nearly got me.'

Dave started to laugh out loud. 'I heard the old bitch could handle herself. I've heard she's flogged Max on occasion.' He wiped away tears of laughter.

'Glad you think it's funny.'

'We'll slip out through a side door when it finishes.'

'I'd feel better if Sam was here,' Peter said pensively. 'He didn't deserve to die that way.'

'Die? Who? Sam?' Dave replied in quick succession. 'He wasn't killed.'

'What!' Peter exclaimed. 'The old bugger's still alive?'

'Well, he nearly died,' Dave continued, 'but he managed to drag himself to a homestead five kilometres away. He was in hospital for three months. That young nutcase Corey fractured Sam's skull and broke his leg.'

'Why didn't you tell me? You know my number.'

'Sam told me not to tell you because he wanted…' Dave was cut off mid-sentence.

'Surprise, young fella!' Peter spun around to see the familiar frame of Sam Saturday, resplendent in a new stockman's hat, moleskin trousers, checked shirt and bootlace tie. Peter also noticed that Sam was using a walking stick.

'I thought you were bloody dead!' Peter stood up and embraced the old man.

'Not too hard,' Sam complained. 'Still a bit sore.'

Peter stood back and admired the stockman. 'I can't believe you survived.' He turned away to wipe his tears.

'Stop the crying, I'm fine,' Sam chastised. 'I'm a tough old black fella. I've had horses roll over me, been gored by a bull and been stabbed in a fight. Do you think some girlie bloke was going to finish me off?'

Their celebration was cut short by the sudden appearance of the bailiff calling Peter's name. He stiffened and patted Dave and Sam on the back before he followed the official.

'Wish me luck, boys,' he tossed at them, with the air of a man who thought that he was the one on trial instead of Max Hillard.

6

Peter and Dave looked desolate as they walked through the lounge of the Townsville Hotel with their first drinks. Sam, on the other hand, looked strangely serene. Peter and Dave had opted for stubbies of beer while Sam was content with orange juice. After sitting down, the three fell silent as they sipped at their drinks. After a couple of gulps, Peter brightened up enough to throw a flirtatious eye at a receptive barmaid who was clearing a table nearby. He then realised he had no interest in proceeding any further. After today's trial, Peter felt like he had been put through the mincer.

'I don't know how you feel,' Peter was the first to break the pall of silence, 'but it didn't go quite as I envisaged. Max's barrister pulled us to pieces. The prick called me an unreliable witness. *A muckraking journalist from a scandal sheet is not a reliable witness.* His own words,' he snorted. 'And no Gloria. What the fuck? Max's defence team are going to shit on us. I can't believe they couldn't locate her even if she has pissed off back to the Philippines.'

Sam and Dave remained mute. Sam finished his drink, then lifted up his hat and picked aimlessly at the band.

'Isn't anyone going to say anything?' Peter looked at Dave, who looked to be on the verge of tears.

Dave drained his stubby in one gulp. 'What's there to say? We should have known it was going to be one-sided. If you're an unreliable witness, then join the club. My apparent unstable mental state added me to that list. I'm glad Mum wasn't here to see this.'

'Today was a bad day,' Sam said finally, after throwing his hat on the table. 'Tomorrow could be different.'

'Why are you so optimistic?' Peter asked.

'The way I figure it,' Sam began, 'Doug's in the slammer, Max's career is finished, I'm sitting with my mates, and I'm alive.'

'I just wish it would go against Max,' Dave said. 'Dumb Doug puts up his hand. Fancy not ratting on Max and taking the fall for him.'

'Max is a cop,' Sam replied. 'Cops don't like going to jail. There's a lot more black fellas in jail than there are cops. Get it?'

The barmaid had finished gathering up the used glasses on the other tables and had sidled up to them, one hand on her hip, looking bored.

'Just another round, thanks, love,' Peter ordered, finally glancing up at her.

A different barmaid returned with their drinks.

'Where are you blokes staying tonight?'

'We're sharing a room here,' Dave replied.

'You derros are staying at the best hotel in town and I'm at some flophouse on the Strand. How the hell does that work?' he complained.

'We can't help our good breeding,' Sam laughed.

'Is there another bed in your room or do I have to bunk in next to you, Sam?'

'You can sleep on the floor,' he returned, 'I'm not having you snoring in my ear all night.'

'Sleeping on the floor would be better than that room I was in. It wasn't even air-conditioned. It was like sleeping in an oven. And the coffee was stone cold.'

'Okay,' Dave relented. 'You can stay with us, but on one proviso.'

'Sure,' Peter replied.

'No bloody whinging.'

MARVELLOUS MURDEROUS MELBOURNE

7

Melbourne

Shazza looked unusually healthy and alert, Peter thought when he kicked open the office door at eight o'clock to see her typing and looking at the word processor's screen. *A pleasant change.* Peter playfully rang the counter bell several times.

'What the hell?' Shazza looked up at him and sneered. 'You look like a frigging politician.'

Peter was resplendent in his new Stafford Ellison suit and carrying a new leather briefcase. Another request from Bob.

'Please don't lower my status from scum journo to scum of the earth,' Peter replied in a mock aristocratic voice. 'Still on the wagon, I see? Don't know if that's a good thing. You sound too witty.'

'Doing my best,' Shazza replied. 'Been two weeks now. If I keep this up I could become a good Christian girl.'

'I think I prefer you drunk or hungover.' Peter smiled. 'You, a good girl? And I'm going to become a choir boy.'

Shazza took a drink from her cup of coffee.

'That's reminds me,' Peter said anxiously, 'is the coffee machine still working? I don't want Mad Dog chasing me around the office.'

'You can rest easy. It hasn't broken down once since you've been away.'

'Thank God,' he sighed.

'So, are you glad to be back from the sticks?' she asked.

'Shit yeah,' he beamed. 'I know for sure that I'll be able to get a good cup of coffee in Melbourne. Back in civilization,' Peter said happily and turned away from the counter.

'Hey. There's a big bunch of flowers on your desk,' Shazza winked. 'Someone thinks you're good in the sack.'

'Really?' Peter stopped dead, flattered. 'I wonder who it is?' *Irmgard. How come she was getting all hot and heavy when he had only rung her once from Townsville. Tread carefully, Peter Clancy.*

'What on earth?' Shazza rolled her eyes. 'Someone thinks he's a big lover boy?'

'Some men have it,' Peter grinned. 'Some don't. I don't.'

A huge bouquet of carnations greeted him when he reached his desk. He read the card.

My darling Peter. Thanks for the story you did on Ted. He was so happy, though I think you've created a monster. Crowds are up. He wants to do a whole revue. Sorry I doubted your sincerity. Hope to see you soon. Lots of love. Concheetah and Teddles.

Peter should have been embarrassed, but instead he felt pleased. Pleased that he hadn't lost a friend and especially relieved he hadn't lost a source of information. He picked up the flowers, cradled them in his arms and moved stealthily down the corridor. He would have made it back to his desk unnoticed, except for Tom Crocker.

Old Tom Crocker, was the journo who took up the slack, who did the stories no one else could be bothered with, including the sex advice column. He had a work ethic that belied his advanced years. And apparently a more than passing interest in horticulture. *How old was Tom? When was journalism invented?* Tom was here before everyone else had started at *The Truth* and would probably still be here when everyone else has left.

'Beautiful flowers,' said Tom. 'From someone special?'

'Not really.' Peter felt himself blush and kept walking. He put the flowers on the floor next to his desk.

'Don't do that,' Mad Dog snarled from somewhere. 'You need to put them in water,' he instructed as he approached.

'I don't have a vase,' Peter replied, a little bewildered.

'You'll probably find one in the storeroom.'

'Thanks, I'll get onto it soon.'

Mad Dog smiled uncomfortably at Peter, who was now sitting in his chair pretending to look at papers on his desk. Peter slowly picked up the flowers from the floor and held them uneasily between his legs.

'I love flowers, especially carnations.' Mad Dog fingered the petals. 'They're a symbol of beauty. Don't you think?'

'Yes, I suppose.' *What the...?*

'But so short-lived. Alive for a briefest moment in time then...' He took a sip of his coffee and leaned in towards Peter, who shifted in his chair. 'Crime writer now, I see. I hope you're up to it. Won't be pleasant.'

'I should be right. I've seen my share,' Peter replied, a little defensively.

'I hope so.' Mad Dog took another sip of his coffee. 'Because you and I are going to be working fairly closely. More than normal.'

'You and me?'

'Bob wants good pictures, see. What's the saying?' he paused. 'If it doesn't bleed, it doesn't lead.' He chuckled for a moment then his face turned sombre. 'So I don't want anyone falling apart on me.'

'No worries about that,' Peter bit back. 'I hope you're up to it, too.' He placed the flowers back on the desk.

'Funny,' Mad Dog shook his head. 'I've seen stuff that would make you go insane. You've never been in a war.'

'Well, then it looks like we'll make a good team,' Peter returned.

Mad Dog took a long time to reply. 'Bob says you have a scanner. You better start listening to it.'

'It'll be on all the time.'

'Only do the hard stuff. Nothing else. I don't want to be woken up for car accidents and domestics.'

'I get it—if it isn't bleeding, it won't be leading. I know the brief. I am the journalist, after all,' he called after him, as Mad Dog sauntered back to his cubicle. Peter was still shoving flowers into the glass vase on the last piece of space on his desk, just as the door to Bob's office swung wide.

'Doing a bit of flower arranging,' he sniggered, barely catching his breath as he approached Peter. A cigarette dangled from Bob's lips, glued there with spit; it bobbed up and down with every word. 'Which admirer is it this time?' he continued.

'Would you believe they're from a five-feet, eleven-inch drag queen?'

'Whatever puts the wind in your sails,' Bob chuckled, admiring the flowers. A line of ash fell on them. Peter flicked it away.

'Purely professional,' Peter replied as he put the finishing touches to the arrangement.

'I didn't know you had another side,' Bob joked, adding in an effeminate voice, 'Drag queens. Flower arranging. Should I be worried?

'Just keeping Mad Dog happy,' Peter retorted. 'Apart from being mad, he's also a bloody florist. And apparently I'm going to be working closely with him.'

'No more than you have before.'

'Good,' Peter sighed. 'To hear Mad Dog speak, we're going into combat together. He's taking the crime column far too seriously.'

'He'll be fine,' Bob reassured. 'And at least he won't be squeamish. As long as you don't mention the war,' he chortled, slapping Peter on the back.

'And this fucking scanner,' Peter slid open the drawer and took out the scanner, still in its box.

'It isn't going to work in its box, now is it?' Bob growled.

'Do I have to keep this on all the time?'

'Yes. Even at night. Sorry mate, it's going to cut into drinking and girl time but I want this column to work.' He pulled open the box and took out the scanner. 'Count yourself lucky you're not a police beat reporter. And you have to listen to everything, day in, day out. You can't even have a piss without taking it with you. Keep it on the priority one channels. You know, the fatal shootings, the homicides. That has to be your focus.'

Bob tossed the scanner at Peter, who thought about letting it go through to the keeper for a brief moment. He stretched out his hands at the last moment and caught it. Just in time.

'Make it your friend. Between this and your sources, I reckon we'll keep ahead of the competition. *The Age* won't know what hit it. Hey?' Bob slapped Peter so hard on the back that it stung.

'Okay.' Peter toyed with the scanner. He could feel his blood pressure sinking quickly into his newly acquired Julius Marlowe shoes, and had the sudden urge for a stiff drink, followed by a second. Was this the crossroad moment that he had dodged his entire long and undistinguished career? Either the enormity of the job was now suddenly dawning on him, or was he just plain shit scared.

Bob detected conflict in Peter's eyes and shifted subjects. 'So, things didn't go so well up there in the boondocks, I hear?'

'I should have expected that Max Hillard would get off,' Peter replied, snapping back from his thoughts with a jolt. 'Now I'm thinking I don't have a story. After everything we did, he walks free.'

Deep in thought, Bob stubbed out his cigarette at a nearby desk. He lit up another one almost as quickly. 'That's easy,' he proclaimed. 'Don't make Max the focus. Open the aperture a little. *Frontier justice, Queensland style. A lesson for Melbourne.* No names, no pack drill. That shouldn't get the lawyers too hot and bothered. How does that sound?'

'I get it,' Peter rejoined. 'Concentrate on police corruption. Its far-reaching effects.' He began to type.

'There's no hotter topic than that at the moment. Everyone's blaming the police for the spike in crime already.'

'That's good,' Peter nodded, adding, 'You're fucking good, Bob,' by way of emphasis.

'In my day, son. In my day. Believe it or not, when my fellow journos were sitting in a pub, I was working the beat.' A lazy smile stole across Bob's face. 'To be honest with you, you're not a bad journo, Peter, but you're bone idle. You have to pull your finger out now. This job could make you. No more titty boom-boom stories for you—this is the real deal. *The Truth*'s going to make you a legend, even if it kills you.'

'Great,' Peter replied. 'I'm looking forward to it.'

8

The Tote was nearly empty when Peter wandered in for his pre-dinner ritual drink at six. Slugger wasn't there. Thankfully. Neither was Irmgard.

She had told him on the phone that she was looking forward to seeing him. A thought drifted into his mind. Maybe Slugger had run off with Irmgard and her friend? Peter grinned to himself. With a wave, he called over Harry, a novice barman who had been leaning over the bar, watching television.

'Where's Irmgard?' he asked.

'You didn't know?' Harry looked surprised.

'I've only just got back from Queensland.'

'I thought she would have told you,' Harry chuckled. 'You were shagging her, weren't you?'

'Yeah. You'd think she'd tell me, wouldn't you?' he replied flippantly. He didn't have a clue what Harry was talking about.

'She left, while you were away.'

Peter zoomed in on Harry's teeth as he spoke. Tar stains. Not a sight for sore eyes after a hard day's work. Peter didn't know which was worse: his needling personality, his scowl or the lank *muffet* on his head, as Peter called Harry's hairstyle hybrid of the muffin-topped mullet. Possibly, it was all of the above. If Peter ever wanted to punch anyone, Hooray Harry would definitely be first in line. He wouldn't want to connect with those teeth, though.

'Obviously,' Peter rolled his eyes. That was another irritant: Harry wasn't the coldest beer in the fridge.

He began again. He knew it all. Filling Peter in on everything he'd missed. 'She said her and her mate were going to travel. Heading to Western Australia, apparently.' He looked Peter up and down and started to snigger. 'You look cut up, mate.'

'You continually dribble shit, Harry,' Peter snapped back. 'Just get me another beer then you can go back to watching *Neighbours*.'

Harry drifted away to the fridge. A snigger for the road.

*

Con and Roula both came around from behind the counter and greeted Peter with a hug when he entered the Apollo at seven. *Someone cares*, Peter thought. *Someone cares. Stop beating yourself up, Peter Clancy. Did you think you were going to have a long-term relationship with Irmgard? You know relationships don't suit you.*

'We missed you,' Con said cheerfully.

'I was only gone for a few days,' Peter replied faintly, 'but I'm glad to see you too.'

'Isn't it good to know someone misses you when you're not here?' Roula smiled and hugged Peter again.

'What are you having tonight?' Con asked, returning to his spot behind the counter. 'If you say fish and chips again, I'm not going to make them. Too much! I know we have the best in Melbourne, but you eat too much the same thing, you have a heart attack.' He clutched his hand to his chest. 'Like the Greeks say, *Pan metron ariston*. You hear that before?'

'All things in moderation. That's Greek?'

'Yes, that's Greek. That's very old Greek.'

'We'll make you something healthy all right,' Roula added, rolling her eyes. 'We'll make you Greek salad and *pastichio*. Much better for you.'

'Okay,' he smiled. 'I don't know if my body will take it but I'll give it a try.'

'Very good,' Roula replied. She shovelled a piece of the *pastichio* into an aluminium tray, while Peter wondered how a concoction of pasta, meat and cheese sauce could possibly be a healthier choice than fish and chips.

'You looking very sad, Peter,' Con fixed his large, dark eyes on Peter like a concerned parent.

'I'm fine,' he replied, scanning the menu on the wall that he already knew by heart.

'I know! That German girl,' Con continued. 'She broke your heart.'

'I'm not the broken heart sort of bloke, you know that.'

'Sure, you are,' Roula interrupted. 'You very soft. I see it in your eyes. I have words of advice for you.'

Here we go, he grinned. Always full of useful advice for Peter which he always found useful to ignore. Maybe, one day he would heed their advice.

'Good family, good food, good woman. And lots of healthy children. That's all you need in life,' Roula declared as she spooned the salad into a separate takeaway container. Con smiled in agreement.

Then again, maybe not. 'I should start to worry,' Peter grinned, pretending to wipe sweat from his forehead. 'I've managed to avoid all of those, so far.'

'But you not too old yet,' Roula continued. 'You still young and not bad looking. You meet a good girl. But not one who like to smoke, drink and go to parties. Okay?'

'Sounds like you want me to marry a nun,' he joked. Con and Roula broke into a hail of laughter.

'Good,' Con wiped his eyes. 'We start looking for one tomorrow.'

9

After dishing up his evening meal onto a chipped plate, Peter settled onto the couch with a comforting can of VB. Feeling the need for relaxing dinner music, he left the couch to slip the latest *Whitesnake* record on his Pioneer stereo (with the turntable and two cassette players combination). It was one of only five items of furniture, the others being a second-hand fridge (with leaking seals), a very old double bed (with sloppy mattress), a battered wardrobe (with one door missing) and a rusty camp bed for pissed guests who didn't mind doing permanent injury to their back. The stereo was the only thing in it that was insurable.

He turned the volume to mild ear pain and fell back onto the couch. All of his immediate neighbours were shopkeepers and Con and Roula had already gone home, so there was going to be no noise complaint. He felt lucky to be where he lived because, if on occasion he turned it up to ear-damaging volume, the surrounding residents always blamed the bands playing at the Tote.

With the VB still in one hand and the instructions to the *fucking scanner* in the other, he sank into the couch, determined that he would learn how to use it, thus making the new position his own. Embracing new jobs and new technology were, admittedly, not his forte. He needed help to change a light bulb. A Luddite.

The sound of Coverdale's vocals filled the flat and overflowed, joining the screech of the Johnston Street traffic, as Peter wrestled with the manual and the scanner's buttons. It responded with a series of farts, crackles and whistles. He wanted to throw it across the room.

Instead of Irmgard for seductive diversion, he had this machine to contend with.

By midnight, after six more VB's, three temper tantrums, four changes of records and a broken hearted depressive moment, he finally conquered his fears, his heartbreak and the scanner, which, in the meantime, he had nicknamed, *The Beast*. He fell into bed, placing the scanner on the floor beside him. His new, dark navy blue Stafford Ellison suit awaited in the broken wardrobe. The phone sat on the pillow next to him. Peter was prepared. Peter was ready. Ready for anything. The Pulse was ready. *Bring it on*. With that, Peter crossed himself and fell asleep.

Peter was skipping along in a field that appeared to be in the Bavarian Alps. He was holding Irmgard's hand tightly as they laughed and gambolled. Reaching a stream—a bubbling one, of course—they fell with unbridled laughter onto the soft verdant grass. Irmgard slipped off her white blouse to reveal her bounteous Germanic breasts covered in a lacy bra. Peter joyfully was unhooking and fumbling with the bra but the noise of the stream was distracting. It crackled urgently.

Cars in the area of Clifton Hill, gunshots have been reported at 92 George Street, repeat…

Peter was rudely snapped out his dream. He sat upright as if a rope was around his neck and he was being pulled towards the ceiling.

Double shooting, two males, 92 George Street Clifton…

He fumbled for the phone and dialled Mad Dog, who answered as if he had been sitting by the phone expecting an important call. No hint of sleep evident in his voice.

'We're on. Double shooting,' Peter flung at him. 'Ninety-two George Street, Clifton Street.'

'I'll be there in three. Just live two streets away.' Silence. Mad Dog must have thrown down the phone.

Peter dived into his new suit pants and a T-shirt. He flung the suit jacket over his shoulder. *Out the door*. He was running down the stairs towards the Stag with the image of a helicopter landing under fire in Vietnam in his head. He threw himself into the car, pulled open the choke and turned over the ignition. The Stag roared lustfully, suddenly injected with adrenaline. He pressed down the accelerator several times just to make sure. *Thank God. The Stag is alive. Don't let me down.*

He propelled the car down the street, its well-worn tyres screeching and shuddering against the bitumen as he hurtled around a corner. He peeked at the speedometer. Twice the limit, and no police, or anyone else, around. *I hope they're not at the shooting yet.* He glanced at his wristwatch. *No wonder. It's five thirty. The Pulse is coming,* Peter thought.

Mad Dog's Harley Davidson was already at the front of number ninety-two, a double storey period brick house, with a concrete driveway down the side. He noted the house's name on a large plaque over the front door. *Serenity.*

Mad Dog wasn't in sight. He'd probably already gone into action. Peter threw open the car door and sprinted across the footpath towards the guttural sobbing of a woman emanating from the house. The sobs turned to wailing, loud and distressing. He could hear a chorus of sirens in the far distance. Groans echoed out of the garage at the end of the driveway.

First glimpse: A grey-haired woman wearing a floral nightie is hunched over, kneeling on the ground in the entrance of the garage, her face and nightie blotched with blood.

Second glimpse: Mad Dog standing over the woman, spooling off shot after shot of the carnage, his face blank. *What the fuck? What the fuck?* Mind reeling, Peter reaches the garage.

The woman is bent over a man sprawled on the ground beside the open passenger door of a BMW, his balding head resting against the wheel. He looks to be the same age as the woman but it's hard to tell. The garage is a slaughterhouse. Blood is smeared across the car door from the man's hand. It's as if a hose has been left on and it is running blood, not water, over the concrete floor. The woman is on the ground, crouching in a deep pool of claret. A thin stream of blood seeps from the man's neck. There is so much blood it obscures the man's face. The woman grasps the man's neck tightly with both hands, trying to stem the flow. Peter stands frozen just outside, the open garage door framing the horror within. It is overwhelming. Mad Dog's camera whirrs. He's still taking photos. He is possessed. The woman screams for help. She screams at Mad Dog, who ignores her.

'Get away, you scum!' The woman picks up a bloody slipper she's been wearing and throws it at Mad Dog. It hits him in the head leaving a gory footprint on his forehead. His camera clicks. She looks down at the man, who is trying to talk. He's turning a dusky blue and drifting in and out of consciousness. Again, he is trying to talk. Peter wants to walk away, but his feet are now stuck to the concrete. He shakes his head and frowns. *None of this is right*, he thinks, yet he can't tear himself away.

'Don't talk, Pat,' she begs. 'Save your strength.' One of the man's red hands reaches up and pulls her head towards his mouth. He mutters to her. Peter observes the scene unfolding, edging forward to hear. A deathbed confession? A final expression of love? A dying will and testament? They both strain to listen.

'Yes, yes, Pat, I can hear you,' she says, stroking his face 'Save your strength. We'll get them.'

Peter is an eavesdropper. He feels ashamed. He can hear the cacophony of sirens now in the street. The woman looks directly at him. Her eyes are dilated and luminous.

'Help him. Help me,' she implores Peter. 'Please. Please help.'

Her voice jolts his mind and Peter suddenly finds himself pulling off his jacket, tearing off his T-shirt and reaching down to cover the man's neck. From observer to participant in a single moment: gonzo journalism at its most authentic. He presses hard against the man's neck in an attempt to staunch the haemorrhage. His blue T-shirt turns crimson in an instant. He keeps pressing down, until his hand aches, but the man has stopped breathing, and the woman's screams become a howl. She has already gone into mourning. Peter feels a hand on his shoulder, jerking him aside.

'We'll take over here, mate.'

Peter looked up the driveway at a swarm of ambulance paramedics, police officers, cameramen and journalists descending like a succession of waves. *When did they appear?* The ambos were already applying CPR and the police had cordoned off the journos who were gathering further up the driveway. He could hear their fruitless protests.

He stood up slowly and moved aside, his legs quivering, nearly buckling.

'It's okay,' he heard himself saying, 'I'm a journo with *The Truth*.'

A police officer tried to shift the woman, but she hung onto the man's torso with both hands.

'I'm not leaving him,' she cried as the police officer tugged. 'I'm staying.'

'You have to let the paramedics help him. They can't help him when you're holding onto him,' the police officer reasoned.

'I'm staying. Fuck off, you copper bastard.'

Another police officer stepped in to assist, but she wasn't letting go. He threw himself into the melee. Finally, the woman was dragged off the man and into the house, kicking, punching and yelling. In the meantime, Mad Dog was jostling with a detective who had covered his camera lens with his hand. Another uniformed officer joined in. Mad Dog was yelling vehemently about freedom of the press as he was frog-marched back up the driveway.

Another officer had taken Peter aside and instructed him not to leave. The officer seemed annoyed, saying something about how Peter would have to answer some questions and congratulations, he had just contaminated a crime scene. Peter mumbled something about trying to help. He attempted to find an eye in the storm: a calm place. He finally found a spot near a child's swing. A doll with one of its arms missing lay near the swing. He could hear men yelling. He looked up to see two thirty-something men pushing their way through the phalanx of police. One had red hair; the other had long hair and a beard.

'He's our father. Get out of the fucking way,' the bearded one yelled, angry spit flying into the face of a young constable.

'We want to see him. We're his sons, you dumb copper cunt,' Ranga added.

The constable, flushed with anger, stood his ground until a tall, wavy-haired policeman, who appeared to be in charge, pushed the constable aside and took the two men to where the victim lay on a trolley. Peter walked back towards the fracas, observing that his neck was now covered in a tight compression bandage that was steadily turning red. Peter still couldn't make out what the man looked like; his face now had an oxygen mask on it.

The bearded son took hold of one of his father's hands and the other leaned over him, dripping tears of grief onto the face of the dying man. The bearded man retrieved something from his pocket and pressed it into his father's hand, then closed it. Peter edged forward: Rosary beads. The monitor on the trolley was alarming. An ambulance officer started CPR.

'We're losing him. Move. Move. Move!'

The ambos were at both ends of the trolley, manœuvring it frantically up the driveway. They hit a bump and the monitor looked like it would fall off the trolley, except that one of the officers secured it without stopping. The wheels rattled as they rolled over the concrete. The sons, the police and the journalists herded themselves behind the trolley and towards the ambulance.

The grey-haired woman darted out of the house, followed closely by a policewoman. The woman had changed into a fresh, green tracksuit with yellow edging. In her urgency she had only zipped up the tracksuit top over her abdomen, leaving her bra exposed. She threw a passing glance at Peter before running up the driveway towards the ambulance. She seemed oblivious to her public display. Peter thought about telling her but decided against it. Maybe the female copper would tell her.

Mad Dog had gone back into action, snapping the trolley as it was pushed into the back of the ambulance. He attempted to take a photo of the woman trying to climb in and being grappled by police, but he was pushed away. The doors were thrown shut and the ambulance screamed away, siren blaring in harmony with the two police cars following it. Peter wanted to go back to the swing and close his eyes. He desperately wanted a stiff drink. He managed to direct his feet back towards the garage. It was cordoned off. He realised his suit jacket was back there and he was wearing nothing but a singlet and pants soaked to the knee in blood.

A line of police officers and ambos were gathered at the doorway of the garage. Peter wanted to blend in. He was a few steps away. Then he noticed. How the hell hadn't he noticed before?

In the congealing pool, Peter saw four bullet casings alongside the still open passenger door of the BMW. Four more on the other side. The driver's door was also open. Two police officers were standing near the door looking down. One has taken off his cap and was running his hand through his hair, pale with shock. Peter could now clearly see what he was looking at. A male torso hung out of the driver's door, the head resting limply in a puddle of gore on the garage floor. The back of his skull was missing.

Then Peter saw his suit jacket draped over a carpenter's bench. He wanted to go and pick it up but an agitated male voice bore down on him from behind. The two coppers looked up in the direction of the voice. It was the wavy-haired detective senior sergeant.

'Hey you,' he barked. 'You. The bloke in the singlet. You can't go in there, you'll be disturbing a crime scene. Don't you touch anything.' With a wave, he signalled one of the other Homicide Squad members to approach Peter.

As Peter backed away from the garage door, he was followed by a senior constable, who cornered him against a fence. A few minutes later, the detective senior sergeant crossed the yard towards him.

'Who are you?'

Peter was still trying to shake the vision of trauma he had witnessed from his consciousness. He concentrated all his energies on the present. The detective was taller than Peter, broad-shouldered with a soft, jowly face, a porn moustache, and that hair. The thought that it might be permed pushed everything else away. The detective's soft face didn't match his rasping voice.

'Peter Clancy. I'm the new crime journalist from *The Truth* and the owner of that coat.' Peter was beginning to feel the brisk Melbourne winter air. He started to shiver. *I need a shirt. I need a shirt. I want my coat back. My tits will freeze off.* 'I heard about the shooting on a scanner and my photographer and I got here just before your lot turned up.'

'If it was up to me those things would be outlawed,' he sneered at Peter.

'I was using my shirt as a compress. For the man who was shot. Can you tell me anything about him?' he continued, wrapping his arms around his body for warmth.

The detective smirked, enjoying Peter's discomfort. He took his time responding. 'I'm the one asking the questions here, mate. You'll be very lucky not to be charged.'

'With what? For trying to save a life?'

'Well, Peter Clancy, porn peddling, muck raking Good Samaritan from *The Truth*, one of the detectives here will ask you a few more questions and then you can go home. But make sure you don't go too far away; I might need to speak to you again. Understood?'

'Understood.' Peter hesitated. 'You can't tell me anything more about the victims? Their names maybe?'

'You have got to be joking. There'll be a press conference for your lot tomorrow at St Kilda Road. You can ask your questions then. That's if you're not dead from hypothermia,' the detective chuckled. He shot a glance at another detective standing nearby with his hands in his pockets, who joined in.

'That's clever,' Peter answered back sarcastically. 'The detective senior sergeant's a comedian.'

'The detective senior sergeant has a name, and his name is Dale McCracken,' he growled as he stepped forward.

'I'll try to remember that,' Peter replied with a smirk. 'Dale McCracken: Senior Dick and part-time comedian. Or is that the other way around?'

'If this is your first day covering crime, then you're already off to a bad start, Clancy,' McCracken snarled into Peter's face. 'I hope it changes along with your shitty attitude. How it works is, if the press are pleasant to us, we give out the necessary information. If not...'

Peter interrupted. 'Wow! I'm starting to get it! You spill the breadcrumbs and we get to eat them. Like chooks.'

McCracken's face flushed crimson. 'Get the hell out of here,' he snapped, 'before you find yourself in a cell.'

'Thanks,' Peter smiled as he attempted to push his way through the two detectives. 'I'll be in touch. And I'd like to get my coat now'

McCracken grabbed Peter on the shoulder. 'Forget your coat. And that crazy photographer you dragged along with you: keep him on a chain. He's interfering with police work.'

'Of course,' Peter retorted. 'I'll return him to the RSPCA today.'

McCracken left Peter to the smirking detective. A few questions and a flash of his driver's licence later, he made his way briskly up the driveway, heading back to the Stag and more importantly, to its heater. *McCracken.* He was vaguely aware of having heard the name before. Was it the same McCracken that Concheetah had mentioned?

The cold had overcome him. Maybe the Beatles could have written a song about the Melbourne winter. *Freeze, freeze me...* Peter's shivering was now competing with his teeth chattering.

As he started to jog to the car, he noticed two men he had presumed were the sons of the dying man climbing into a Mercedes parked immediately behind the Stag. An older man was getting into the back seat. When he got closer, he recognised the older man. It was Slugger. *What the fuck? Slugger?* Peter called out, but the Mercedes was already down the street before he had reached the footpath.

He jumped in the Stag, switched on the ignition and turned the heater to maximum. Saved from frostbite, but only just. He looked around. Mad Dog had already gone. A smile of satisfaction stole across Peter's face. Thanks to modern technology, he had scooped the other papers. Then he realised. He hadn't been able to discover the names of the victims. He fell out of the car and went to the mailbox. No mail. He thought of asking the neighbours but that was likely to cause problems, considering his lack of apparel. How was the headline going to read? *Mystery men shot mysteriously. One man mysteriously dies. Shit!*

10

After a quick change of clothes back home, Peter swung by Slugger's flat on the tenth floor of the Housing Commission high-rise on Hoddle Street, just opposite the Collingwood Town Hall. As expected, Slugger wasn't answering. There was a note attached to the door with a tack. Peter glanced up and down the corridor before tearing it open. It said in a manic scrawl: *To the nurse. Gone to help friends. Slugger.*

He reattached the note to the door and ran to the lift as soon as he heard its doors grind open. At St Vincent's Hospital he was recognised at the front door by a cop and given his marching orders. However, he was able to get out of the cop that the two men were both now deceased.

Shazza stopped typing the moment Peter pushed open the front door. She didn't say a word but made a series of hand gestures at him and then down the corridor. She then mimed a large belly with both hands. It was Bob. *Got it,* he gestured back with a thumbs-up. Shazza returned a thumbs down. *Shit. I'm in deep trouble.*

Peter trudged to his desk where Bob was waiting, arms akimbo, mandatory cigarette dangling from his mouth. Mad Dog was sitting nearby looking flushed. He had removed his bandana to reveal long hair twisted into bits of twine.

'Got there first,' Bob muttered.

From past experience, a quiet Bob was not a good sign. Peter stiffened, waiting for the onslaught.

'Congratulations.'

'Thanks to the scanner,' Peter replied with a faint smile.

'That's good,' Bob returned, his voice growing in volume. He took several frantic puffs on his cigarette then stubbed it out. 'But what in the fuck happened after that?' he asked menacingly, his voice increasing yet again 'Pray tell?'

'We got great photos and a great story,' Peter rejoined, on the defensive. He looked at Mad Dog for support but only got a vacant stare.

'I've just had the police commissioner on the phone saying that you both acted like a pair of fucking cowboys,' Bob bellowed. His face florid, he pointed at Peter. 'Not wearing a shirt?' He shook his head.

'I was…' Peter attempted to reply but Bob cut in.

'And Mad Dog thinks he's at the fall of Saigon.'

'You wanted a story and we did what we had to do, Bob,' Peter argued. 'We're not social workers.'

Bob sucked in a deep breath and softened. 'All right. But some words of advice. Are you listening, Mad Dog?'

'I hear you, Chief.'

'You don't have to be the cop's friends, but it might help. If you can't, then at least be diplomatic. And Peter, don't render assistance. It clouds your judgement. Remain detached. No matter how you much you want to help. Remember, you're not part of the story.' Bob paused for another breath. 'And as for you, Mad Dog, the war is over. Repeat. The war is over. Most of the photos you took can't be published in a paper, not even ours. Do you think the public is going to want to see pictures of locals with their heads blown apart? Bodies undercover and background photos only, all right?' He stopped to light a fresh cigarette.

'But I thought that's what you wanted,' Mad Dog grunted.

'In case you think I don't know what I'm talking about, I'll tell you: In my younger days, when my gut was smaller, when I only smoked two packs a day and only drank a bottle of Jameson's a day, I was a crime reporter for the *New York Post*. That's right boys, the *New York Post*. And before that I was a special correspondent during the Israeli Six Day War. So, I think I know what I'm talking about.'

'Got it, Chief. Loud and clear.' Mad Dog threw a mock salute. 'Under control. Can I go?'

'Go on. Piss off.'

Mad Dog stood up, grabbed his bandana and headed towards the coffee machine.

'This Detective Senior Sergeant Dale McCracken,' Bob continued, 'I presume he's a right pain in the arse?'

'A fucking bleeding haemorrhoid, Bob,' Peter replied.

'When you go to the press conference tomorrow, I want you to be humble. Don't be the pain in the arse you usually are. We need the cops on our side. You can't do this job without them. Until you can say that the commissioner is your major source of information, we have to work in with the cops. '

'All right. I suppose I overstepped it.'

'Okay,' Bob smacked his hands together. 'We have to concentrate on today's deadline. What have you got?'

'Two men shot at a house in Clifton Hill. One man dead straight away and the other died in hospital.'

'Know who they are? Know what they were up to? I'm sure they weren't two innocent men going off to work. They must have form.'

'Cops weren't speaking. Couldn't talk to any neighbours.'

'Come on, Peter,' Bob snapped, 'it's not flipping amateur hour. The other papers probably have that information already.' He banged his hand on Peter's desk. Peter was beginning to regret accepting this 'promotion'. Catching people having affairs was starting to seem much easier.

'One of my sources was there,' he recalled, 'but I couldn't speak to him. He was getting in a car with two men who I presumed were the sons of one of the men who were shot. I haven't been able to find him since then.'

'His name?'

'Slugger Douglas,' Peter replied. 'He's a punch-drunk ex-boxer. Comes in the Tote and rambles on about his boxing days. Says he used to work for the Painters and Dockers after he gave up the fight game. Supposedly. He doesn't usually take his psych medication so he's not the most reliable. But he's the one who gave me the information about Tony Donarto and the starlet.'

'I remember him. Saw him fight at Festival Hall when I was a kid. Had a powerful left hook.'

'He seems to know the family,' Peter added.

'They don't sound like the Brady Bunch, do they?' Bob joked.

'Maybe they're the last ones standing from the Painters and Dockers' days. There wouldn't be many of them left on the street. Most of those old union blokes are either encased in cement or in jail. And the Painters and Dockers Union got deregistered a few years ago. So who are these people?'

'Is that how he knows about Tony Donarto?'

Peter drummed the desk with his fingers. 'He would never let on. Old bugger.'

'Don't worry about that. Okay. If we go with what we have,' Bob sighed heavily. 'We'll be just saying the same stuff as the other papers.'

Peter was deep in thought. 'O'Connor, O'Gara, O'Toole, O'Lara,' he rattled off. 'Slugger mentioned a name once: *I have to go and see Mrs O'…she needs my help…Mrs Oooo*,' He picked up a pen and threw it in frustration. It bounced off the back partition.

'O'Leary,' Bob suggested. 'O'Leary Stevedores. Maybe?'

'O'Leary. That's it!' Peter exclaimed.

'They're a family company. They run the container traffic at South Wharf. The O'Learys set themselves up after the union went guts up. I think there are three sons.'

'Maybe only two now,' Peter surmised, adding, 'How do you know the O'Learys?'

'They're big patrons of the St Kilda footy club. I've met them at functions. Solid blokes. I think one of them may have played a few games in the seniors.'

'Mrs O'Leary was helping a bloke who I presume was her husband.' Peter was thinking aloud. 'He was balding. I could see grey hair. She called him Pat. That's it, Pat.'

'Are you sure,' Bob exploded. 'Are you sure?'

'Plain as day.'

'Pat O'Leary disappeared two years ago,' Bob reached for a critical cigarette.

'Come again?'

'The rumour was that he got murdered after dogging on the union officials and that he ended up in pieces in the bay.'

'Well, that can be ruled out,' Peter replied.

'Or that he pissed off to a South American country. We go to press,' Bob bellowed and flung his arms around cheerfully. 'Mad Dog, get those photos developed pronto. The ones that can be printed.'

'Done, Chief.' Mad Dog emptied his cup of coffee.

'I don't know how you did it, Peter,' Bob said as he grabbed him in a bear hug. 'You fucked it up from start to finish and you've still scooped it. Well done. We're ahead of the pack already.'

'It's a talent I've developed. Just fucking up in the right place, at the right time.'

The headline read: *A Dead Man Returns and Ends up Dead.*

11

Peter was starting to worry about Slugger's disappearance. Scenarios were whirling through his head a lot faster than the Housing Commission lift that was laboriously dragging him up to the tenth floor.

Slugger knew a lot more than his brain-damaged thinking let on, but the medications might not have been working yet. Without them, Slugger knew absolutely nothing. He was in the terminal phases of FITH syndrome. Peter banged on Slugger's front door with no response. He then tried to endear himself with the onsite manager, a grizzled old dear with a face like parchment. He played the concerned relative and *could she please let him in? Poor Slugger may have had a fall and be lying unconscious on the bathroom floor. Please?* Not a hope in hell, although Peter did manage to elicit that Slugger had gone out early this morning and hadn't returned yet, and that the nurse had also been around looking for him. That was all—after slipping the old bitch twenty dollars. *Rip off.*

After that encounter he went by the Tote, hoping to find Slugger holding up the bar with another disjointed fight story, as Peter drowned himself in a load of celebratory Victoria Bitters for a job well done. Peter was even going to shout the bar, provided it wasn't full. The first disappointment of the night was that Slugger wasn't in and no one had seen him for a couple of days. Hooray Harry had the first beer lined up, even before Peter sat down. The second disappointment was when Peter gave up the celebration halfway through his fourth beer.

The events of the morning kept running through his head. The balding man lying on the garage floor bleeding like a stuck pig, his

wife screaming for help. Blood, blood and more blood. He hadn't ever
seen that level of carnage. And Peter had thought he'd seen it all. Then
there was Slugger. Where was he?

*This story is going to explode and I need Slugger. I have to be at the
epicentre not on the periphery. It's my story. I'm the headline around
here.* Peter put down the half-empty fourth glass when his hands
started to shake, splashing beer over the bar. He sat stunned, watching
them as if they weren't part of his body. He grabbed hold of the bar,
but the shaking wouldn't stop.

'You okay, mate?' Harry said. 'You're as pale as a ghost.' He sidled
up to Peter.

'Must be the dim sims I ate at lunch.' Peter attempted at a joke until
his arms joined in. Peter felt his whole body convulsing.

'You're in shock,' Harry commented, matter of factly. 'Shock.
I know that.'

'What?' Peter was beginning to feel nauseated. He hopped off the
barstool and looked in the direction of the toilets on the other side of
the bar. Too far away. He edged closer to the door.

'I had it after I was in a car accident ten years ago,' Harry reminisced.
'Me mate's head was in me lap. His eyes were…'

'Got to go.' Peter staggered out of the door, his hand clamped over
his mouth. He got as far as the house next door before vomiting into
the gutter. After straightening himself up, he wiped his mouth with
the back of his hand.

'You want another beer and some greasy dim sims to wash it
down?' Harry called out from the doorway.

'Next time it will be on your fucking lap. I promise that.'

Peter staggered back to the flat and dropped onto the bed without
removing his clothes. He could only summon enough energy to turn
off the scanner before falling into a stupor. *Fuck the scanner. I don't
need it,* were his final conscious thoughts before succumbing to the
exhaustion.

He didn't know whether it was the shouting or the thumping at the
front door that brought him, in degrees, out of his sleep. It sounded
urgent, whoever it was. He still felt too paralysed to get out of bed
but was alert enough to check the alarm clock. Ten-thirty. *I just
want to sleep. I don't care if you're dying out there. I don't care.* Then
again, maybe it was Irmgard. *Irmgard, mein liebes Fräulein.* With that

thought he willed himself to haul his body upright. *She's returned!* But as he neared the front door, Peter discerned that the shouting was a man, a frantic man. Peter was reluctant to open the door. For all he knew, it could be a psychopath with a blunt axe on the other side. He had just picked up the phone to call the police, when he heard a familiar name called through the door. *Jack!* He put down the receiver and scurried to the door.

'Where in the hell have you been?' Peter shouted as he threw open the door.

'I've been knocking and calling out for the past fifteen minutes, Jack,' Slugger breathed with relief. 'I was nearly ready to knock down the door.'

Peter waved him inside and closed the door, after looking around to see if Slugger had company. Slugger was in wild-eyed and dishevelled. Peter had seen him like this many times before. He looked as if he was being chased by demons. *He hasn't taken his psych pills today for certain,* Peter thought, as he directed Slugger to the couch. Slugger sat down tentatively, perching himself on the edge of the seat.

'Do you need your pills, Slugger?'

'They can wait,' he replied in a nervous staccato. 'There's too much to do. Too much. Way too much.'

'How about a cup of coffee?' Peter asked as he headed towards the kitchen. 'I'm going to make one. How about a bite to eat?'

'All right,' came the snappy reply. 'But I have to tell you something first.'

Peter turned on his heel and sat on the couch, next to Slugger. 'Oh yes? And what's that? What do you want to tell me?'

'It was a bloody bad day today.' Slugger was shaking. Hard to tell if it was from shock, or if he was just missing his meds.

'Certainly was,' Peter replied. 'That's an understatement.'

'I saw you there. Didn't have time to talk.'

'I know.'

'Did you know? Pat O'Leary's dead,' Slugger sighed with grief. 'And his son, Mickey. Good boy was Mickey.' He lowered his eyes.

'I heard.' Peter wiped the last, crusty vestiges of sleep from his eyes. 'They had a lot of blood on them.'

'Ivy's devastated,' Slugger continued. 'She's a good woman.'

'Who's Ivy?'

'You saw her. She was there.' He wiped the trickle of tears, running down his face. 'That was her husband and son that died.'

'How do you know her?'

'Too many questions, Jack. I don't know if I can keep up.'

Okay, Peter thought, I'll try a different approach.

'You're talking to me different now. Like I'm on the TV. Talk to me like you were me mate, Jack.'

'Sounds like you were a good friend of hers, Slugger,' Peter remarked after a long pause.

'We go back a long way. I got an eye out for her when I'm up and about. Haven't been well enough to do that lately. She's a good woman,' his voice trailed off.

'Is she a relative?'

'She's family. That's all I'm going to say.'

Blocked again. Can't you just break down and tell me? 'So why haven't you mentioned the O'Learys before? How do you know them?'

'It was none of your business,' Slugger returned curtly. 'You're a good bloke but you're still a reporter. The O'Learys are good people. They really are.'

'At least you think I'm a good bloke,' Peter quipped. 'But I didn't think good people got shot like that, Slugger. I just don't get it.'

'You probably think it's your business to find out?'

'Well, I've sent a story to press with my fucking by-line on it. I've had Pat O'Leary's blood all over me and, before today, I didn't know him from Adam,' he replied. 'I'd like to think it is my business now.'

'I don't want Ivy upset by the papers hanging around. She's always been pretty fragile. Now with the killings and the papers, I don't know how she'll handle it. It could put her over the edge.'

'The thing is, Slugger, the press are going to be swarming all over this. They love these kinds of stories. Do you want all these journos coming after Ivy like a pack of dogs?'

'Of course not,' he shot back. 'And I don't want her boys thrown into it either. They're good people.'

It was interesting, Peter thought, that Slugger had to keep telling him that the O'Learys were good people. It was starting to arouse his suspicions. 'Or do you want me asking the questions? That'll keep them off Ivy. It's an offer. You know me. Good bloke. Good journalist.'

'I didn't think of it that way,' Slugger replied. 'I wish I could get all the reporters to stay away, but you'd be the best one to deal with, I suppose. You wouldn't upset Ivy and the boys too much.'

'I don't want to upset anyone, Slugger. I just want to get behind the truth before the vultures start making up their own. And that's what's going to happen.'

'But you won't ask Ivy lots of hard questions and make her cry?' Slugger asked. 'They always make people cry on the TV.'

'It'll be like a gentle conversation,' he assured Slugger. 'I promise you.' He found the word interview made people defensive.

'If you do, I'll get upset,' he added as he clenched his left hand.

The famous Slugger left hook, Peter thought. *It'd probably still put me in hospital.* 'So I'll see you tomorrow?' he asked as he headed to the kitchen to make the long overdue coffee. 'First thing tomorrow we go and see Ivy?'

'Has to be now, Jack,' Slugger insisted. 'Or you won't get another chance.'

'Now?' Peter checked his watch, 'It's eleven. Will she still be up? What about her boys?'

'I've just come from being with her. This is the only time.'

'I guess I'd better forget about the coffee, then.'

With Slugger sitting in the Stag's passenger seat and Peter in the early stages of caffeine withdrawal, they soon arrived at Slugger's flat. Slugger smiled when he noticed the quizzical look on Peter's face. The ancient lift had a sign, written in wonky, fat, red Texta letters, which Peter immediately recognised as Slugger's: *Lift Brocken Down.*

Slugger led Peter to the urine-soaked staircase adjacent and galloped up the stairs, taking some of them two at a time, while Peter huffed up behind him, struggling to keep up. A small, yellow light illuminated the front door. Instead of letting himself in with his key, Slugger rang the bell. Twice. Peter cautiously hung back in the shadows ready to scarper in the event of trouble. Was Slugger trying to set him up? Was Slugger having a hallucination? The door opened before he had time to run every scenario through his head.

'Did you bring him, Slugger?' Ivy slurred expectantly, as she ushered him in. From a distance, Ivy didn't seem as grey as she been the last time Peter had seen her. Maybe she had found the time to go to the hairdresser, although that was unlikely. Most possibly she was wearing a well-fitting wig.

She was still a looker for a woman in her sixties; her face seemed devoid of the ravages of aging. Peter surmised that was thanks to a good plastic surgeon. She was still wearing the same tracksuit of that morning, but zipped up to the neck now.

Slugger grabbed Peter by the arm. 'I've got him,' he responded as he pulled Peter out of the gloom. He was propelled over the threshold and greeted with an air kiss from Ivy. *The old dear's had too much Valium, too many brandies, and way too much trauma*, he thought.

'I should thank you,' Ivy smiled faintly as she planted another kiss on Peter.

'What for?' He looked to Slugger for help. Slugger responded by slapping Peter on the back.

'I told you,' said Slugger.

'For trying to save Pat's life today.' She took hold of Peter's hand and led him past a punching bag dangling from the ceiling and into Slugger's tiny lounge room to a gold and burgundy brocade sofa. Slugger's taste in interior decoration evidently stretched from sixties chic all the way to baroque.

'I don't know if I was able to do much,' Peter replied.

Slugger followed closely behind. A pug dog came from nowhere and latched its teeth onto Peter's pants. Ivy kicked away the dog.

'Get away, Pugsley,' she chastised.

As if in protest, the pug squatted and urinated on the rug near the sofa. Peter felt he was the only one noticing. The dog headed to a corner of the room to sulk and scowl at him. Ivy took her seat in an adjacent recliner next to a table covered with bottles of medications and a half empty bottle of brandy. She indicated for Peter to sit on the sofa next to her. Slugger chose to stand in the other corner, in front of an enormous framed picture celebrating his boxing career in photographs.

'At least you tried,' Ivy sighed. 'You might be a reporter but you still have a beating heart. I didn't think you people had hearts at all.'

'How are you feeling now?' Peter asked. He looked to Slugger for reassurance. Slugger gave a thumbs up sign.

'Oh, you know. Just managing to hold it together,' she said as she bit back tears. She reached for a glass of brandy and took a sip. 'Don't usually drink but it's calming my nerves. Not easy to see your husband and son die like that.'

'Or any way, I imagine. What do you think happened today, Ivy?'

'I don't know,' she replied vaguely. 'It's like a dream. I just keep seeing blood everywhere. It's surreal.'

Peter cringed when the word *surreal* came out of her mouth. He hated the word. That and 'literally'. He could see Slugger giving him another thumbs up sign from the corner of his eye. *So far so good.*

'Do you have any idea who might have done this?' Peter said cautiously. He had thrown the cat among the pigeons now. Slugger stepped forward.

'Don't upset her too much, Jack,' he warned as he leant into Peter's ear.

Peter shook his head with annoyance and waved Slugger aside. 'Why did you want me to come here tonight?'

'To tell my side of the story and to thank you,' Ivy replied after taking another sip. 'Slugger said you could be trusted with telling the right version, not a made up one.'

'But you haven't really told me anything yet, Ivy. You must know something. Give me something.'

'All I know is that Pat and Mickey have been shot,' she cried. Slugger rushed forward to comfort her. He sat on the armrest and folded his arm around Ivy. He then kissed her on the head. She continued, 'And I really don't know why or who.'

'They're dead for some reason. Was it to do with Pat's reappearance?'

'The coppers keep asking me if they had enemies. I don't know,' Ivy replied despondently. 'I thought Pat was dead. And my boys and me, we're just hard working people. We have no enemies.'

'She doesn't know,' Slugger said angrily. 'That's what you have to put in the paper.'

'I'm really confused right now. You asked me to come here and you don't tell me anything?'

'I'm an honest woman,' she wept, 'and now you're picking on me.'

'Answer me one question, then' Peter began. 'Where did Pat go to for two years when it was assumed he was dead?'

'He went away on business to South East Asia,' she stammered, her eyes flicking around the room. She picked up the brandy glass and drained it. Peter had one of the best inbuilt bullshit meters in the business and it was off the scale.

'That's it, Jack,' Slugger jumped out of the corner and stomped towards Peter. Pugsley saw it as an opportune time to start tearing at Peter's pants again. Slugger kicked the dog away and grabbed Peter by the arm, pulling him off the sofa.

'Do you believe that, Ivy?' Peter managed as Slugger dragged him by the shirt collar through the lounge. He thought briefly of resisting but Slugger, even in his advanced years, was stronger than he. 'Are you towing the party line, Ivy?' he continued as grabbed hold of the punching bag and held on tightly with both hands. Slugger had finally run out of puff and was having trouble dislodging him. Ivy responded by pouring herself another drink and avoiding eye contact. Peter held on firmly. 'What about you, Slugger?' Peter turned to face him.

'I don't want to hit you, Jack,' he said with a hint of sadness. 'Don't force me.'

'Fine.' Peter released his grip on the bag and continued walking through the lounge room, 'I'm not getting hurt to get a story.'

Slugger followed Peter all the way back to the Stag.

'Wait, Jack,' Slugger said finally, as Peter was opening the car door. 'We need to talk.'

Peter stopped. 'I thought we'd already done that—or tried to.'

'This is off the record,' he said. 'You know what that means, don't you?'

'Of course I fucking know what that means. You're going to tell me what really happened and I can't use it. Like taking a beautiful woman to bed and finding out she has an extra appendage.'

'Ivy doesn't know anything,' Slugger began. 'The boys always kept her in the dark.'

'Where did she think Pat went for two years?'

'She thought he was living with two Thai women in a beach villa in Phuket. He was having a mid-life crisis.' Slugger stopped for breath. 'Or that's what she was told.'

'Lucky him,' Peter replied. 'So why did he come back if his every need was being attended to in Thailand? Sounds like he'd already died and gone to heaven, except he comes back here to die. This time for real.'

Slugger began to shift uneasily on his feet. 'Not saying anymore,' he blurted. 'I've helped you enough.'

'You know,' Peter began, slamming the car door behind him and drawing nearer to Slugger. 'I'm starting to get this.'

'What do you mean?'

'You bring me here tonight on the pretext that Ivy is going to tell me everything, when you know she knows stuff all.'

'I don't get you.'

'I write a sympathetic story about the O'Leary widow and the filthy press leave her alone. Maybe everyone will leave the family alone. You're thinking like a lucid man all of a sudden.'

'You should be a bloody writer. Talk about fantasy land.'

'Was that your plan? Why are you protecting her, Slugger?'

'I'm going inside.'

Slugger walked away, over the lawned frontage of the high rise. Peter followed.

'Why are you protecting her? Off the record. You worked for them on the docks, didn't you? You were the standover merchant?'

'Leave me alone,' Slugger cried as he spun around and pushed Peter to the ground.

Peter fell onto the soft grass and lay there, winded momentarily. Slugger rushed over to him and pulled him up by one arm into a sitting position. 'I'm sorry, Jack,' he whined. 'I didn't want to hurt you. I don't hurt mates.' He squatted down next to Peter.

'Part of the game, I guess,' Peter croaked, shaking his head. He pulled a blade of grass out of his mouth.

'Ivy's my lover,' Slugger gushed. 'That's why I look after her.'

'Say again?' Peter shook his head with disbelief.

'Promise you won't publish this?'

'Okay,' Peter agreed reluctantly. 'It's just between you and me.'

'Ivy and me became an item not long after she married Pat. When I was the best boxer in Australia and she was the best looking sheila in Melbourne. Not that anyone knew we were seeing each other. Pat was always at work and I had an unhappy marriage. We sort of found each other.' Slugger chuckled at the memory. 'Ivy and me would meet at the Windsor every Friday for a bit of a cuddle. I had money in those days. Our afternoon delight, we called it. You know. If Pat had found out—whew! He would've…' He took a deep breath, 'But we loved each other so much that we were planning to run away. I wanted to go to the States and fight. Make some really big money.' He paused, brow wrinkled. 'Then Ivy fell pregnant. Just before the big fight with the Yank.'

'Did she have the child?'

'He's an O'Leary now.' Slugger flopped onto his backside, supported by his arms.

'An O'Leary?'

'Yeah,' Slugger whispered painfully. 'If I hadn't been knocked out that night, it would have been all different. All different.' He slumped forward as his voice trailed away.

'The fight that nearly killed you?'

Slugger nodded. 'When I woke up everything was different,' he continued. 'My brain wasn't what it was and I couldn't fight anymore. Then the money ran out. The house went, the car, the friends. The missus left. That didn't worry me at all. It was not having any bloody money.' He wiped his eyes.

'What about Ivy?'

'Ivy stuck by me all the way.' He took a deep breath. 'Pat didn't catch on that the boy wasn't his. In fact he got me a job at the docks. I became his trusty sidekick, you might say. Funny that, when I'd been sleeping with his missus.'

'She gave up thinking about leaving Pat O'Leary?'

'Ivy's a good woman,' he bristled. 'She would never leave Pat. Not with kids and a growing business.'

'I don't understand. You loved each other.'

'I told her to stick with Pat. What could I give her? Only barely function when I'm loaded up on bloody pills.' He began to sob. Peter placed an arm around him. *This is one of the saddest stories I've ever heard*, he thought. *In the top ten. And I've heard it all.*

'You gave her up?'

Slugger pulled out a long, white handkerchief and blew his nose vigorously.

'What about the boy?' Peter continued.

'Tommy's an O'Leary now,' Slugger continued. 'He's the eldest. Turned out to be a real go-getter, you know. Head of the family. It would have been different if he'd stayed with me. No future there.'

'Does he know you're his father?'

'No. I'm Uncle Slugger,' he replied through gritted teeth, 'and he is never to know. Get it?'

Peter stiffened as he watched Slugger clench and unclench his fists.

'Between you and me,' Peter nodded.

'I'm telling you as a mate. Off the record.'

'I know. I know. He wasn't the one that got…'

'No, that was Mickey.' Slugger paused. 'Poor bloody kid. He's the youngest. What a horrible way to go. Tommy's the red haired boy. '

'So why did Pat and Mickey get knocked over, Slugger? You'll remain anonymous,' Peter questioned. 'You hang around them. You must know something.'

With that statement, Slugger leapt up and headed towards the front entrance. Peter followed suit, only more slowly, at a safe distance, until the entry door.

'How should I know?' Slugger tossed over his shoulder as he opened the door. 'I've got a scrambled brain remember?'

'I'll see you at the Tote sometime,' Peter replied, as the door swung open. Next to the lift stood Ivy, now dressed in a fresh nightgown.

'Take care, Jack. Could be a chilly wind,' Slugger said as he and Ivy got into the lift and the door, with sign still affixed, closed after them.

Peter eased the Stag away from the kerb and headed back around the corner into Johnston Street, his sleep-deprived mind racing with every scenario he could conjure up at twelve-thirty at night. So close to home, it was hardly worth starting the engine. *Pat O'Leary returns from his suck–fuck paradise in Thailand, only to be gunned down by Ivy O'Leary, Thomas O'Leary, an unknown other party, or even Slugger. Take your pick. It's become an Agatha Christie novel without the poison or the butler.* Peter wondered if Slugger could operate a gun in his state of mind and with his shaky hands. In his state of mind? What were Slugger's parting words? *Could be a chilly wind.* And was that a wink just before the lift door closed? Peter was sure Slugger had winked as he said it. *Wink?* Peter stopped the car and threw it into neutral. What was Slugger trying to say? Suddenly a chill came over Peter, as if he had been lowered slowly into a pool of freezing water.

12

The press conference room was already swarming with journalists from all the television channels and the dailies by the time Peter stepped nonchalantly through the door and pushed his way to the front. He hadn't seen so many journos gathered in one place since the last happy hour at the press club. Now they were all turning up to try and get the best scoop since the Hoddle Street massacre. *Swim in my wake*, Peter thought, *Peter Clancy has just entered the building. Remember, I am the headline. Woodward and Bernstein. I'm both. All rolled into one. Eat my runny shit.* Sure, it was arrogant but you had to be to deal with these fuckers. A pack of starving, worm-ridden dogs. They'd eat their offspring or sell their grandmothers for a story.

Peter noticed the stares, heard the snide comments as he elbowed his way to the podium. *How could Clancy scoop us? He's from that pornography rag. A hack for a porno rag. Clancy should stick to what he knows. Tits and bums. It won't last. Clancy's pissed more times than sober. Lives at the Tote.* Peter smirked as he looked left and right. At last. He had recognition from his esteemed colleagues, even if it was begrudging. At that moment, it felt better than a Walkley.

Some well-known journalists gathered close to him and even Gavin, his long-estranged ex-friend, stood nearby. Peter wanted to yell out, *I thought you were going to become editor of The Age. What happened?* His musings were soon interrupted by the arrival of an entourage of police through a side door. They were packing heat today. Police Commissioner Stapelton led an ensemble of detectives, including Dale McCracken, who looked sharp and self-important in a silver grey suit. No matter what rank they were, uniformed or not, you could always pick a copper, like you could always pick a nun. Apart from the cropped hair, coppers had battle-hardened stares, eyes devoid of emotion. As a result, Peter had always found it difficult to read a copper. They were all hard bastards, nearly as hard as an old journo. The commissioner wasted no time getting down to business. He tapped the microphone several times.

'A heinous crime was committed two days ago in Clifton Hill,' he began, 'but before I speak more about the victims and the circumstances of their deaths, I would like to warn you that attempting to gather the names of the victims or speculating on what occurred before the police have released the details will not be tolerated. I repeat: Will not be tolerated.'

Peter could feel Stapelton's gimlet eyes piercing him from the lectern. Their eyes met. *Fuck you,* Peter thought, *we both have a job to do.* He grinned back.

'I'm not naming the newspaper in question here today, but its editor will be receiving a terse warning directly from me as soon as I leave this press conference.'

The commissioner's gaze moved from Peter to Dale McCracken. McCracken stepped forward and stood at the commissioner's right side. Peter felt all the eyes in the room fixing on him. He looked over at Gavin, who had his best sneer on for the occasion. The journos could sense weakness; one of the pack about to succumb. Let's finish him off. So they thought. *I'm ahead of the pack.* Peter smirked at Gavin, who looked away. *Or should I say, I'm the pack and they're the mob of sheep.*

Commissioner Stapelton continued. 'Detective Senior Sergeant Dale McCracken has extensive experience in homicide and organised crime and will be heading up the investigation. As you probably know, he led the investigation into organised crime on the docks five years ago.'

The commissioner tapped McCracken on the shoulder and stepped away. McCracken preened, running his hand through his hair and adjusting his tie, before approaching the microphone. McCracken looked confident. McCracken was an organised crime expert. *Maybe these were no ordinary murders?* Peter pencilled his thoughts into his notepad.

McCracken spoke without using notes. 'It appears that Patrick O'Leary and Michael O'Leary, his son, were victims of a crime committed two days ago at their home in Clifton Hill. Both victims appear to have been shot at close range as they were leaving for work. Both were taken to hospital where they were pronounced dead. We suspect they were shot multiple times by an unknown assailant or assailants. We are attempting to ascertain whether it was a random killing or if it was organised. At this stage, there are no suspects and no one is assisting us with our enquiries. We would urge the public to come forward with any information that is relevant to this case.' He paused to take a sip of water.

McCracken was right to the point. Peter speculated that he probably wanted to answer as few questions as possible. And no hard ones.

'I will be heading up the investigation team, which will consist of detectives and uniformed officers and based at St Kilda Road. I would be grateful if you would pass on any information you gather directly to me before publication. Time is of the essence in this case, and I don't want the investigation hampered by press interference and speculation. Questions? Briefly...'

Peter waved his arm furiously. 'Detective Senior Sergeant McCracken,' he began.

'Mister Peter Clancy—we meet again,' McCracken leered as he pointed his finger towards Peter. His comment was greeted by chuckles. 'You have a question?'

Cockhead, Peter thought. *Well, I'm not here to admire your suit.* 'Will you be largely concentrating on organised crime because of your extensive experience in that field?'

'That was only my resume, Mister Clancy,' McCracken bit back. 'Don't get this case and my resume mixed up.'

He smoothed his moustache. Another opportunity for everyone to laugh at Peter's expense. Before Peter could follow up with another question, someone else cut in. It was an inane query about when the case would be solved. *Dumb,* Peter thought. *It's amateur hour here in Smallsville.* He threw up his hand.

'Question,' Peter called out.

'Mister Clancy,' McCracken laughed. 'Looks like someone had a good liquid breakfast this morning.' The journos sniggered.

'Patrick O'Leary disappeared two years ago. It was assumed that he was dead. There were theories then that he was murdered due to his evidence to the Costigan Royal Commission. Any reason why he suddenly returned from the dead?'

McCracken's lips started to move but nothing was coming out as he searched for an appropriate reply. He looked down and shuffled some papers on the lectern.

Got you, smart arse.

'You can't answer the question, Detective Senior Sergeant, or you don't want to?' Peter interrogated.

McCracken's head shot up. His eyes were slitted, his face sanguine. 'That information is confidential.' McCracken was fuming. 'I will not be disclosing any information about Patrick O'Leary at this conference. No further questions. Thank you.'

He gathered his papers and stormed from the podium, but not before throwing a final menacing glare at Peter. With McCracken's and his team's departure, the journalists quickly began to dissipate. Peter scribbled some notes into his pad before closing it and slipping it into his coat pocket. A familiar throat clearing alerted Peter that Gavin was standing directly behind him. He turned around slowly.

'How to win friends and influence people. Looks like the Detective Senior Sergeant and you are old friends.' Gavin was ever the cynic.

Peter wondered why he and Gavin had ever been mates at university. Once the fun-loving, bohemian savant, Gavin had now reinvented himself as a caricature of Roger Moore, resplendent in a tailored woollen suit, leather shoes, and an acquired posh accent. Where was the martini? Obviously he was having trouble losing his throat-clearing habit. *Gavin Jenkins, you're a long way from the working class government housing shithole of Inala in Brisbane.*

'Gavin,' Peter began, holding out his hand but dropping it quickly when he noticed that Gavin wasn't going to reciprocate. In a single, fluid motion, he tucked the hand into his trouser pocket. 'What's with the accent?' He turned away and began to walk towards the exit with Gavin close behind. 'Are you turning into James Bond?'

'Well, I do work for *The Age*,' Gavin replied. 'I'm a sub-editor now.'

'You're nearly there,' Peter increased his walking pace from leisurely to brisk as he left the press room in an attempt to pull away from Gavin. Gavin kept following closely.

'Is this how you treat old friends, Peter?'

Peter stopped and swung himself around. Gavin hovered between him and the exit, preventing Peter from pushing open the *get the fuck out of here* door.

'Friends?' he said. 'That wasn't how we left each other at the wine bar, as I remember. How are the English lords by the way?'

'Okay,' Gavin began, 'we didn't part on good terms. I accept that, but because we're old mates I have a proposal.'

'Oh yes, and what's that, Gav?' Peter shot back. 'You'll teach me how to speak like Alec Guinness so I'll get a job at *The Toff*. I mean *The Age*.'

'Still caustic, embittered and bolshie, I see,' Gavin sighed, placing his hand on Peter's shoulder. 'I've been following your crime column closely. It's very good. You've finally hit your stride after all these years.' Gavin cleared his throat. Again. 'Here's my proposal…'

Peter removed Gavin's hand from his shoulder. 'If you're offering me a job, I'm not interested, Gav. Now, if you don't mind, I have to get back to the office. I can feel another scoop in me waters.'

'A twenty-five per cent pay rise if you come and work for us. How's that sound?' Two uniformed policewomen eating their lunch were trying to pass. Gavin blocked the doorway.

'I'm not interested.' Peter pushed Gavin aside so the women could enter, and smiled at the officers.

'You're a fool if you stay at *The Truth*. Everyone knows it's going broke. You'll be out of work in six months.'

'Still not interested,' Peter shouted as a herd of policemen approached.

'I'll be at the wine bar in Hardware Lane at five,' Gavin managed to call out, as he was swept up in the group.

'He's not interested,' one of policemen joked, as the others laughed as the door swung shut between them.

13

Shazza was sitting bolt upright looking studious, a pair of reading glasses perched at the end of her freckled nose and typing as if her life depended on it. Peter banged on the counter bell several times. She ceased typing and peered over the rim of her spectacles.

'You're really annoying me.' Peter grinned. 'Where have those long and painful hangovers of yours gone? I miss them.'

'You're a sadist, Peter Clancy. Why would you want to see a sweet innocent girl like me in such a position?' she snapped back. 'I don't have any intention of ever having one again, unlike yourself.'

'We'll see,' he smiled and gave a wink.

'I'm not going to break, Clancy.'

'There's a big piss up at the press club on Friday. Drinks are half price. I'll even pay.'

Shazza looked uncomfortable and squirmed in her chair. He could see beads of sweat gathering on her forehead.

'No,' she stammered as she removed her glasses, 'I won't. I'm not giving in.'

'Admit it,' he laughed, 'you nearly broke.'

'You're an evil bastard aren't you?'

'I just hate to see a great relationship between you and the bottle break up.'

'Piss off,' she retorted, as she pushed her glasses back on and resumed typing furiously.

The office was eerily quiet and empty, except for the hissing sounds of the coffee machine and the presence of Mad Dog, who was standing over it stabbing randomly at the buttons.

If the coffee machine is broken and Mad Dog sees me, he'll come after me. Mad Dog turned around. *Too bloody late.* 'Is it running okay?' Peter said tentatively.

'Running like a dream,' Mad Dog whispered as he stroked the coffee machine. 'It's a real work of art. You know you can get better coffee if you show it some love.'

Peter wondered what Mad Dog had been finding in the pantry lately. 'I suppose,' he replied vaguely, and moved past Mad Dog into his cubicle. He flopped into his chair and after gathering his thoughts he began to type. Then he looked up with a start. Mad Dog was hovering over him like a vulture over a carcass.

'The other morning was full-on, wasn't it? Lock and load all the way, baby,' Mad Dog chuckled. 'Haven't seen that much bloodshed since the Tet Offensive.'

'It was crazy. Part of the job, I guess.' Mad Dog grabbed Peter in a bear hug and squeezed. He could feel and smell Mad Dog's rancid, canine breath on his face. He sat rigid, too afraid to move, attempting to overcome the nausea that was rearing up into his mouth. *Help! I'm being attacked by a Mad Dog. I'll get rabies.*

'If you need to cry, need to scream, I'm here. Just let it out. Let it out, man.' Mad Dog shook Peter several times. *Not the brown acid, Mad Dog. Not the brown acid.*

'I'm fine.' Peter was able to squirm away from Mad Dog. 'I don't need to cry or scream, but if I do, I'll let you know.'

Mad Dog stood back and adjusted his bandana, which had slid off his head onto his neck. 'We're a team, baby. The lock and load team.' He adopted a kung fu stance and snapped off several punches and kicks into the air. At the same time, Bob was calling out from his office.

'Got to go!' Peter bounced out of his chair and dashed to the safety of Bob's office like a hundred metres sprinter.

Bob was screwing the cap off a new bottle of Jameson's just as Peter flew into the office. 'You're keen, Clancy. I don't think I've seen that kind of response from someone since I waved five hundred in front of a hooker,' he said dryly, pouring a measure into two glasses.

'No, it's Mad Dog,' Peter puffed as he lowered himself into the chair. He reached for the whiskey glass and downed the contents in one gulp.

'What about Mad Dog?'

'He's getting madder. If that's even possible.' Peter motioned Bob to pour him a refill.

'I noticed,' Bob replied. 'He was singing to the coffee machine before you came in. I think it was *War Pigs*.'

'Does this have anything to do with what happened yesterday?' Peter asked, taking measured sips this time. 'Maybe he's getting combat fatigue. The other day might have set him off.'

'Probably. I've seen it before.' Bob paused to light a cigarette. 'Not only soldiers get it. I've seen a few correspondents lose it over my time. I saw an American bloke when I was in Saigon jump out of a window at the Hilton Hotel screaming he couldn't take this anymore. Right in front of me.'

'What are you going to do?' Peter ventured. 'He might hurt someone. Especially me, if that coffee machine shits itself. I'm the coffee machine mechanic, remember.'

Bob leaned back on his chair. 'I'll give him a week off,' he said. 'He just needs a rest.'

'I frigging hope so.'

'Progress?' Bob changed the conversation and put his hands behind his head. 'What's the latest?'

'I was over at Slugger's last night,' Peter explained. 'The Widow O'Leary is staying with Slugger Douglas. She wanted to talk to me.'

'What was she doing there?'

'It seems that they go back a very long way. Let's call them "friends".'

'Bloody excellent, Clancy,' Bob bellowed as he shot forward in his chair.

'She didn't know much, or at least that's what she told me,' he began. 'She didn't seem all there, as expected. She said that the old fella had gone to Thailand to do business for two years.' Peter wasn't going to mention what Slugger had confessed to him. *Never rat on your sources.*

'Still great stuff,' Bob added. '*Years of Anguish for Widow as She Waits.* Then he returns and is gunned down in a hail of bullets. The human angle. Now a grieving widow. Again,' he rattled off. 'Ask Mad Dog for a photo from the other day. A nice emotional one.' He picked up his glass and drained it.

Peter rose from his chair. 'Okay,' he said slowly.

'By the way, the police commissioner rang me. I believe you know him: Jack Stapelton.'

'That was quick. And?' Peter felt his blood pressure rise as he sat down again to listen.

'Full of frigging piss and vinegar,' Bob spat, his face growing crimson. 'The stupid bastard thinks he can dictate to us what we write—well, bugger him. I've dealt with tougher cops than this silly bastard. And New York cops are the toughest. If he thinks they can feed us information and we cheerfully print it…Those days are over because *The Truth* has just entered the ring.'

'Let's brawl, then.'

There was a sudden crash from outside Bob's office. Peter threw open the door and ran up the corridor towards the kitchen, as Bob waddled behind. He found Mad Dog clutching the broken remnants of the coffee machine. Broken shards from the jug were scattered nearby. Shazza had leapt up from her desk and was watching the scene unfold from a safe distance.

'She's dead,' Mad Dog said. 'I've had enough of this shit.'

'Settle down,' Bob soothed him. 'We'll get another. A better one.'

'Can't do this anymore, Bob.'

'I told you, Mad Dog, we'll get a new coffee machine.'

Peter watched Bob placating Mad Dog as if he were a child.

Mad Dog leaned against the kitchen bench, fatigue and resignation written all over his face. 'Not just the coffee machine. All of this.' He waved his hands around.

'I was about to suggest that you should take a week off.'

'A week's not enough,' Mad Dog replied. 'I'm going home.'

'What do you want me to do for you?' Bob stubbed out his cigarette and tossed it in the sink.

'You, Bob? Nothing. Mad Dog is going home,' he announced. He pulled himself up and glanced around, as if playing to a crowd. 'Mad Dog is going home,' he repeated. 'Never to return. Carol Comely has just left the building.' He put down the coffee machine, strode past his desk and out the door.

'Carol Comely?' Peter said.

'That's not the full horror. Carol Sisyphus Comely. Maybe his parents wanted to raise a tough boy. Or a girl. I promised him I wouldn't tell anyone.' Bob gazed at the door, looking as if he half hoped Carol might change his mind and return. 'I'll ask one of the lads to check up on him later. See if he's all right.'

The incident had shaken Peter.

'You all right, Clancy?' asked Bob. Losing one was bad enough, but

The Truth couldn't afford to lose Peter too. 'Go home. Rest. Come back tomorrow.'

Peter nodded. A double murder. A crazy photographer. The police on his back. And now there was no coffee. It had been a rough week thus far.

14

If there was a time to have a drink, this was it. This was condition critical. Mad Dog's derangement was to blame. It was unsettling. Peter almost tripped with anticipation as he entered the door of the Tote. The barman was pouring his first VB as he slipped onto the barstool in his favourite corner of the bar. *I'll only have five pots,* Peter told himself as the barman placed it in front of him. *I really need it today.*

Peter lifted the glass and sipped eagerly at the froth. Much better. All stress is floating away. Who needs meditation when you can have a hard-earned Vic. Vic Bitter. The Victoria Bitter ad jumped into Peter's mind. Hard men quenching their dusty throats after a day on the station or down the mine. *That's me. A hard man and a pretty bloody stressed one at the moment.*

'There've been people here asking for you,' the barman said.

'What's that?' Peter murmured, snapped back to reality.

'Two blokes,' the barman continued. 'One's wearing a cowboy hat.'

'Slugger?' Peter reasoned aloud. 'But he doesn't wear a cowboy hat.'

'No. No.' The barman replied and pointed to the other side of the bar, near the juke box. 'Those two blokes. The Abor…'

Peter caught sight of Sam and Dave waving at him. 'Bloody hell!' he called out as he leapt off his stool. 'I didn't expect to see you here.' Peter hugged Sam and then moved onto Dave.

'Settle down. We only saw you two weeks ago,' Sam laughed. 'We thought we'd take a look at the big smoke,' he added. 'See how the other half live.'

'It's such a surprise. How did you know I'd be here?' Peter asked.

'We just asked the taxi driver. Do you know where Peter Clancy camps?' Sam laughed.

'Sure.'

'You're always talking about the Tote Hotel,' said Dave.

'Sounds like your second home,' Sam observed.

'It's where I come to relax. Drinks? My shout.' Peter waved to the barman.

'Lemonade for me, thanks,' said Dave.

'Small shandy, barman,' said Sam.

'Okay. I'm celebrating with two old ladies, but I'm going to still enjoy it.' Peter was just happy to surround himself with his mates. Friends he could count on.

Two hours later, with Peter increasingly merry and relaxed, Sam began trying to persuade him that they should get something to eat.

He reluctantly agreed. 'We'll have the usual home cooked meal. How about that?' he slurred back at Sam, as he gathered his change off the bar.

'Do you cook?' Sam asked, a little perplexed. 'Only, I don't imagine you being able to boil an egg.'

Dave appeared equally puzzled.

'Sam was right,' Peter joked as he led them down the road, then darted across Johnston Street between the traffic with Sam and Dave in his wake. 'I'm flat out opening a can of baked beans. It'll be home cooked. At my real home, The Apollo Café.'

Roula must have glimpsed Peter from the corner of her eye as he entered. Without looking up, she said, 'You having guests tonight, Peter?' as she wrapped a bundle of fish and chips for an elderly man.

Con wiped his hands on a towel hanging over his shoulder and came out from behind the counter. 'Hey, Peter,' he said, slapping him on the back, 'you bring in new customers?'

'They're friends of mine, Con. From up north.' He turned towards Dave and Sam, adding, 'Con and Roula are my Melbourne family. They've adopted me. Without them, I'd starve. And I'd miss Easter and Christmas entirely.'

'He come and eat with us every Greek Easter. I make the *yiros* and Peter, he bring the beer and a big appetite,' Con chuckled. 'Is good to meet you. I am Constantinos.' He pumped Sam's and then Dave's hand. 'And she is my wife, Roula.'

'Samson Clancy,' Sam replied, 'but everyone calls me Sam.'

'Dave Tindall.'

'Very good,' Con said. 'So, you both family of Peter? From up north?'

'Not really,' Sam ventured. 'We're more old friends from way back who have come for a visit. See the big smoke.'

'Oh,' Roula said. 'Plenty to do in Melbourne. Lots of Greeks here. Almost as many Greeks here as in Athens. Must be a good place.'

'You staying long?' Con asked as he returned to his place behind the counter.

'Until Peter kicks us out,' Sam winked at Peter.

'Then, one day you must come to our place. We'll have Roula's *arni me patates*—roast lamb with potatoes—a little *rigani* on them, they melt in the mouth. Okay?'

'Only if we're not imposing,' Dave replied, looking at Peter.

'No. No. Peter like family. He comes to our place to eat sometimes, when Roula thinks he get too skinny,' Con joked. 'Any Sunday, Peter,' he continued. 'You bring them for lunch?'

Peter was embarrassed by the extent of their hospitality. He'd never reciprocated. He never could. 'All right, but it's my turn this time.' He couldn't cook, but he could char a sausage as well as anyone. 'Next weekend, a barbecue at Yarra Bend, all right? All you have to bring is yourselves.'

'You sure?' said Con doubtfully.

'Of course I'm sure. Bring the family. We'll all be there,' he glanced at the boys.

'Okay. We be there. Twelve o'clock, Greek time.' Con laughed. 'Which is mean one, maybe two…'

'One o'clock. Aussie time.'

Roula shrugged. Sam and Dave looked equally surprised. 'So, I get you a big meal tonight? Something extra nice for your guests,' she laughed.

'They're country boys so they want to eat lots of meat.'

'Or fish and chips. They look good,' Sam interrupted. 'I'm not fussed. I'll eat anything right now. Even the backside off a dead cow.'

Peter squirmed.

'Then you have three extra special souvlaki. We make the best,' Con thumped his chest. 'But this one, I make extra special for you.'

'What's that?' Dave asked.

'Souvlaki,' Peter repeated. 'Lamb.'

'No worries, is extra good. You come back and tell me if is no good. But I know you love it.' Con started preparing their order.

Peter noticed Dave still looked anxious. 'Sam and Dave have never eaten Greek food before. Where they come from, a Chinese take away is considered high dining.'

Con laughed. 'They come here every day for more after they eat this one. Is very good.'

Roula busied herself warming the pita bread on the grill, while Con sawed off chunks of barbecued lamb. The boys salivated, watching her smear the pita with garlicky yogurt and loading it with the lamb and salad. She rolled the lot up and pushed three fat cylinders towards them, wrapped in white paper and squeezed into plastic sleeves.

The boys were gathered around Peter's flimsy 1960s dining table, tearing mouthfuls from the now half-wrapped parcels.

'Good tucker, this,' Sam announced, biting into a piece of meat. 'Best lamb I've ever tasted.'

Dave nodded and wiped juice from the corner of his mouth. 'Really good.'

Peter took another mouthful. 'This is only the start. You're gonna love eating in Melbourne. There's everything here. And if it's not good, it soon closes down.'

'I wish those people would come up north,' Sam remarked. 'Clarkes Flat would love this.'

'You reckon they would?' Peter jibed. 'I doubt they'd try it. They'd think it's too exotic or spicy. All they like is their cold beer and burned barbecued steaks.'

'Hey!' Dave bit back. 'We're not all rednecks. There are some open-minded people there. We've just met a lot of rednecks lately because of all the crap with Max. Don't forget, you came from there.'

'Precisely,' said Peter. '*Came* being the operative word.'

'Okay, boys,' Sam raised his voice, 'enough of the arguing. We have to think about camping arrangements.'

'I'm not sharing mine,' Peter joked.

'I'll sleep on the floor,' Sam suggested. 'I brought my swag.' He pointed to a rolled up khaki ground sheet, tied with a cracked leather belt. Inside were Sam's clothes, bedding and a bag of toiletries.

'You can have the fold-out bed in the spare room, then,' Peter told Dave.

'Lucky me,' he sighed. 'I just saw it. Will it last the night?'

'It'll be fine.'

'I hope so. My back isn't the greatest.'

With Dave looking maudlin, Peter decided to steer the conversation in a different direction. 'So, what do you want to see while you're here on holidays?'

'We haven't talked about it,' Sam replied.

'I could take you to a Collingwood game this weekend at the MCG,' Peter said as he wrapped up the bundles of paper. 'There's lots to do.'

Sam and Dave were silent. Sam lowered his head and fidgeted with his feet.

'For two blokes who are supposed to be on holidays you don't look very excited.'

Another long silence. Dave finally spoke. 'We're not actually here on holidays, Peter.' He looked at Sam anxiously.

'What's wrong?'

Sam pulled out a note from his shirt pocket and handed it to Peter. He unfolded it and read it out aloud.

The only good nigger is a dead nigger. Prepare to die, coon.

Peter screwed up the paper and threw it on the floor. 'Disgusting. Must be something to do with the case.' He reached into his trouser pocket and retrieved his wallet. He took out a crumpled note. He gave it to Sam to read.

If we ever see you in Queensland again you're dead, Clancy.

Sam handed it back to Peter who scrunched it up as well. 'It was left for me at the motel I was staying at.'

'I got one too.' Dave read his out:

You're a traitor and traitors are going to die.

He ripped it into several pieces and sprinkled the pieces on the table.

'Looks like we're members of a select club,' Peter attempted to joke. 'I wouldn't make anything of it.'

'Those notes were only the beginning,' Sam murmured.

'Beginning?'

'Someone ran me off the highway when I driving from Clarkes Flat to Prospect Hill five nights ago. I just managed to avoid a tree.'

'It could have been a drunk driver?' Peter conjectured.

'Then someone started shooting in my direction when I was backing up the car,' Dave sighed.

Peter's eyes widened with disbelief. 'That's terrible,' he said.

'Lucky it was dark and there was a rock to hide behind because I reckon they would have got me.'

'You didn't see who it was?'

'Landcruiser ute,' Dave replied. 'Could be anyone.' Dave turned to Sam. 'Tell Peter what happened to you.'

'I was staying at the caravan park near the beach in Townsville when I heard the window breaking and then next minute the van was on fire.'

'What the hell!' Peter exclaimed.

'Someone threw a Molotov cocktail in through the window,' Sam added.

'They've been following the both of you. Is it Max, you think?'

'Max or his devoted supporters, I'd say. Could be his wife, for all we know,' Dave said as he stretched out in the chair.

'It's madness,' Peter shook his head. 'It's the wild west.'

'So that's why we're here,' Sam lamented. 'I've always wondered how you live down here.'

'Queensland is a big state. You'll eventually find somewhere to live away from Max,' Peter observed. 'You won't have to stay here forever.'

'Wherever we go in Queensland, the cops are going to know and some of them are going to tell Max,' Dave said. 'And I should know. I was once one of them.'

'Well,' Peter assured him, 'you're going to be safe in Melbourne. No Max or his henchman will get you here.'

'Don't go and live back there for a while,' Sam added.

'You don't have to worry about that,' Peter replied. 'With that thought, I need a beer.' He hopped up from his chair and went to the fridge, retrieved a VB and pulled off the tab. 'Nightcap,' he said. 'Sorry I didn't offer, but you two like the lolly water. There's some in here, if you want it.' He returned to the table and sat down.

'Thought you were cutting down,' grumbled Sam, glaring at Peter. 'So this place is safe?' He stood and picked up his swag. 'Can you leave your house and car unlocked?' He undid the strap around the swag and rolled it out.

'I would strongly advise against it. This isn't a country town. So, if I leave you the key to this place you have to make sure it's locked up. The druggies will break in and steal everything.'

'But we can walk around the city,' Dave asked. 'We're not going to get robbed, are we?'

'Of course not,' Peter laughed and took a final drink from the can before crunching it up. 'This isn't New York. You can even walk around the city at night. I feel a lot safer here than up north. I think they're mostly friendlier here than up there.'

'We believe you, maybe,' Dave replied up as he got up from the table. 'So what's happening with your crime column? Anything exciting?'

'A father and a son got gunned down in their garage as they were going to work.'

'Hey, you said it was safe here.' Sam stopped making up his bed.

'Excepting psychopaths, there's always a reason why people get killed like that.'

'They've either dogged on someone or they owe a debt,' Dave surmised.

'So you're safe, Sam,' Peter grinned, 'for the moment.'

'Those psychopaths,' Sam asked nervously, 'where do they hang out? Are they around here?'

'You have more chance of being struck by lightning than being killed by one of them. So don't worry about it,' Peter sounded a little annoyed. 'They don't all live in Melbourne, as we all know by now.' With that statement, Sam appeared to relax. He slipped off his clothes down to his singlet and underpants and crawled into his swag.

'Smells like the bush,' Sam said as he stretched out and snuggled into his pillow.

'Dave, I've been meaning to ask you,' Peter continued, 'you know a bit about photography.'

'It was part of the private investigator course. Why?' Dave replied.

'The crime photographer at *The Truth* went crazy yesterday and we need another one in a hurry.' Sam's eyes popped open and he sat bolt upright in his swag.

'Is he one of the mad blokes? The ones that kill people with axes?'

'Sure was. He nearly chopped my head off,' Peter teased. 'No, he just went crazy. He was in the Vietnam War. Go back to sleep.'

He continued talking to Dave. 'So what do you reckon?'

'Yeah. Sounds all right. I could do that.'

'Come in and meet the boss tomorrow morning,' Peter called out, as he headed to the bathroom. 'If he likes you I'll need you to cover a funeral I'm going to.'

'Have you got a job for me?' Sam asked. 'I don't want to sit around here all day.'

'I don't know if they'll be much work for a stockman in Melbourne,' Peter laughed.

'I can do more than that,' he replied defensively. 'I've done a few things in my time. Crocodile shooter, labourer, boxer, truck driver. I worked on the wharves in Darwin. I've done a bit, you know, young fella.'

'I'll ask around,' Peter yawned. He smiled wryly. 'I know…I know a drag queen who runs a club. Maybe you could be one of her dancers. You'd look good in a sequinned dress and feather boa.'

'Piss off, young fella,' Sam said as he threw his pillow in the direction of Peter.

15

'I assume you've seen a bit of blood and guts, being an ex-copper?' Bob asked as he eyed Dave up and down from behind his desk. Bob pulled out the familiar bottle of Jameson's and three glasses from the top drawer of his desk.

'Enough.'

'You drink, Dave?'

'No. I used to get bad hangovers,' he replied quietly as he fidgeted in his chair.

Bob poured out two glasses. 'Unlike your mate here,' he grinned as he handed a glass to Peter. 'If I thought you two were going to get on the piss all the time, forget it. You're not on drugs?' he asked.

'No way.'

'You haven't got a psychiatric condition?'

'Of course not,' Dave replied uneasily, looking at Peter.

'It's a good chance you'll go mad hanging around Clancy,' Bob laughed. 'Peter probably told you about the last bloke. I don't want a repeat of that.' Bob drained the remnants of his glass. 'You seem a quiet bloke, Dave. A solid country boy.'

'I guess.'

'I like that. I was one of those once. Came from Wangaratta. Now look at me,' he tapped on his gut. 'Good. I want someone dependable. On time.' He glanced at Peter.

'Why are you looking at me?' Peter asked.

'You have other qualities, Clancy,' Bob said. He turned back to Dave. 'And you know a bit about cameras?' he continued.

'I did a private investigator's course. Cameras are a major part of the job.'

'Good.' He poured out another scotch. 'How are you going to find living in the big city? You're not going to get frightened by the noise and all the people?'

'I lived in Brisbane for two years.'

Bob and Peter laughed.

'Brisbane,' Bob teased, 'that's a country town.'

'I'll teach him the lay of the land, Bob. Don't you worry,' Peter grinned as he slapped Dave on the back.

'All right. The job is yours.'

'Great,' Dave and Peter replied in unison.

'But don't let me down,' he warned as he checked his watch, 'I don't want any stuff ups, especially now. We could be onto the biggest story this paper's ever done so I don't want anything missed. No pressure, Dave.'

'I work better under pressure, Bob,' Dave assured him.

'It's nine-thirty. You'd better get down to Saint Pat's for the O'Leary funeral to get a good position. It's going to be a big one.'

Peter sculled his glass and both men jumped out of their chairs.

'I know I'm throwing you in at the deep end, Dave, but I've always found it a good way to learn. Now piss off.'

'We're gone, Boss.' Peter threw open the office door.

Hundreds of mourners were already filing into the grey monolith of Saint Patrick's Catholic Cathedral when Peter and Dave arrived in Cathedral Place to take up a vantage point among the media throng opposite the entrance. They managed to push in beside a camera crew from a commercial television station, who were reluctant to yield an inch to accommodate them.

'Give us some room here, you pricks,' Peter complained as he jostled in beside Barry Pritchard, a tall reporter with a blond tipped muffet, a surfer's tan and a huge ego. He was known in the Melbourne journo community as *Ilmo. I Love Myself Only*. Ilmo was not a trained journalist, although he was once a ruck-rover for Carlton. Which were two big reasons for Peter to really dislike him.

Barry Pritchard easily pushed the lighter Peter back onto the street. 'What the hell are you doing here, Clancy?' he laughed. 'Shouldn't you be in the pub?'

Dave stepped in and elbowed Barry out of the way. Barry nearly tripped on the kerb.

'Don't argue, mate,' Dave glared at Barry, who took a step back when he realised he was outclassed by the infinitely younger and more solid Dave.

'Yeah don't argue, Ilmo,' Peter said as he wriggled in beside Dave. 'This bloke is an ex-Queensland cop.'

'You *Truth* blokes are a bunch of bloody cowboys,' Pritchard said as he adjusted his tie. 'Gutter press.'

Peter laughed. 'Not me. But it looks like you are, Ilmo.' Barry was actually standing in the gutter. 'Don't get the leather shoes dirty.'

Suddenly all attention was drawn to two long hearses coming into the street followed by three black limousines. The convoy pulled into the cathedral's courtyard. Dave lifted the camera and started snapping.

'Good, Dave,' Peter encouraged. 'Don't hesitate.'

The mourners in the limousines streamed out and headed up the front steps of Saint Patrick's. Other mourners who had not made it inside took up positions in the courtyard and spilled onto the street. Peter noticed Slugger getting out of the second car. He looked dapper but also bewildered, in a suit that looked brand new. One of the O'Leary boys waved impatiently at him to join them.

'That old bloke's a friend of mine,' Peter remarked to Dave as he pointed out Slugger to him.

Dave left the footpath to take a few shots from closer in. Peter grabbed him on the arm when he noticed Ivy O'Leary getting slowly out of the first limousine, assisted by one of the funeral attendants. 'That's the widow, in the veil,' Peter instructed Dave. 'Get a picture of her.'

Ivy was dressed totally in black, as expected, her face partially obscured by a long black veil. Peter could still detect no emotion on her face, although she was pale as she moved to stand beside her sons and Slugger. She lifted her veil when the first coffin was hauled from the hearse and touched it with one hand. It was draped in St Kilda Football Club colours. The second coffin followed, also draped in St Kilda colours. At the sight of the second coffin, Ivy started to cry. She laid her cheek against the coffin and kissed it. The attendant held her tightly by one arm. With that cue, a bagpiper at the entrance of the cathedral started to play *Danny Boy*. The coffins were slowly lifted up the cathedral steps and into the dark interior.

'That's it?' Dave asked.

'No, we'll wait around until after the service,' Peter replied.

'These O'Leary's know how to put on a funeral,' Dave observed, as he lowered his camera. 'I haven't seen anything like it.'

'They made their money off the wharves,' Peter replied. 'By honest means. Apparently.' They walked back to the footpath. 'Hopefully it won't take long,' he added. Unfortunately, it seemed he was wrong.

'You must be getting thirsty, Clancy,' Barry Pritchard joked when they returned to their original position.

'Hey, Barry,' Peter snapped back, 'your make-up's running.'

One hour later the bagpiper reappeared and started playing again at the entrance of the cathedral.

'About time,' Peter yawned. 'Same thing again. More photos of the funeral party. Don't make it obvious.'

The two left the kerb again to get closer to the proceedings. They positioned themselves near a tree at the entry to the courtyard, about two hundred metres distant. Dave kept taking photos of the first coffin and the pallbearers, of which Slugger was one. He continued until the second coffin was loaded into the hearse. The pallbearers assembled on both sides of the hearses like an honour guard. Peter tapped Dave on the shoulder.

'Let's get a better shot.'

They moved closer. Maybe too close. They were the only media people standing next to the hearses. The other media contingent remained on the footpath.

'Where's your respect?' a mourner yelled at them. A man shoved Peter backwards. He only regained his balance by grabbing hold of Dave.

'Maybe we should go,' Dave frowned, as he lowered his camera to his chest.

'Get a picture of the cars leaving and we'll get out of here. It's getting too hot.' Peter knew from past experience that the media's presence at prominent funerals could cause tensions to rise. Funerals and post-trials: prime times for journos to be turned into punching bags. Taking pot shots at the press was the way some people released tension.

Peter was the first to notice that some of the pallbearers had begun to notice them. Except for Slugger, they all looked to be solid, young, hardworking men, obviously men off the docks who probably worked for the O'Leary's, and had that *don't fuck with me* persona. Robbie O'Leary broke from the pack first and raced towards Peter.

'Time to go,' Peter hastily warned Dave, as Robbie O'Leary threw a wild punch at his face. 'The camera. Don't let them grab it,' he blurted as he managed to duck the punch.

Dave had just enough time to lock the camera in a vice-grip, as a bear of a man in an ill-fitting suit attempted to snap the camera from him. Dave's hold on it was stronger and the bear gave up and turned his attention to Peter, pushing him back into the throng of mourners.

The archbishop who had officiated at the funeral was now standing at the first hearse waving his hands frantically at the crowd. 'Move backwards, away from the cathedral,' he called out.

Two priests scurried, still in their vestments, down the steps of Saint Patrick's and started to move the crowd away from the hearses with trained precision. The crowd quickly complied. It was as if the archbishop was Moses and he had just parted the Red Sea.

With the push, Peter had fallen backwards against a legendary ex-football player from Carlton who seemed in no particular hurry to move for anyone, including the archbishop.

'You're in a bit of a bloody pickle here, aren't you, son?' The player laughed as he righted Peter back onto his feet.

Dave grabbed hold of Peter by one arm and pulled him back through the dispersing crowd. Peter's new suit coat, which he'd only replaced the day before out of his own money, was torn and he could feel blood trickling from his nose. Hand cupped over the flow in a futile attempt to prevent further damage to his outfit, Peter was just able see two policeman running towards them, narrowly followed by Barry Pritchard and his crew. He also glimpsed Slugger attempting to reach the fracas.

'Stop it, Robbie,' Slugger implored, as he shoved aside one of the priests and another pallbearer who was trying to reason with him.

'Scum journos,' Robbie O'Leary cried as he grabbed Peter from behind. 'And you're the bloody worst, Clancy.' Robbie spun him around and landed a punch in Peter's midriff. He doubled over. Meanwhile Dave kept pulling at Peter's arm. For a moment, he was strung out between them like a rag doll.

'Keep moving,' Dave instructed.

'I'm fucking trying,' Peter cried as he doubled over again.

'How dare you interview Mum after her husband and son had just been killed. Scum bastard!' Robbie yelled.

He spat at Peter, just as a police officer seized Peter by the collar. He was still clutching his abdomen as a second police officer grabbed him. 'What in the frig did I do?' he swore.

'Language!' one of the priests said tersely. 'We are on holy ground.'

'Yes, Father.' Even in immense pain, in fear of his life and under threat of imminent arrest, Peter, the ex-Christian Brothers' boy, gathered enough of his senses to apologise. Robbie pulled away from the police officer and attempted to land another haymaker on him. Slugger grabbed the punch before it landed on Peter and turned Robbie's arm behind his back.

'What are you doing, you stupid old man?' Robbie cried with pain. The police officer now took hold of Slugger.

'Leave him alone, Robbie, he's a mate,' Slugger yelled. 'He was invited. Ivy and I invited him to my place the other night.'

'What?' Robbie intoned. 'You did what?' Then Robbie exploded and twisted out of the Slugger's grip. 'You punch-drunk old bastard!' His body shuddered as he shoved Slugger to the ground. Slugger fell on his back but slowly raised his head and shook it. The police officer, now in a state of total confusion, grabbed Robbie again.

'We should have put you away years ago. I don't know why Mum wanted you around,' Robbie cried. Ivy came from out of the crowd and fell on Slugger.

'Leave him alone, Robbie,' she cried as she cradled Slugger's head in her hands.

'Why, Mum. Why?' Robbie sobbed. Passive now, he appeared to lose all strength and allowed the police officer to lead him away.

Peter was attempting to straighten up when he saw Barry Pritchard and a camera in front of him.

'Looks like you're going to be on the news tonight,' Pritchard grinned as he shoved a microphone in Peter's face.

'Piss off, Ilmo, before I shove that up your arse,' he growled, covering the mike with his hand.

***

'I'd like a drink for every time a Truth journo has been shoved around,' Bob sighed as he tapped his desktop, deep in thought. Peter was slumped in Bob's office chair having his cuts and abrasions attended to by Shazza, who was saturating a cotton ball with Mercurochrome. Dave was sitting in the other chair, wincing as she started to dab it onto Peter's forehead.

'Shit,' Peter cried out as Shazza patted an abrasion, 'I don't want any more pain. I've had enough.'

'You're a sook, Peter Clancy,' Shazza laughed. 'Hold still.'

Bob seemed unaware of commotion going on in his office. His strumming on the desk became faster and harder. 'Well, we can forget about the O'Leary family wanting to talk to us, can't we? I just wanted us to look slicker, more professional. Keep the fence-jumping and the stunts away from the public eye. Can you do that Peter? Can you please try?'

'All right, Bob,' Peter replied meekly.

'This has organised crime written all over it,' Bob resumed. 'Everyone's ready to explode. I can feel it. I can taste it. I was in New York during the Mafia turf wars, so I don't care what you do to get the edge on the competition. Oh, and I have one more thing to tell you: I'm bringing in an old colleague of mine to help out.'

'An old colleague?' Peter started. 'I think we're right with this story, Dave and I.'

'You know how it was going to be a weekly crime column,' Bob added. 'In view of what's happening, I'm going to expand it to twice a week.'

'So? We can handle that, no worries, Bob.' Peter paused to reflect. 'Is this because of today?'

'No. No. It's nothing to do with that. Stella Reimers will bring a wealth of experience to the job that you don't quite have yet, Peter. She is the best crime reporter I've ever seen. And New York is a tough place. I've been to war zones that are like holiday resorts compared to New York back in the seventies. She's tough and she gets results.'

'So now I'm a frigging cadet. This is my time, Bob. My chance. Do you think I want to be a sleaze merchant forever? Fuck you. Fuck Stella Reimers,' Peter snapped and stood up to leave.

Dave grabbed him by the arm. 'Relax, mate. Let's hear Bob out.'

Peter hovered over the chair, but didn't sit.

'Here's my vision for you and Stella. You're going to be a team,' Bob persisted. 'A team of investigative reporters. Like Woodward and Bernstein.'

'Woodward and bloody Bernstein,' Peter shook his head. 'What's so good about them? Even the movie was boring.' Bob had his best poker face on. 'Do I have a choice?'

'You have two choices, Peter,' said Bob. 'You can be part of the team or not be part of the team. I'll get someone else. That's it. The story is going to be huge.'

Peter sat down as he thought. 'So how is this team going to work? We can't be doing the same thing.'

'Stella starts tomorrow.' Bob beamed. 'We'll talk about it then.'

'That it?' Peter said as he rose again.

'I know you might be pissed off at the moment but this is going to work. I promise.'

'It better,' Peter sighed and looked at Dave and Shazza. 'This story deserves it.'

***

Peter and Dave arrived back at the flat a little after five.

'Sam. Where are you?' Peter called out, as he opened the door. He threw his bag on the dining table. 'You sleeping again?' he yelled into the silent flat.

Dave padded across to the spare room and looked in. 'He's not here.'

Peter glanced around, hoping Sam had left a message. 'He hasn't left us a note. So where is he?' he wondered. 'If he's gone for a walk he won't be able to find his way back. Sam's never lived in the city.'

'Maybe we'd better go and look for him,' Dave suggested.

'Where do we start?' Peter fumed as he reached for his car keys. 'Melbourne isn't actually small.'

'He's got a limp so he shouldn't get too far,' Dave remarked.

'Don't count on it.'

They drove around Collingwood without success. Then they checked the Tote and the Apollo Café. Still no Sam.

'I'm going to ring the police,' Peter said anxiously.

'Waste of time,' Dave replied. 'It's too soon. They won't even take down a report.'

Some of the regulars at the Tote agreed to check a few of the laneways in exchange for beer, but Peter couldn't just sit on his hands and wait. 'I'm going back to the flat,' he told Dave, 'in case, by some miracle he manages to return there.' Dave had no reason to stay at the

Tote, so he left a few moments later and followed Peter back to the flat.

Peter was fumbling for his key when a rusted Kombi wagon with faded blue paint pulled up beside him and the side door slid over. Sam eased himself out and called back to other passengers.

Been in Melbourne for a couple of days and he has friends already? How, Sam, how?

'Thanks for the lift,' Sam waved. 'I'm all for it. Right on, bro,' he laughed. He turned around and noticed Peter's stony face. The Kombi roared away belching smoke.

'Have a good time?' Peter interrogated.

'Where did you go?' Dave asked. 'We've looked all over the place.'

'I didn't hang around here. No bush here.'

'Where the hell did you go?' Peter asked.

'Not really sure. I went that way,' he pointed west, towards the city. 'I ended up in a park, a big one, with a fountain and a grand old building.'

'The Exhibition Building? How did you get there?'

'I walked,' Sam replied. 'And after that, I walked through the university. It was only a couple of streets further down. Bought myself a copy of *Das Kapital* while I was there. Funny, some of the kids were staring like they'd never seen an Aborigine in a book shop before.'

'Bloody hilarious,' said Dave.

'Maybe they never saw one reading Karl Marx before,' Peter added.

'So, then I was going to walk back home, but I only got as far as Fitzroy before I got tired. Walking in the city's not like walking through the bush, you know. It's hard on the feet. I was sitting on a bench when some brothers asked me if I had a smoke and we started talking. Good people those city brothers,' Sam said cheerfully. 'Peace and love. Land rights. They're all for it. They gave me a lift back here.'

'Good for them.'

'I'm glad you had a good time, Sam,' Peter chuckled, 'but have you ever thought of telling us where you're going?'

'I would have, but I couldn't find a pen.'

'Here, have one of mine.' Peter took a pen out of his shirt pocket and handed it to him. 'No excuse, now, okay?'

'One thing with all that walking. It's made me hungry. No bush tucker to nibble on in the city.'

Dave laughed. Peter thought briefly about cooking them all

something for dinner, but decided on another home cooked meal from the Apollo instead. Why mess around with perfection?

They perched in front of the television with a pile of fish and chips as Dave lay in front of the set, clicking through the channels and finally settling on the ABC.

'You don't want to watch that,' Peter remarked casually.

'I want to watch the news. It'll be on in a minute.'

'Yeah, me too,' said Sam.

Peter was outvoted. He thought of leaving, but Dave encouraged him to stay.

'It shouldn't be that bad,' he said.

'You reckon?' Peter growled. He checked his watch. Seven o'clock. The news and the lead story. *Scuffle erupts at prominent businessman's funeral. Truth journalist involved in the fracas.* He looked away. It was going to be a train wreck.

'Hey, that's you, young fella!' Sam pointed a chip at the screen. He shifted himself to the edge of his chair, straining to see the screen. 'What are you doing lying on the ground?'

'I was tired,' Peter exploded as he leapt off the couch, 'what do you think?' He grabbed his wallet and headed for the front door.

'Where are you going?' Dave called out as he fled.

'To the Tote. I need to debrief with Victor and Bob.'

'You want us to come?' Sam asked.

'I want to be alone for a while,' Peter said as he closed the door.

Sam and Dave exchanged quizzical looks. 'Why's he going all white fella on us all of a sudden?' Sam asked.

'He had a bad day today,' Dave replied. 'And he knows he'll probably have another bad one tomorrow.'

16

Peter arrived at the office early, feeling heavy and bleary-eyed. Contrary to his original plan, he'd returned home after only one VB and spent most of the night tossing and turning and thinking about Stella Reimers. At four o'clock in the morning he drank a glass of port and finally convinced himself that he was being stupid and childish. How could he be threatened by someone he hadn't met? It was ridiculous. *Peter Clancy threatened. Peter Clancy intimidated. Not on your...*

He sensed a different atmosphere in the office as he walked down the corridor towards his cubicle. It was a hint of perfume. Then he heard a new voice: an assertive, loud, hammer-drill of a New York accent. It was reminiscent of New York during rush hour: not that Peter had ever been there. *One day.*

His guts twisted tighter and tighter as the voice grew louder. He hadn't been this stressed since his first day as a cadet journalist. That old, familiar Peter Clancy coping mechanism was kicking in. *I want to run. Over hill and dale. Run. Until I find a pub.* Stella Reimers spun in her chair when she heard Peter approach. *Too late.*

Great! he thought. *She's in the next cubicle next to me. Team bonding. I hate team bonding.*

Stella bounced out of her chair as if she'd pressed an ejector button, just as Peter threw his bag on his desk.

'So, you're the infamous Peter Clancy?' Stella proclaimed, thrusting her hand towards his. 'Pleased to meet you.'

Peter had prepared himself to dislike Stella, yet he liked her accent. He always liked the New York accents. It was up there with his other

101

favourites: Cockney, Aboriginal and Irish. She wasn't what he'd expected. She didn't look like a journalist who could reduce New York cops to blubber. He expected a woman in black, a Cruella DeVille type, who ate puppies for breakfast. What he saw was an attractive, bottle blonde in her forties, well coiffed and finely tailored—more corporate than journo, more real estate agent than body-counting crime investigator. Maybe she did a better job of camouflaging her darker side than Cruella.

Peter took her hand. She pumped it harder than he'd expected. 'Me too,' he said.

'Feels clammy,' she observed. 'You feeling okay?'

'Just…' he stumbled. 'Just a bit…' He scratched for words.

'Not contagious are you?'

'Just feeling a bit under the weather.'

'That's what people say when they're hung over, isn't it?'

'Yeah. Sorry,' he replied. 'It's part of the Aussie way of life.'

'No need to explain,' Stella laughed. 'I spent a year here as a college student. I lived with a family in Sydney. My God, it was backward. Like stepping back in time thirty years. No brewed coffee in the coffee shops.'

Peter nodded. He thought of his recent experience up north. Some places hadn't changed.

'The beaches were so pristine and the sea was like a jewel,' she continued. 'Men were mates and women were sheilas. And me, I was the Yank. From what I've seen thus far, things have changed. Improved.'

'We joined the rest of the world. At least Sydney and Melbourne have. Large parts of Australia are still instant coffee.'

'How about we go out for coffee and bagels? Bob tells me there's a cafe around the corner that sells them and he says they're not half bad,' she suggested. 'I'm starving. You eat bagels?'

'Of course,' he replied. 'Although I think I just need a drink.' He caught Stella smiling. 'And by that, I mean a coffee.'

***

'I saw you on television last night,' she commented as they finished ordering and sat at the nearest table. 'You don't mind putting yourself in the line of fire.'

'Embarrassing,' Peter cringed. 'Got too enthusiastic.'

'No.' She shook her head. 'You showed gumption. I like that. Initiative. You're as much a part of the story as the story itself.'

'You think so?' he brightened. 'Thanks. *The Truth*'s always had a reputation for assertive reporting. The other papers in Melbourne are softer in their approach. They like to build relationships. We prefer to break them down.'

'Word of advice: Fuck the other papers. You have to eat them.' Stella's bagel arrived. She smeared it with cream cheese and bit into it. 'Most of my stories came from the streets or tip-offs, not from press conferences and press releases. You have to get in there and shake it around.'

Peter gazed at her with admiration, although he felt as if he might have just glimpsed Stella's inner Cruella. Was it possible to admire someone and be shit scared of them at the same time? As he pondered, Bob wandered into the conversation, sallow-faced Bill Symes riding his coat tails. Bill was the kind of senior journo who never shared a lead. Stella wiped her fingers, stood up and kissed Bob on both cheeks. Bob motioned to Bill to find himself somewhere else to sit.

'How's my crime reporting team settling in?' Bob asked, as he grabbed another chair from the next table and eased himself into it.

'You know what? The bagels really aren't half bad, the coffee's good and so's this guy. I mean bloke,' she laughed. 'Early indications are he's got balls.'

'He has,' Bob chuckled. 'He just needs me to twist them every now and again.'

Stella laughed loudly. Peter didn't.

She pushed her half eaten bagel away and sipped her double espresso. 'Bob has brought me up to speed with what's happening with this O'Leary story,' she told Peter. 'It's got the sense of a Mafia war about it.'

'You don't think it's a straight out murder. A crime of passion?' he asked.

'In my experience...' she hesitated. 'The way I figure it, they're rich. They run the dockyards. Dockyards are the epicentres of crime everywhere. They've pissed someone off. They definitely stink. There'll be more going down. You wait and see.'

'That's why it's important to have your scanners with you at all times,' Bob stated.

'I've got mine.' Stella took her scanner out of her handbag. 'Thanks, Bob. Most places I've worked I've had to buy one myself.'

'Where's yours, Peter?' Bob asked.

'I must have left it at home.'

Bob looked unimpressed. 'If you want to stay on this story, Peter,' he spat, 'you better get your scanner. That scanner's got to be more important to you than a well-earned shit. Get it?'

'I get it. I'll go home and get it now, okay? Sorry.' He took a last mouthful of coffee and bounced out of his chair.

Stella's scanner crackled into life.

Report of two shots fired at Footscray Market. Cars in the area of Footscray market…

'Already?' Peter stopped in his tracks.

'Better go,' Bob ordered. Peter and Stella exchanged glances. 'You're both going. Hurry.'

'Where's Dave?' Peter asked.

'Last I saw, Dave was flirting with Shazza at the front counter. I'll tell him to meet you at your car.' Bob was already headed towards the office as his voice trailed off. Peter was surprised to see how briskly he was able to walk when motivated.

'Which car?' Stella asked.

'The Stag.'

'The Stag?'

Peter replied, 'It's a car.'

Dave barely managed to squeeze his camera bag plus his six-foot frame into the back seat. Stella looked anxiously at Peter as she watched him turn the ignition over several times.

'Does this old bucket go?'

'Slow start but a quick finish. Nearly there,' he replied, as the motor began to whine into life.

'The body will be in the damn morgue before we get there,' Stella remarked in frustration.

The Stag roared, blowing a plume of smoke out of the exhaust. Peter slipped it into gear and put his foot down. The Stag spun away from the kerb.

Stella grabbed hold of the dashboard. 'That's more like it. Don't worry about breaking the law. The cops will all be at the shooting.'

After breaking every road rule and running over a bin on the footpath for good measure, the Stag arrived at the Footscray Market, occupants safe if a little shaken.

'What's this place, then?' asked Dave.

'Looks just like an indoor market to me,' Peter remarked as Stella rolled her eyes.

'Like the meat packing district back home,' she observed, reading the names on the advertising boards. 'It's run by Italians.'

The car park was already teeming with police, ambulance and media.

'Shit,' Peter said as he flung open his door, 'the place is crawling.'

Stella had already jumped out and was heading towards the action. 'I'll go for the police,' she yelled, as she scurried in her high heels towards the police cordon. 'You look around the periphery.'

Peter crossed his arms and leant against the Stag as Dave assembled his camera. 'I might as well stay in the car,' he complained, 'she's claimed it for herself.'

'Stop whining,' Dave replied. 'We've got work to do.'

While Stella was ingratiating herself with the police, Dave and Peter rushed towards a refrigerator van emblazoned with the words, *Donarto's Fruit & Vegetable Distributors*. The police had taped off the crime scene from the back of the van to the loading dock area.

'What a frigging mess!' Peter said to Dave. 'It looks like a bloody fruit salad.' In the midst of the scattered boxes of peaches, apples and pears lay a man in a pool of blood.

Peter pushed his way through the media scrum. 'Shit!' he exclaimed as he caught a glimpse of the body right before an ambulance officer lowered a sheet over it. 'The poor bastard's face is blown off. My God!' He felt a wave of nausea and looked away at Stella, who was throwing questions at Dale McCracken. The diversion settled his stomach. McCracken's face was illuminated like a neon sign. Peter grinned. *The Yank attack dog is onto you, McCracken. Go on, Stella, bite the bastard!*

Dave was clicking off shots of the body, camera propped over Peter's right shoulder. 'Probably a sawn off shotgun at close range.'

'Over here,' Peter grabbed Dave and led him away to where Tony Donarto was being loaded into the back of an ambulance. Tony was sitting upright, holding a bandaged hand and looking grey with shock. Dave reeled off another series of shots.

'Fuck you!' Tony yelled as he pulled the sheet up over his face. 'Have you bastards no respect?'

'Everything okay, Tony?' Peter shouted back. Tony's eyes fixed on Peter.

'Clancy, you prick,' Donarto spat out. 'I'm not saying anything to you. Scum pig. I could still be deputy mayor except for you, you bastard.'

'Do you know what happened, Tony? Was this an attempt on your life? Any comments we can print?'

Tony was being pushed into the back of the ambulance. He grabbed the loose oxygen mask off his face and threw it at Peter, hitting him in the chest. The ambulance officer shoved Peter off to the side and slammed the door shut.

'Take care, Tony,' Peter waved. He turned to Dave. 'I wonder who the great Tony Donarto's been upsetting?'

Dave tapped Peter on the shoulder and motioned him to look at Stella and McCracken.

'They suddenly look friendly,' Peter declared. 'What's going on there?' He thought about rushing over there and interrupting, but he figured Stella could have her moment. Just then, he noticed a solitary man propped against the truck parked alongside Donarto's, trying to light a cigarette. His hands were shaking so much that he kept dropping the lighter, picking it up and repeating the whole process without success.

'Take a look at this guy,' he said to Dave. 'He looks pretty shaken up.' He started walking towards the old man. 'I'm gonna check him out.'

The man had given up trying to light his cigarette in favour of drawing his hands through his wispy hair.

'Need a hand?' Peter asked the man, as he picked up the lighter. He noted the man's bloodied apron.

'Very bad for my nerves. All of this,' the man said in faltering English.

Peter held the lighter to his cigarette.

'*Molto grazie.* Thank you. Thank you,' the man stammered as he sucked back on the cigarette.

'It's a very bad thing,' Peter agreed. 'One man dead, another injured. You look like you could use some help as well,' he added sympathetically. 'Did you see everything?'

'You from the police?'

'No. From the paper. I'm just trying to find out what went on. I'm Peter.' He held out his hand.

'Gianni.' The old man refused Peter's hand. 'But I can't talk to you. You make all this sound bad.' He took another drag on his cigarette and looked away.

'It won't be like that, Gianni. I just want to know what you saw. I won't even mention you.'

'No. Sorry.' He threw his cigarette on the ground and stamped it out.

Peter looked at Dave and shrugged his shoulders. 'You see that woman over there?' Peter pointed to Stella who was now having a heated argument with a journalist from one of the television stations.

'She very angry,' Gianni replied.

'She's my boss.' Peter embellished. 'If I don't have some information to give to her she'll bust my balls.' He looked pleadingly at Gianni.

'Why do I care?' Gianni retorted. 'Your balls, not mine.'

'Let's see if this helps.' Peter pulled his wallet from his pocket and offered two fifty-dollar bills.

Gianni shoved the notes in his pocket. 'No photos of me, all right?' He glanced around nervously.

'Promise.'

'They pull up in a white Commodore. I no see their faces because they wear hoods.'

'How many?'

'Two. They shoot Frank as he unloading the truck. Mister Donarto, he hit too, but he okay. He jump behind a bin. Then they go. Like that.' Gianni moved away from the truck. 'I go now.'

'Just one more question,' Peter asked, blocking Gianni with his body.

'Be quick. I gotta go.' Gianni was looking anxiously past Peter and Dave to a group of men, who were gesturing him to come to them.

'Did you notice anything interesting about the shooters?'

'One man run into the other one and he swear at him.'

'Anything said?'

'"Stupid prick", I think. Like that. I don't know for sure.'

Gianni left a puzzled Peter and Dave standing beside the truck.

'Not sure that helped us much.' Peter waved at Stella to signal that it was time to leave.

'Marvellous Melbourne, all right,' Stella laughed as she slipped into the passenger seat of the Stag. 'More like murderous, marvellous Melbourne.'

'So what did Dale McCracken have to say for himself?' Peter asked as he turned on the ignition.

'He thinks you're an asshole,' Stella smiled.

'That's complimentary of Dale. Really? And here was I thinking that Dale and I were great mates,' he replied sarcastically. 'Dickhead.'

'And we could be in the midst of a family feud,' she beamed. 'Now that could be exciting.'

'Between who?'

'The O'Learys and the Donartos. Apparently they had a falling out. Over a woman.'

'How do you know that?' Peter asked as he stopped for a red light.

'From McCracken, of course. What a sweetheart.'

'Just like that?' he retorted. 'He would never have told me that.'

'Well, he doesn't want to ever date you.'

'What the hell!' Peter exclaimed as the car behind began sounding its horn. 'Are you going to go out with him?'

'Probably,' she replied in a matter-of-fact way. 'He's not really my type though.'

'This sounds a lot like honey-pot journalism. Now I'm really starting to feel redundant.'

'Hey, buddy,' she snapped back, 'I just want some information. I'm not going to sleep with him. You have your techniques, I have mine.' She opened her purse and took out her lipstick. As she applied it, she added, 'So, what did you find out?'

'Two shooters wearing hoods in a white Commodore. One swore at the other. That's it.'

'Anything else?'

'They traumatised an old Italian bloke.'

'See?' she grinned. 'We both brought home some of the bacon.'

Peter let the comment pass. 'Couldn't get anything from Donarto. He still remembers my story about him and the soap opera bimbo.'

'I'll have to work on him, too,' Stella burst out laughing.

'Probably. He hates me as well. You, on the other hand, seem to have a way with my enemies.'

***

Bob tilted back on his chair, hands behind his head, looking like a proud father as Stella recited the details of the shooting. Peter sat quietly, wishing he could join Dave and help process the photographs.

'Get this written up, you two, and we'll have it out tonight. We won't even have to wait for the press conference tomorrow. Good work.'

Peter rose from his chair.

Before you go,' said Bob, 'have you heard from Slugger recently?'

'I haven't seen him since the funeral.'

'Peter was telling me about him. Do you think you could find him?' Stella asked.

'Eventually,' Peter responded. 'I know all of his haunts. Hopefully he's not back in the mental ward.'

'If you can get him to talk,' Stella mused, 'we may be able to find out what's happening between these families.'

'You look for Slugger,' Bob commanded, 'and you don't have to come into the office until later.'

'I guess so.' Peter snuck through the door.

'Someone's got their knickers in a knot,' Bob remarked as Stella disappeared behind the partition separating Peter's desk from hers.

As Stella had busied herself with the article, Peter occupied his time by finishing off a fake letter to the editor and unpacking a new coffee machine on his desk. Since Mad Dog had had his meltdown, he had felt guilty that he'd somehow contributed to Mad Dog's psychosis by not maintaining the old coffee machine properly.

'So you're the coffee specialist around here?' Stella interrupted and sat on his desk.

'I just knew how to keep a buggered coffee machine operating,' he replied, 'until Mad Dog smashed it.'

'I heard. Poor guy. I've seen a lot of journalists take drugs and drink too much. And the failed marriages. You know the story.'

'And we get paid shit for the privilege. Gotta wonder why we do it.'

'Because we don't know anything else. You really think you could be an accountant?'

'Some days I tell myself I could.'

'Don't delude yourself.' She fingered the coffee machine. 'Hey! You didn't pay for the machine?' she asked.

'No. I managed to coax some money out of Bob, which is unusual. He's usually as tight as a fish's arse. '

'He hasn't changed,' she laughed.

'Bob told me that you and he worked together in New York.'

'*New York Post*, in fact,' she replied.

'The *New York Post*,' Peter repeated. That was something to put on a CV.

'Only the frigging best. We shared the crime circuit. Bob was one of the best reporters I've seen. He could get a lead story out of a stone.'

'So what brought you to Melbourne?' he questioned. 'We don't actually get American journos arriving here in droves.'

'I wanted to catch up with Bob. He's a great mate. I owed him a favour. And he wanted me to add my expertise to his new crime column.'

'So, he didn't trust me to handle this on my own?' Peter pushed the coffee machine aside.

'That's not what this is about. Bob wants the best crime column in the country. Remember, I did this for ten years in one of the toughest cities on earth. If you want my input,' she shot back, 'fine. If you don't: fine. I'm here to help. That's all.' Stella got off the desk.

'Sorry,' Peter apologised. 'I'm sounding like a jealous kid at the moment.'

Stella nodded her head in agreement. 'I'm not here to take over your column. I'm not here to diminish you.'

'You're not? What about today. You wrote the story. It's your by-line.'

'It's ours,' Stella leaned over Peter and tapped him in the back of the head. 'We're a team, remember? I said it and I mean it. Get that into your thick antipodean skull.'

'So we're Woodward and Bernstein?' Peter laughed.

'Better than them. Clancy and Reimers.'

'So where to from here, Reimers?'

'How about a drink tonight? To christen the partnership?'

'Maybe,' he sounded doubtful.

'Don't worry, Peter. I don't want to sleep with you, in case you were thinking that.'

'That's a relief. No offence.'

'None taken.'

Okay, meet me at the Tote,' Peter said. 'At seven. It's dark, the bands are loud and the carpet sticks to the bottom of your shoes. Dress accordingly. I'll draw a map for you.'

'We're going to make a great team,' Stella grinned. 'The rest of the media won't know what hit them.'

17

Sam and Dave sipped orange squashes at the bar as Stella and Peter cemented their working relationship with a long series of bourbon shots.

'Aren't you two drunk by now?' Sam complained, his stomach churning with hunger. 'You should be.'

'We're journalists,' Stella joked. 'Booze is one of the major food groups. We need it to get up in the morning. We need it to sleep. We need it to think. Vitamin B.' She held up her glass in a toast. Sam didn't reciprocate.

'Food,' Peter replied. 'If it wasn't for the Apollo Café I'd have died of scurvy years ago. You know I reckon I've eaten more meals in the Stag then at a table. Terrible, isn't it.'

'Eating in cars,' Stella chimed in. 'And the sleeping in cars. Chasing a story. I'm too old for that now.'

'We're fucking crazy,' Peter slurred as his finished off his sixth glass of bourbon. 'My shout.'

'No more for me,' Stella waved her hand. 'I want to be able to get out of bed in the morning.'

'I thought you'd be able to handle yourself?' he teased.

'One of the best lessons I've learnt in life,' said Stella as she got off the stool and checked that nothing had stuck to her skirt, 'is to never attempt to go drink for drink with an Australian journalist. I learnt that from Bob Connolly once in a bar on the Lower East side.'

'I should call it a night too,' Peter added. 'I don't want a hangover clouding my judgement.'

Sam started to laugh.

'I don't reckon you'd be able to function without a hangover.'

'I just have them on the weekends. Remember?'

'Well they must be bloody long weekends,' Sam replied, shaking his head.

Peter had given up waiting for Slugger to appear, when he heard a piercing scream coming from the rear lane. It pierced the hum of the bar and the background music. *A screaming, fucking banshee,* Peter thought. *No; more like Ian Gillan with testicular torsion.* It was enough to sober him up.

Mary Riley, an old backstreet boozer, appeared in the doorway babbling incoherently. She only started to make sense when her lower dentures fell out. She stooped to pick them up but her stomach was too big and her arms too short. No one seemed inclined to help her. They were accustomed to seeing her dancing to the bands that played at the Tote, looking for all the world as if she was having an epileptic seizure. Perhaps she was dancing to the music in her mind. Mostly, Mary was totally sloshed but now she was as sober as a babbling person could be.

'What's wrong, Mary?' Harry the barman leaned across towards her. He only looked mildly concerned, probably for the same reason as everyone else. She was hyperventilating and started to stagger. He darted from behind the counter and buttressed her, as she began to sink to the floor. 'Someone,' Harry called frantically, as he tried to keep her enormous frame upright, 'grab a chair.'

Peter snapped a chair from where they were sitting and rushed it to her. He was able to throw the chair under her before she hit the floor.

'What's happening, Mary?' he asked as he watched her slowly regain her breath. 'Take some slow, deep breaths.'

Mary was well known to Peter. She had even propositioned him several times. He had always politely declined.

'Horrible. Bloody horrible,' she cried. 'Out in the lane. Behind the pub.'

'What? What's in the lane? Did you see something?'

'Bloody horrible,' she repeated. 'Out there.' She pointed in the direction of the lane.

'Get her a drink,' Peter threw down a five-dollar note. 'I can't get any sense out of her.' Harry went back to the bar.

'Me teeth,' Mary pointed to her mouth. 'I can't talk without me teeth.'

'You can certainly frigging scream without them, Mary,' he quipped as he looked on the floor. He found them lying near where Stella was standing.

Stella jumped higher than if she'd seen a dead rat. 'You're not going to pick them up?

'The things you do in the name of journalism,' he grimaced as he picked them up delicately between two fingers. The others looked away.

'Here,' he said as he dropped the plate into Mary's left hand and wiped his fingers on his pants. She slipped them into her mouth. The barman returned with a glass of Mary's favourite rum. She drank it down in one gulp.

'Now I can speak,' she announced. 'That's better.'

'Speak then, Mary. Speak, for fuck's sake.' Peter rolled his eyes.

'In the laneway,' she began. 'I've been trying to tell you. There's a body lying in the rubbish.'

'A body?'

'Is the person dead?' Stella asked.

'Well, he's not fucking moving, love,' Mary shot back. 'He's all covered in rubbish. Shocking.'

'We better have a look.' Peter looked at Stella and then at the barman. 'Can you ring the cops?'

Harry already had the receiver in his hand and was dialling. He handed Peter a torch.

'Okay. Let's check it out,' Peter murmured as he stepped out onto the footpath.

'It'll just be some old, dead wino,' Stella added as she followed. 'Used to see more dead winos in New York than pigeons in Times Square.'

'You coming, Sam?' asked Dave as he got up to follow.

'I think I'll wait here. Seen enough dead bodies, thanks.'

Peter, Stella and a few of the others dribbled out of the pub and into the laneway. The body was lying in a heap of rubbish and overturned bins, just as Mary had reported, as if he'd suddenly dropped dead while rummaging through them. Peter shone the torch over the mound. The only parts of the body that were clearly visible were the legs. The rest was obscured by a pile of rubbish in black plastic bags that had been thrown out by the pub. The pants and shoes looked familiar. Peter inched forward and stood over the body.

'Should I see who it is?' he asked.

'I guess someone had better check in case he's still alive,' said Dave.

'I'll let you do the honours,' Stella looked away and put a handkerchief over her mouth. 'You sure you want to look? Something smells and I have a hunch it's him.'

'I think I might know who it is,' Peter replied as he delicately peeled back the pub's detritus of beer cartons and food waste from the corpse. 'Bloody hell!' He reeled back in horror as he recognised the body. Despite the early stages of decomposition and a gaping wound in the forehead, the identity of the body was unmistakable.

'It's Slugger!' He suddenly felt like vomiting. Stella kept her handkerchief clamped over her mouth.

Dave leaned forward to take a look. 'Pretty certain he's dead. Don't move anything else, Peter.'

Peter wiped his mouth on his handkerchief. 'Still a cop at heart, eh, Dave?'

Dave shrugged. Peter went back to the body and pulled a squashed beer carton over it.

'Your source?' Stella remarked as she lowered the handkerchief from her face.

'And a good one,' Peter sighed. He turned to Dave. 'What do you reckon happened?'

'Probably fell over. Happens a lot.'

'He was strong as an ox, but always having falls. Legacy of having his head beaten too many times in the ring, I guess,' added Peter. 'I wouldn't be surprised if Slugger was behind the bins having a piss, and fell over.' He blew his nose.

'You were fond of him?' Stella eyed Peter, searching for clues.

'I felt sorry for him. And we had some funny times. I shouldn't be thinking about having just lost my main source, yet that's exactly what I keep coming back to.'

'It's all right, Peter,' Stella comforted. 'All right, okay? Sometimes it's hard to separate the man from the journalist.' She took a final look at Slugger. 'I think I'll call it a night. The police might want to hear what you have to say about Slugger, but I'm going home.'

Peter looked at Dave. 'Let's get Sam and go home. I've made enough statements to the police to last a lifetime.' He stood with his head bowed for a moment, in silent prayer. *Goodbye, Slugger. God bless*

 'Let's go,' he said.

***

Peter and Stella were once again in Bob's office, contemplating the events of the previous night. The mood was solemn. Peter was sitting forward in his chair, head in his hands. He only raised it every so often to sip the whiskey Bob had poured for him. Stella had passed on the whiskey, but was pacing around the office. Bob rested his elbows on the desk, pawing his glass.

'I know what everyone's thinking,' Peter broke the long silence, looked up and placed his glass on the desk. Stella stopped pacing and sat down.

'My stories depend on sources in the street,' he began. 'I don't do well sucking up to authorities, the big wigs. That's my style. I've gone out of my way to piss off the top end of town.'

'We know that, Peter,' Bob threw in. 'That's part of your charm.'

'But in this instance, it's not going to work.' Peter scratched his head. 'Look at the sheet. McCracken and Donarto hate my guts. I'm going to get shit out of them. The O'Learys are only going to beat me up if I go near them again. And my only way into this story is now dead. I'm fucking dead in the water.'

'Do you think you could snuggle up to Ivy O'Leary again?' Bob asked.

'I only got that interview because Slugger set it up.'

'Where in the hell does that leave me?' asked Stella.

'Seems to me you're doing fine with McCracken and I'm sure Tony Donarto will be the same. That's where the leads are going to come from. You may be able to bend the O'Learys too. Who knows?'

'You want off the story then, Peter?' Bob asked as he picked up the whiskey glass.

'What's the point of having me *on* the story? My main source is dead.'

'Your theatrical sources,' Bob suggested. 'What about them?'

'They're only good with society gossip stuff. You know: which politician's sleeping with whom. Nothing to do with this.'

'What about all the sources you've used over the years? I thought you had a busload of them. These puppies of yours.'

'I've lost many of them,' Peter admitted. 'I should have found replacements but…' His voice trailed off. 'Sorry.'

Bob leaned back in his chair and looked at Stella.

'I think Peter would be a great loss, Bob,' she spoke up. 'I think he should remain on the team. I need someone to guide me through this crazy place.'

'I get it and I'm grateful. Thanks, Stella,' Peter replied. 'But I think you're able to handle yourself without me.'

'I don't do sentimentality. You're a fine journalist, that's all. It's pure self-interest.'

Sure it is. Like throwing a starving dog a bone. I've worked you out, Stella. You're more considerate than corporate.

'Today,' Bob interrupted, thumping the table. 'I want you to bring a major breakthrough to the table, today.' He stopped to take a drink of whiskey and look Peter in the eyes. 'And I don't care how you get it. Use that commando journalism of yours. Get me something or you're off the story.'

'Bob,' Stella questioned, 'is that wise?'

'My decision, Stella.'

As Peter sat studying his hands and contemplating his future, Bob gave Stella a wink.

'Okay.' Peter put down the still three-quarters full glass. He stood up and puffed out his chest. 'You want a fucking breakthrough? I'll give you one.'

'Clancy, you are so predictable,' Bob laughed. 'You love being backed into a corner, don't you?'

'All right,' Peter replied. 'So, I have a healthy ego.'

'So you're still on the story?' Stella asked.

Peter shrugged his shoulders.

'You have twenty-four hours,' Bob repeated as he held up a finger. 'One day.'

'Where are you going to start?' Stella asked. 'You're back to square one.'

'Fucked if I know,' he said. 'I'm going to have to go out there and find it, I guess. Maybe it will fall into my lap.'

'Let's hope so,' said Bob.

Peter could hear a commotion spilling out of the reception area as he was walking back to his cubicle. It sounded like Shazza was having a heated argument with someone. A very noisy argument. As he approached his desk, he caught every other word. Shazza was saying his name. Loudly. A woman responded. Equally loudly. *Peter Clancy*…He continued walking past his desk, all the way through to reception. It was exactly as he suspected. The woman having the loud confrontation with Shazza was Her Highness.

Concheetah was wiggling a gloved finger at Shazza while simultaneously tossing her feather boa around her neck. Shazza was standing with her hands on her hips, freckled face blazing with anger. Peter stood behind them, unnoticed, smiling, as the two went head-to-head.

'You don't get it, do you? I need to see Peter Clancy,' Concheetah argued. 'I'm a close friend of his. You think I'd waste my time coming all the way here if it wasn't important, you stupid girl?' She growled in her best tenor: 'Get him now.'

'I can't. He's busy, I'm telling you,' Shazza fumed. 'You'll have to wait.'

'Don't you know who I am?' Concheetah raised herself up to her full height. Six feet four, in heels.

'I don't care who you are,' Shazza shot back. 'I wouldn't care if you were the Queen.'

'Stupid peasant girl. I'm more than a queen. I'm a diva.'

Just then, the water cooler next to Peter belched. Concheetah spun around and caught him grinning.

'Have you been enjoying this?' she asked as she threw back her head in disgust.

'I was wondering who was going to attack first.'

'Sheeee,' Shazza elongated the vowel for emphasis, 'sheeee wants to see you.' That said, Shazza sat down and continued typing.

'How are you, darling? It's very important, you know,' Concheetah cooed as she planted a kiss on both of Peter's cheeks, leaving smears of red lipstick.

'In future, if Shazza tells you I'm busy, maybe you should just wait for me quietly in the reception area.'

'Darling, that sounds *so* hoi polloi.'

'Where's Ted?' Peter asked.

'He had to take a break from his act. His prostate has been playing up. Poor dear will probably need an operation.'

'So what did you come to tell me?'

'I can't talk here,' she whispered into his ear. 'Very hush-hush.'

'Then you'd better follow me to my desk,' he said as he pointed down the corridor, in the direction of his cubicle.

'Oooh, how exciting,' she gushed. 'Going into Peter Clancy's inner sanctum.' Concheetah's comment was met by a chorus of wolf whistles.

'Just try and tone it down,' Peter suggested, as they walked down the corridor.

Concheetah inhaled. She always played to an audience. Any audience. 'My dear fans all, Queen Concheetah is here.' She waved at the journalists, who had pushed themselves away from their desks to catch a glimpse as she passed. Peter felt himself blush. *There's going to be hell to pay.* He pulled out a chair when they reached his cubicle.

'Sit,' he ordered pointing to the chair.

Concheetah looked about Peter's messy desk, disdain on her face, as she lowered herself onto the chair. 'Positively post-apocalyptic, my dear,' she sniffed. 'I'm coming back here to do a makeover.'

'No, you won't!' Peter snapped back, grabbing a chair from the other cubicle and sitting face-to-face with Concheetah. 'I don't want my work area turned into a fucking bordello.'

'You, my dear, have no taste.' She rolled her heavily made up eyes, 'I could teach you. Teach you lots of things.'

'Coffee?' he retorted.

'You don't have anything stronger?' she whispered. 'I know you journos like to keep a bottle or two in the desk.'

'Okay,' Peter sighed and reached into a desk drawer. He pulled out a flask of whiskey and two plastic cups. 'My emergency rations. Not your usual poison. Will this do?'

'Of course.'

He half-filled both cups and handed one to Concheetah. 'I'm pretty busy, so you'll have to make it quick.' He took a sip from his cup.

'Cheers,' she lifted her cup and took a sip. 'Of course, you don't want to spend a lot of time with me…You're embarrassed aren't you?'

'I assure you that I'm not.' He looked around just as Stella peered over the screen of her cubicle and smiled. 'It's just that I'm on a deadline and I don't have anything.'

'Let's call it kismet, then, my dear. This might help you.'

'Shoot.'

Concheetah leaned forward. 'There have been a multitude of drug overdoses in St Kilda in the past two weeks. I found someone dead on the footpath in front of the club, last Thursday morning, the needle still stuck in her arm. A young girl, poor thing. She looked so angelic. She's someone's child. Everyone hates druggies, but I feel sorry for them. It's not their fault they have an addiction. Why not help them?'

'I agree,' Peter replied. 'Is that what you wanted to tell me?'

'You're not impressed?'

'These kinds of things happen all the time,' he countered. 'It's not actually earth shattering news. Obviously someone is cutting it too pure or is new to the game.'

'I began to wonder why would you want to kill your customers? Isn't that bad for business? That's why I thought I should tell you.' She asked as she upended her cup to drain the dregs. 'Something's rotten in the state of Denmark.'

'What about the cops? Shouldn't they be interested?'

'The cops couldn't give a shit,' Concheetah retorted angrily. 'They'd love all the druggies dead.'

'Maybe they would, but there'll always be more to replace them, I guarantee it.'

'So you're not interested?' She flicked the end of her feather boa.

'I can't see the relevance to what I'm doing at the moment.'

'You're working on the O'Leary and Donarto shootings? You're really in the thick of it.'

'Okay? You think there's a connection?'

'With the deaths? I'm not sure about that.'

'Then you think they have a connection to each other? I've been trying to work it out,' said Peter, 'but I've hit a brick wall. I don't see how the families are connected.'

'You should have asked Her Highness Concheetah, first,' she smiled as she tweaked Peter's cheek with her left hand. 'You're a very naughty boy.'

'Do you know them?'

'Not well, but we have been introduced. Two of the O'Leary boys, a couple of Russian brutes from Sydney and Tony Donarto used to come into the Velour Lounge together, every so often. But that was a while back.'

Peter's eyes widened with interest. 'Which of the O'Learys?' His interest meter was sitting at maximum. He grabbed his notepad from his desk and scribbled into it.

'Robbie.'

'And?'

'I don't know the other one.'

'Friendly?'

'Of course. Very cosy. Plenty of drinks, laughs and women who weren't their wives. High-class hookers. Only the best.'

'How recently?' Peter continued scribbling.

'Haven't seen all of them together in the club for about a year. Of couse, Donarto and his hooker friend were regulars until we had words a few weeks ago.'

'You don't know why the others stopped coming?'

'No, my dear. The O'Leary boys stormed out of the club one night and I never heard another thing about them until now.'

'Interesting,' Peter said as he tapped his pen on the notepad. 'You mind if I introduce you to my partner? Is it okay for me to share this?'

Concheetah preened her hair with her hands. 'You know how I hate playing to a crowd,' she sighed, 'but if you must.'

He spun around in his chair. 'Stella,' he called, 'I may have something.'

'That was quick,' Stella called back. 'I'm coming over.'

'Who's the lovely lady?' Concheetah said as she stood up for Stella.

'Concheetah, meet Stella Reimers, and vice versa,' Peter introduced the pair, closing up his notepad.

'It's a pleasure,' Stella smiled as she held out her hand and shook Concheetah's.

'You're an American!' she remarked with admiration. 'I love Americans.'

'New Yorker, in fact.'

'Fantastic. Andy Warhol. The Factory. Lou Reed. Studio 54. I love it. What are you doing in this backwater?'

'Let me tell you, Melbourne ain't no backwater, lady. No way,' Stella replied. 'Not how this story's going down.'

Concheetah giggled. 'You sure are new to this place. And I ain't no lady.'

Peter interrupted the love-in. 'Concheetah was just saying that the O'Learys and Tony Donarto used to come into the club until they had a public tiff about a year ago.'

'Unlikely friends,' Stella surmised. 'Maybe they were business associates?'

'I'll keep my ear to the ground,' offered Concheetah.

'Thanks,' Peter replied.

'You must bring Stella to the Velour Lounge for some decent, decadent entertainment.'

'The Velour Lounge?' Stella repeated. 'Sounds fantastic.'

'Darling, you'll think you're in New York,'

'The information,' Peter interjected. 'What's your take on it?'

'We're getting closer,' said Stella. 'But we just don't know how close it is yet. Damn.'

18

Peter and Dave opened the door of the flat to the scent of corned beef boiling. It was warm and familiar and, after the Antarctic blast of a Melbourne winter's southerly, more than a little welcome. Sam was standing over the stove in singlet and shorts with a tea towel hanging over one shoulder, ladling potatoes and pumpkin out of the simmering pot.

'You blokes are home early.'

'I haven't had corned beef since I was a kid on the station.' Peter smiled as he hovered over the stove drinking in the smell. 'Potatoes in their jackets. Tomato sauce on the meat. Yum.'

'Mum used to make this every Sunday,' Dave added as he was drawn into the kitchen to inspect the pot. 'She used to be such a good cook.'

'It'd taste better in a camp oven over an open fire,' Sam said. He replaced the lid of the pot and shooed Peter and Dave away. 'Stop hanging around! Don't upset the cook. Out!'

'It's a pity you can't build a campfire in Collingwood, isn't it, Sam?' Peter laughed as he reached into the fridge to retrieve a can of VB and a bottle of soft drink for Dave.

'Where did you get the corned beef?' Dave asked as he poured out a glass.

'At the butcher's. Where else?' Sam said shaking his head.

'Is there a butcher around here?' Peter asked as he flopped onto the couch.

'Just up the road,' Sam replied. 'I suppose you've never been to it.'

'The only place I've bought food around here is the Apollo. Okay—I know I should cook for myself more.'

'You, cook?' Sam sniggered. 'I'd like to see that.'

'Thanks for the vote of confidence. I have cooked noodles in the past. Boiled eggs. Oh, and that's right,' Peter recollected, 'I once cooked apricot chicken for a girlfriend. She was a babe. I thought I'd be in after I cooked her that. Unfortunately she became an ex-girlfriend soon after that.'

'Why's that?' Dave asked.

'I left the chicken out too long,' he replied sheepishly, 'and she got food poisoning.'

Sam and Dave burst out laughing.

'Fuck. I don't know why she was so upset. I got the frigging trots, too!' He sipped at his beer. 'We'd just gotten into bed and we were getting all hot and bothered when it happened. She rushed to the toilet and closed the door. For the rest of the night. She wouldn't let me in.'

'You didn't?' Sam laughed.

'I tried to get to the Tote but it was too late.'

'Where did you end up?' Sam asked as he pulled three plates out of a cupboard.

'Have you ever shit yourself and spewed at the same time?' Peter continued. 'That bloody happened.'

'Not in the flat?' Dave chuckled.

'I managed to get down a laneway, thank God. And went about my business in privacy with my arse in one bin and my head in another.'

'Disgusting.'

'Tucker's up, boys,' Sam was already dishing up the meal.

'Still feeling hungry, Dave?' Peter teased. 'After my story?'

'Starving.'

'Bugger. It didn't work.'

'I don't mind cooking,' Sam commented as they sat down to eat, 'but I wouldn't mind doing some work. I'm getting a bit stir crazy in this pokey flat.'

'I haven't been able to find you anything, Sam. I have been asking around,' said Peter.

'I'll have to go back to Queensland if I can't get anything around here. I'll take my chances with Max.'

'Don't do that, Sam,' Dave advised. 'It's not going to be safe.'

'I want to do something. I can't just lie around here.'

'You think you have problems,' Peter said as he hopped off the couch.

'Where are you going?' Sam questioned.

'To the Tote. I can't think here.'

'Do you go to the pub every time you have a problem?' Dave asked.

'Just about,' Peter shrugged. 'Some people go to shrinks, I go to the Tote. What's wrong with that?'

'Nothing, I suppose,' Dave ventured.

'Bullshit, it's nothing. Listen here, young fella. I've told you this once before. You drink too much,' said Sam.

'I can cut down. I could even stop drinking altogether if I wanted to. I've done it before,' Peter retorted.

'I've seen plenty of good men go bad because of that stuff. Do it for one day. Just one,' continued Sam. 'Don't drink for one day.'

'Okay, I'll do it. But not today. I've got a lot on my plate.'

'Why don't you talk to us about it?' Sam asked. 'We may be able to solve it.'

'Sure. How are you going to help me find a way back into this story?'

'Well, I'm definitely a genius,' Sam laughed, 'and Dave must be close to one, cause I'm teaching him everything I know.'

***

Even at six-thirty in the morning, South Wharf was a flurry of frenetic activity as gantry cranes, forklifts, trucks and men moved together in a close, at times, to the uninitiated eye, shambolic choreography. Long gone were the days when teams of men used nothing more than brute strength and trolleys to unload cargo from the bellies of ships, risking their health, and receiving only basic wages in return. Now, the machines outnumbered the men and cargo was enveloped in large metal containers. Containers that could be removed from the desks of the ships and placed on the waiting trucks within minutes. Where once hard living old wharfies would have taken two days to unload a ship, now it could be done within hours.

To Sam, who was picking his way through the men and machines, it seemed pointless that he should even ask for a job on the wharves. He could lift and carry any load, despite being middle-aged, no worries, but his only claim to fame was that he had once worked on the docks in Darwin. He'd never worked in a busy port like Melbourne. He wanted to turn around and find something else to do. But what? Jobs custom made for Aboriginal stockmen from far north Queensland were rare. He was making a mental list of everything he couldn't do in a big city. And then he smelt the sea and a strange calm overtook him.

Whenever he smelt it or saw it, he thought of the times he had spent with Annie all those years ago, eating crab or fish and making love on the beach in Darwin. He missed Annie every day. Even though she had died ten years ago, it still hurt like a fall off a bucking horse.

A forklift blew its horn impatiently at Sam. He called out to the forklift operator as he passed, but the forklift had whizzed away before Sam could shout '*Where is…*' Still, he pressed on and eventually found a ramshackle demountable building that had *Office* scrawled in paint on the front door. Two burly men wearing jeans and leather jackets stood out front. It took Sam several minutes to convince them that he wasn't from the media or the cops.

'Have you ever seen a blackfella in the police force or on television?' he asked the men.

They had no response to that.

The office was a mess of different smells: tea stewing in an urn, photocopy toner, sweat and stale tobacco. It was equally full of visual clutter: rusty filing cabinets, a sink piled with empty cups, and sheets of paper stuck on a noticeboard. Sam's eyes settled on the bearded man and a stout, short, middle-aged woman with bleached blond hair gelled into spikes, sitting together behind a new computer. It looked to Sam like the woman was trying to teach the man how to use it. He alternated between stabbing at the keyboard and scratching his beard with frustration. Another man—tall, irritated, red-haired and business groomed—was shouting into a phone. *Fuck* surged out of his mouth.

'Excuse me,' Sam muttered as he removed his stockman's hat. 'Is this where I come for a job?'

They each continued on without noticing Sam.

'Excuse me?' Sam raised his voice a notch.

The woman lifted her gaze from the computer screen. 'What do you want?' she asked brusquely. Her accent was so broad that she sounded like a parched crow.

'Got any work?' Sam repeated nervously.

The bearded man looked up and laughed. 'I didn't think any of you blokes had the ability.'

'I'm here to work, all right?' Sam answered back, only barely containing his anger.

'What's your name, mate?' the woman asked, her voice softening as she looked Sam over.

'Samson Clancy,' he replied. 'But everyone calls me Sam.'

'I didn't think blacks had names,' the bearded man smirked. 'Just blackfella. What are you doing here anyway, Abo? Did you walk off the mission and get lost?'

Sam clenched his fists. The man might have been younger, but Sam could have had him on his arse before he had enough time to jump out of his chair. Instead though, he relaxed his hands and smiled widely at the bearded man.

'That's enough!' the woman chastised, rapping the man in the back of the head. 'Sam's looking for work, so enough of the racist comments.' She stood up and smiled back at Sam.

'Just a joke,' the bearded man sulked.

'The name's Babs,' she began, 'Babs Bell. What sort of work do you do?'

'I'm a jack of all trades. Mainly worked in the bush but I've worked in the city too. Worked on the wharf in Darwin for a while.'

The man on the phone tried to drop the receiver back onto the hook but missed. 'Fuck! Fucking prick!' He replaced the receiver carefully and pulled a chair in beside Babs. He looked Sam over.

'We don't need any jack of all trades around here,' the bearded man smirked again.

'I do the hiring and firing around here, Robbie, remember?' the suited man interjected.

Robbie turned his gaze back to the computer screen. 'Sure,' he said timidly as he started tapping, 'you're the boss now, aren't you?'

'They're brothers,' Babs added, shaking her head in despair 'Always been like this.'

'Whatever,' Robbie pouted.

'I have no problem with Aboriginals, unlike my brother. But he's not the human side of this organisation,' the suited man announced, 'I am. The ones I've met are tough, honest people. Shame they get treated so badly.' The suited man stood up and held out his hand. 'Tommy O'Leary.'

Sam shook hands.

'Take a seat, Sam.' Tommy pointed to a chair near a wall. Sam pulled it over and eased himself into it. 'Been in trouble with the law?' he asked.

'Do I have to answer that?' Sam replied uneasily.

'Do we look like the law?' Babs smiled displaying badly stained teeth.

'I haven't been in trouble for a long time. Not since I was a young bloke,' Sam replied. 'I try to avoid trouble.'

Robbie rolled his eyes.

'We like to give people a second chance. We find that people give us more loyalty that way.'

'We don't like fucking cops either, blackfella. They still think everyone's crooked, like the old painters and dockers days. They're always sending in undercover cops to find out what's going on. Sometimes they come here looking for a job. You can pick 'em all right. You can almost smell the pricks. I'm still not too sure about you. You don't look like you're from around here,' Robbie sneered as he stuck his head over the screen.

'I'm down from Queensland,' Sam stammered. 'I've got relatives down here. I want to stay with them for a while.'

'Are you joking, Robbie?' Tommy laughed. 'Look at him. Does he look like a cop to you?'

'Just saying. You have to be careful.' Robbie looked down at the screen again.

'Honestly, I'm not that keen on them myself.' Sam replied. 'I don't like the bastards picking on us.'

'So, you're looking for a job?' Babs interrupted. 'Can you operate any machinery?'

'I've operated a forklift, driven trucks. I can lift.'

'Not a lot of lifting these days, although sometimes muscle power is needed,' Tommy added.

'You look too old, Abo,' observed Robbie. 'You won't be able to keep up. And you'll probably go walkabout on us.'

'I can work like a blackfella,' Sam joked.

Tommy and Babs laughed. Robbie didn't.

'I can give young fellas a run for their money,' he continued. 'No worries.'

'Show us what you've got, then,' Robbie said and pointed to the metal filing cabinet. 'Let's see if you can lift that.'

'Okay.' Sam rolled up his sleeves and went over to the cabinet. 'I'm up to it.'

'You don't have to.' Tommy held out his hand to stop Sam. 'It took two men to bring it in here and that was empty. I don't want you to kill yourself. My brother is just being a prick.'

'I'll be right,' Sam replied, brushing Tommy aside. He stood in front of the cabinet and took several deep breaths, as he wrapped his arms around it in a bear hug. With another deep breath, he gripped the cabinet and slowly lifted it off the ground. 'Where do you want it, then?'

'Put it down, Sam,' Tommy said, 'before you blow a gasket.'

Sam slowly lowered the cabinet to the ground and stretched out his arms and then his back. 'I must be slipping. I could have lifted two of those once, one under each arm.'

'Not bad, Abo,' Robbie nodded in quiet approval. 'It must come from eating all that goanna.'

'Actually, you've come at the right time. Just so happens that we're short on men at the moment,' Tommy stated, 'When do you want to start?'

'Well, I'm here,' Sam replied. 'Might as well be today.'

'Right then. We can get the formalities done later. Welcome aboard.' Tommy shook Sam's hand again. 'I'll show you the lay of the land and then we'll get you started on a forklift.'

'You've got to go,' Robbie interrupted as he pointed to the clock on the wall. 'You've got to take Mum to the funeral.'

'I nearly forgot.' Tommy grabbed his suit jacket off the back of the chair. 'Babs can fill you in. Won't be long.'

'Sorry to hear of your loss,' Sam said with respect.

'No, no one close. Some old friend of Mum's,' Tommy replied dismissively as he headed for the door.

19

Northcote Cemetery. Mid-morning

An icy drizzle fell on the few mourners gathered around the grave. Peter raised the collar of his coat and shivered. Twelve mourners, including himself and an aging Catholic priest. The priest was reading out the service like he was an auctioneer, intent on getting it over and done with before the rain set in.

Poor Slugger Douglas.

Most of the mourners were from the Tote and the housing block. Ivy O'Leary stood near the priest, wearing the same veiled hat she wore at the previous funeral. Occasionally, she lifted the veil to wipe away a tear. Slugger—the greatest Australian boxer never to win a world title. Here he was, being buried in near-anonymity. But that was only part of the reason felt Peter sad. That, and Slugger and Ivy's secret.

Now Slugger was nearly buried, Ivy's secret would be safe, or so she probably thought. Peter looked back at the cars parked on a crest behind them. Tommy O'Leary stood against a black Mercedes with his arms folded, checking his watch. Waiting. Looking bored. How ironic, Peter thought; if he only knew.

The priest sputtered out his final words, closed the service book, nodded at Ivy and was gone. Maybe the priest also knew. The gravedigger moved in as the mourners drifted away. Peter was intrigued by how the wealthy and influential were laid to rest in golden splendour, like Patrick O'Leary had been. If you were neither, it all ran like a takeaway order. Get in, get out. Take a number, take a grave.

Someone had mentioned something about a wake at the Tote. Peter was the only one who showed any real enthusiasm. The murmurs that came from the others were washed away in the drizzle.

The mourners had already evaporated by the time Peter reached his car. Tommy O'Leary had got back into his car and turned on the ignition. Probably trying to warm himself up. Peter turned to see Ivy walking closely behind him. After his last encounter with the O'Learys, it was best to avoid a confrontation. Another punch-up at a funeral was too much. Sure, he was supposed to be a hard-edged journo, but he wasn't a punching bag.

He looked at Tommy who was watching him like a hawk, rubbing his hands and peering over the steering wheel. Peter quickly opened the door of the Stag, keen on an early exit. He felt a tap on his shoulder and stiffened.

'Mister Clancy,' said Ivy breathlessly, 'Mister Clancy. I have something for you.' Ivy O'Leary held out a small package wrapped in brown paper, bound on all sides by string.

'Missus O'Leary!' Peter looked at the package and then at Ivy. She looked like she'd aged ten years since the last time he'd seen her. 'Sorry, I didn't hear you. How are you going?'

Tommy tooted the horn of the Mercedes several times and waved at Ivy to hurry.

'I thought Slugger would be around for a few more years,' she blurted, as she shoved the package into Peter's hands.

'What's this?'

'Slugger wanted you to have it,' she nodded. 'It's a book of his press clippings from when he was a fighter.'

'Thanks, Ivy. It's an honour.'

'Well. He liked you. Always said you were too good a bloke to be a reporter,' Ivy smiled faintly. The Merc's horn blew again.

'There's a wake at the Tote. Will you be there?'

'Got to go,' she said with a hint of annoyance. 'My son apparently needs me.' She smiled thinly and scurried away to the Mercedes.

The wake was as solemn and as poorly attended as the burial had been. No one seemed sufficiently motivated to relate a humorous story—or any story—about Slugger. Wasn't that the purpose of a wake? Maybe they hadn't known him. They were nevertheless happy enough to turn up and drink. In silence.

Peter ordered another round for the few mourners in an effort to loosen them up. Maybe there weren't any stories to tell. He wanted to tell them about Slugger and the German backpacker, but changed his mind out of respect for the old bugger. Instead he broke into a disjointed and tuneless version of *Danny Boy* in a last ditch effort to get the wake going. It was Slugger's favourite song. His concession to the deceased was to change the words to *Slugger Boy*. All Peter's recital achieved was a hasty dispersal of the mourners to all parts of the bar. Peter was left alone as he sang *...in sunshine and in shadow,* accompanied by slow claps from Harry the barman.

I tried, Slugger. I tried.

***

Peter was relieved to be back in the office. He had brought Slugger's book with him, in the hope of reading through it during lunch. He could hear Stella swearing from her cubicle and thumping the typewriter keys. She was an old fashioned girl in some respects.

'Are you all right?' he called as he shoved the book aside. 'What's happening?'

'Nothing's happening,' Stella barked back. 'That's the trouble.'

'Let's talk.'

She appeared holding an open notepad in one hand and pulling her chair behind her.

'No luck?' Peter threw his legs on the desk and slumped back in his chair.

'No one's talking,' she announced. 'Donarto doesn't return his calls. McCracken still wants a date but won't talk. I got chased out of the market by a mob of angry Italian men. How about you?' She leafed through her notepad. 'Nothing else. Nothing.'

'There may be progress. I hope.' Peter lowered his voice. 'A mate of mine went for a job at the O'Leary company this morning. Undercover stuff. He's my last hope.'

'Going out on a limb. Do you know if he got the job?'

'I'll know tonight. What about your date with McCracken? Still going?'

'I'm not looking forward to it but maybe he'll be more forthcoming with any information.' Stella shrugged her shoulders. 'What can I do? I've got to try something. Short of bribery, bugging.'

'That sounds a bit like Watergate.'

'It's been done,' she winked.

'We're at an impasse, then, aren't we?'

Stella nodded and folded her arms. They stared at each other silently.

'How was the funeral?'

'The host was dead, as expected, but the guests seemed just as dead. Poor Slugger. He deserved better.'

'I don't like poorly attended funerals,' Stella said. 'Funerals should be grand. They should be a celebration of a good life.'

'Ivy O'Leary was there.'

'Really? Were you able to get an interview?'

'Not with one of her brawny sons watching us.'

'But you were able to talk to her?'

'She gave me a book of Slugger's press clippings. Back when he was a boxer.' Peter unknotted the string and tore off the paper. The two battered exercise books bulged with pieces of yellowed newsprint.

'Great,' Stella snorted as she glanced at the books. 'You'll be able to write a good obituary about him. I'll leave you to it.' She hopped off her chair and wheeled it back to her cubicle.

Peter flipped open the first book to reveal a pile of carefully cut-out newspaper clippings: Slugger's career, year by year. He smiled when he saw a young and fairly handsome Slugger shaking the hand of the then premier of Victoria. It seemed that he was looking at another man. A man full of dreams and aspirations. A man much admired by the public.

Peter flicked through both books, hoping to find a misplaced picture of Slugger and Ivy, but that would have been asking a lot. Then he found the headline about Slugger being expected to die in hospital after his last fight. And after that, nothing.

Peter continued thumbing through the empty pages. Three pages from the end he found a sealed envelope. He tore it open. A letter written on new paper. He unfolded it and began to read. *Dear Mr Clancy,* written in a neat, well-formed hand.

Stella didn't know what she heard first, the sound of his chair crashing to the floor or Peter shouting at the top of his lungs: '*Oh my God! Oh my God! Stella! Bob! Anyone! Come here!*'

Stella got to Peter first, closely followed by the rest of the office.

Shazza ran down the corridor carrying the office first aid kit and shouting, 'Not again!' Peter had tears in his eyes and a huge smile at the same time.

'Not you too,' Bob said anxiously, as he lurched out of his office. 'What are you putting in the bloody coffee?'

'No. It's all right. I'm not going mad. Look!'

Peter brandished the letter wildly in front of Bob. He snatched the letter and opened it carefully, reading the first few lines. The others gathered in.

'In my office now, you two,' he ordered, pointing at Stella and Peter. 'The rest of you have work to do.'

Bob shut the door behind them, sat down and placed the letter on the desk. 'Dear Mr Clancy,' he began reading aloud:

You are my last hope. I want to end the madness. As you know, my husband and my son are now dead. I don't want my other boys to die too.

It sometimes seems as if everyone around me is dying. Even Slugger has gone.

My boys have never told me exactly what they do. I was never involved in the business, but I know in my heart that it's been rotten for a long time. I'm worried they're involved in drugs somehow, but I can't be certain. I'm no addict myself and I don't think the boys are. They never tell me anything but I know something is wrong.

Everyone thought Pat was dead, but he was in Asia all this time. I knew he wasn't dead. I couldn't tell you that. The boys said he was setting up a business there. I wondered why he stayed there so long. Then Pat came back to sort things out, all of a sudden. He arrived one night and next day he was dead.

Mr Clancy, I would rather have them safe in jail than dead. Slugger said you could be trusted to help me. He said you wouldn't use my name. Please don't try and find me, as my boys are sending me overseas for a rest. They think I'll have a nervous breakdown if I don't go. Please do whatever you can to make it stop. Yours truly, Ivy O'Leary.

Bob looked up. Peter noticed that his hands were shaking. He folded the letter and placed it in his trouser pocket.

'We can't name her,' said Peter, 'or give away any clues to the identity of who gave us this.'

'I know.' Bob reached into the drawer for the whiskey. 'Her life could be at risk.' He filled three glasses with Jameson's. 'I need a stiff drink.'

Stella took the glass and put it to her lips. She took a swig, shuddered and put the glass back on the desk. 'Why am I drinking this? I hate whiskey,' she grimaced.

'Do we run with something now?' Peter asked Bob.

'Let's look at what we've got before we go getting overexcited. We have two families at war. We have Ivy's vague theory about what's been going on behind the scenes, but that's all there is. She won't go on the record and, even if she did, we don't really know why these families are at war.'

'So we'll need to build on Ivy's information,' Peter chipped in.

'You both know what we need. Key players. A way into the story. How the operation works. Any other inside information we can gather.'

'I know what Dave would say about this,' Peter frowned as he drained his glass of scotch. 'Aren't we obstructing the law?'

'First of all, Dave's paid to take photographs, not to have an opinion. Secondly, it's in the best interests of the public. Crimes don't all have to be solved by the police. All right?' Bob winked.

'I'm way ahead of you, Bob. I have an acquaintance trying to get on the inside, as we speak.'

'So, what you're saying is you're already obstructing justice by sending your mate to the wharf. Do you think McCracken would be happy with that?'

'Probably not,' Peter smiled.

'Let's hope your friend gets a job there. I'd say they'd be pretty antsy at the moment,' Stella sighed. 'If he succeeds, it could open up a can of worms.'

'I'm telling you both now,' Bob warned, 'we have to keep this under wraps. This is strictly between the three of us.'

'Sure. But Sam and Dave will have to know what we're up to, won't they?' said Peter.

'Who the hell's Sam?' asked Bob.

'You've heard me talk about Sam before. Sam Saturday. He's the mate who's trying to get the job at the wharf.'

'Can we trust them not to tell anyone?' Bob clenched his hands. 'Stella?'

'Well, you already know Dave. Sam seems pretty straight up to me. And he's the last person anyone would ever suspect. No offence, Peter,' she said.

'None taken. All three of us have been through this type of stuff before. I'd follow Sam and Dave into hell.'

'Okay. Okay. It's a need to know basis with Sam and Dave. Get me?' Bob took a deep breath and turned to Stella. 'What about this date with McCracken?' he asked. 'Do you think it will lead anywhere?'

'Could lead to love.'

Stella slapped Peter playfully. 'It has worked for me before,' she grinned.

'McCracken comes across as someone who keeps his cards close to his chest. I have a feeling you won't get much out of him.'

'I have to try, Bob. I have been wondering why he did ask me out on a date so soon.'

'Isn't it obvious?' Peter teased.

Stella smirked. 'Okay. Let's try and keep it above the waistline, you bastards.'

***

Sam was cooking again by the time Peter got home from the office. 'I thought you'd be passed out on the couch,' he remarked as he wandered into the kitchen.

'I could do with a back massage.' Sam was bent at forty-five degrees, stirring a large pot of stew. 'I'd ask you to give me one, only you've got soft hands.'

'Fuck off,' Peter replied. 'Why don't you ask Dave when he gets back?' He peered at the contents of the pot. 'So, you got yourself a job?'

'Part forklift driver, part office boy.'

'How'd you do it? Get them to hire you, I mean.'

'Jedi mind control—blackfella's version.'

'Excellent.' He slapped Sam on the back. Sam shuddered.

'Careful,' he stiffened, 'I had to lift something heavy.'

'Never known you to complain. Must be bloody bad.'

'I'll be right. Not worn out yet. Those O'Learys are supposed to be tough, hey? If they're tough, then I don't have a worry in the world.'

'So,' said Peter steering the topic back to business, 'anything interesting happen?'

'Let's see. Tommy O'Leary is the boss and Robbie is the brother without the brains, but with the brawn.'

'That was obvious at the funeral. What else?'

'There's an office lady there who keeps them in check. She seemed real happy to see me. And then Tommy left to go to a funeral not long after I got there.'

'Slugger's. I saw him there.' Peter paused, thinking of how Sam could ever be considered a honey trap. 'Anything else?' he asked.

'Two blokes turned up after lunch. Tough. Hairy. Like bikies, you know the sort. They looked like trouble.'

'See or hear what they were up to?'

'Too busy working. I couldn't hear anything, but they looked pretty matey with Robbie.'

'And?'

'They left after an hour.'

'I know I don't have to tell you how important it is for you to be careful. If you feel that you're in danger, get out of there, pronto.'

'These blokes are pretty bad,' Sam remarked.

'Drugs and death: I reckon that's their business. Just keep your wits about you,' Peter added. 'You're not James Bond.'

'No. I'm better.' Sam laughed as he dished up dinner. 'I'm the black James Bond.'

***

Peter rolled from one end of his saggy bed to the other, cuddling two flat pillows. Something had woken him up, but he didn't know if it was Sam's shrill snoring coming from the other room or Dave, who occasionally cried out from night terrors. Peter needed noise to sleep, just not that kind of noise. He remembered once lying on a trolley in an accident and emergency cubicle at the Royal Melbourne for six hours with a broken hand and having the best sleep of his life. Of course, the liberal supply of morphine might have been a contributory factor.

He needed the hum of the traffic and the chatter of people on the street to sleep, but it wasn't working tonight. He checked the alarm clock. Twelve-thirty. He fell back onto the pillows and stared at the ceiling. He had an idea why he was clock-watching: It was the story, rattling along in the back of his mind. The rattling had become so loud that it had woken him up in the middle of the night. He always got like that with big stories. They took over his life and enveloped him in a battle between self-doubt and elation. At that moment, he was definitely in doubt mode. He wondered if this was how soldiers felt when they were about to go into combat.

He sat up again, pressing his eyes with his palms, sufficiently awake to contemplate whether he needed something to send him back to sleep. A beer perhaps, or something stronger? He rolled out of bed and was drifting towards the kitchen when his eyes were drawn to the glass pane in the front door. Was that a shadow? Then a gentle rap on the door. Peter stopped dead. Another gentle rap. He bent double so he couldn't be seen from outside and crept towards the door. Should he wake the boys? Although he couldn't make out the identity of his midnight visitor, there was something familiar about the outline. He unlocked the door quietly and peeled it open.

'Stella?' Peter whispered. What was it with these surprise home visits?

She had already started walking back down the stairs, but she turned when she heard Peter's voice. 'Sorry. I thought you might still be awake but when I realised you weren't...I decided to leave. Shit. You know what I mean,' she murmured.

'I was awake. Couldn't sleep. Do you want to come in? I was going to have a drink,' Peter opened the door wider.

Stella peered in through doorway and caught a glimpse of Dave sleeping on the couch. 'I shouldn't.'

'There's something wrong, isn't there?'

'We have to talk,' she stammered. 'In private. I need to tell someone otherwise I won't be able to sleep.'

'You've got sleeping problems too.' Peter yawned. 'Okay. Meet me down at the Stag. It's parked out front. We'll talk there.'

Stella was leaning against the Stag, her arms crossed tightly against a chilly wind blowing off the bay. Peter had thrown on an old tracksuit and slippers. He held two Milos in faded mugs.

'You Aussie guys really know how to impress, don't you?' she smiled as Peter unlocked the passenger door.

'If you'd phoned to say you were coming I'd've worn a better tracksuit.' He crossed to the driver's side and unlocked his door. Once inside the cabin, Peter turned over the engine, flicked on the heater and the overhead light. It flickered into life and bathed the cabin in a faint glow.

'Brilliant,' Stella remarked as she looked up at the light. 'I can barely see anything in here.'

'Your eyes will get used to it,' Peter replied, handing her a mug. 'This will make you feel better.'

'It's warm,' Stella flinched as she reluctantly took a sip. 'But what the hell is it?'

'You've never tasted Milo before? It's a little like cocoa, I guess.'

'I was expecting something stronger.'

'I'm trying to cut back,' Peter admitted, taking a sip. 'Ran out of milk, so it's a bit watery. Sorry.'

'I think I'll stick to bourbon,' Stella grimaced.

Peter took another drink. 'Is this about your date with McCracken?'

'In a way,' she replied. 'At least, that's how it started out. It's not how it ended.'

'What do you mean?' Peter revved the engine. The heater fan sped up and the light grew brighter.

'Do you mind if I turn that off?' Stella clicked off the light and the fan sped up again. 'Makes me feel a little like we're on show. Well,' she began, 'I went on the date with McCracken. I don't know why. It was the Dale McCracken appreciation show. My God, that man has an inflated view of himself.' She took a tentative drink. 'I guess I might learn to like this if I live here for another twenty years.'

'Did he disclose any gems of information, apart from himself?'

'He actually said something complimentary about you,' she smiled.

'Sure he did. I'd make good road kill, or something like that?'

'In his own words: you're a tenacious prick.'

'I like that!'

'I got nothing out of him about the investigation. He was very evasive. I reckon he thought the great Dale McCracken would be able to get me into bed.'

'And?'

'Not that I'd ever tell you, but he only managed to give me a sloppy kiss in the car park.' She sighed with relief. 'I got out of there as fast as I could.'

'You woke me up in the middle of the night to tell me that?'

'But it's what happened afterwards,' she continued. 'That's when it all went down.' She shifted around to face Peter. 'McCracken went off all angry. I was about to start the car and drive home,' she fell silent and looked past him out the window.

'Are you all right?'

'I've been in this kind of situation before,' she resumed. 'I started the car and next minute this guy jumps in the front seat, reaches across me and pulls the keys out of the ignition. It was frightening.'

'What did he look like?'

'He was wearing a ski mask. He was a big guy. That's all I could tell about him. And he had an Australian accent.'

'Did he try to…'

'Thank God, no, he didn't,' she replied. 'He wanted to give me information about McCracken.'

'What information?' Peter sat up straighter.

'All he said was that McCracken's on the take. And he has the evidence to prove it. He gave me this.' Stella clicked the light back on and wedged the mug between her knees. She took a folded manila envelope out of her handbag and handed it to Peter.

'It's a photo,' he said as he took it out of the envelope. He held it up to the light. 'Shit!'

'I know McCracken's there,' she resumed as she looked across to study the photograph. 'I'm not too sure about the other guys. Those women look like hookers.'

'They do.' Peter held the photograph closer and rotated it. 'I suppose the other blokes could be Tommy O'Leary and Tony Donarto.'

'If you're right then it sure is interesting company he keeps.'

'I guess cops have the right to as much kinky sex as the next guy,' Peter surmised. 'It's who they fuck *with* that's the real problem.'

'The ski mask guy says he has more. Much more. He says that this is just the tip of the iceberg.'

'Did he say when he would see you again?'

'He just said he'd be in touch.'

'Have you told Bob?'

'Not yet. I didn't want to wake him.'

'Thanks,' Peter began, 'but you don't mind…Ah, forget it.'

'That's what teamwork is all about, buddy,' Stella laughed. 'I know you're not used to working with a partner, but this is what teams do.'

Peter gave a wry grin. 'Do you think it is safe to go back to your place tonight?'

'Concerned for my welfare, Clancy? Are you inviting me to stay in your flea-ridden apartment?'

'If you feel frightened,' Peter replied. 'You're welcome, of course.'

'I'm fine—all in a day's work,' she rejoined. 'I'd feel a lot safer with my handgun and can of mace but they wouldn't let me bring it into the country. But I can still handle myself without them.'

'I'm sure you can. Shame about the gun, though.' Peter rolled his eyes.

'You don't like guns?' Stella observed.

'I'm not a fan. In my experience they're big, noisy things that put holes in people, sometimes for no apparent reason.'

'We'll have this argument another time. Better get some sleep.' Stella handed Peter her mug, shoved the envelope back into her handbag and opened her door.

'Good luck with that.' He switched off the engine and watched as Stella disappeared down the lane. *Thanks a lot. How the hell am I supposed to sleep now, Stella?*

20

Peter had already been at work for a half hour before Stella arrived, bleary eyed and unusually dishevelled. He was congratulating himself on his self-restraint, when the urge to ask Stella whether she'd been able to get any sleep got the better of him.

'You look like a train wreck,' he blurted.

'Thanks. Right back at you.'

They sat together in Peter's cubicle, too impatient to start any work. Stella fidgeted with the envelope, occasionally looking up the corridor.

'Hurry up, Bob,' she muttered, 'where are you?'

Peter stared at the blank sheet of paper in his word processor while sipping a cup of coffee. 'I think I can hear his wheeze coming up the steps.' He cocked his head to listen.

'That's Bob? I thought that was a vacuum cleaner. My God, Bob. Stop smoking!' Stella exclaimed. Everyone assumed those few steps were going to kill Bob sooner or later.

Please don't let it be today, Bob, Peter thought. *We really need you today.*

'What's wrong? Looks like neither of you have slept a wink,' Bob gasped as they loitered about the door to his office.

'Too much happening to sleep. It's party time, Bob,' Stella said, grimly holding up the envelope and flicking it across Bob's desk. 'McCracken, Donarto, O'Leary. Only this time, we're invited.'

Bob tipped the photographs onto his desk and raised his brows. 'What do we have here?' he said as he studied them. 'Well, it certainly looks like them.'

'Do you want to run with it now?' Stella asked.

'Too soon,' Bob grumbled as he gathered the photographs together and put them back into the envelope. 'Let's see how far this goes.'

'It might be all we get.'

'Let's see if this bloke turns up again. Don't be too hasty.' Bob leaned back on his chair, deep in thought. 'Meanwhile,' he resumed, 'where do you want to keep these?' He handed them back to Stella. 'I suggest they be put somewhere no one would suspect, under lock and key.'

'Peter can have them,' Stella said as she gave the envelope to Peter.

'Are you sure?' Bob asked.

'Yeah?' Peter added. 'Why me?'

'I trust you,' Stella smiled. 'And that apartment of yours will be perfect. Three men living in two rooms. No one would think of breaking into a place like that.'

'Don't lose them,' Bob warned pointing his index finger, 'or I'll cut off your nuts and feed them to you.' He watched Peter squirm. 'I mean it.'

'What about Stella's safety?' Peter asked. 'This bloke could be a psycho.'

'Stella can handle herself. I've seen her in action,' Bob chuckled, imitating a karate chop.

'Stella's fine,' she looked at Peter. 'I'm no dainty little princess.'

'All right,' Peter said, holding up his hands, 'I hear you loud and clear. Won't mention it again.'

He just got the last syllable out when the scanner in Stella's hand started to screech.

Report of a single shot heard at 15 Acacia Drive, Templestowe. All cars in the vicinity...

'Hey,' Peter exploded, 'that's Tony Donarto's.'

'See what comes of speaking of the devil?' said Stella, fumbling with the scanner. 'Do you want me to go, Bob?' She bounced out of her chair throwing the scanner into her handbag.

'Yeah, go.' Bob snapped. 'The Donartos are yours. Go. Peter, you stay here, with me.'

'I'll take your car, Bob,' Stella blurted as she rushed to the door.

'And take Dave with you.'

'Yeah. Yeah. Got it.' She swung open the door.

'One more thing, Stella.'

'Yeah, Bob? I'm in a goddamned hurry.'

'Remember, we drive on the left side of the road.'

Stella slammed the door but not before flicking Bob the bird.

'Sorry, Peter, we needed to talk. Did Sam get the job?' Bob asked, still grinning.

'I don't know how he did it, but he's working a forklift for the O'Learys.' Peter said. 'Now we wait for Sam to pass on any information.'

'I half wish he hadn't got the job,' Bob exhaled.

'You mean that?'

'Well, think about it. If we get caught we're in a big shit. Really big shit. And anything could happen to Sam.'

'Sam's willing to take the risk. I'm willing to take the risk. If you are, Bob...'

'I don't have too many more years of this, so what a way to go out. A story that could take us to the top. It would make the other papers really take notice of *The Truth*. Isn't that what we all dream of?'

'You reckon that deep down all journos are either really insecure little creatures or total egomaniacs?'

'Mostly both,' Bob laughed.

'Or just FITH,' Peter returned with a snort.

***

Peter stared at the same empty page on the word processor. He typed a sentence, then stopped and backspaced over it. *This teamwork stuff sucks.* Peter tore the paper out of the processor and threw it on the floor. *I'm in the office typing empty words while Stella is out gathering the juicy details. What justice is there in that? Teams usually play ball at the same place at the same time. But not us.*

Peter grabbed his coffee cup and stood up when his phone rang. He let it ring several times before snatching the receiver off the hook. 'Yeah?' he said curtly.

'Someone wants to talk to you, Peter,' Shazza replied. 'I'll put him through.'

'Who it is?'

'I dunno. It's a man,' Shazza answered. 'He's speaking very softly and he's difficult to understand. All I could make out was *Peter* and *urgent.*'

Peter toyed with telling the man he was busy.

'He sounds stressed.'

'All right,' he said, 'put him through.' He heard a click. 'Who is it?' he began.

'It's me,' the voice murmured.

'Sam?' Peter said urgently, 'What's wrong?'

'Can't talk too long,' Sam began, 'I'm using the phone in the office. They've gone outside.'

'Okay.'

'A lawyer's here. The police are on their way. Sorry, got to go.' The phone went dead.

Peter threw down the receiver and ran into Bob's office. 'Sam's rung. Said something about the police going round to the O'Leary's.'

'What are you doing here? Fucking go!' Bob replied waving his hand furiously at Peter. 'Don't wait to tell me.'

By the time the Stag screeched to a halt on South Pier near the security checkpoint, a squad of uniformed police, detectives and the rapid response group had already enveloped the area. The stupid bastard in the box wasn't letting anyone in, unless they were police. That was, until Peter pulled out the warrant badge that he kept in his box of tricks: his *Cunning Kit*. Well, it had fallen out of a copper's pocket in the Press Club toilet and Peter just hadn't gotten around to returning it.

They've come prepared, he thought as he ran towards the cordon around the office. The police were here in force but where was the media? *Beaten to the punch once again by Peter Headline Clancy*. None in sight. *Ilmo, where are you?*

Peter saw McCracken lead Tommy O'Leary out in handcuffs first, then another detective followed with Robbie. Strangely, both Tommy and Robbie looked relaxed. This, despite having an array of guns trained on them. *Too calm*. Peter could see Sam consoling a middle-aged woman crying near the office doorway. *That must be Babs Bell*. The police were carrying out stacks of files and boxes.

Peter sneaked close to the first unmarked police car, the one he assumed would take the O'Learys to the police station. He guessed right.

'What are you doing here, Clancy? Only police allowed in,' McCracken growled as he pushed past him, gripping Tommy's hands, which had been cuffed tightly behind his back.

'I was fishing nearby and I heard the commotion,' he smirked.

'In a suit?' McCracken sneered.

'What's happening here?' asked Peter.

'No comment.'

Peter turned his attention to Tommy. 'Do you know why you're being arrested, Tommy?'

'Fuck off,' Tommy retorted, spitting in Peter's face. To add insult to injury, McCracken laughed as he pushed Tommy into the back seat. Peter backed away, hastily got out a handkerchief and wiped the spit off his face. The second detective led Robbie past in handcuffs, just as Peter shoved the handkerchief back into his pocket.

'Any comments about why you're being arrested, Robbie?'

Robbie replied in the same manner as his brother, but this time Peter was prepared. He jumped aside as the wad of spit shot in his direction, whistled past him and landed near his shoe.

'What are you people?' Peter responded angrily, 'a mob of fucking alpacas?'

Peter watched as Sam continued to console Babs and the police continued to remove reams of papers from the office. It crossed his mind to attempt to get an interview with Babs, but thought the better of it. No reason to further jeopardise Sam's tenacious position.

He had turned to walk back to the Stag when he caught a vision of her. Of *her*. He stopped dead. She was a woman of around thirty, attired in a filmy white dress with a pastel woollen cardigan over it, collar out, pearls around the collar. She floated out of the office behind the police, an English rose in a field of Patterson's Curse. To complete the look, she had a Hermes scarf wrapped loosely around her shoulders. She was the model Sloane Ranger, a Lady Diana clone, right down to the peaches and cream complexion and soft blue eyes. Peter nearly tripped over himself as he tried to approach this vision of pure loveliness. Her thick blond mane was shaped into a purdey. Like Lady Diana. It was his secret, his deepest darkest secret that no one should ever know. Ever. He was in love with Lady Diana. His secret fantasy. To work in London, then, in the event that Charles and Diana ever divorced—which everyone knew would be never—he'd be first on the scene to offer succour and support to the poor girl.

Now, she was standing on South Wharf calmly talking into a mobile phone the size of a brick.

Who needs to be available at all times? Those stupid things will never catch on. Peter caught her attention by waving inanely just as she finished her conversation. She put the phone into a leather satchel slung over her shoulder and looked back at Peter with those dewy blue eyes. She smiled radiantly. *My God!* He felt himself becoming a dizzy schoolboy again. *Even her teeth are pure white.* He wanted to touch her.

'You're a journalist, aren't you?' she asked. Her accent betrayed a private school education. To the uninitiated, it might have even sounded a little public school English. 'You are, aren't you?'

Peter's heart threatened to leap out of his chest and his breathing increased. *What the hell is wrong with me? It's not Lady Diana.* He considered telling her that he was an aristocrat that just happened to be in the area. *Would you like to come back to my Bentley for a bottle of Moet and some canapés?* 'I am,' he replied meekly. He felt himself breaking into a lopsided smile that could belong in a terrible school photo.

'You're Peter Clancy?'

'How did you know?' he stammered. 'Is it that obvious?'

'I read your column,' she replied. 'I think it's the best in Melbourne.'

'Really? Wow. That's great.' Peter felt as lightheaded as if he'd downed a six-pack.

'Poppy,' she said, as she held out her hand. 'Poppy Reynolds.'

'Poppy,' Peter cooed as he shook her hand. *Her skin is like velvet.* 'Poppy.'

'You like long handshakes?' she asked coolly as she slipped her hand away from Peter's.

Where's my composure gone? 'Sorry,' he stumbled. 'The reactions from the O'Learys sort of threw me.'

'To be expected.'

'How do you know them?' Peter's composure was returning.

'I'm their solicitor.'

'Their solicitor?' he repeated aloud.

'Do you find that fascinating? Or strange?' Poppy said curtly. 'Is it to do with the fact that a woman is representing the O'Learys?'

'No. No,' Peter backtracked, 'I just thought Frank Galbally would be doing this. I thought the wharves were his turf.' He'd met Galbally on occasion when he had been invited by Bob to watch a Collingwood game in the members'. One of Australia's greatest criminal lawyers, Frank Galbally was a mesmerising character with a large dash of Irish charm. He seemed more the O'Leary type than Ms Poppy Reynolds. A passionate advocate of the underdog, Galbally was, a defender of many a Painter and Docker.

'Frank's been taken ill and he's asked me to take care of the O'Leary family in his absence.'

'Do you want to tell me why they have been arrested?'

'Of course not. I'm a lawyer. I don't talk to journalists.' She smiled faintly. 'Got to go.'

'Right,' Peter replied, barely masking the pain in his voice. 'So, I'll see you around? Give my regards to Frank.'

Poppy smiled at him once more and glided down the wharf towards the silver, soft-topped Alfa Romeo Spider that was parked near the Stag. Unabashed, he continued to watch her. When she was two hundred metres away from him, Poppy turned around.

'If you come down to St Kilda Road later today you might find out more.'

He kept observing Poppy until she reached her Alfa and drove away, right up until the car could no longer be seen. Then she was gone.

Peter returned to the office feeling giddy, as if he'd just been on his first date. The office was empty. He popped his head through the doorway of the staff room, even though he knew it was rarely used. He was surprised to see Dave and Shazza sitting together, sharing a Chinese takeaway. Peter stood there, unnoticed. She was instructing Dave in the use of chopsticks. *Cute.*

They turned around when Peter cleared his throat. 'You both look cosy,' he teased.

Dave put down the chopsticks and picked up a fork. 'Want to join us?' he asked. 'I know you like Chinese food.'

'Not now. Too much to do,' he replied with a wide grin as he leaned against the door.

'You survived?' Shazza asked.

'Yeah,' Peter said vaguely. 'The O'Learys are now in jail.'

'What's wrong with you?' Shazza asked, leaning across the table to take a closer look at Peter. 'Have you been drinking?'

'No,' Peter blushed. 'Just happy at the moment.'

Dave interjected. 'You probably want to know what went on today. Stella can fill you in on what happened to us.'

'Well, then,' Peter announced as he straightened up, 'I better go and find her.'

'You sure you haven't been drinking?' Shazza asked again.

'Shit no,' he retorted. 'Can't a man be happy with life without the booze?'

Peter tapped softly on Bob's door. There was no answer. He usually barged in anyway, but he felt somehow gentler, calmer, and so he turned the handle and swung the door open ever so slowly to reveal…

Holy shit!

It was an autonomic reaction, in the same league as a dying man's last gasp for breath. Peter tried his best to divert his eyes away from what he was seeing. Yes, it was Stella and Bob. But not as he had expected, seated on opposites sides of the desk making polite conversation. No. Stella was sitting astride a totally naked Bob and they were both in the deep throes of passion. Peter might have had enough time to quietly extricate himself without being discovered, except for Stella's wild head-toss in his direction. She caught sight of him shuffling backwards, head down, out of the office.

'You should…knock,' Stella managed to gasp.

Peter held out his hand in a stop motion. 'Just popped in to tell you that the O'Learys have been arrested,' he blurted before easing the door shut.

He tried his best to work on the O'Leary arrest story but to no avail. His fingers sat limply on the keys. He just couldn't get the scene of Stella and Bob coupling out of his head. He'd accidentally caught friends in bed with their girlfriends before, but Stella and Bob! On the desk. Totally unexpected. Was Bob's health up to shagging a woman younger than himself? There was that, too. *Bob looked like he was really straining. Dirty old bugger. Maybe Bob wanted to go out on a shag high. My God,* Peter thought, *there I go again. Focus on the story. On the story.* Though it was comforting for him to know that love was alive and well in *The Truth* air: Dave and Shazza sharing an intimate takeaway. Stella and Bob. Maybe Peter and Poppy, the Sloane Ranger? And what about Sam?

It was another ten minutes before Stella emerged from Bob's office, adjusting her dress with one hand and trying to push her well-shagged, tousled hair back into its original arrangement with the other. Peter pretended to type when she reached his desk.

'You said the O'Learys were arrested?' No apology, no excuses. Business as usual.

'Yes. I'll go to St Kilda Road later for an update. I met their solicitor,' he said trying not to look at her. 'And you?'

'There was a drive-by shooting at the Donarto house. Someone sprayed the stone wall surrounding his mansion. No one injured. He wasn't there, but his elderly Italian mother was screaming at the police in front of the house. I was hoping she'd attack one of them so I could get a better story.'

Peter smiled dimly and looked up at Stella. 'Funny.'

'Who needs a Doberman when you have an Italian mother guarding your home, right?'

Peter smiled faintly again.

'Well, at least I thought that was funny.' She realised that they would have to discuss the elephant in the room sooner or later. She decided it had better be sooner. 'It's about what was happening in the office.'

'Well. I didn't expect to see Bob and you having a shag.'

'Shag?' Stella asked vaguely.

'Sexual congress. Intercourse. Coitus. Whatever you want to call it.'

Stella turned away so he wouldn't see tears welling in her eyes. 'Can you keep a secret?' she pleaded.

'Of course I can.'

'Bob and I were close in New York. We were lovers, in fact, but we never lived together.' She sighed. 'Then our careers got in the way and other complications happened. And then that was it. Bob came back to Australia and I stayed in New York. I thought that was the end of it,' she continued, 'but Bob got in contact a year ago. And we reconnected. Now I'm here.'

'So you didn't come to Australia to see the wide horizons and cuddle our fluffy marsupials,' Peter grinned.

'No, not really, but I am glad to be working on this story. And I'm also glad to be working with someone like you.'

'You're a suck, Stella,' Peter blushed. 'But it's wasted on me.'

'Suck?'

'Someone who ingratiates themselves,' Peter shook his head. 'I'm really going to have to teach you our slang.'

***

Four o'clock in the afternoon. Four o'clock on an overcast Melbourne afternoon. St Kilda Road Police Complex. Another press conference. Another press conference packed with the flotsam and jetsam of Melbourne's media. *This story is growing by the minute.* Peter almost expected journalists from the *Woman's Weekly* to be there. Well, didn't he just overhear a journo saying he was from *Australian Playboy*? *They all want a piece of the carcass.*

He took up position again near the rostrum. He didn't have to shove his way into that privileged slot near the speaker. He breezed into pole position. *They're depending on me to open up this story and dig into the shit the deepest.* They were waiting for him to make the moves. Or the mistakes. Peter Headline Clancy? Or Peter Fuckup Clancy. He wondered why he'd bothered to come. It would just be a formal announcement of the arrest of Tommy and Robbie O'Leary. *That's it. Blah, blah. But where was Poppy?*

The media pack didn't have to wait long. Police Commissioner Stapelton appeared from a side door followed by two uniformed minions. Where was McCracken? Peter was expecting a gloating, preening McCracken to be there bathing in the glory, but Dale was a no-show. Jack Stapelton got down to the nitty gritty, pronto and presto.

'You may have heard that Thomas and Robert O'Leary were arrested today on suspicion of the murder of Aldo Morosto and the attempted murder of Anthony Donarto at Footscray Market,' Stapelton announced. 'They were questioned and later released without charge.'

'What in the hell?' Peter exploded.

'Please restrain yourself, Mister Clancy, or I'll have you removed,' Stapelton growled back.

'Sorry Commissioner,' Peter replied sheepishly, causing the media pack to titter.

'I'll continue and without interruption. In a late development, two men known to police, James Machowicz and Rodney Eastern, were taken into police custody and confessed to the murder of Aldo Morosto and the attempted murder of Anthony Donarto. I'll take a few questions,' Stapelton concluded.

The room erupted into a series of shouts but Peter was able to get his heard first: 'Are you sure that these men are the culprits, Commissioner?'

'A confession is fairly conclusive, don't you think, Mister Clancy? Another question,' Jack asked as he surveyed the room.

'Did these men work for the O'Learys?' a female journalist behind Peter asked. *Good question*, Peter thought.

'No comment. But, as I said, these men are well known to the police. One more question.' Jack looked around the room.

'Are the police getting any closer to solving the O'Leary murders?' Peter shouted above the throng.

'You seem to be the squeaky wheel today, don't you, Mister Clancy?' Stapelton shook his head. The pack laughed as per usual. 'Yes. We are confident we are getting close to solving those murders. We are pursuing several lines of enquiry at present.'

'Blah, blah, blah, ad nauseam,' Peter muttered to himself. 'This press conference is over.'

Stapelton grabbed some sheets of paper from the lectern and made to leave.

'Tell me, Commissioner,' Peter called out, as Stapelton tried to ignore him and head towards a side door, 'why has Melbourne been turned into a shooting gallery by a bunch of thugs? Why has this been allowed to happen?'

Jack Stapelton spun on his heel and glared at Peter. He was crimson.

Don't have a stroke, Jack. At least, not before making a comment, please.

'The damn impertinence of you, Mister Clancy,' Stapelton barked, shaking the papers in his hand at Peter. A minion opened the door and Stapelton was gone.

'I didn't mean to upset the old bugger,' Peter remarked to another journalist.

He loitered around the police station for another fifteen minutes, hoping that Poppy might appear or just float out of an office or down a corridor. Dejected, he returned to his office. He had just thrown his coat on the desk when he heard Bob summoning him.

Stapelton. The dobber.

'I've had a phone call from the police commissioner,' Bob announced, even before Peter could grab a chair. 'I thought he was going to have a frigging heart attack on the phone this time.'

'Okay. Maybe I shouldn't have said that Melbourne was a shooting gallery for thugs. Too late to apologise?'

'He wants to ban you from all press conferences,' Bob shook his head.

'Can he do that?'

'Well, I said that it was against the principles of press freedom, so we made an arrangement,' Bob replied.

'What is it?' Peter asked dryly.

'You can go to the press conferences but you can't ask any questions.'

'What the fuck?' he roared. 'You didn't agree?'

'For the moment,' Bob exhaled, 'we need to start having a friendlier relationship with the police.'

'None of those journos there ask the hard questions,' Peter complained. 'They expect me to do it because I work for *The Truth*. Remember, we don't give a shit who we upset.'

'I hate to say it, Peter, but this time you're wrong. Try to remember that we're not in the business of pure sleaze anymore,' Bob countered. 'We can't go around antagonising everyone. Some people, but not everyone. We have to be in with the police, or at least seen to be. When I was in New York I'd hang out with them at their watering hole. The information I picked up during those drinking sessions was immeasurable.'

'Why the change of heart?' Peter asked.

'Because we're getting close to getting the biggest story this paper has ever had. I can bloody feel it. And I don't want you to stuff it up because you have a problem with authority.'

'I have a problem with authority?' he chuckled.

'You do.'

'Okay,' he said throwing up his hands. 'Blame the fucking sadistic Christian Brothers then, all right?'

'Let it go, Peter,' Bob replied calmly. 'Let it go. You work with authority, not against it. Or bloody pretend to.'

'What do I have to do, take Dale McCracken out for dinner? Send Jack a bouquet of flowers?'

'Of course not,' Bob rolled his eyes. 'Just be less abrasive. Act more BBC.'

'I can do that.' Peter replied in a mock upper class English accent. He rose from the chair.

'About the…' Bob said awkwardly.

Peter paused. 'It's fine, Bob. No more said.'

'You don't want to talk about it?'

'Of course fucking not. I don't even want to think about it. I'm not a pervert.'

'Our secret?'

'You don't have to worry about me telling everyone. You have enough dirt on me. I've got to have at least one on you.'

Peter had hoped to get home early but it was a bad day. And this time he needed a drink. He arrived back at the flat before seven to find his dinner—a plate of lamb chops and boiled vegetables—on the table. *I miss my Greek takeaway*, Peter thought as he eyed the meal with disinterest. Sam and Dave were crashed on the couch, watching the television.

'Thanks for cooking again. Looks like you've had dinner,' he said as he sat down at the dinner table. He picked up a knife and fork and commenced eating. 'It's cold!' Peter put down his utensils.

'If you had a microwave,' Dave replied, 'or you could just warm it up in the oven.'

'Can't be bothered,' Peter grumbled between mouthfuls. He felt too hungry to worry about how cold it was.

'Where were you, anyway?' Sam asked without diverting his eyes from the television.

'I was at the Tote,' he responded. 'I had a bad day. I needed a drink.'

'Good days. Bad days. You always need to have a drink,' Sam observed. 'Maybe you should have a drink-free day.'

Not again. 'Maybe I should have a hot dinner,' he retorted angrily.

'Quiet, you two,' Dave interrupted. 'It's the news.' Dave got off the couch to turn up the volume. 'The O'Leary arrests.'

'I can tell you all about that,' Peter interjected.

'Shush,' Sam said. 'I want to see myself on the TV. I reckon I'll look like that bloke in the Shaft movie.'

'Thomas and Robert O'Leary were arrested today,' the newsreader began.

'That's me with Babs,' Sam said cheerfully pointing at the television screen. 'Never been on the tellie.'

'And in a dramatic twist, they were later released without charge after two men stepped forward, admitting they had murdered Aldo Morosto at Footscray Market and attempted to kill Anthony Donarto.'

'What!' Dave exclaimed. 'I don't get it.'

'I could have told you,' Peter said as he picked up a chop with his hands and gnawed on it. 'Did you think the O'Learys were going to do the dirty work?'

'Quiet,' Sam pleaded.

'The two men, whose names are Rodney Eastern and James Machowicz, were detained at St Kilda Police Station and will be charged,' the newsreader continued.

'It's them,' Sam shouted at the screen and bounded off the couch to point at the television. 'It's those blokes.'

'Who?' Peter asked.

Dave jumped off the couch to turn down the volume.

'Those blokes,' Sam stammered, grabbing hold of Dave, 'the ones I was telling you about. The hairy ones.'

'What are you talking about?' Peter said impatiently pushing his meal aside.

'Those bikie looking blokes I saw with Tommy and Robbie in their office the other day. The ones they were all friendly with.'

'I frigging knew it!' Peter exclaimed as he stood up so quickly that he nearly knocked over the chair. 'I knew this was going to happen.'

***

The morning found Stella, Peter and Bob huddled again in Bob's smoky office. Planning the next move.

'That guy found me again,' Stella shivered as she reached for a cigarette from Bob's packet on the desk. Peter noticed her hands were shaking as she lit one and inhaled deeply. 'I needed that.'

'I didn't know you smoked,' Peter remarked.

'I'd given up for two years before last night.'

'Did the informer come back?' Bob asked with concern.

'I'm getting softer,' she exhaled loudly. 'Last night I went out for a walk along the river and he grabbed me again.'

'In a ski mask again?' Peter asked.

'You bet ya,' she replied as she stubbed the cigarette. 'It was the same guy. Tall, well built, Aussie accent.'

'Did he hurt you?'

'Sort of,' she shrugged. 'He pulled me into a bush from behind then made me lie on the ground, face down with my arms by my side. Even though he was wearing a ski mask he still didn't want me to look at him. That was kind of creepy.'

'What did he say this time?' Bob questioned.

'Same thing; he has a lot of dirt on Dale McCracken. I wonder if the ski mask is in the police force.'

'I've heard some interesting rumours about what happens down at St Kilda Road,' Peter added.

'Yeah,' Bob added, 'I've heard them too.'

'All of the top brass are bugging each other, apparently,' Peter chuckled. 'They go outside to talk.'

'Sounds toxic.' Stella shook her head, 'Sounds like the New York police.'

'So he didn't add any more?' Bob tapped the desk.

'He gave me another envelope.' Stella took another plain, yellow A4 envelope out of her handbag and handed it to Bob.

'Okay,' Bob took out three photographs from the envelope, spread them across his desk and examined them closely. He shook his head and dropped them back on the desk. Peter picked up one, Stella another.

'Bloody hell,' Peter spoke first. 'It looks like Led Zeppelin on tour.'

'Urrgh,' Stella squirmed. 'It's a sex orgy.'

'Looks like McCracken's fu... sorry, I mean, having intercourse with the woman wearing the leather mask. From the angle, I'd say the photos were taken through the window.' Peter took a closer look.' That mask hasn't got any holes for the eyes, only the mouth. I guess the reason's obvious. That's creepy.'

'What the?' Stella commented, as she looked at the same photo. 'Oh that! It's called a dog mask, which is exactly what it looks like. Notice the lacing along the side? That mask would cost a lot of money. This guy's a real S&M devotee.'

'So how do you...' Peter began.

'Not what you think, buddy boy. I was a crime reporter in New York,' Stella laughed. 'Give me a break.'

Peter continued to examine the photograph. 'And she's giving the other guy a blowjob. I don't recognise him. All you can see is his lower torso. Shit, this woman's a real multi-tasker. From the looks of it, I'd say she's a high class pro.'

'I'm surprised how detailed the photos are,' Bob cut in as he continued to look them over. 'I agree they've been taken from outside. The photographer's got in really close, though. I wonder how they didn't notice him? Still, they look pretty professional to me.'

'Do you recognise this man?' Stella interrupted, holding one of the photographs in front of Peter and pointing a red lacquered fingernail at a naked man.

Peter examined it closely, turning it around. 'Difficult to tell,' he said. 'His head's bent head down over that naked woman. Looks like he's snorting lines of coke off her back. I have to say, the hairline does seem familiar.'

'Who do you think it is, then?' Bob asked.

'Well, I've never seen him naked, thank God,' Peter sighed, 'but I hazard a guess that it's Tony Donarto. That's just pure speculation.'

'Tony and Dale,' Bob stated, 'But none of the O'Learys.'

'Not invited?'

'Maybe it's just not their scene. I wonder if my guy's one of their associates, then?' Stella theorised.

Bob gathered up the photographs and returned them to the envelope. 'Shame we won't be able to publish these photos uncensored. It'd make one hell of a story.'

Stella pushed the envelope back across the desk to Peter. He reluctantly picked it up.

'Add them to the others. You have put them in a safe place, haven't you?'

'Of course,' Peter hesitated, suddenly realising that the last place he'd seen the previous photographs was when he had thrown them onto the rear seat of the Stag. *Why am I being entrusted with these? I can't even find a clean pair of socks on a good day.* 'But, shouldn't they be put in a safe or somewhere really secure?'

'If someone wants those photos,' Bob remarked, 'they'll come after Stella or me first. By that time, you would have found another safe pozzie for them.'

'Fine. Fine,' Peter repeated as he threw up his hands. 'It looks like I'm the guardian of the porn.'

'Whatever you do, don't leave them lying around in your car,' Bob said as he looked Peter in the eye. 'And for fuck's sake, don't lose them.'

Peter wiped a bead of sweat from his brow and put the handkerchief back in his replacement suit pocket. His third suit so far. 'Why do you think Stella was the one chosen?' he changed topic.

'I'm a woman,' she began. 'I look vulnerable. Or so he thinks.'

'I have another thought. You're new to town. Any other journo might recognise his voice. Just a theory.'

'Nice theory,' Bob thought, 'but let's move on. You said Sam saw Machowicz and Eastern at the wharf having a group hug with the O'Learys? They won't do a full stretch in Pentridge, that's for certain. Frank Galbally will make sure of that. The O'Learys would have rung Frank as soon as they were regarded as suspects.'

'Apparently, Frank's not doing it. He's ill,' Peter replied. 'A girl called Poppy Reynolds is doing it.'

'Never heard of her.' Bob drummed the table with his fingers. 'She'll have to be good. What's she like?'

'Pretty. Cool. She wouldn't tell me anything. Looks a little like Lady Di.'

'I wonder what the O'Learys think of that?' Bob smiled.

'So where do we go to from here?' Peter asked. 'Do we run with it now?'

'We wait,' Stella interrupted. 'I think the O'Learys are planning more.'

'I agree. What was it Conceetah told you about some Russians?' Bob asked.

'Nothing,' Peter replied, 'except that they were from Sydney.'

Then that's what we should follow up. Stella, pack your bags. You're on the next flight to Sydney. Let's find those Russians.'

'What about my secret informer?'

'Let Peter handle him. I've got a feeling about this.'

'Okay, Bob, but it's a needle in a damn haystack. Where do I start looking?'

'Start at King's Cross.' Bob paused for a moment. 'And we're really dependent on what Sam is bringing out of there. He's getting some good stuff but if he's in danger, get him the hell out of there.'

'I won't risk his life, Bob,' Peter declared. 'No way.'

'What about the lawyer?' Stella asked. 'This Poppy you've been talking about? Can you get close to her? We really need to know why the O'Learys and Tony Donarto have declared war on each other.'

'She's not going to tell me that,' Peter said dismissively. 'She's protecting the O'Learys. Why would she want to tell me anything?'

'We have to try,' Bob growled. 'Some lawyers like to talk. Some of them certainly like the sound of their own voices.' He paused for breath. 'Use your charisma on her. By the sound of her, she seems pretty ditsy, dressing like Lady Diana. Now, why doesn't she dress like Princess Margaret? She's more my style.'

'Get close? I'd love to,' Peter blurted, as Stella and Bob exchanged glances. 'What I mean is I'd love to be able to do that. It's going to be difficult. I've tried ringing her but she hasn't returned my calls.'

'Forget that,' Stella suggested. 'You gotta go to her. Invade her personal space.'

'Use that animal charm of yours,' Bob teased.

21

After trying to be charming and ingratiating himself to the receptionist, Peter soon found himself back on the footpath in front of Grace and O'Connor in William Street. The receptionist had the personality of a piranha. He sat on the bench directly outside, staring up at the three storey Victorian bluestone, despairing that this would probably be the closest he'd ever get to Poppy. Grace and O'Connor was one of the most prestigious law firms in Melbourne, an Irish Catholic firm that had sprung from humble origins, representing the unwashed, the unwanted and unrepresented, as well as the masses of Irish peasantry who had arrived in Melbourne during the gold rush and never left. The firm had prospered alongside its clients. It was their privilege to represent the doyens of Melbourne's Irish Catholics as well as the Catholic Church and the Australian Labor Party, both cornerstones of Melbourne society. And, once it had been registered, the Painters and Dockers Union.

Now it seemed they also represented the O'Learys. If only he could find out about that relationship. *If only.* He sat there for another ten minutes, thinking, scanning the entrance in the hope that Poppy might appear. *It's times like these I need coffee.* He wandered into the adjacent coffee shop and ordered his usual double espresso.

He pulled up a chair in the corner nearest the window, overlooking Grace and O'Connor's front door and waited. And waited. It was his hunch that Poppy would have to come in for a coffee sooner or later, assuming that she was a caffeine addict, like most Melbournians.

By the fourth espresso Peter was wired and ready to give up, when Poppy floated into the café. The very sight of her sent his heart thumping out of his chest. Poppy always seem to float. She was ethereal. Either that or he was in the throes of a caffeine overdose.

He was hovering, ready to stand up and meet her at the counter, but she noticed him first. She exchanged a few words with the waiter and then glided towards him. Peter felt dizzy and had to sit down again.

'I haven't seen you here before, Mister Clancy,' Poppy purred, pulling out the chair opposite him. Peter was taking deep deliberate breaths and wishing he had ordered tea.

'Call me Peter. Please,' he stammered, 'please join me, if you'd like.'

'As I said,' she repeated, 'I haven't seen you in this coffee shop before.'

'I just happened to be in the area,' he lied, 'and I was desperate for a coffee.' He knew he had being caught out when Poppy raised one eyebrow.

'Would I be wrong if I assumed that you're telling me porky pies, Peter?' she responded icily. 'You know what I do for a living. Are you trying to test my lie detector?'

Peter felt himself breaking into a cold sweat. Fortunately, she was momentarily diverted by the arrival of her order. She picked up her cappuccino and sipped, observing Peter as he fumbled in his trouser pocket for a handkerchief that wasn't there. He picked up a napkin and wiped his hands.

'Okay,' he admitted, 'I've been trying to contact you but without success. I went to the office but the receptionist gave me the quick heave-ho.'

'So you met Roxy the Rottweiler and survived? We call her our receptionist and attack dog. You're persistent, I have to admit. I guess that's the nature of your job,' Poppy chuckled. 'It's an admirable quality.'

'Gee, thanks.'

'You already know that I can't really disclose any information to the press.'

'Would it help you if it was all off the record? You know, in confidence. I just wanted to clear up a few background details. For my own peace of mind.'

'Off the record? That has to be consensual.'

'It does.' He matched her tease and raised it. 'So I'd be consenting and you'd be consenting.'

'Mmm. But I have another request,' she said as she brushed back her hair. 'No recorders or listening devices.'

Interesting, Peter thought. He could always tell those who were media savvy and those who weren't. The uninitiated always merged journalist with spy, for some reason. They assumed all journalists were outfitted with electronics. He was surprised by Poppy's naivety. 'Nothing of the sort,' he declared, opening up his jacket. 'I don't even have a pen and notepad.' He, like so many old-school journos, had trained his mind to remember verbatim what was said at an interview. Even ones who drank as much as Peter. It was a talent ranked equal to shorthand.

'I can't talk about the details of the coming hearing,' Poppy replied, frowning.

'Of course,' he reassured her. *Shit. Not going to get anything here.*

'So I don't know if I can help you much.'

'Okay,' he began. 'But the O'Learys are clients of your firm. For how long?'

'Off the record,' she emphasised. 'They have been clients of the firm for a long time.'

'Years?' he ventured.

'Decades.'

'What sort of work have you done for them?'

'All manner of work. The family is one of our big clients.'

'Do they keep you busy?' he asked.

'Well, they operate one of the most successful family companies in Melbourne. They have many interests.'

'Anything to do with importing goods from South East Asia?'

'As I said, the family has many business interests. South East Asia is the main focus,' she replied evasively.

'Okay. I'm going to bite the bullet here,' he said. 'I'm not interested in wasting my time or yours. Is one of the commodities they import heroin?'

A wry smile curled one corner of Poppy's lips. She took a slow, deliberate sip from her coffee. She lowered her cup and stared at him intensely before replying. 'That's rather fanciful, Peter. The O'Learys have worked hard for their money. And honestly.'

He pondered both her statement and her non-verbal cues. He always theorised that he could pick a lie by the number of blinks, mouth movements and speech stumbles. She might have an inbuilt lie detector, but he had the best bullshit meter in the business—only his bullshit meter wasn't registering that well with Poppy Reynolds.

'I know they were connected with the Painters and Dockers Union,' Peter continued.

'If you had done your research you have known that Patrick O'Leary spoke out against the corruption of the union at the Royal Commission.'

'So, why did he disappear for all those years and suddenly reappear recently like a long-lost Nazi? I'm confused.'

'You have a rather fertile imagination,' she said with a schoolgirl giggle. Peter thought it was cute. 'Have you ever thought of leaving journalism and becoming an author? You could be the next Frederick Forsyth. Possibly.'

'You like Frederick Forsyth?' Peter asked.

'One of my favourites. And Robert Ludlum.'

'Really,' Peter's eyes widened. 'Same here. We'll have to compare books sometime.'

'I think we're getting off track. Or is that your intention?'

'No. I'm not here to confuse you, Poppy. If I do that I'll only confuse myself. Where was I again?'

'We were discussing Frederick Forsyth,' she smiled.

'Yes.' He began his questioning again. 'Do the O'Learys and Tony Donarto know each other and, if so, how do they know each other?'

Poppy sipped her coffee again and looked away. For a moment he detected that she was either looking very uncomfortable or his bullshit meter was bullshitting him.

'They have been business associates in the past,' she offered after a long silence.

'What sort of business?' he asked quickly.

'They had an importing business.' She stared back at Peter as if she was challenging him to blink first. 'Coffee from South East Asia.'

'Coffee? Do they grow coffee there?'

'In Vietnam.'

'I always thought it came from Brazil,' he observed. 'You said they were in business. Past tense.'

'It didn't work out. The government wanted too much. Communist governments aren't sharing, benevolent entities, you might say. Off the record, of course.'

Peter suspected that she reinforced the 'off the record' statement whenever he closed in on the action.

'So this is what I think happened. Feel free to interrupt. Patrick O'Leary was there, somewhere in Asia, happily running a Vietnamese coffee plantation for years. The government—or someone else—gets greedy and it all falls apart. He returns to Australia. He reports back to Tony Donarto that the coffee plantation has gone belly up and they call it quits. Happy ending? No. Next minute, Pat's dead and his son is dead. All over coffee. And you didn't interrupt me. Interesting,' Peter said as he raised his left eyebrow at Poppy.

'I didn't, did I?' she said uneasily. 'But that's exactly how it played out. It's all off the record, of course.'

'I'm going out on a limb again here, Poppy,' he began. 'Is there a war going on between the O'Learys and the Donarto camp?'

'War sounds rather strong,' she replied. 'Maybe there are other people involved. Maybe it's all just a coincidence.' She checked her wristwatch. 'Have to get back.'

'And why haven't the police arrested any of the Donarto camp? They seem to have concentrated on the O'Learys.'

Poppy grabbed her handbag. 'You'll have to ask someone else that, Peter,' she smiled. 'So, you fancy yourself another Frederick Forsyth, then? This could be an interesting back-story to your book. It will be a great book. But I don't know if you should use coffee as the cause of all of the friction. After all, it is only coffee.' She arched her eyebrow and rose from her chair.

Peter stood up. 'Well, thanks for the background information,' he said.

'I guess that means you'll stop pestering me,' she murmured.

'If something comes up, can I contact you?'

'I think I've given you all the off-the-record information I can supply. You wouldn't want me to lose my job because I'm an informant?'

'But we haven't compared our book collection yet,' Peter grinned.

'You're very forward,' she replied with mock indignation, 'to think you can lure me into a corner both professionally and personally.'

'Forgive me for trying,' he shrugged.

Poppy shook her head and left the table. She stopped when she reached the door. 'Donnini's. Friday at seven. I don't like to be kept waiting. You do like Italian, don't you?'

Peter nodded in agreement. 'Italian's fine. And by the way, neither do I.'

***

I'm walking on sunshine, Peter sang in his head as he hurried along William Street back to the Stag. Or possibly he was singing it out aloud, judging from the strange stares he was getting from passers-by. *So what. I'm happy. I've done a good interview and got a date out of it. How good is that? Now get back to the office and get down the information.*

Yes, he could memorise whole interviews, only these days not for very long. He was already beginning to wonder what it was Poppy had said about the coffee plantation, exactly. He was still humming when he reached his cubicle back at *The Truth*. Katrina and The Waves. He dropped into his chair and started scribbling keywords into a notepad as quickly as he could. O'Leary, Tony, coffee, Vietnam and, of course, the most important: the date on Friday night. Now he could relax.

From the adjacent cubicle, Stella was belting out *New York, New York*, Ethel Merman style. *If I can make it there, I can make it anywhere...*

'Why are you singing?' he asked as he spun his chair around towards her.

'Why are you?' she rejoined. 'By the way, that's a lousy song.'

'I'm coming over.' He sauntered around to Stella's cubicle, adding, 'Ethel.'

Stella was leaning back on her chair. She looked very chuffed with herself. He pulled up a chair beside her.

'He wants to do an interview,' she announced happily, but I'm flying to Sydney.'

'Who? The informant?'

'No. No. Tony Donarto.'

'The great Tony Donarto wants to speak to *Truth* reporter Stella Reimers?' he laughed. 'I don't believe it. You were able to persuade him? He hates the media, especially *The Truth*.'

'Tony Donarto rang me,' she explained. 'Wants to clear the air. He feels victimised. In his own words.'

'Why you? You'd think Tony would love to be on television preening himself in his expensive Italian suit rather than go to a paper.'

'He says he trusts us.'

164

'After what we did to him?'

'I know. Go figure. Anyway, I told him I'm outta here and he'll need to speak to you.'

'And what did he say to that?'

'He agreed. But he wants to be paid for the interview or he'll go to a TV channel.'

'And he needs the money?' Peter shook his head. 'You didn't agree?'

'Bob did. He said it might break open this story and we can print it as an exclusive.'

'You've done well. Where are we doing the interview?'

'He'll call you to let you know. You'll be okay?'

'You worried about me or Donarto?' Peter chuckled. 'Will you be okay in Sydney?'

'I'll be fine. I'll keep you in the loop. Shame Bob won't buy me one of those new cell phones.'

'It would never fit it in your handbag.'

'Okay, wiseguy. How about your leads?'

'I did an off-the-record, cryptic interview with Poppy the solicitor.'

'What did you find out?'

'That the O'Learys grew coffee in Vietnam.'

'I didn't know they grew coffee in Vietnam,' Stella replied. She reached for a book buried at the back of her desk. 'I'll check my facts-of-the-world book.' She opened it and started poring over its well-thumbed pages.

'Interesting reading.'

'I like to get my facts right,' she commented as she turned over the pages. She stopped at one page. 'Coffee producing countries in the world.'

'I'm surprised there's a market for this useless trivia,' Peter remarked.

'Well, waddaya know? Here it is,' she pointed her finger at a line on the page. 'It does grow coffee. Remind me why you were asking about coffee-growing in Vietnam.'

'Poppy mentioned that the O'Learys and Tony Donarto had been in business together. Wait for this: They were once in the coffee-growing business. They even owned a plantation there. I have my doubts about it being a coffee plantation.'

'I think you're right. I don't think it was a coffee plantation. She's given you some clues, hasn't she?'

'It's not coffee,' he replied. 'I think it's heroin.'

'Maybe that's how they've imported it. In coffee cans. I've heard of it being done by that method before. Back in the States.'

'Pity the interview was off the record,' he remarked.

'Seems Pretty Poppy has pointed you in the right direction. I don't understand why she even went that far. It's a cryptic clue, isn't it? She's telling you why these two parties have fallen out.'

'Maybe I'm just a bloody good interviewer. I've always been good at reading between the lines. I have a theory that people give out cryptic clues even when they are trying to cover up the facts.'

'Nice hypothesis, professor,' Stella teased. 'You certainly have a healthy ego. I think she may have an agenda. Don't know what it is, though. She's trying to tell you something.'

'Agenda? Interesting theory. I'm taking her out on a date on Friday. She may tell me what it is then.'

'Mixing business and pleasure can be tricky, as you've seen. Good luck.'

'Good luck with the Cross. Wear two pairs of knickers, though, and give Sydney my regards,' Peter laughed.

22

Of all the hundreds of containers that were unloaded on South Wharf during the week, Sam noticed that the O'Leary brothers paid special attention to a pale blue twenty-foot container with the lettering KTV marked on it. Since the arrests of Eastern and Machowicz there had been a staff shortage, and Sam had been promoted from forklift driver to a straddle carrier operator.

It was a gigantic piece of machinery with no room for error. Sam, in his usual quietly confident manner, had picked it up after three instruction sessions with Tommy O'Leary. He saw it as his mission to challenge those white folks who thought the black man was less intelligent than they were. And there were other benefits, aside from the extra pay. A straddle carrier operator sat at the very top of the crane in a central cockpit with views both front and rear. It was a perfect position to keep an eye on the activities of the wharf.

The KTV container had not been stacked, but sat isolated at the end of a row of containers. And the O'Leary boys always checked on it several times a day. They didn't unlock it, but they walked around it, inspecting the metal skin and the locks diligently. Sam had told Peter and Dave about the container in dinner conversation over his homemade shepherd's pie.

From his cubby in the sky, Sam could see the O'Leary brothers mostly arguing and occasionally talking as they inspected the container. The other people who had showed interest in the container were two customs officers. Sam had seen the O'Learys and the customs officers opening the container one day. It didn't appear to be a normal inspection. The four of them had emerged after ten minutes, all jokey and friendly. Sam assumed being friendly to the wharf operators wasn't part of Customs' job descriptions.

After a friendly chat with Babs, Sam learned that the brothers engaged their own security firm on the wharf. O'Leary Security. According to Babs, the security guards consisted almost exclusively of ex-cons who were no strangers to violence, but as loyal to the O'Learys as the Waffen SS were to Adolf Hitler. Through good old Babs, Sam had also ascertained that containers were at a high risk of being broken into, either through cutting the door locks or cutting through the metal wall. It had happened several times in the past, although it didn't happen anymore. The brothers had found the culprits, she told him. When he asked if the thieves had gone to jail, she fell silent.

Good old Babs, Sam thought. She was a solid stick who didn't mind a yarn. And she was a good sort. A bit rough around the edges, but he was always a sucker for a woman who showed an interest. Maybe he would ask her out on a date. But the main job at hand was to find out what was going on with this container. Babs was his source, first and foremost. It was like a movie, Sam thought. Like *The French Connection*.

Sam switched off the crane for lunch and climbed down the steps. He saw the O'Leary boys climb into their black Mercedes and speed off. He slipped across to the container. He walked around it. Touched it. There were locks securing the doors. No way in without breaking in. Stumped, he leaned against the container. He smelt cigarette smoke. Stiffening, he peered around the corner of the container.

'Interesting, isn't it?' Babs rasped between puffs. 'This container. Of all the containers on this wharf. This is the most interesting.' She stubbed out her cigarette and walked up to Sam.

'I was wondering if I had to move it,' he lied. 'It doesn't look safe here.'

'I wouldn't move it, Samson.' She approached him, reached out and stroked his face. 'I think it's the safest frigging container on this wharf. The boys would get very upset. Don't you think?' She stroked his face several times more, then lowered her hand. 'You're a good looking man aren't you, Samson?'

'I scrub up all right,' he said smiling faintly. He didn't know whether to be aroused or frightened. Was Babs Bell onto him?

'You've been looking me over for a while,' she said flirtatiously.

'Well, you're the only woman on this wharf. You certainly beat looking at Tommy and Robbie.'

Babs chuckled. 'I like dark skinned men,' she cooed. 'Always have. You look more manly. More sexy. You remind me of Isaac Hayes.'

'I won't disagree, Babs,' Sam smiled. Was she luring him into a false sense of security, he wondered. If she was it felt bloody good.

'What are you doing tonight?' she asked. She reached down and picked up her cigarette butt. 'The boys don't like litter on the wharf.'

'What do Melbourne girls like to do on a first date? I'm not the restaurant sort of bloke.'

'Bugger restaurants,' she replied. 'And besides. I'm not a Melbourne girl. More Wodonga.'

'We could go to the pub,' he suggested. 'Though I'm not a pub bloke either. I'm not a drinker.'

'Come over to my house. I'll cook you dinner. Good wholesome food. How would you like that?'

'I wouldn't mind that,' he blushed. 'If that's all right with you?'

'Of course, love,' she smiled and stroked his face again. 'Meet me at the car park after work. I only live in Port Melbourne.'

'You don't care if I'm not dressed for dinner?'

'You can always slip into something more comfortable when we get to my place,' she winked and then walked away.

***

Sam was finding it difficult to relax. He shifted uneasily in the battered beanbag and sipped occasionally from a can of soft drink as he watched Babs standing over the stove with a cigarette dangling from her mouth, stirring a mixture in a frypan that smelt like fish. For all the efforts Sam made, his eyes still drifted back to the two snarling German shepherds flanking him in the lounge room. He was thankful that the dogs were restrained by thick chains attached to a heavy oak table and out of reach of him. Manson and Ripper growled every time he moved. He hoped that dinner would be on the table soon. And the knocks on the door? They hadn't stopped since he'd arrived. Each knock sent Manson and Ripper into fits of barking and pulling at their metal chains until they were taut.

Sam could see who was coming to the door if he stretched up. Sometimes it was a secondary school child, or a person in work clothes, but usually it was a procession of wasted shells of people staggering to Babs Bell's door. Sam knew that these people weren't friends, or collecting donations or hawking products. He wasn't too sure why the Bells were popular at first, until a chill that ran down his spine. Then he saw Babs grab a baseball bat from behind the door and shake it in the face of a skeleton person. The skeleton person begged but was pushed away. Sam wondered how he could have been so naïve. This wasn't Hollywood. This wasn't a sleazy tough guy with a New York accent dealing drugs down a side alley. It was Babs Bell, a woman old enough to be a grandmother, dealing the same stuff from a suburban house in Port Melbourne. He peeled himself slowly out of the beanbag. He had to get out of here.

'Dinner,' Babs called from the kitchen as she dished up the meals onto four plates. 'My favourite, Sam.'

'What's that?' he stammered as he adjusted his shirt.

'Tuna mornay,' she replied softly. She reached into a cupboard by the door and pulled out a cardboard sign with the words *Don't Disturb Or Else* written on it in crayon. She opened the door and placed the sign on it, slammed it shut, locked it, then marched towards the kitchen. Brushing past Sam, she grabbed two plates that were piled higher than the other two and returned to Manson and Ripper.

'It's their favourite too,' she smiled as she placed the plates next to the dogs. No sooner had she put down the plates than the dogs devoured their meals and were looking for more.

'I'll get them a bone each after we eat,' she stated as she grabbed the plates and walked to the dining table. The dogs settled as she and Sam sat at the table. The chain rattling stopped.

'This looks nice,' Sam lied, as Babs placed the dish in front of him. Sam thought it smelled strange. Like rotten fish. It wouldn't be the worst meal he ever ate. Fried kangaroo guts held that honour. He was grateful when the telephone rang and Babs scurried off to answer it.

'Yeah,' he heard her say, 'I need you to help me.' Apparently the conversation wasn't proceeding quite as she had planned. Next thing Sam heard was Babs yelling down the phone, 'One night is all I'm asking for, one fucking night and we'll be set up for life.' A pause and then, 'You will? Seen sense at last, hey? I'll tell you when, Buddy. Nah, nothing like that. Yeah, I'll call you. Bye-bye love. Bye-bye sweetheart.' Then she resumed her place at the table as if nothing had happened.

'That's my grandson, Buddy. Still lives in Wodonga. He's a bit of a rough nut, just like his dad was. Before his dad disappeared.' She took a mouthful of food and chewed as she spoke. 'Yeah, Lionel disappeared nearly ten years ago. I blame his father.' Another mouthful. 'The bastard was always in jail and when he was out, he used to bash us senseless. Knocked Lionel around so much that he damaged his bloody brain.'

'That's...sad,' Sam replied with as much sympathy as he could muster.

'Buddy's on a disability pension now, too,' she continued. 'He has trouble controlling his impulses.'

'That's terrible.'

'Hmm. I'll take Manson and Ripper outside with their bones.' She stood up, unchained the dogs and led them out the back door.

Sam sighed. Whatever feelings he might have had for Babs were waning by the minute. He couldn't really be attracted to a drug-dealing granny, could he? He told himself that, from now on, it was just a bit of sex. And a great deal of important information. He had to continue the relationship. No matter what.

'That's better,' Babs sighed after she closed the door. 'It's good to have some peace.'

'You brought your son up by yourself?' Sam asked.

'Yep. On me own. Lionel's father got shot in a bank robbery a long time ago. But I reckon the frigging coppers set him up. Anyway. That's another story. I've had a few men since his father but they're all the same. They just want to root ya and bash ya and hurt your children. Got any children, Sam?'

'Never had the privilege. I had a woman, but she died up north. Ten years ago.'

'That's sad,' she said as she touched Sam on the shoulder.

'Can't be sad about it,' he reflected. 'Just have to get on with it.'

'You're a good man, Sam. You and me deserve a bit of happiness.'

Maybe he'd been too quick to judge her. 'I guess.'

She reached across the table and began to kiss Sam on the mouth. He responded by clutching her around the shoulder and pulling her towards him.

'Looks like the horse hasn't been out of the yard for a while,' she laughed as she pulled away and undid her blouse.

'How did you know?' Sam grinned as he reached for her again.

'You can kind of tell with a man,' she smiled looking down at Sam's groin region.

'Sorry.'

'Don't be sorry,' she replied. 'Let's go somewhere more private. My bedroom, perhaps.' She took hold of Sam's hand and tugged gently.

'I could do with a rest,' he winked.

***

Sam awoke to hear the dogs barking playfully in the yard. Babs had pulled back a curtain and was looking out of the bedroom window.

'Something wrong?' he asked in a trance. He rolled to his side to see her naked, smoking a cigarette. Babs's body was surprisingly well-toned. The light streaming in from the street bathed her in a silvery halo. Sam could feel himself getting aroused.

'Want to come back to bed?' he said playfully patting the side of the bed where Babs had lain. The lovemaking had invigorated him. There had been many women and lots of lovemaking in his life, but this was one of the few times that he felt connected both physically and emotionally with a woman. Not since Annie.

'Soon, darl,' she replied. 'Just checking the dogs.'

'You love those dogs,' he stated as he rolled back on his back and placed his arms behind his head.

'Yeah, I do,' she said as she closed the curtain and stubbed out the cigarette. 'I'd be buggered without them.' No sooner had she closed the curtain then she reopened it again, 'Everything's fine. Good.' She closed the curtain for the last time.

'A bit of a rough area? Sam asked.

'Well, it isn't Toorak. Unfortunately there's a few derros and druggies that live here,' she replied as she slipped back in beside Sam. He flung his arm across her, as soon as her head hit the pillow.

'Can you just hold me?' she pleaded. 'Just cuddle me, darl.' Her outstretched arms intertwined with Sam's. He tried to kiss her but she turned her head away. 'The sex was some of the best I've ever had. Got a few things on me mind.' They held each other without speaking for what felt like an eternity.

'Everything will be all right, Babs,' Sam whispered.

'I hope so,' she replied as she looked at the curtains. 'I hope so.'

172

'You want to tell me about it?' he said as he stroked her hair. 'I'm an Aboriginal version of a social worker.'

'I bloody well hope not,' she snapped. 'Those cunts. Pardon me French. Those mongrels took Lionel off me when he was a little tacker. I had to fight the frigging Department for years to get him back. They reckon I was an unfit mother. Load of bullshit. Lionel got raped in foster care. Poor little bugger. Fucked him up good and proper.'

'Sorry about that,' Sam replied.

'I don't really want to say anything,' she ventured. 'You're a good man, Samson, but I don't want to involve you in me troubles.' She pecked him on the forehead and sat up on the edge of the bed. He shifted closer to her and lay against her, rubbing her back.

'That's nice,' she cooed. 'I could write a bloody book about what I've done, what I've seen and what I shouldn't have seen,' she chuckled. 'It would curl your hair. I'm telling ya.'

'I can't wait to read it.'

'Once I get Buddy and me set up, I'm going to do something about it. I've even started a night class in creative writing. People seem to like tragedy-made-good books.'

'You sound keen, Babs,' he observed. 'When do you reckon you'll be set up?'

'Pretty soon. Just a few loose ends to tie up and that's it.'

'So you won't be living here anymore, I suppose,' he remarked as he continued to gently rub her back.

'I'll be out of here so quick the Department of Housing won't even know about it. And we'll live on a farm where the dogs can run around all day and Buddy can ride his motorbike. And I'll be able to run some cattle and horses. And some chooks. You have to have chooks on a farm.'

'Where's the farm going to be?'

'I'm looking at a place near me old hometown. Wodonga,' she replied. 'Wodonga's a shithole but there's some good land near the mountains. There's a place I really love that's got a stone fireplace and a big kitchen. All set on fifty acres. And beautiful views of the mountains. I'm going to put a deposit on it soon.'

'The O'Learys are going to miss you,' he stated.

'The O'Learys.' Babs's voice dropped. 'I've worked for them for a long time. They've got their money's worth out of me. Doing all their office work. Being their gofer. They made a lot of money over the years and they paid me minimal wages. Not even a bloody bonus or a ham at Christmas. Enough of them.'

'But you seem to run the office and the business.'

'You tell 'em that. I don't want to talk about them anymore. It was better when the old fella was in the country.'

'I'm going to miss you, Babs.' He sat up beside her on the edge of the bed and placed his arm around her.

'You don't have to miss me,' she kissed Sam on the lips.

'What do you mean?'

'I might need a good man around the place,' she winked.

***

Peter was about to write up a piece on a priest who wanted a sex change operation, just so he could join a contemplative order of nuns. He knew it wasn't strictly true, but he needed to fill some empty space. He hoped it would be a sellout across the newsagencies in Melbourne. It would be on the television. In everyone's conversation. Peter had typed the first line when the phone rang.

'What the…?' he said aloud as he snatched up the handset and yelled into it. 'I'm frigging busy, Shazza!' He cradled the handset between his shoulder and his ear and continued to type as if life itself depended on it.

'A little bit stressed?' Shazza ventured.

'Yeah,' Peter softened. 'Sorry. Is this important?'

'Could be. If you think a phone call from Tony Donarto is. He wants to talk to you.'

'I almost forgot. Scum. Put him through.'

'Love to,' she said as she transferred the call.

'Hello, Tony?'

There was a pause. A deep breath. 'Clancy. This Stella. She said I should talk to you,' Tony said.

'I know. She's gone to Sydney and I'm your man. Funny how things work out.'

'But I wanted to talk to her, not you, you cocksucker.'

Peter held the handset away from his ear. 'As I told you, she's in Sydney. You could fly up and talk to her there. There was silence on the other end. 'Tony. You still there? You can always talk to me,' he braved, 'if you need to talk to someone.'

'You?' Tony snapped back, 'you nearly ruined my life. The wife would have left me except that we're Catholics. *Vaffanculo. Tua madre si da per niente.*'

'My mother was a highly principled woman, if you want to know. Fuck you indeed, Tony,' Peter replied.

Another silence. 'You speak Italian, you prick?'

'Enough to understand you. We're in Melbourne, remember? Little Italy?'

'All right,' he hesitated. 'I'll talk to you. On my terms.'

'You'll talk to me?' Peter repeated with a jolt. What was happening? Tony Donarto had good reason to hate him and now he wanted to confess all? 'The same interview as Stella?'

'But it'll cost you extra because I have to put up with your fucking ugly face.'

Peter thought briefly of putting the phone down to confer with Bob but something in Donarto's voice was desperate. Peter had a hunch. 'Sorry, no deal.'

'What do you mean? Stella was going to pay me a thousand.'

'Yes, but as I told you, she and the money have gone to Sydney. There's nothing left in the pot. Besides, you don't need a thousand quid, Tony. You want to talk to me, so let's talk.'

'You come to my house in Templestowe in one hour. I'll wait for you there.'

'All right. I'm bringing a photographer.' Peter was thinking he might need Dave for security. He also knew that Tony would like the idea of a photograph, vain creature that he was.

'Make sure you bring a good photographer,' said Tony. 'I have a public image.'

Thinks he's Marcello Mastroianni.

Armed with a cash cheque just in case, signed by a reluctant Bob and with Dave in tow, Peter arrived at Tony Donarto's within the appointed hour. Of course, Templestowe Tony's was the ugliest mansion in a street filled with ugly mansions. The whole suburb was overflowing with parvenus. It was the destination of choice for nouveau riche Italian and Greek families who had outgrown their inner city cottages and their working class lives. They had replaced the battered, cardboard suitcase with Fendi, their native tongue with English and they had realised their dreams. In Templestowe.

Each white mansion was doing its best to outdo the next in over-the-top extravagance and bad taste. Tony Donarto's was by far the most ostentatious. It was a three-storey villa that looked like it could have been designed by Liberace. Peter and Dave stared at it open-mouthed for a moment as Peter pulled the Stag up in front of a wrought iron gate, pressed the intercom and announced himself. He looked at the stone wall surrounding the house. The bullets holes had been plastered over. *I guess they lowered the tone of the neighbourhood.* The gate swung open slowly.

'He's done all right,' Dave said. 'You don't see houses like this in Clarkes Flat.'

'Or anywhere in Queensland,' Peter added as he engaged first gear and drove up the paved driveway. It was lined with marble statues, one every few metres, right up to the front door.

'They look like the real thing,' Dave said as he stared at them.

'You think so?' Peter doubted anything was real. 'Where are the slaves?' he added as he stopped the Stag behind a Ferrari.

'Slaves?' Dave pondered. 'Hey, look at that. That's a Daytona!'

'Well it isn't a Kingswood, that's for certain,' Peter snorted. 'We're here to work, Dave, not admire the view. And stop being so bloody country. We're not in Kansas anymore, Dorothy.'

Dave made a harrumphing sound and grabbed his camera bag.

'And here's the slave or something out of his personal zoo.'

A huge ape of a man lumbered towards them. He was dressed entirely in black: black pants with a black skivvy and jacket. His biceps were so thick they projected from his body almost at right angles. He had all the demeanour of a nightclub bouncer or, worse still, a contract killer.

'I hope he's been fed,' said Dave.

Peter opened the door and stepped out. Dave followed. The ape-man crossed his arms and eyed Peter and Dave up and down before speaking. He might just as easily have been looking at a pair of stray dogs shitting on his lawn.

Have I just walked onto a Godfather movie? Please Mister Mafia man, please don't whack me.

'I'm Peter Clancy and this is my photographer, Dave Tindall. We're here to see Mister Donarto. He's expecting us.'

'Inside,' the ape-man tilted his head towards a cathedral-sized wooden door.

'Thanks.' They walked in the direction of the ape-man's head.

'I think the bloke is wearing a pistol,' Dave whispered, as they approached the massive entrance.

'You think? I wondered how long it would take you to notice,' Peter replied as he wielded the heavy iron knocker.

'No. Just go in,' ape-man called from behind them. A smirk crossed his face as he waved them inside.

'Stay calm.' Peter opened the heavy door. 'It's not the first time I've seen people carrying weapons. He's not going to pull it out. It's all show. Macho crap. This isn't a movie.'

'Comforting,' Dave replied.

They stepped through the doorway, only to be assailed by the interior. It was part Roman, part Renaissance, part Confederate, but mostly high-class brothel. They kept walking, gawking at the tapestries hanging on the walls, the marble colonnade to the side, the gold and crystal chandelier that cascaded from the double height ceiling right down to the travertine floor, and encircled by a massive mahogany staircase, of the kind Vivien Leigh favoured.

'Wouldn't surprise me if Tony appears in a purple toga,' Peter shook his head.

'What's this with slaves and togas?' Dave whispered.

'Roman history, David. It's all Roman history.'

'Looks more like nineteen-fifties Hollywood to me. Too much.'

Peter called out, 'Tony. We're here.' His voice echoed. They waited.

'Where is he?' Dave asked.

'Probably putting on his best toga.'

'How long should we give him?'

'I don't want to stay here much longer,' Peter replied. 'This place is starting to creep me out.'

'Tony,' Peter called out again, this time louder. 'Anyone?'

There was a rustle from further inside the house, then an elderly woman's voice muttering in Italian. The voice drew nearer.

'Someone's coming,' Dave remarked.

'Nonna?' Peter hypothesised.

The voice was getting louder and more agitated.

'She sounds pretty pissed off,' Dave said nervously.

'Just wait,' Peter replied. 'We've probably woken her up.'

Nonna Donarto soon appeared through a doorway wearing a black dress, a black scarf and a crazed, wide-eyed stare. She was swinging a meat cleaver in wild arcs in their direction. For an old woman, she moved swiftly and soon the cleaver described semi-circles just short of their faces. Peter and Dave both dived backwards as the blade shaved their cheeks. They spun around and sprinted for the entrance.

'Time to go,' Peter shouted. 'The door. Open the door!'

Dave got there first and pulled it open. The cleaver sailed past Peter's head and thudded into the wooden door, as Nonna Donarto screamed abuse.

Outside, still alive, Peter scanned his body. *Not missing any body parts. Maybe messed my pants.* He slammed the door behind him. 'You all right?' he panted.

'I wasn't expecting to be attacked by a crazy woman,' Dave replied. 'She nearly got you.'

'For a pensioner, she's pretty strong.'

The old lady was still screaming inside the house and rattling the door, trying to get out.

'What's dear old Tony up to?' Peter wondered. 'Is the bastard trying to kill us or is it some kind of joke?'

Roars of laughter from the direction of the cars drowned out Nonna. The ape-man was standing near the Stag, doubled over with laughter. Tears streamed down his cheeks and ran through the stubble on his face.

'Someone thinks it's funny,' Dave commented as they walked to the Stag.

'I didn't know gorillas could laugh,' Peter said. 'I hope he laughs so much he pisses himself.'

'Mamma didn't kill you?' the goon said between bursts of laughter. 'She thinks all strangers in the house are Americans from the war. She's a little…crazy…you know.' He traced little circles with his finger around the side of his head.

'And you didn't warn us?' Peter spat at him. 'We wouldn't have gone in.'

'Mister Donarto said you would think it's funny. He said you have a strange sense of humour. Mister Donarto also said that you like catching people off-guard.'

'Really. Can you see me laughing? I'm not even laughing on the inside. Okay. I get it now. It's Tony little act of retribution.' Peter snapped as he swung open the door to the Stag. 'By the way, where is Tony?'

'He's not here,' the ape-man replied.

'What the…? Where is he?'

'Mister Donarto is at St Francis's church in the city. He wants to meet you there.'

'But he told us to come here. What's your name?'

'Marco. And now he says for you to go there.'

'And how do I know this isn't just another stunt? Another humiliation?'

'He said that if you want the story, then you have to met him at St Francis. Pronto.'

Peter toyed with the idea of telling Marco exactly where Tony could shove his story. Then he remembered Stella. 'On our way,' he replied. 'If you let us out, Marco, we'll be there. Pronto'

∗∗∗

Peter zipped down Lonsdale Street, flew past the back of the Myer department store and did a U-turn, just as the lights at Elizabeth Street turned green.

Dave looked at him, shaking his head. 'You drive like a racing car driver.'

'Well, Peter Brock and I do have at least one thing in common,' he responded.

'What's that?'

'Good old Collingwood, forever,' he grinned as he stopped the Stag a little further up from the church and snapped on the parking brake.

He and Dave passed by the tablet that pronounced St Francis Melbourne's oldest Catholic Church. As far as Catholic churches went, Peter was prepared to concede that this one was exceptionally pretty and modest, and so much more inviting than that bluestone mammoth, Saint Patrick's, up the road. They entered the church through a side door, where Dave stopped momentarily to genuflect, before walking slowly towards the front of the church.

'I hope this isn't another joke,' Dave whispered.

'What next?' Peter looked around the church. 'We're going to be set on by a mob of crazy nuns?'

'Why a church?' Dave remarked.

Peter scoured the pews. 'Over there. Is that him?' In the gloom he noticed two men sitting together in the pew closest to the altar.

'Is that a priest with him?' Dave wondered, drawing closer.

'What's going on?' Peter asked, as he stood in the aisle next to Tony.

The priest replied with a loud shush. 'You're in a church. Lower your voice.'

Tony grinned. He was his usual oily self. His suit was tailored, his hair dyed, his manner reeking of arrogance and expensive aftershave. The priest looked like any other Catholic priest: pinched and intimidating. Tony beckoned Peter and Dave to sit behind them. By force of habit, Peter found himself genuflecting before taking the seat closest to Tony. Dave took his seat a little further away and started taking his camera out of its case.

'No photographs in here,' the priest waved a bony finger at Dave. He immediately stopped and repacked the camera.

'This is Father Kennedy,' Tony announced, looking at the priest with admiration. 'He's been the parish priest here for many years. A good priest, a good man of God. He's here to help me sort out this mess.'

Mess, thought Peter. *Interesting.*

'And you have been a good provider to the church, Mister Donarto,' Father Kennedy replied.

Peter thought how it was funny that priests always seemed to have a special place for wealthier parishioners and another place for the rest of the congregation. In his experience, the special place was called hypocrisy.

'You met my dear mother?' Tony said softly as he turned to Peter.

'How is your mother?' Father Kennedy interrupted.

'Very frail, Father,' Tony replied. 'Very frail.'

'She didn't seem very frail when she was running at us in a banzai charge with a meat cleaver.'

'You're referring to Missus Donarto? She would never do that,' Father Kennedy said.

'She's very frail and unwell, Father,' said Tony.

'I must go and see her, then.'

'That would be very good. It'll help her feel at peace,' he replied as he patted the priest on the back.

Peter grinned as an image of the priest being chased around the mansion by Nonna wielding an axe flashed into his mind. Then back to the job at hand. The interview.

'Why have you been wanting to talk to us Tony,' Peter asked.

'Before we begin,' Tony replied, 'there's the question of the donation.'

'The fee for the interview?'

'The donation. We agreed,' Tony continued. 'I give you an interview and you make a donation.' Peter felt for Bob's cheque in his breast pocket. 'To the church.'

Peter took out his wallet instead of the cheque, opened it up and withdrew a ten-dollar note. Tony took one look and shook his head. 'More than that.'

He took out a twenty. Again, Tony shook his head. 'You have to be joking.'

Anything more and I'll have to cash the bloody cheque myself and keep it. Peter opened up his wallet and offered Tony the entire contents.

'That's better.' He pulled out a handful of fives, two fifties and snatched the twenty still clasped in Peter's hand. Tony turned to Father Kennedy. 'This is a start. For the renovations to the church, Father,' Tony declared as he tucked it into his shirt pocket.

'Oh, thank you, my boy. Thank you,' the priest said.

For a moment Peter thought the priest was going to kiss Tony Donarto's hand, as if he were the Pope himself. After all, Tony was wearing a large gold ring on his finger. Of the many reasons he had left the Catholic Church, Peter reflected, this was probably the main one. A church that based it doctrine on the acquisition of wealth and the courting of the wealthy and influential simply didn't match what he had been taught during religious instruction. Give to the poor, et cetera, et cetera. Or perhaps he was just mad at the nuns and brothers who had thrashed him throughout his long, dark years in the Catholic education system. In time he might forgive. In time.

'I want to clear my name here,' Tony announced, dramatically looking up to the heavens. 'Before God.'

Father Kennedy put his arm around Tony.

'Why do you have to clear your name, Tony?' Peter asked.

'I've been dragged into this…this mess. This mess that the O'Learys have created.'

'Won't all this be brought up in court?' asked Peter.

'I am a respected businessman and former…former because of you,' Tony pointed a finger at Peter. 'Former deputy mayor of Melbourne.'

'How well did you know the O'Learys?'

Tony stiffened before replying. 'We were in business together. Growing coffee.'

'So I heard. And it didn't work out.'

'Yes, that's right' Tony continued. 'They were too violent. Too skip.'

'Skip?' Dave asked.

'Skip. It's what some European-Australians call Anglo-Australians. You know, Skippy the bush kangaroo?' Peter explained.

'I got out of the business but they got angry,' Tony continued. 'They threatened me. Threatened my family. That story you did on me—they told you all that, didn't they?'

'I don't disclose my sources, Tony,' Peter replied. *Had Slugger been fed the information by the O'Learys? Maybe.*

'Good for you!' Tony pretended to sob. Father Kennedy patted him like he was burping a baby. The crocodile tears flowed until the priest handed him a tissue. Tony continued after wiping his face, and took another tissue from a box next to him. Father Kennedy had come prepared.

'You see?' Tony continued, 'I am an innocent man. Aldo was an innocent man.'

'So you think the O'Learys did all the shooting? Peter questioned.

'Well they caught the men, didn't they? Those two thugs worked for them.'

'But it all seems to have started after Pat and Mickey O'Leary were killed in their garage.'

'My theory is this—this is what you paid money for, so listen closely. It's very important,' he took a deep breath and continued. 'That family are not nice people. You see? They always fight among themselves. The father, Pat, he was okay to deal with. But the sons. No good. No good. They fight each other. Those boys even treat their mother badly. No one should be disrespectful to their mamma.'

'So you think it's a family feud and you've been drawn into it?'

'Yes. For sure. That's it. I'm an honest businessman who made his money honestly. I did business with them. I trusted them. Bad idea. Very bad.' Tony finished with a dramatic sigh and looked at the priest for comfort.

'Is it possible,' Peter began slowly, 'that the brothers are importing illegal substances into the country?'

'You mean…drugs?'

Peter observed that Tony's eyes were darting around in their sockets. 'Maybe,' Peter continued. 'All this seemed to be pointing in that direction, but you're probably right, it's a family feud. I've met the O'Leary clan and got punched to the ground for my troubles.'

'I declare before God, I do not know anything about drugs,' Tony declared loudly, looking upwards at the crucifix as Father Kennedy patted him on the back. 'When you get into bed with dogs, you wake up with fleas. And I'll be telling the court that. I hate drugs. They destroy the innocent. I give money to help them get off drugs. Don't I, Father?'

'Yes. You do.'

'I have my hunches, but nothing's been proven yet,' Peter added. 'About the business.'

'Yes. Of course,' Tony sighed.

Peter thought it sounded a lot like relief. 'Is that all you were going to tell Stella? You have to be joking, Tony. You have to give me my money's worth, at least.' Peter closed his notepad and shoved his pen into his coat pocket, rueing his hundred and forty-five dollars, but glad that he hadn't handed over the cheque. 'One more question. Are you afraid for your life?'

'What do you bloo…Sorry, Father. What do you think? I can't sleep. I have had to hire security. I'll be happy when these O'Learys are locked away. Pity it's not the whole lot of them. Not just those thugs that work for them.'

Peter thought for a moment before replying. 'Let's wrap it up.'

'Do you want to take my photograph?' Tony asked anxiously.

'Of course,' Peter chuckled.

'How about in front of the church?' Dave suggested.

Tony Donarto was adamant that he should pose holding his hands in prayer in front of the church but after gentle persuasion from Dave it was decided that he would look better looking up at the church. Like an innocent altar boy. As Tony Donarto stood solemnly in front of Saint Francis's church affecting the pose that Dave wanted, Peter had already composed the headline: *Tony Donarto: God's Good Man.*

'What did you think of that,' Peter asked as he slipped the Stag in behind a group of cars at a traffic light.

'I don't know,' Dave said with bemusement. 'Is he going out of his way to tell everyone he's Mister Good Guy?'

'I bet he's employed a public relations firm to work on his image. I bet you. The court case is coming up and he wants to tell the public that he's a good man.'

'Quite the celebrity, isn't he?' Dave remarked.

'He loves the spotlight. Always has done. I'm surprised they haven't given him a role in *Neighbours*,' Peter stated as he accelerated away from the green traffic light.

'Do you think he's innocent? Dave asked.

'I've never heard that he's involved in anything illegal. That's interesting. But what was more interesting was how Tony reacted when I asked him about the drugs.'

'He did his best to dodge and weave around the question. But he could be scared.'

'Shit,' Peter barked as he screeched the Stag to a stop.

'What?' Dave looked around.

'That useless prick just pulled out in front of me without indicating. Fuck!' Peter said as he blew his horn. He engaged first gear again and accelerated.

'I thought it was something important.'

'I'm sure the traffic is getting worse,' Peter complained. 'Everything is changing. More traffic. More criminals. More shit going on. Everything is changing.'

Peter checked in with Bob as soon as he got back to the office. Shazza told him she hadn't seen Bob come out of his office for hours. He knocked on Bob's door. There was no response. He knocked harder.

'Yeah,' Bob yelled, 'come in.'

Peter entered the office to find Bob unscrewing the cap of a bottle of whiskey and pouring two glasses. There was an empty bottle sitting in the waste paper basket. The ashtray overflowed with cigarette butts.

'I was wondering when you'd come by,' Bob slurred.

I've never heard Bob slur his words, Peter thought. *Ever.* Bob had the same alcohol carrying capacity as an elephant. He pushed the glass of whiskey in Peter's direction. 'Thanks,' Peter picked up the glass, took a sip and placed it back on the desk.

Bob threw his back and plonked the glass back on the desk after he had drained half of its contents.

'Are you okay?' Peter asked.

'Of course I'm okay,' he replied. 'Don't you think I am?'

'You seem to be taking Stella's vacation hard.'

'I shouldn't care that she's putting her arse on the line, infiltrating God knows what organised crime syndicate for me?' Bob emptied the rest of the glass and poured a refill. 'I should be the hard-arsed editor that doesn't care. Maybe you should be the hard-arsed editor. You don't seem worried about her.'

'Of course I care,' Peter said. 'I really like Stella, but she's only gone to Sydney, Bob. I want her back as much as you.'

'Sorry, mate,' Bob sighed as he leaned back in the chair. 'I guess when you have a personal involvement with someone it makes it bloody harder.'

'That's why I'm worried. We're all worried about you.'

'I keep thinking about the photos and the type of scum she'll have to mix with to get information. Maybe we should hand the photos over to the police and drop this whole story. What's a headline when there could be a person's life at stake? It's a grubby fucking game, isn't it?'

'It's your call, Bob,' Peter replied. 'I'll go with whatever you want.' He took a drink.

'I haven't heard from her for two whole days. I just keep hoping that she's safe.

'Why don't you have some time off, Bob? Go to Sydney. See Stella.'

'And what? Leave you in charge of the paper? You couldn't organise a piss up in a brewery, Clancy.'

'You're the boss.'

'Bloody oath. And what did the great Tony Donarto have to say for himself?'

'He declared his innocence before God. We did the interview in Saint Francis Church. Strange.'

'He's slick,' Bob shook his head. 'And slippery. I have never heard of him being involved in anything illegal. You know that? He's the Teflon man'

'We'll see,' Peter replied.

'What plans now?'

'I'm meeting Poppy the solicitor for dinner tonight.'

'Business or pleasure?'

'Both, I hope,' Peter confessed.

'Just be careful,' Bob lectured. 'It's a delicate balancing act. I've done it. Just be careful.'

'When haven't I been careful?' Peter teased.

Bob rolled his eyes. 'Try and get some information out of her before you jump into bed with her. Please.'

'I'll try,' Peter winked.

23

Friday night. Lygon Street

The street was jumping as people strolled along the street looking for a restaurant to eat in. Adding to the buzz were the spruikers, the under-employed waiters urging them to come in and dine in their establishment. All very European.

Peter avoided the spruikers and met Poppy in front of Donnini's. Poppy was dressed in her usual Lady Diana-inspired ensemble. Her dress was pastel again, but this time with a hint of cleavage. She looked absolutely beautiful. Peter could hardly look away as he opened the restaurant's door for her.

'You look fantastic,' he said. *Steady on, bloke.*

'You look good yourself.' Poppy looked Peter up and down. 'You have the right body for a suit.'

'Thanks. I get to buy a new one every other week.'

'Really? You're made of money.'

'Not really. In this job, I tend to go through them pretty quickly.'

'Ah ha.'

An Italian waiter wearing a starched apron and a pencil thin moustache showed them to their table tucked away in a corner. Softly lit. A hint of Italian music playing in the background. It looked romantic. Felt romantic.

They sat down, ordered drinks and looked at the menus.

'Ever been here before, Peter?' Poppy asked, as she sipped her glass of Chianti. The waiter returned promptly to take their orders and place a small plate of homemade bruschetta on the table, which

187

Poppy pushed towards Peter. 'I mean, have you ever brought any of your many, many dates here?'

Peter bit into a slice of bruschetta as she spoke. He chewed the mouthful as he considered how to answer her. 'Only the ones who read Frederick Forsyth novels.' He smiled. 'Truthfully?'

'I find the truth is always a good place to start,' she purred. 'Especially for someone who works there.'

'Actually, the truth is, I'm too busy with work to stray too far from home. I'm always running on deadlines.' In fact, Peter had last gone to Donnini's with Michelle two years earlier at her insistence and on the understanding that she would pay the bill. How things had changed.

The waiter scurried over with Poppy's entree and positioned it in front of her. 'You work hard to avoid coming across as the romantic sort of guy,' Poppy said. 'So are you trying to impress me with your work ethic?'

'I can be as romantic as the next guy when I need to be. With you, I'd prefer to just be myself.'

'Can't you be both? It is possible, you know.' She slipped one of the plump oysters out of its shell and swallowed it. Whole. 'It's okay to admit to being romantic.'

Peter swallowed. 'And what about you?' he said. Do you have a romantic streak in you?'

'With the right person, I can be persuaded,' Poppy smiled, picking up a second oyster.

'So, tell me about yourself,' Peter asked.

'Not many men ask that. They usually only want to talk about themselves. Does this have anything to do with you being a journalist and me being the O'Learys' lawyer?' she asked playfully. 'Are you interviewing me again? Are you trying to soften me up so you can catch me off-guard?'

'No. I'm interested in you,' he replied. 'I left my notepad at home. And I don't use recorders.'

'Okay. Not much to tell, really,' Poppy began softly. 'Grew up in a middle class house in Mont Albert. Went to Methodist Ladies College. Father a solicitor, as was Grandfather. Mother a housewife. Went to Melbourne University and got a law degree. My resume in a nutshell. And here I am. I love my job. Of course. I like expensive jewellery and designer clothes and going overseas every year. And you?'

'I lived on a cattle station in North Queensland until my father was killed in a horse riding accident. My mother and I then lived in a small town. I went to a private school, which I hated. When I left school I studied journalism at Central Queensland University. I've had a few jobs but I've worked for *The Truth* longer than anywhere else. I used to do the big scandals but I've been promoted to crime. Apparently it sells more newspaper than scandals at the moment. I love my job too. I'd like more pay and more sleep, but I can't imagine myself doing anything else.'

Poppy laughed. 'You've led a rich and interesting life. And sounds like at times it was a sad one.'

'It was hard to lose my father,' he admitted. 'I was very angry and sad. I took a lot of anger out on my mother. Poor Mum, it must have been hard for her. Funny, I'm only starting to realise that now. I envy anyone who had a stable upbringing. Yours sounds idyllic.'

'Yes, sounds like it,' Poppy said vaguely as she watched a couple entering the restaurant. 'It doesn't exist, you know.'

Peter was puzzled by her reply. As he was mulling it over, the waiter arrived with the main meals. Veal scaloppine for Poppy and lasagne for Peter.

'Yours fine?' Poppy asked as she cut at her meat slowly.

'Really nice,' he said cheerfully.

'That's good. It's a nice restaurant.'

'You really can't go wrong here,' he replied awkwardly.

They fell silent as they continued eating. Eventually Peter looked up from his meal to Poppy. She looked forlorn. He placed his knife and fork on the plate.

'I can sense we're falling into that horrible dilemma that first dates suffer.'

'What's that?' Poppy looked up from her meal.

'The dreaded small talk dilemma. And that's the start of something far worse.'

'What's that,' she grinned.

'The awkward pauses that grow longer and longer. Pretty soon you're trying to talk about the décor just so you can talk.'

'No. We can't let that happen,' Poppy's grin turned into a laugh. 'Forgive me. I was thinking about work. It's been a stressful week.'

'Do you want to talk about it?' Peter asked. 'Here's my proposal:

Let's talk about work now. Then it's all out of the way. After we talk about work we'll talk about politics and religion.'

'Forget the politics and religion,' Poppy said as she pushed aside her plate. 'Not my favourite subjects. Let's get the work thing out of the way. You go first.'

'I don't know if you know him…Tony Donarto?' he began. 'I did an interview with him today.'

'Of course I know him,' she replied, 'but not well. I met him when I was doing the legal work for their business partnership.'

'Your opinion?'

'Do I have to assume you're interviewing me again and I have to say off the record?'

'I'm not at work. This is strictly social.'

'What do you say in newspaper-speak? "A source has disclosed…"' She folded her hands together and rested her chin against them. 'I got the feeling that Tony Donarto didn't know what he was getting involved in. He's not an astute man that way. His father was the more business savvy of the two and Tony's just been fortunate to inherit a sizeable fortune. And don't print that or I'll have to hunt you down,' she laughed, and took a mouthful of wine.

'I won't. Promise.'

'Here's my take on things. Tony is just too successful a businessman to want to get caught up in illegal activities. Like him or hate him, he's an identity. He has political aspirations. Do you know Tony Donarto wants to be the first Italian-Australian premier of Victoria? I bet you didn't know that.'

'No. I didn't, but it figures.' Peter said with a jolt. 'You don't want to share that source?'

Poppy smiled and continued. 'The O'Learys are a very different kettle of fish.' She rested her hands back on the table. 'They're a leftover from the old Painters and Docker's Union, as you know. Their business methods are a lot different to Tony Donarto. I think it's a shame they're not as entrepreneurial.'

'You're being brutally honest. About your client, I mean.'

'Funny, I needed to talk about that. It's actually feels good. I don't have anyone at the firm I can debrief to. I can't tell the O'Learys, unfortunately. I'm their solicitor.'

'You don't like representing them?'

'This is purely social intercourse, right? I'm very naughty telling you this,' Poppy sighed, 'but strictly on that basis, no, I don't. I have to paint a picture that all my clients are innocent. The picture can be very abstract at times. The O'Learys, for instance. Enough said.' She raised one eyebrow.

Peter had a sip of wine. 'We both work with the public but you and I have different relationships with people. I'm an enemy unless they're a source and you are like an ally.'

'Yes, my relationship with my clients is like an uneasy alliance—or more like strange bedfellows.'

'I guess so. People I deal with usually hate me and vice versa. It's a great symbiotic relationship like that. Why are you telling me this, by the way? The other day you were keeping your cards close to your chest.'

'All this small talk, all this verbal sparring—it's not everything. You know why we're here, don't you?' Poppy flicked her hair.

'We enjoy each other's company? We like Italian food?' Peter suggested. 'No, forget that. The truth is, I think you're very attractive and I'm hoping we're both on the same page. I'm going all out, here. I nearly walked off the wharf into the sea that day I saw you at the dock. And the coffee shop; my heart was running at a steady one hundred and fifty after five coffees and, when you came in, it went to two hundred.'

'Most girls would think you're crazy,' she grinned. 'I can imagine them saying they have to go to the ladies and then disappearing out of the back door.'

'Then why aren't you?' Peter leaned across the table and fixed his blue eyes on her.

'You're a man who doesn't give a shit. You're a man who's led a different life. Conventional men are boring. I find that rebellious streak very attractive. And the blue eyes—well, that seals it.'

'Do you want dessert, then?'

'I've had enough to eat,' she said. 'I'd rather relax at your place. Or mine, perhaps? Somewhere a little more secluded.'

'If you come to mine my two flatmates would get in the way.'

'Then it's mine. I have a flat nearby. I live alone. Follow me.' She picked up her handbag and stood up. 'Are you coming?' she said over her shoulder.

Peter's Stag followed Poppy's Alfa as closely as he dared, so eager not to lose her that he nearly rear-ended her twice. Was he excited? Yes. Was he aroused? Of course. He was thirty-something and he had just dined with a beautiful, sexy and intelligent woman. Of course. It was a warm, romantic Melbourne night. Or a warmer than usual winter's night.

But he began to have second thoughts. Maybe it was too rushed. A great first date and then it all implodes. But then again, maybe he'd read far too much into it and Poppy was simply inviting him in for a nightcap and a play of her latest CD. *Why drag it out if you're attracted to someone? Why go through the ritual of going out on five or six dates before the possibility of a passionate snog?* There was the possibility that after five dates it would fade out. As Peter's hero, Hunter S Thompson, once said: 'Buy the ticket, take the ride.'

They pulled up outside a nondescript block of flats. Three storeys of brown brick cubes stacked on top of each other. A 1970's assault on architectural design. But while it was a nondescript building, it certainly wasn't a nondescript address. No working class location for Poppy, no bohemian chic, oh no. They had pulled up in South Yarra—a blue ribbon, silvertail, top-end-of-town suburb. Home to powerbrokers, captains of industry, airbrushed celebrities and successful criminals. *This woman has style*, Peter thought as he stepped out of the Stag.

Poppy had parked in her bay and was waiting for him by a set of external stairs.

'Nice place,' he commented inanely. He accidentally brushed against her breasts and felt the heat of her body. He placed his arm around her shoulders and one around her waist and pulled Poppy closer until he could feel the contours of her body against him. He could feel the outline of those breasts. A romantic poet would liken it to being kissed on the face by a gentle breeze, but Peter was earthier. For him it was like being stung by a jolt of sexual electricity. He let his self-restraint slip. He wanted to kiss her.

'You're an impatient man, Mister Clancy,' she cooed, easing away. 'My neighbours might think we're exhibitionists and that sort of thing simply isn't welcome in this neighbourhood.'

Poppy's apartment looked like a Laura Ashley showroom. There was an overabundance of floral and pastel, from the curtains to the cushions, from the coffee table to the couch. And all tied together by a floral frieze that ran around the entire apartment. It was exactly how he imagined Lady Diana would decorate. A little too English, too twee. There were the obligatory travel statements: photos of Paris by night, and that black and white print of the young man and woman kissing in Paris. The one that seem to be displayed everywhere. Ad nauseam. Then there were the Lladró figurines a china cabinet. More nausea. A Melbourne University degree hung in pride of place next to the Paris pictures. It all set the scene. This was an apartment for a successful professional woman going places. *My place is a concrete tank compared to this place. You can have the floral shit and the dust collectors, though.*

'How do you like my flat?' Poppy asked as she hung her handbag on a hatstand, shrugged off her coat and made her way to a drinks cabinet. Peter took off his suit coat and hung it over Poppy's.

'I really like it,' he lied, gazing up at a small chandelier. Chandeliers were another of his dislikes. His eyes wandered from there to the cabinet with the figurines, past them to a set of photographs of Poppy at play: Poppy skiing with friends, Poppy at the top of the Eiffel Tower, Poppy standing next to a grenadier guard.

'I have a pretty good selection of alcohol,' Poppy announced, 'but I prefer a muscatel at the end of an evening.'

'That suits me.' He looked away from the pictures to the more alluring vision of Poppy pouring drinks. 'Looking at those pictures makes me want to travel.'

'Why don't you?' she asked, as she handed him a glass. 'I love travelling. It broadens the mind.'

'I'd like to work in London. It's always been an ambition of mine. To work for the *Times*—not one of the tabloids.'

'What's holding you back?'

'I like Melbourne too much. It has everything I need. Or maybe I like living in a rut.'

Peter drew in the syrupy drink. 'A nice drop,' he announced as he examined the glass.

'Yes. It's good. You really should go. London is an amazing city to live and work in. I worked in the City for two years. I loved it. Representing all manner of villains at the Old Bailey.'

'I'll think about it. I don't have any ties. Not expecting any anytime soon.'

'No failed marriages? No girlfriends?' Poppy teased, placing her hand on Peter's shoulder. 'I've heard you journalists are hard people to live with.'

'Never been married or engaged. I've always been footloose and fancy-free. I've never even lived with a woman.'

'Quite the playboy, aren't you?' Poppy slid her hand off his shoulder and took hold of his hand. She put her glass down.

'Playboy?' Peter laughed, 'More commitmentophobe.'

Their eyes locked onto each other. Peter leaned forward to kiss Poppy on the lips. She smiled and pulled away.

'Let's take those blue eyes of yours and sit on the couch,' she suggested, gesturing towards a pink floral couch. Peter quickly drained the reminder of his glass and returned it to the cabinet.

'Let's get comfortable,' he said. 'Have you got any music? I mean, if we're going to relax on the couch we need something atmospheric.'

Poppy crossed to a three-in-one German stereo. 'What sort of music do you like? I have an eclectic collection, but I particularly like Sting, Meatloaf, Bruce Springsteen. And a little jazz.'

Peter winced and wondered if he could ever see past her musical tastes. 'How about a little jazz?' *If you want to stop my romantic ticker, just play Stung or bloody Meathead.*

Poppy shut the drawer, picked up a CD and read it. 'How about Miles Davis? *Kind of Blue.*'

'Perfect.' He was a hard rocker but there was always time for Miles and Miles was ideal for what he thought lay ahead. *Miles Davis plus jazz noir equals romance. I hope.*

What floated out of the stereo speakers was like a gentle, intoxicating zephyr. Poppy settled back on the couch and cuddled in next to Peter. The music pulled them together in an embrace and soon they were kissing passionately. *She's so beautiful,* Peter kept thinking. *A perfect woman. I want her. I want her.*

Poppy lay down on top of Peter, their lips still fixed together. He felt the roundness of her breasts on his chest. *I've got to have her.* He tried to loosen the buttons of her blouse with one hand, while running the other up and down her slender legs.

'It's all getting hot and heavy,' she gasped as she squirmed away from him. She sat up, adjusting her blouse.

'Is something wrong?' Peter asked as he too sat up. 'Am I being too forward? I can't help it. You're just so beautiful.'

Peter tried to touch her but Poppy pulled away. She folded her arms across her body and looked down. He couldn't have imagined Poppy ever looking vulnerable but now she did.

'Sorry, but I don't want you to think I'm a complete slut. I'm not that type of girl. I find you really attractive but I don't want you to think...' Her voice trailed off.

'I'm sorry too,' Peter replied. 'I got carried away. It's only the first date and I had wanted to come across as the suave gentleman. We can always start this again—I mean, go out on another date.'

He was about to stand up but Poppy grabbed his arm and pulled him back on the couch. 'Really, I don't want you to go,' she confessed. 'I'd feel really lonely if you went.'

'We can sit here and talk. We haven't got to know each other yet. I don't even know what football team you follow.'

Poppy smiled faintly and unfolded her arms. 'You could have persisted. 'Although, to be honest, I don't like being dominated.'

'I'm not going to persist if you don't want me to. I'm not a caveman.'

She edged herself closer to Peter and pecked him on the cheek. 'That's what I like about you. You're all rough and ready on the outside, but underneath lurks a gentleman. You're David Niven and Peter Finch rolled into one.'

'David Niven?' Peter shuddered, 'Do I look like a weedy Englishman?'

'You're much, much better.'

Peter leaned towards Poppy and lightly kissed her on the lips. 'Is that too forward, Miss Reynolds?' he joked as he pulled away, 'I don't want to take too many liberties, but I find you most awfully pleasing to the eyes. I shall have to speak to your father.'

'Funny.' She grabbed Peter's head with both hands and kissed him hard on the lips, mouth open, her tongue caressing his.

Peter exhaled. 'Wow. I'm lost for words.'

'Tell me,' Poppy demanded, 'do you like women to take control of the situation?'

'You take control of the situation and I'm happy to follow. As long as it ends in the same result for both parties, who cares?'

'I like your answer,' she replied as she undid her blouse. 'I like being in charge. It really turns me on.'

Poppy took hold of Peter's right hand and placed it on her breast and let him caress it. She moaned softly.

'You have beautiful breasts,' he whispered. He attempted to lean in to kiss her breasts but she stopped him.

'How much can I control you?' Poppy questioned.

'As long as it doesn't get too painful.' His mind returned to his deep and meaningful relationship with Amber the stripper. Every time they were locked in a passionate embrace, Amber liked to bite Peter's neck, and when they were making love she would rake his back with her fingernails. After a short while, the missionary position was taken off the menu.

Poppy took hold of Peter's hand and pulled him off the couch. 'You'll have to follow me to find out,' she winked.

***

Peter arrived home relatively early—at nine the next morning. He expected to be met by a worried Sam and Dave at the door. Not the case. There were two notes sitting on the kitchen bench, one from each of them, saying they'd be staying elsewhere for the night. Sam at Babs's house and Dave at Shazza's place. Shazza and Dave? Peter didn't see that coming. He'd noticed the long conversations between the two of them and the occasional shared lunch. Shazza and Dave. Everyone was hooking up. There was a glimmer of hope for him and Poppy. *Poppy! What a night!* He was walking on sunshine—that dumb song again—but exhausted after a night of lovemaking.

Where did Poppy's energy come from? How had he kept it up? *Peter Clancy, you sly dog. Yes, and what an explosive night.* He rubbed his sore wrists. The impressions from the handcuffs were still there. *Not that unbearable but I'm getting educated.* And where in the hell were Sam and Dave? He was desperate to relate his exploits to the boys. Or maybe not. He had feelings for Poppy.

There was a knock at the door. 'Did you lose your keys, you old tomcat,' Peter laughed as he swung open the door, expecting to see either Sam or Dave. It was Con.

'Sorry,' Peter laughed, 'I thought you were one of the boys.'

'We're still coming for lunch today,' Con asked. 'The barbecue?'

'Today? That's right. I invited you.'

'Of course. Of course, Peter,' Con shook his head with amusement. 'You invite us a whole week ago.'

'I must have forgotten. Sorry,' Peter shrugged.

'Is all right for the barbecue, yes? Or you want to make another time?'

'No, no, it's fine. At Yarra Bend. Twelve o'clock Greek time.'

'You really need a good woman,' Con's voice rang with despair as he examined Peter's state of dishevelment. 'If you lucky enough, maybe she even help you dress yourself. You look like… you look like a beggarman.'

'I've only just got home.' Peter tucked his shirt back into his pants, noticing that was at half-mast. He did up his fly quickly and brushed back his hair.

'You had big night, eh? Looks like you didn't get much sleep.'

'I had a very restless night. Just couldn't settle. If you know what I mean.'

'I think I know what you're talking about. I meet this girl today? If you happy, you make Roula happy. She worry too much about you.'

'We'll see.'

'Do you want us to bring anything?'

'No, nothing.'

'If you sure.' Con turned and walked back down the stairs.

Peter quickly closed the door and headed for the phone. Thoughts of rejection ran through his head. Funny, he was always the one doing the rejecting, but this time the shoe was on the other foot. Did she want to see him again? Was it just a one night stand? And so soon? But he had to try. He had to see her again. The sooner the better. *Stuff caution. Caution's for boring people.*

He made a quick call to Poppy, happy to have a reason to talk to her. To Peter's delight, Poppy had agreed to come along the minute he asked her. She told him she had been to Greece several times and loved the culture. Then he made an inaugural outing to the supermarket. By the time Dave and Shazza, Peter and Poppy and Sam minus Babs arrived at Yarra Bend, about thirty members of the extended Theophilis family had already descended and commandeered several tables and an electric barbecue.

Rebetiko music blared from a stereo sitting alongside its speakers on a folding table. Chattering women were depositing mountains of food on the long wooden tables while the men were gathered around Con, who was attending to pieces of lamb rotating on the charcoal-fuelled rotisserie he had brought along. By the look of things, they had arrived very early.

The adults were drinking wine out of water glasses and talking loudly over each other. Con and Roula's children dodged in and out, between the adults, with their cousins. For the uninitiated it was probably an assault on the senses, but Peter had been to their house many times.

Everyone turned as they approached. Dave and Shazza looked uncomfortable, but Poppy seemed unfazed. Sam glanced at the trays of pink pork sausages nestled in Peter's bags and the plastic container full of coleslaw and then at the meat rotating slowly over the coals.

'I prefer the look and smell of their tucker,' he said.

Roula darted towards them, grabbing Peter with both hands and planting kisses on each cheek. 'You here at last,' she announced. 'Everybody, you know Peter. And these are his friends.'

Peter introduced the others and glanced at the tables piled with salad, cooked greens and pita. 'I told Con to tell you not to bring anything.'

'Yes, yes,' she said. 'But what you bring? What we eat? One sausage and some lettuce?' She looked at Dave's Esky. 'And plenty beer. No good.'

'This isn't like a normal barbecue, is it?' Dave commented to Sam. 'No cheap sausages, warm beer and cold hospitality here.'

'I'd better tell you now,' Peter warned them as Roula returned to distribute paper napkins. 'Most people are going to want to kiss you. Even the men.'

'What the…' Sam stiffened.

'Don't worry. It's a tradition. I always found the people in Greece really friendly, even to complete strangers,' Poppy laughed.

Peter introduced Poppy to Con, leaving the others to introduce themselves. He cracked open beers and handed them around, then fed coins into the electric barbecue and laid the sausages on the hotplate. He found the end of a bench to perch on. To his surprise, Poppy sat on his lap, chatting about her last trip to Santorini. Dave and Shazza settled themselves opposite, with Sam alongside.

While Peter's sausages fizzed, Con pulled the pieces of meat off the spit and deposited them onto platters and placed them on the tables.

'Good tucker,' Sam announced. 'Better than yours. I think I'm going to become a Greek.'

Poppy slid off Peter's lap and squeezed herself in beside him. 'A Greek Aborigine?' she said. 'Hilarious.'

'You two look cosy,' Sam observed. 'For only a second date.'

'Pissed off that Babs didn't come today?' asked Peter.

'I asked her, but the dog was sick or something. She had to take it to the vet. She reckons someone tried to poison it.'

'Who'd do something like that?' said Poppy 'That's awful.'

'Some people are just plain evil,' continued Sam, eyeing Poppy. 'Peter says you're a high-rolling solicitor. And from what I saw, you're a mate of the O'Learys.'

'Well, I don't know about that.' Poppy replied defensively.

'I saw you at the wharf the other day talking to Tommy and Robbie.'

'I talk to them all the time. Not that it's any of your business, but they're clients of mine.' She paused to take a sip of wine. 'So, do you work for them? I didn't see you there.'

'Well, you wouldn't. I was too busy working,' Sam grinned. 'I bet those boys keep you busy, too.'

Poppy put down her fork. 'Are you trying to say something?'

'No. Just saying that defending crooks must be hard.'

'If I'm not mistaken, those men you call crooks employ you, don't they?'

'Wasn't talking about the O'Learys. They have to be good blokes for giving me a job. All I was saying is it's a lawyer's job to defend crooks. Must be hard to do.'

'They're not crooks,' she snapped at Sam. 'They're a respectable family.'

Peter interrupted and glared at Sam. 'Don't worry about Sam. He likes to dig. Like an old busybody.'

Con looked from Sam to Poppy and back again. He stood, turned the music up and began to sway. 'Opa! Opa! Let's dance!' He took his serviette, whipped it around and started to dance to Zorba the Greek. 'Come on, Peter, Poppy. Enough beer. Opa!'

Roula got up and took hold of Con's shoulder. 'Come on, Peter!'

Grateful for the distraction, Peter nudged Poppy and gestured to the others. He and Sam joined the end of the line, while Poppy grabbed the other end of Con's serviette and led the dance, kicking in time with the music, faster and faster as the pace increased.

The rest of the afternoon passed in a swirl of dancing, food and wine, while Poppy and Sam did everything to avoid each other.

Peter hoped he would be able to drop off the others first and spend the evening at Poppy's. He was crestfallen when she excused herself, saying she would have to go home and work on a brief for an upcoming committal hearing on Monday. He was pissed off with Sam at the same time.

They all helped Con and Roula pack up, Sam depositing the rubbish into bins while Poppy gathered up the leftovers, not daring to look at each other. In the Stag, Poppy sat in front with Peter while the others crammed into the back for the trip home. The journey to Poppy's apartment passed in silence.

She pecked him on the cheek as they pulled up. 'I might see you in court on Monday?'

'I hope so,' he replied.

She looked at the others. 'Nice meeting you. Bye.' She slammed the door and hurried off.

Peter was already jumping on Sam before he'd pulled away from the kerb. 'You couldn't be nice to her, could you? Thanks, Sam. Thanks!'

'I was just saying I'd seen her at the docks. What's wrong with that?'

'You upset her,' Peter bristled, 'and because of you, I might not see her again. You stuffed it up for me.'

'That's interesting,' Dave interjected. 'You don't usually give a shit about whether you see a woman again.'

'Sorry, young fella,' Sam sniggered. 'I didn't realise you were sweet on Poppy.'

'Well I am. Shit. Why can't I like someone? Just be happy for me.'

'You have weird taste in women. You've never been sweet on me,' Shazza laughed, 'and I'm hot.'

'I just wanted everyone to be nice to her. But Sam gives her the third degree and you guys give her the cold shoulder. I have great friends. Thanks, everyone.'

'But we were nice to her,' Shazza retaliated. 'She barely spoke to us. I think she thinks she's better than us because she's a lawyer.'

'Shazza,' Peter replied, 'sometimes you sound so bloody working class.'

'Fuck you, Peter Clancy,' she snapped. 'And guess what? Dave'll be keeping me warm tonight. Just because you'll be sleeping alone from now on, don't blame us.'

Dave nudged Shazza in the ribs and mouthed 'shut up' at Sam. No one said another word until they were heading down Johnston Street, not far from Peter's flat.

'You and me have been friends a long time. I didn't want to say it,' Sam ventured, 'but I'm not sure about that Poppy.'

'What the hell is it now?' Peter despaired. 'Is this pick on Peter night?'

'I can't put a finger on it,' Sam continued. 'You know when you have a horse you're not sure about, or someone you're working with. It's in the eyes. You know. In the eyes.'

'In the eyes? I'll fucking give you in the eyes. I've had enough,' Peter shouted as he screeched the Stag to a stop in front of the Apollo café. Everyone bounced around like bobblehead dolls. He threw open his door and stormed up the stairs leading to his flat. Dave turned and glared at Sam.

'I just have a feeling. Maybe I'm a silly old blackfella. Too superstitious, too old fashioned. But my gut says she isn't what she says she is.'

'Let him work it out, Sam,' Dave replied.

'Yeah. Yeah. I'll drop it,' he declared. 'If he's fallen in love, he's fallen in love with the wrong woman.'

24

Monday. *The Truth* Office

Bob designated Peter to cover the committal of Eastern and Machowicz at the Magistrates' Court.

'They confessed to the murders, but they reckon they're not guilty of the crime. Go figure. I want you to cover the committal, but don't fucking fall asleep,' Bob warned. Then it dawned on him that Peter probably had at least one good reason to stay awake. 'Oh, that's right. Pretty Poppy is the defence counsel, isn't she? Keep your eyes on the road, all right. Not on her.'

When Peter arrived at the Melbourne Magistrates' Court, Dave was already standing in front of the building together with all the other media scum and onlookers. They were all hoping for a glimpse of the accused, but Peter was hoping to catch a glimpse of Poppy. Ilmo and his camera entourage had already set up. Ilmo's muffet appeared to be getting higher and higher, the eagle wedge at the back thicker and more defined.

'Clancy,' Ilmo called, 'try not to get assaulted today.'

'I hope it rains and your hairdo collapses,' Peter retaliated. 'You deserve a Logie just for best hairstyle in a news program or documentary.'

A titter passed through Ilmo's camera crew, but the prisoner van arrived before Ilmo had time to think of a retort. The crowd pushed forward for a closer look, held in check by a line of police. Cameras clicked and Ilmo pressed ahead of the others, calling out, microphone

202

poised to catch a sound bite. Just then, Poppy glided past on her way to the court entrance, catching Peter's eye. While the others jostled to capture candid shots of the prisoners, Peter was jostling for a better view of Poppy in her conservative navy suit. She was a flash of colour in a black and white picture.

Peter called out as she passed. 'Poppy!' He waved his arm like a besotted schoolboy. 'Over here.'

She turned as she heard his voice. Her eyes softened and Peter's heart rose. She smiled the most radiant smile he'd ever seen. *Poppy.* She was saying something but he couldn't hear her. Then she disappeared inside. Ilmo had dropped back and was making some smart-arsed comment to him but Peter didn't care about Ilmo or anything else. *Poppy.*

He entered the courthouse and found his way to the public gallery. He would be sitting there for the rest of the day and possibly the next few, as vital testimonies and evidence would be given. The prosecuting counsel was an older man, instructed by a younger, well-groomed man in a pinstripe suit. Poppy and her instructing solicitor appeared, and exchanged greetings with the prosecution. The young man's eyes lingered on Poppy a little too long for Peter's liking. He would have liked to yell out that she was his. She was now wearing a wig and a black gown over her suit. Peter had never seen anyone else make that crusty old outfit look sexy.

The hearing commenced not with a crescendo, but with long and boring legal submissions. As the hearing recessed for lunch, a clerk from Poppy's firm handed a note to Peter. He tore it open. From Poppy. And the world was in glorious technicolour once again. *Meet me at my apartment at seven. xxx. Poppy.*

Three crosses. *You know what that means,* he told himself as he fumbled with the note. What was the old country and western song? *I can't wait to touch her, kiss her, lay with her.* But first he had to sit through this bloody hearing that everyone in Melbourne seemed excited about except him. Peter was only excited about tonight. *Tonight.*

Back from lunch. Peter pulled out his notepad and pen as the witnesses were called to the stand. The rest of that day and the next passed in a blur, as he sat through the hearing during the day and made love to Poppy during the night. Running on three hours sleep.

Snatching a nap here and there in the gallery but recording the vital information. *Peter Clancy: man of action. The multitasker.*

On the third day, Poppy cross-examined the prosecution's witnesses. Enter Mister Public Relations himself: Anthony Donarto had been called to the stand. Tony looked around the courtroom as if he was about to perform to an audience. Peter was reminded of an aging Italian crooner with an oily toupee singing in a Las Vegas lounge. *I did it my way? I cast my fate to the wind?* And the drama continued.

Yes, he had been in business with the O'Learys but he had not received all monies that had been due to him and had decided to end the business arrangement a long time ago. The coffee plantation in Vietnam, Tony was quick to add. Yes, he had been upset but he had never threatened to kill anyone. He didn't know that Pat was in Melbourne. If they could have met, this mess could have been sorted. No need for anyone to be shot. Tony also had to add that he was a peaceful man, as he gave a forlorn look to the magistrate; that he had given so much to this great city of Melbourne, to a city that had given him and his family so many opportunities. And the tears began. *Poor Tony.* Peter had a hunch and looked around. He was right. To his far left sat Father Kennedy, hands clenched, eyes fixed on Tony. *In silent prayer?*

The fucking trial of tears, Peter jotted in his pad.

Tony Donarto was milking this for everything. *These people are doing a better job than most actors you'd see at the movies*, Peter thought. The best courtroom drama he had ever seen. Then suddenly Tony Donarto's testimony was over.

Peter wanted to leave, but Dale McCracken was called to the stand. Dear Dale had a mediocre tale to tell. No evidence to suggest that Tony Donarto had ignited this whole bloody bushfire. Machowicz and Eastern had willingly confessed to the killings, no coercion or verballing required. All the police had to do was record it. Forensics gathered from the car showed nothing remarkable. No twists in the Eastern and Machowicz tale. No fingerprints, no weapons to be found.

Then it was Poppy's turn again. Patrick O'Leary had been like a father to the defendants. The O'Learys hadn't known anything about the shooting. Eastern and Machowicz acted alone in the shooting at Footscray Market. It was self-defence. They were innocent. Nothing was planned, nothing.

Peter scrutinised Tommy and Robbie O'Leary, who were there minus Ivy. The brothers looked relaxed. The defendants appeared to be towing the party line.

That's right, Eastern and Machowicz had acted alone. *Again.* They had been caught unawares and they really hadn't planned anything when they went to Footscray Market that day. They were there for a friendly chat with Donarto and Morosto, that was all.

The prosecuting barrister asked, if they had done this on impulse, why had they worn ski masks and gloves during the shooting?

Poppy had it covered. It happened to be a cold day. Anyone check the records? Well, we did. It was minus one that morning. A very cold day indeed. They'd gone for a friendly chat because Eastern and Machowicz knew the O'Learys had been in business with Tony Donarto. There had been a falling out. What type of business? Importing coffee from Vietnam. *The coffee again.*

Pat O'Leary had saved their grimy lives from a never-ending cycle of drugs and jail. He'd given them a fresh chance. The two had witnessed Tony Donarto threatening Tommy and Robbie at their office on South Wharf. Donarto had been so angry that he had picked up a stapler from the desk and had thrown it at Tommy O'Leary's head, injuring him. Machowicz had personally pulled the two apart. Eastern and Machowicz had gone to Footscray Market that day to speak to Donarto, that was all. What happened after that happened in self-defence. They didn't bring the guns. Morosto's own weapons were only turned on him after he'd threatened them first.

Everything became mundane after that, except Poppy, who performed through it all looking amazingly fresh and composed; her voice, her argument always mesmerising and commanding. Even Frank Galbally would have been impressed. Obviously, the intense, edgy sex really agreed with her. On the other hand, after a night with hardly any sleep Peter was ready to lie down on the floor of the gallery and go to sleep. And then the magistrate deliberated. Peter caught a glimpse of Poppy. She looked at him and smiled.

Eventually, the magistrate adjourned the case for McCracken to file a charge sheet for manslaughter. It meant that, instead of murder and attempted murder, Eastern and Machowicz were probably going to stand trial for the manslaughter of Aldo Morosto and reckless conduct endangering Tony Donarto's life. Tony Donarto erupted, yelling profanities in Italian, and stormed out. Tommy ran his finger across his throat when he saw Tony. No love lost there. Obviously. The O'Leary brothers cheered like their team had won the footy final. The magistrate was not impressed. The O'Learys were escorted from the court. Peter wanted to hug Poppy on her success but he would be doing that in the comfort of her bed in a few hours. And it was all over. *Get to the office. Type up the story. Get it out. Then hopefully home to bed for a quick restorative before a long night.*

'Shit,' Bob commented, as Peter crawled into his office. 'You look as buggered as a shagged-out mongrel dog. Ever thought of just sleeping with the girl occasionally? You don't have to shag her continuously. I need you at your best.'

'How could you tell?' Peter asked. 'I haven't told you.' He edged his way onto a chair and sat bolt upright in case he suddenly found himself falling asleep.

'Pretty Poppy still?' Bob pulled out the familiar Jameson's and two glasses. He shoved one in the direction of Peter.

'Drink,' Bob urged. 'It's a good pick me up.' Peter picked up and had drank half the contents before Bob added, 'So your mate Sam is covert on the dock and you're shagging their lawyer.'

'It gets better.'

'How can it?'

'Sam is sleeping with the clerk who works for the O'Learys. How about that?'

'Why do the police bother with bugging devices when they could use you randy bastards? Is this some Queensland thing?' Bob shook his head.

'We're getting some great information. Sam reckons there's a very precious container waiting to go somewhere.'

'So, the more he shags the clerk, the more the information will come?' Bob chuckled, still shaking his head.

'Seems to be working out that way.'

'Bloody hell. What's with you blokes from up north? Weren't there enough women up there to keep you satisfied?'

'It's a hard way to gather the information,' Peter grinned, 'but someone has to do it. We're like honey-pots. We get the information.'

Bob drained his glass and leaned back on his chair, looking up at the ceiling. 'If we don't get caught we'll have awards and accolades flowing out of our arses. We'll be the toast of Melbourne. But if we get caught…' his voice trailed off, 'we're well and truly fucked.'

'It just seems how it worked out,' Peter observed.

'At least Dave's keeping it in his pants,' Bob said. 'He's the quiet one.'

Peter smiled. 'You didn't know? Dave's seeing Shazza.'

'Shit,' Bob remarked, stroking his head. 'What's wrong with me? I would have known all that once. Bugger.'

'You've had a lot on your plate lately, Bob.'

'I guess so,' he sighed. 'For the first time in a long time, I feel I need a break. But I can't until Stella comes home and this story is put to bed.'

'Do you have any news on Stella?' Peter asked.

'Seems there are an awful lot of Ruskies running businesses in Sydney. She's trying to narrow the field.'

'We have to be optimistic.'

'If anyone can find that bloody haystack needle, she can.'

Peter postponed his restorative for an hour or so by popping into the Tote for a recuperative. *I need a Victor Bravo or two.* Dave and Sam would be expecting him for dinner but he was fed up with having to be places at certain times. To be honest, he was sick and tired of living with blokes. It was better when he lived by himself. No one to answer to. This had never been his style. Although perhaps he was more stray cat than lone wolf.

It was over his third VB that he seriously considered what it might be like to live with a woman. He had only ever lived with his mother and that had been a disaster. Just the thought of it had sent cold shivers down his back and made him slightly bilious. A couple of years ago, Michelle had pestered him to try it. He had nearly succumbed, but then she had gone all gushy and announced she was going to totally makeover his flat. Peter began to shiver. Enter the Monet print and scatter cushions. Then he gave Michelle a lame excuse that he needed time. How long, she had asked. *Is eternity too much?* He told her they had to be really certain, as this was the first stage of something that could lead to marriage and babies. He'd painted such a gloomy picture that even Michelle had started to baulk. He had described living together as if it was going to be the start of a virulent, infectious disease. Mission accomplished. Soon after that they had broken up. Exit the Monet picture. And the scatter cushions.

He had felt safe until now. Of course, Peter was probably getting ahead of himself. He and Poppy were still at the let's-have-sex-at-every-opportunity-and-anywhere stage. Yes, it was only early in the relationship. More wild sex was needed before the possibility of cohabiting could really be considered. *I can handle that.* But this time, he didn't feel like he was having post-traumatic stress at the mere thought of it, and that was a major step forward. Was he cured? *My hands aren't shaking.* Peter finished his third VB and headed home.

He didn't notice anything unusual when he entered the flat until he saw Sam and Dave sitting at the kitchen table, bolt upright, as if they had been tied to their chairs. A look of dread was painted all over Sam's face. Peter looked around the immediate area. No signs of imminent danger. He was about to speak when he saw Dave. He wore the same look as Sam.

Dave said nothing except to flick his eyes from Peter to Peter's bedroom and back in rapid succession. A rustling noise came from the bedroom. Wardrobe doors slammed. Furniture was turned over.

Peter asked in a whisper, 'Who the hell is that?'

Before Dave could answer Dale McCracken thumped back into the kitchen.

'McCracken!' Peter exclaimed.

'Not expecting to see me?' McCracken chuckled as his eyes darted around the flat. 'I was in the area and thought I'd drop in for a friendly visit.' He reached down, opened a kitchen cupboard and pulled out the contents. 'You've got a real shit pile here, haven't you? Poking your nose around everyone's business doesn't seem to pay much. Why would you bother?'

'Have you got a search warrant?'

'I don't need one,' McCracken smirked. 'See any signs of forced entry? The boys invited me to stay. We're good friends and this is only a social call. For the moment.'

'So I can come over to your house, or hovel or whatever rock you crawled out of, and do the same thing,' Peter retorted.

'That's uncalled for, Peter. Why don't we have a friendly chat?' McCracken beckoned him to sit. 'Take a seat, here, next to your friends. They've been missing you.'

Peter's eyes narrowed. He studied McCracken. For all his bravado, he detected McCracken was nervous. *Unless it's very well concealed, my hunch is he's unarmed.* So why hadn't Sam and Dave thrown him out?

'Why are you really here, McCracken?' Peter asked. 'It's not for the stimulating conversation.'

'Must be really draining being a smartarse all the time. If I were you, and thank Christ I'm not, I'd be thinking about my future. It doesn't look so bright at the moment.'

Peter frowned. 'Get to the point or get out, McCracken.'

'Where do I start? Peter Clancy, investigative reporter from *The Truth*, can't get a break in his story. Boo hoo. Peter Clancy isn't afraid to bend the rules to keep ahead of the pack. He has that reputation. How can he get information on the O'Learys? No, he's not going to use traditional means of news gathering, is he? No. His mate Sam, over there, is going to go undercover and do it for him. Very clever. But not really. Fucking idiots!'

'Actually, I thought it was pretty clever,' Peter mused.

McCracken thumped the table. 'Shut the fuck up!' He stared at Peter menacingly. 'You didn't see that in your efforts to fill that paper of yours with lies and half-truths, you put a major police operation in jeopardy?'

'Bullshit! There's no police operation happening on South Dock. Apparently the O'Leary brothers can spot an undercover cop from a mile away.'

'Sorry the police commissioner didn't run it past you first, Clancy. Police have other means of infiltrating the O'Learys' operation which you haven't thought of.'

'Their coffee importing business?' Peter smiled.

'Don't be a fucking idiot,' McCracken snapped back. 'Clancy, you've overstepped your mark and I'm shutting you down.'

'You do whatever you want, McCracken, but you'll soon realise you can't do a thing,' Peter spat out. 'The press is mightier than you.'

'Well, I'm shutting down your little covert operation. It's the least I can do.' McCracken smirked. 'If you or any of your mates go back to the docks for any reason, I'll know about it. I'll make sure the O'Learys are told exactly who you are and why you're there. Consider yourself lucky. I could have you arrested for interference in a police operation and I could also report you to the press council for unethical behaviour. You'd have to find another job. Maybe one that suits your level of skill. How about a bottle shop attendant?'

'You're an arse, McCracken. You can't do this.'

'So sad isn't it?' McCracken laughed. 'Life's shit, then you die.'

'If the police are holding all the cards as you say, Detective Senior Sergeant, then why are you here?' Dave piped up. 'Why would you guys be worried about some blackfella—sorry Sam—sleeping with his boss? Seems to me we might just have something you don't.'

McCracken shifted uneasily. *This is personal*, Peter reflected. *Nothing to do with any police operation.*

'Can't see how we're threatening anything. If you let us keep the story,' Dave said, 'I'm sure Peter'd give the police a good rap as a bonus. I've seen it work.'

'Think yourself brighter then these other two?' Wouldn't be hard,' McCracken observed.

'I was in the Queensland Police. I know a thing or two.'

'Is that so?' McCracken sneered. 'Well, we like to think we're a bit smarter in the State of Victoria. So I'm going to pass on that offer. And, for the record, you are as big a fucking idiot as the other two. What is this? The Three Stooges?'

Peter had been thinking of offering to share information with the police but changed his mind. *I'd like to shove my fist down his throat. Fuck him.* He headed for the bathroom.

'Where do you think you're going?' McCracken asked.

'For a piss. Want to watch?'

The contents of the bathroom cupboard were spilled across the floor. A bottle was on its side, cap ajar, slowly leaking cologne. Peter picked it up and crossed to a large stack of dirty laundry that lay in a musty pile in the corner of the bathroom. It reached nearly to his waist.

He inspected the washing pile and sighed with relief. It hadn't been touched. *I guess no normal human being would, not even Dale McCracken.* He reached into the dirty clothes tentatively, like he was reaching into a radioactive slagheap.

'What are you doing in there?' McCracken called from outside the closed door. 'Hurry up or I'll come in.'

'I'm coming,' Peter called. *Yes, still there.* Two envelopes were lying towards the bottom of the laundry pile, on top of some women's underwear. *Is it that how long since I've done a full wash? Irmgard's underwear.* He picked up one of the envelopes, opened the door and returned to the kitchen, where McCracken was making himself a cup of coffee.

'What's this all about?' McCracken asked as he watched Peter take out a set of photographs.

'What in the hell are you doing?' Dave whispered, 'You're bloody crazy.'

'We're buggered,' Sam shook his head.

'I don't know if you'd call them party snaps,' Peter grinned, 'but it looks like everyone was having a good time. Especially you. The look on your face is priceless.'

'Give me a fucking look at them,' McCracken put his coffee on the table and attempted to snatch them out of Peter's hand.

Peter anticipated him and sidestepped. 'Careful, Dale. You don't want to damage them before you have a look.'

'Give me a look, you cunt,' McCracken roared, 'or I'll give you the flogging of your life.'

'You can have a look, Dale,' Peter responded calmly, 'but if you tear them up I have another set deposited in a bank safe. For emergencies. You just don't know what's going to happen. Have a careful look at these photographs, as they could be career changing.'

'Fucking prick!' McCracken glanced at the photographs. He dropped them on the floor and grabbed Peter around the throat with both hands and squeezed.

Dave pulled McCracken off and pushed him into a chair. Peter picked up the photographs with one hand, coughing and holding his throat with the other. He laid the photos in front of the deflated McCracken.

'Now, tell me if I'm wrong,' Peter coughed again. 'That's definitely you. Look! See: the guy having doggie sex with the woman wearing the leather mask.'

'Can't tell,' McCracken grunted as he looked away.

'These photographs are reprints. Maybe they look a little grainy to you, but I think they're a good reproduction. The originals are clear as a bell. What do you think, Sam?' Peter handed the photo to Sam.

'Do people do that?' Sam reeled. 'That's bloody crook.'

'Don't worry about the content,' Peter said. 'Do you think that's Detective Senior Sergeant McCracken in the photo?'

Sam took another look at McCracken, slumped over the table with his head in his hands, and then looked at the photograph. 'I reckon it's the same person,' he said softly.

'The girl, I presume, is a prostitute. Dale? Are you there?'

'She's nothing,' McCracken murmured.

'And that's Tony Donarto snorting white powder off her back. He must wear a corset when he's dressed, because he looks a lot fatter naked.'

'Where did you get these, you piece of shit?' McCracken asked quietly.

'Someone gave them to one of our journalists. Stella.'

'A fucking pervert with a camera!' McCracken replied. 'You really are a piece of work, aren't you, Clancy? You fucking belong in the gutter with that trash paper of yours to keep you warm.'

'I'm just doing my job. Society expects their police officers to be uncorrupted, don't they? We don't want to have a crooked police force running around like they did in Queensland for years. Do we?' He picked up the next photograph and dropped it in front of McCracken. 'This is my favourite,' Peter commented with a chuckle.

Dave stood up to take a look. 'That's gross.'

Sam turned away in disgust.

'I didn't know you could do that,' Peter continued. 'But the girl wearing the leather mask's pretty nifty. Is that cocaine she's snorting off your erect penis? Yep, seems like it's your dick, Detective Senior Sergeant. I'm very envious.'

McCracken took a deep breath. 'What in the fuck do you want? If this stuff gets printed I'm fucked.'

'I know,' Peter patted him on the back. 'I'm not here to destroy you, Dale. I just want your co-operation. You let me have this story without any interference from the police and we'll give you what we know.'

'We know the O'Learys aren't importing coffee from Asia. You haven't got anything we don't already know. We just need to catch them moving it,' said McCracken.

'But, Dale, you're not in a position to argue. We've got the upper hand, remember?' Peter grabbed the photographs and slipped them back into the envelope. 'Plus we've got the benefit of pillow-talk.'

McCracken looked at Sam with a bewildered look.

'He's a real stud,' Peter commented. 'Hot stuff.'

'He's not sleeping with one of the boys?' McCracken asked. 'I didn't think they were gay.'

'Not them,' Peter laughed. 'Their clerk, Babs.'

'Babs Bell?' McCracken shook his head. 'She doesn't know shit. She's an old pro with a retard grandson who deals dope out of the front parlour on the side. She does the clerical stuff at the docks. We know all that. We've questioned her before.'

'Here's something you don't know. She's got a plan to sort out the O'Learys and we know what it is. We could let you in on it, as long as you don't interfere with our story, and you save all the best information for us. Dale McCracken takes down the O'Learys and it's a *Truth* exclusive.'

McCracken studied his hands.

'It's a win–win, Dale.'

'All fucking right,' he growled.

'So we have an agreement?' Peter smiled.

'I guess so,' he snarled again. 'Which leads me to the photos.'

'I presume you won't want them published?'

'What do you fucking think? When it's all over, you bring me both sets of photographs and you destroy them in front of me after the arrest. Can I trust a scum piece of shit like you to do that?'

'I guess you have to, Dale, don't you? And I think you have me all wrong. I have ethics and morals, but if I detect corruption, I'll bend them in whatever way I can to achieve a result.'

'You fucking prick,' McCracken sneered. 'You've won tonight but one day, one day, when you least expect it, Clancy, I'll burn you.'

'So we're done?' Peter concluded.

'I'll be in touch.' McCracken rose from the chair still glaring at Peter. 'Shit coffee, by the way.'

'You made it, Dale,' Peter retorted, 'not me.'

25

'You okay in there?' Babs called to Sam as she cuddled up in bed. Waiting. Waiting for Sam.

'Fine,' Sam replied.

'You sound like you're in pain.'

'No. No. My…my haemorrhoids are playing up,' Sam called. 'That's what you get for sitting on horses all day.'

'Have you got the cream to put on them, love?' Babs asked. 'I've got me own supply if you need some.'

'Always have my own supply,' Sam sighed. 'That's better.' He emerged from the toilet naked and pounced onto the bed and into Babs's open arms.

Sam was still thinking himself lucky that he had a bare chest or the tape would have left a mark when he pulled off the wire he'd been wearing. That would have been hard to explain away. Placing the bug in the bedroom and in the lounge had been easy. He hoped it was all worth it. He was still thinking about the frigging wire when he entered Babs.

He was woken from his post-coital slumber by Babs blowing in his ear. 'What?' he muttered as he rolled away from the irritation. 'What's happening?'

Babs watched him with a wide smile.

'You want some more love?' Sam murmured and reached out to Babs.

'No,' she murmured with satisfaction, 'I've had my fill. Black men are always the best. Black is beautiful, hey?'

'If you want another feed,' Sam smiled as he shook himself awake.

'No, Sam. We have to talk about the future.'

'Future?' he replied vaguely. 'More sex I reckon.' Sam tried to grab hold of Babs, but she pushed him away.

'Well we can't live on that forever. Not at our age. You'll give me a frigging heart attack.'

'What are you trying to say?'

'About me plan. The one I've talked about.'

'Where you help yourself to that heroin stuff the O'Learys brought in that container?' he said loudly.

'Will you keep your frigging voice down!' Babs scolded. 'There could be someone listening outside.'

'With those wolves of yours?' Sam chuckled. 'I bloody doubt it.'

'Look, just shut up for the moment. I want you to drive the car, all right? Buddy and I are going to do the break in and I want you to drive the car.'

'Why me? I'm no getaway driver.'

'Yeah but you've pinched things before,' she replied. 'You told me. All those cattle up north, then the…'

'That's enough now,' he interrupted.

'You know what I mean. You want to get ahead. And being an Abo you'll be able to see and hear things that we can't.'

'When did you have it planned for?' he asked.

'The next full moon…that's over the next two days.'

'In the next two days?' Sam repeated louder.

'So. Are you in or are you out?'

'Okay. Yeah. All right,' he responded. 'Count me in. I want to retire and I don't want to do it on some old age pension. End up in some stinking nursing home. I've worked frigging hard for white fellas all my life and I deserve bloody more. This poor black fella has nothing to show for it. I'm in.'

'There's another thing, Samson. It's about us.'

'You know,' Sam said, 'I'm pretty sweet on you.'

'Me too.' She pecked him on the cheek. 'I never thought I'd ever fall for a man again. You're one of a kind. You're a real special bloke.'

'I'd just about given up on being with a woman.' He kissed Babs on the lips.

'You know, I put a deposit on the farm,' she said excitedly. 'I can't wait to take you there. You can see the mountains all covered in snow from the kitchen window.'

'Are you going to run any cattle?'

'Of course. And I want you there to help me run them.'

'Me?'

'You stupid black bastard. I want us to be together. I want to live with you, Sam. You're my everything.'

'I'd love that.'

Babs smiled. 'You see, life's nearly perfect. Live with me, Sam,' she cried. 'I need you in my bed. Now and forever.'

'You want me here. Now?' He glanced at the bedside table.

'You're not going home tonight,' she said as she smothered his neck and face in kisses. 'You're bringing your swag here, darl.'

'That's so good Babs. So good,' he said as he looked again in the direction of the bedside table.

***

Peter rolled across Poppy's king size bed in discomfort and sat up.

'Do as you're told,' she said gruffly as she pushed Peter onto his back, straddled his chest and took hold of both his arms. She was wearing nothing but a lace G-string and a bra. He attempted to take hold of her bra and remove it. 'Don't touch what you can't handle, you piece of shit!' She pushed his hands away, then reached for the silk scarves tied on either side of the iron bedpost.

Peter pretended to resist but Poppy had already wrapped the scarves around both of his wrists and pulled tightly. His arms were stretched taut. He waited expectantly for what would happen next.

'Much better than those handcuffs,' he moaned as Poppy rubbed her hands over his chest and down his stomach, finishing when she reached his groin.

'Not yet, scumbag,' she growled as she again reached into the bedside drawer and retrieved a leather blindfold. She slipped it over Peter's head.

'I can't see anything,' he teased. 'Help me, mistress!'

'I'm not your mistress,' she barked. 'I'm your dominatrix. But just call me Slut.'

'All right. Slut.' He thrust his hips forward. 'You like that, Slut?'

'If you want me to service you with my mouth,' she replied, 'you'll do as you're told.'

'I'll do whatever you say.'

'Thought you'd agree,' she laughed as she started to stroke his groin. 'You know what I want to do, scumbag?'

'What?'

Her hand wrapped around his penis. Peter groaned with pleasure. 'I'm going to suck your member,' she whispered in his ear, 'then I'm going to cowgirl fuck your brains out of your head.'

***

Peter was lying asleep against Poppy's back as she stirred from her slumber. He awoke with a jolt.

'I'm still alive,' he laughed. 'For a moment there I thought I died and gone to heaven.'

'The French call it la petite mort,' she replied softly. 'Little death.'

'Sounds better in French. A perfect description.'

He turned to look at Poppy's face. She was radiant but her eyes were red.

'You okay?' he asked as she stroked her face, causing her to flinch. 'You look like you've been crying.'

Poppy snapped, 'I'm allowed to get emotional. I'm not here to be fucked by you, have you pump your sperm into me and have your petite mort. I find it hard to connect emotionally sometimes. That why I like control. All right?'

'Hey, I'm not just here to fuck you. Sorry I came across that way. I love being with you, and not just physically.'

'Do you think less of me because I like it a little…kinky?' she asked as she rolled over to face Peter.

'It's a bit of fun,' he smiled. 'It's adventurous.'

'You have the most beautiful eyes,' she commented as she ran a hand gently over his eyebrows. 'The best come-fuck-me eyes I've ever seen.'

'Thanks. You have the best…the best everything. Especially your breasts. They're perfect.' He ran his hand over her left breast and gently stroked it. He reached over to place his mouth on her nipple but Poppy pulled away.

'You didn't really answer my question about the…you know… bondage.'

'I love it,' he beamed. 'It heightens everything.'

'You really like it?'

'Of course.'

'Most men I've been with want to dominate the proceedings,' she explained. 'Missionary style. Doggie style. Same old. They want to call the shots. I don't want to be a possession.'

'I think it's good to mix it up.'

'So you like to dominate too?'

'No, it's not that,' he clarified. 'I want to lie on top of you sometimes and look into your eyes. Your face is so beautiful.'

'I don't know if I can do that.' Poppy shuddered. 'That's really intimate.'

'Can I ask a sensitive question?'

'The one about why I can't be that intimate?'

'Yeah. That one.'

'Okay.' She turned her head away. 'When I was younger, I was with an older man who liked to treat me as his fuck-toy. He initiated me into sex but it wasn't healthy.' She wiped away the tears in her eyes. 'And ever since I've had trouble getting close. I love sex, but when it comes to intimacy, I feel funny.'

'It's okay,' Peter said gently.

'You're a real dark horse aren't you, Peter,' Poppy smiled. 'I thought you just wanted to fuck me but it looks like you want to know the real Poppy Reynolds.'

'You don't mind?'

'I don't mind.' She rolled to face him again, 'I may even get used to you being the dominator occasionally.'

***

Peter sat at the small table in Poppy's dining room, sipping an espresso and basking in the warmth of the sun streaming through the windows onto his naked body. Poppy came to the table with the paper and her coffee. She was swaddled tightly in a dressing gown.

'You look comfortable,' she laughed, tracing the outline of his obliques with the tip of her finger.

'The sun feels so good,' he replied.

'You need to get outdoors more.'

'Maybe we should fuck outside more,' he smiled.

'Kinky.'

'So what's on the agenda today?' Peter asked.

'Same old thing,' Poppy replied dryly. 'What about yourself?' She flicked through the newspaper.

'You should be reading *The Truth*,' Peter remarked. 'I expect to break a huge story in it very soon.'

'Not the O'Learys?'

'Yes. No. I can't say.'

'Interesting.' She closed the paper and took a drink of her coffee. 'If it's the O'Learys then I'm rather pleased about it.' She smiled enigmatically.

'Should you be saying that? They're clients of yours.'

'Not any more, thank God.' She downed the remainder of her coffee.

'I'm surprised.'

'They were upset that the firm didn't do more for Eastern and Machowicz. Reckon they should have gotten off. So they've taken their business and gone elsewhere.'

'You don't seem too upset about it.'

'They weren't my favourite clients.' She took a deep breath. 'And the partners aren't too upset that they've left. We were always chasing them for fees.'

'So it's all looking shaky for the O'Learys,' Peter commented.

'It all has to come to an end. Besides, they're remnants of a bygone age. It's all changing. Just like Melbourne. Even Melbourne couldn't remain a backwater that shut down on the weekend. It had to compete with the world.'

'Melbourne's not a backwater. At least, I don't think so.'

'Depends on what you're comparing it to, I suppose. Compared to New York it's positively primitive.'

'Compared to Clarkes Flat, it's New York.'

'Hmm.' She looked out the window. 'All I know is that everything's in a state of flux. Nothing remains the same.'

Peter gathered her up, opened her gown and gazed at her body. 'You're eternal,' he said. 'Everything else can go to hell, as far as I'm concerned. You'll never change.'

'She sighed. 'Even me. We're changing all the time, you know. Even me.'

26

Peter had just returned to his desk after his morning debrief with Bob. He thought Bob was worried unnecessarily about Stella. So, she'd uncovered a connection between a group of Russian businessmen and a stevedore company. So what. Then her sources had disappeared inexplicably. Unfortunate, but leads often went cold. He was hoping she'd be coming back soon.

The sound of a crashing lamp emanated from Bob's office, closely followed by a heavy thump. Peter froze and listened. He ran to Bob's office, collecting Dave as he went. Dave dived through the door first, almost tripping over Bob who was lying on his side, his face a dusky blue.

Dave fell to his knees and felt Bob's neck for a carotid pulse. 'I think he's had a heart attack. He's got no pulse. Get an ambulance!' He struggled to roll Bob over onto his back and motioned to Peter to help him.

'Call an ambulance, someone! Bob's had a heart attack,' Peter shouted down the corridor as Dave pulled back Bob's head, pinched his nose and started mouth-to-mouth.

'Can you do chest compressions?' Dave asked between breaths.

'I can try. A nurse girlfriend taught me how.'

'A compression for every five breaths…Go!'

After three cycles, Dave checked for a pulse. 'Nothing. Keep going.'

'The ambos will be here in five,' Shazza called as she rushed into the office.

'Wait out front for the ambos, Shazza,' Dave directed between breaths.

Peter was running out of steam.

'Come on,' Dave bellowed at Peter, 'pick it up.'

'Come on, Bob,' Peter yelled, 'you can't have a holiday now. We need you on the job.'

'Stop!' Dave instructed. He felt again for a carotid pulse. 'He's got a faint pulse,' Dave sighed with relief.

'Thank God,' Peter smiled feebly. 'Thank God.'

'Let's keep going until the ambos arrive,' Dave instructed.

After that, everything became a blur. Peter only barely remembered the paramedics arriving, one of them intubating Bob, the bleeping sound of the cardiac monitor, the worried looks on the paramedics' faces as they rushed him on a trolley up the corridor. Then the hospital.

Peter sat in the waiting room of the coronary care unit feeling as if he'd been there for hours—which in fact he had. Others had come and gone, but he sat and waited. Sat and waited. None of the nursing staff was imparting any information. He was asked about Bob's family. To Peter's knowledge, Bob was a swinging single. The only woman he'd ever seen Bob with was Stella.

It was well into the afternoon now and still no news. Peter had asked the nurses for information so many times that they were now doing their best to avoid him. He lay down and dozed on the waiting room couch. In his semi-sleep he heard a woman's voice.

'Are you Peter Clancy?'

Peter jolted upright. The voice belonged to a petite, grey-haired woman. She stood over him.

'I am. Yes. Peter. Yes,' he muttered as he shook himself fully awake.

'Did you want to see Bob?' the woman asked gently.

'Of course. How's he going?'

'Stable but he's on life support.'

'And you are…?' Peter asked as he surveyed the woman. 'Sorry. Are you a doctor?'

'I'm the ICU consultant. Beverley Cross. Would you like to see Mr Connelly?'

Peter followed Dr Cross into the coronary care unit, overwhelmed by the bright overhead lights, the cacophonous machine hum and the purposeful activity. He followed her into a cubicle opposite the nurse's station. The man in the bed was bloated and unconscious, lying semi-upright, the tube in his throat contorting his face with terror and pain. But where was Bob Connolly, the editor of *The Truth*?

It took a while for Peter to recognise his boss, covered in a mess of wires and tubes. It was only his wild mat of grey-black hair and the scar on his forehead that gave Peter the cues. The ECG monitor bleeped out evidence of life. Bob was still here, but only just.

A nurse that looked like she was fifteen moved confidently and effortlessly among the medical paraphernalia like a ballet dancer. Peter hung back from the bed, positioning himself near an IV infuser, wondering what to do.

'Did you want to say anything to him?' she asked. 'He can still hear you.'

'You'll be all right, Bob,' he muttered uneasily into Bob's ear. 'We'll be having a Scotch again in no time.'

Bob's hand moved, his fingers rising and falling.

'Look,' she smiled, 'he knows you're here.'

'I think he's probably feeling around for that drink,' Peter chuckled. 'So how's he doing?'

Dr Cross led Peter out of the cubicle. 'I prefer he doesn't hear anything negative. He's had a massive heart attack. Without you and your colleague giving him resuscitation, he would have died.'

'So he'll be all right?' Peter asked.

'He's very unstable at the moment. Once he stabilises, he's going to need a quadruple bypass. He's a fighter.'

'*So it appears.*'

'Should I hang around?' Peter asked. 'I don't want to get in the way.'

'The nurse said you've been here for hours. You might want to go home and get some rest. If anything happens, we'll call you. Since he doesn't appear to have any next of kin.'

'Fine. No worries. I'll just say goodbye to Bob.'

Peter returned to the cubicle as she walked away, leaving him to conduct an inane, one-sided conversation. After a while, he checked his watch. It was five o'clock. *Hometime.*

'I've got to go home and have a rest, Bob,' Peter muttered with a yawn.

He got more of a response from Bob than from the nurse, who was now sitting at a desk recording results into a chart. Peter stood up, retraced his steps to the lift lobby and dozed on his feet. He woke when he heard the lift bell pinging. *Shit,* he thought, *I forgot to phone Stella. She'll think I'm an uncaring prick.* Peter sprang to life and headed towards the lift doors. Out of the lift stepped a woman. She looked familiar. She wore sunglasses, a trench coat with the collar pulled up and denim jeans. *Odd.* The woman must have felt his glance. She turned her head slightly as she hurried past him towards the intensive care unit.

'Stella!' Peter shouted as the doors closed. 'Stella! Wait! It's Peter.'

Stella turned and stopped. Her face was stained with tears and running makeup. 'Sorry!' she spluttered. 'I can't talk. I have to see Bob.'

Peter nodded and turned back towards the lift again. This time, he stepped in when the doors opened and pressed the button. He was too tired to think of anything as he descended. He got his second wind when the hospital doors opened to the freezing dusk air. It sucked the breath out of him. *Bloody Melbourne winters.*

He walked slowly back to the Stag, parked two blocks away. He was thinking of Stella. Stella and Bob. He and Bob. Then just Bob. He thought about praying, but couldn't quite get himself to do it.

***

Babs and the dogs were going beserk. Sam was standing impassively on the porch with his hands in the air, watching the drama unfolding before him and wondering who was louder, the dogs or Babs. He judged it was Babs. She was berating the two uniformed police officers, not only for pulling Buddy out of bed to arrest him, but for also threatening to shoot the two dogs if they weren't chained up. Two other police officers had their pistols drawn and Detective Senior Sergeant Dale McCracken appeared oblivious to the din. Babs followed them up the garden path as they towed a wailing Buddy, his crumpled legs dragging. She followed, delivering her impassioned plea interspersed with threats and expletives.

'Leave him alone. He only come down from Wodonga today to see his Nanna, you cunts. He doesn't deal drugs, you stupid copper bastards,' she bellowed into a constable's ear as he hauled Buddy along.

'Nan! Nanna!' Buddy cried like a lost child.

'You can't arrest my grandson,' Babs pleaded. 'He hasn't done anything wrong.'

McCracken stepped in and pulled her aside. 'Take it easy, Babs. We'll probably have to keep him overnight. It'll take that long to get any sense out of him.'

'You can't do that!'

'Well, the offences are serious.'

'It wasn't him selling dope to the schoolkids. It was someone else.'

'We'll sort that out. You can come to the station, if you want. Your poor little grandson's probably going to need a tit soon by the sound of him,' McCracken hissed.

'Nan! Nanna!'

'Copper cunt.' She threw a wad of dried dog shit, narrowly missing McCracken.

'I could throw you in a cell with the little prick,' he snapped.

'Nan! Nanna!'

'Shut up, Buddy,' she screeched. 'I'll be there as soon as I can.'

'Got things to do, Babs?' McCracken enquired.

'I've got to sort out something,' she replied. 'I do have a fucking life.'

'Want to get in a few more fucks with the Abo? Do you love it black, Babs? Black is beautiful?' McCracken sneered.

'I hope you're not charging him,' she said, jerking her thumb towards Sam.

McCracken looked back at Sam, who still had his hands in the air, and laughed.

'Copper bastard!' she snarled, 'I hope yours fucking drops off one day.'

Babs caught up with Buddy, threw an arm around him and kissed him on the cheek as they pushed him into the back of a police van. 'I'll be there as soon as I can. Stay strong. Don't tell the cunts anything.'

'Touching,' McCracken commented. 'Madonna and child.'

Babs glared at him and walked back to her house. An elderly female neighbour was watching the events from the side fence as she pretended to water a vegetable garden.

'What in the fuck are you looking at you fucking old fossil bitch?' Babs threw towards her as she reached the veranda. 'Get back in ya house and die!' She slapped Sam's hands down as the police car and the van pulled away. 'Don't show these bastards that you're scared, Sam. The mongrels get off on it.'

'When a copper's pointing a gun to my head,' Sam exhaled, 'I can't feel relaxed.'

'Shut up your whingeing for the moment,' she remonstrated. 'I'm trying to bloody think.'

'Worried? About Buddy?'

'Nah. He'll be right. I need a break from him for a while, anyway. Of course I'm fucking worried! I'm worried about tonight.'

'Cancel it until Buddy gets out.'

'We can't cancel it, Sam.' Babs slammed the door behind them in frustration, 'It has to be done tonight. I have to have the bags to the distributor early tomorrow morning.' She pulled a crumpled packet of cigarettes out of her top pocket, lit one and inhaled deeply. 'It's a full moon tonight. I need a full moon.'

'I could give you a hand as well as driving the car. I'm a blackfella. I know something about moving around at night.'

'Driving the car's one thing, but I don't want to put you in any danger,' she said as she kissed Sam on the cheek. 'Do you really want to help me?'

'We're in this together, darl.' He kissed her back.

'What a bloke you are. Where have you been all my life?'

'What about Buddy?' Sam asked. 'Shouldn't we go to the police station?'

'He's grown up,' Babs said dismissively. 'He'll have to sort himself out. Getting that smack out of the container tonight is far more important. It's our future.'

***

McCracken was leaning against the Stag with his arms folded as Peter approached it after leaving the hospital. 'Nice car,' he commented as he walked around the Stag. 'Maybe you should look after it. It could do with a clean.' McCracken looked in through the driver's window. 'Disgusting,' he remarked. 'That pizza box's almost as mouldy as your jocks. Do you live out of this car?'

'I like to camp in it sometimes. You could buy if you want,' Peter commented as he slipped his key into the door lock. 'I'll throw in the pizza box and the jocks for free.'

'Going somewhere?'

McCracken stood nose to nose with Peter. Peter matched his gaze. There was something in McCracken's eyes that reminded Peter of Max Hillard. It sent a shiver down his spine.

'How did you know I was here? Are you fucking following me?'

'Yes. Yes, I did. It's the fucking FBI around here. You're under surveillance all the time,' McCracken laughed. 'I asked the bloody receptionist. She even told me your boss was in hospital. Touching. You're visiting your boss. You must be after his job.'

'Don't mistake me for yourself, Dale.'

'It's happening tonight,' McCracken continued. 'Eleven-thirty it all goes down.'

'Sam's in?'

'Buddy's out, Sam's in.'

'Good. Dave and I will be there with bells on.'

'You can give me the photos now.' McCracken held out his hand.

'Not until after the operation is over,' Peter said. 'When I know Sam is safe and the O'Learys arrested. By, the way, if anything happens to him…'

'Sanctimonious cunt,' McCracken snapped, grabbing Peter's collar with both hands and shaking him. Peter did his best to remain composed, which just made McCracken mad. He threw Peter against the car and hovered over him with clenched fists. 'I want them now,' he growled.

'Of course, Dale. You'll get the photos when I say you'll get the photos. You hurt me or Sam, and we go straight to press.'

'Cunt,' McCracken barked as he punched the car window. He cradled his hand, trying hard to disguise his pain.

'They don't make cars like this anymore. Thick isn't it?' Peter chuckled. 'Reminds me of someone.'

'Fucking prick, Clancy.'

'Yes, she's a classic.' He rubbed his hand over the roof. 'As promised, Dale, you'll get the photos once it's all done and dusted. When the crims are locked away and Sam is safe.'

'Make sure you bring them with you tonight, prick, if you want to write another bullshit story for your arsewipe paper.'

'You threatening me, Dale?' Peter sighed. 'That's not nice.'

'Threat?' McCracken laughed as he walked away. 'That's not a threat, Clancy, that's a police fucking direction.'

✳✳✳

George 'Putty Face' McKenna surveyed the Tupperware container of chocolate crackles with childlike anticipation. Putty Face was one of the security guards employed by the O'Leary family, a crusty, middle-aged stand-over merchant from the old Painters and Dockers days. And he had the battle honours to prove it.

His nose had been battered into a wad of putty from a bashing with a lump of wood, his face was deeply scarred and he had a steel plate in his skull from a brutal clout with an iron bar. All on separate occasions. He had been heavily outnumbered. Putty Face had fought like a wild bull and had managed to inflict major injuries on his attackers. His skull split, he had still bitten off the ear of one attacker and glassed another in the throat before being overwhelmed by superior numbers. He was tougher than a brick shithouse and as formidable as a Tiger tank.

Only last week he had caught a young thief scaling the security fence. Putty Face had reefed him off the fence like he might a cat and had given the thief a proper roughing up. The boy had been crazy enough to pull a knife on the old heavy. He was later found tied to a pier support at St Kilda, the tide lapping his chin. Shaking with cold and terror, he told the police he couldn't remember anything.

Chocolate crackles. They were Putty Face's favourite indulgence. He sniffed them as he stirred his cup of tea. Good old Babs. She was always giving him treats for the night shift. Chocolate cake, cheesecake, Anzac biscuits. But chocolate crackles! Before she had given the game away, Babs had excelled at giving out other treats. But he'd have still preferred chocolate crackles over a roll in the hay.

He picked one up, peeled off the patty-cake paper and took a bite. The melting chocolate, the chewy, coconut-laden rice bubbles made him squirm with pleasure. He thought they were so good, like bloody angels dancing on his tongue. After eating the first crackle and wiping away the chocolate ringing his mouth, Putty Face picked up another. And another, until he had eaten all eight of them. Then he leaned back in his chair and patted his belly. After finishing his cup of tea, he rested his head on the desk and nodded off for an hour.

Putty Face woke with a slight rumbling in the abdominal region but thought nothing of it. Probably that salad his missus had made for dinner. His missus was always trying to shove rabbit food down his neck. She was always telling him he had to lose weight, he had to be healthy. All it did was upset his bloody guts. He looked at the clock. It was time to do a walk around.

He grabbed his metal torch and headed out into the brisk night. The rumbling in the guts continued, growing in frequency and intensity. By the time he got back to the guard box, the rumbling had turned into a growl. Then it upped another gear. He felt a sudden urgency. He flung open the door and started to run. A bomb was threatening to explode inside him. He wondered why the toilet was so far away. His putty face lathered with sweat, clutching his guts and holding onto the torch, he ran as hard as his gammy leg could muster. Another injury from another fight.

He dropped the torch and began unbuttoning his trousers, even before he reached the toilet. He threw open the door as he was pulling off his underpants. He turned his arse towards the bowl. Then it happened. It was like a volcano erupting in a confined space. It had sprayed across the walls and floor like a burst water main before Putty Face had the time to prop himself onto the toilet. He sighed with relief as he sat, and it kept flowing. And flowing. The chocolate crackles had definitely worked.

***

Even on a crisp Melbourne night, even as his guts twisted into tight knots with apprehension, Sam couldn't help but admire the shimmering light that glinted off the water of Port Phillip Bay. It reminded him of winter nights spent camping by the river back at the station, and waking up to throw more wood on the fire. He was homesick. Homesick for his homecountry.

Sam coasted Babs's battered Holden Commodore sedan up to the high wire gate that secured the O'Leary wharf operation. A guard box stood near the locked gate. Sam noticed that its light was on but he couldn't see anyone inside. Sam looked at Babs, who seemed relaxed.

'What about the security guard, Babs?' Sam asked anxiously.

'He should be going on an extended break right about now.'

Sam glanced through the small window of the illuminated guard box. Suddenly, a man leapt up and ran out, fumbling with his trousers

'Putty Face will be indisposed for a while,' Babs chuckled. 'Let's open those locks.'

Sam drove slowly down the row of stacked shipping containers until they reached the blue one.

'Stop here,' Babs instructed.

She jumped out and ran to the rear of the car. Sam turned off the engine and followed her. She opened the car boot and retrieved a shopping jeep, about a dozen plastic bags that looked like they contained flour and a forty-five semi-automatic pistol. She pulled a full magazine from her pocket and snapped it into the pistol.

'What are you doing?' Sam whispered anxiously as he picked up a pair of bolt cutters. 'You didn't tell me about the bloody gun.'

'Just in case,' she replied as she tucked it into her jeans. 'You can put them bolt cutters back in the boot, we won't need them. I've got the keys. Took them out of the safe this arvo.'

'And you can put back the gun. I don't want a gun being waved around,' Sam held out his hand. 'It's stressing me out. Please, Babs. I got shot at once. Please.'

'All right,' Babs relented, 'before you have a frigging breakdown on me.' She leaned in through the passenger window and threw the weapon into the glove box.

They hurried to the door of the shipping container, Babs following Sam with the shopping jeep, its wheels squeaking.

'Can't you shut that bloody thing up?'

'Can you see anyone?' Babs shook her head. 'It's as quiet as a cemetery.'

'What about the security guard? He could come out at anytime,' he said as he reached up with the keys.

'Don't worry about him,' Babs smiled as she took a look around. Sam opened the first lock.

'Tell you about it another time,' she continued as she removed the lock. 'Two more and we're in the money.'

Sam opened the other two locks, and began to peel open the heavy steel door.

'Honey, we're home,' Babs chuckled as she scrambled through the open door first, pulling the jeep in behind her. Sam turned on a torch as they entered. The container was full of pallets of Asian food.

'Point the torch over there,' Babs directed. 'We're not after frigging Singapore noodles. We want the coffee.'

'There,' Sam said as he noticed a small pallet of large tins, stacked two high and wrapped in thick plastic. The tins had labels with Asian lettering and the word 'Coffee' emblazoned on them.

Babs tore open the plastic, pulled out a tin and snapped the lid with a screwdriver taken from the shopping jeep. Sam shone the torch into the open container.

'It's just coffee,' Sam remarked.

'No, its not.' Babs said as she punched her hand into the coffee grains and removed a plastic bag about the size of her two hands placed together. She held it up to the torchlight. 'This is pure Asian-grown heroin.' She placed the bag into Sam's free hand. 'This is what a fortune feels like. Worth more than fucking gold. A dozen bags of this when it reaches the street will be worth ten million dollars.'

'Holy smoke,' Sam fingered the bag briefly then handed it back to Babs. 'It looks like baby powder.'

'Well, the bags that are going back on the street have baby powder in them, amongst other stuff.' She took a white bag out of the jeep, shoved it back into the open tin and sealed it. She continued the same substitution process until all the heroin had been exchanged.

'You keeping all this?' Sam asked.

'I fucking wish,' Babs smiled as she put the last pure bag into the jeep and zipped it shut. 'I get ten per cent of the street value. Not a bad night's work, hey?'

'That's a million bloody dollars,' Sam reeled. 'What's that even feel like?'

'Like a life of freedom. Let's go.' She turned and headed to the container door.

'Who gets the rest?'

'The bloke's a real mover and shaker. He's frigging ruthless but he pays well. So we better shake our arses and get out of here. He wants his stuff tonight. We have to drive out to Coburg after this. Don't forget the locks.'

Babs walked briskly back to the car. Sam closed the door slowly, slipped the three locks back on and sealed them. He met Babs at the back of the car as she was wrestling the shopping jeep into the boot.

'All those years of putting up with other people's shit. I'm so excited I want to shout,' she smiled as she closed the boot.

'Don't do that,' Sam said as he looked anxiously up and down the wharf. 'Can we get out of here? This place is making me nervous.' Sam hopped in the driver's seat alongside Babs.

'This is where we're going.' She pulled a small advertising handout from the glove box and flashed it in front of Sam. He took a quick peek.

'You'll have to show me,' he said as he engaged first gear.

'No worries.' Babs wound back the seat and put her feet up on the dashboard. 'How many stereo shops are there in Coburg?'

She closed her eyes started to hum 'Eye of the Tiger' as Sam put his foot on the accelerator. She opened them again when he suddenly slammed on the brakes.

'What are you doing?'

'We have company,' he replied as he slipped the gear stick into neutral and placed his hands on the steering wheel.

27

Babs sat bolt upright when she saw Tommy O'Leary reaching into the open window of the car to shove a pistol against Sam's head. She noticed that the pistol had a silencer attached to the barrel.

'Tommy?' she gasped. She then felt a pistol being pressed against the side of her head. 'What are you…'

'Not expecting us, were you?' Tommy said softly. 'A little birdie told us you'd be here. Where's George, by the way?'

'On the shitter,' Babs stammered. 'I dosed him up on Laxettes.'

'That's different,' Tommy stifled a grin.

'And don't forget your dear little Robbie, you traitor slut,' Robbie snarled. He threw open the door and dragged Babs out of the car with one hand and threw her to the ground. 'Stay there, bitch,' he said as he kicked Babs in the back of the head. She cried out in pain.

'Out of the car,' Tommy directed Sam.

Sam slowly got out of the car and put his hands in the air.

'Over by your girlfriend,' said Tommy. He shoved Sam towards Babs. 'On the ground. Face down.'

Sam looked at Babs. She was bleeding from the back of her head and sobbing. 'You don't have to hurt her,' he pleaded as he sat on his knees.

'Lie down,' Tommy snarled and pushed him down. Sam dropped onto his face. He could feel blood seeping from his mouth. He spat it out onto the cold, cement wharf. 'You're in no position to bargain, Abo.'

'You're beyond hurting, Babs,' Robbie said as he kicked her in the head again. 'I hope you know some prayers. Isn't that what people say before they're executed?'

Babs sobbed louder.

'Of all the people who you'd think would stab us in the back,' Tommy said sadly as he hovered over a prostrate Sam with a pistol. 'I would never have guessed it would be you, Babs. You were like a member of the family. And you've shit on us from a great height.'

'What a big fucking mess you nearly caused. Bitch!' Robbie ranted as he delivered another kick, this time in Babs's back.

'And very clever. Substituting the good stuff with shit. A nice retirement nest-egg. Killed some of our best customers,' Tommy added.

'I only did it because I was forced to,' she turned her head and looked up towards Tommy. 'They said they'd kill me. Please, Tommy. Believe me. You're the sensitive one. Please believe me.'

'Who's they? Donarto?'

'I can't say. I know I'm going to die but if he finds out I dobbed he'll kill Buddy for sure.'

'Tell us, you stinking whore!' Robbie reached down and grabbed the back of Babs's hair and smashed her head into the concrete. A stream of blood gushed from a laceration in her forehead.

'I'm not telling. And I'm not afraid to fucking die,' she cried, 'but I want Buddy to live.'

'So maternal of you, Babs. Here's is the plan.' Tommy leaned down on one knee and spoke gently. 'If you don't tell us, we're going to kill you and Sam. You probably know that by now. We'll throw you in the family cabin cruiser, take you out past the heads and dump you. We can't let you live. Just can't. You see that, don't you?' He stood upright again. 'So if you're not going to tell us, we'll have no choice. No choice at all.' He paused to scratch his face and nodded to Robbie.

'Please let my grandson live. He wasn't part of it,' Babs begged.

'We won't touch him,' Tommy replied in a soft reassuring voice.

'It's praying time, Babs,' Robbie snarled. He put the pistol to the back of her head and pulled her up to her knees. 'You may as well be in a kneeling position, like church.'

'Sorry, Sam,' Babs said, as she took a final look at Sam, crossed herself and glanced upwards. 'Our Father who art in Heaven, hallowed be Thy name, Thy kingdom come, Thy…'

'Taking too long,' Robbie complained as he pressed the pistol hard into the back of Babs's head and pulled the trigger twice. The bullets thudded as they entered her brain. Her body fell forward and lay still, a torrent of blood flowing from her shattered skull. Sam wanted to turn his head, take a last glimpse of Babs but he didn't dare. His eyes filled with tears.

'One down,' Robbie said as he reloaded, 'one to go. Do you want to do this one Tommy?'

'I guess so. Anything to say?' Tommy stated as he pressed the pistol into the back of Sam's skull.

Sam took a moment to answer. 'You blokes weren't bad to work for.'

The brothers laughed.

Sam continued. 'You don't have to kill me. I have a really bad memory. You know I won't even remember what happened here tonight. Put me on a plane to Darwin and we'll leave it at that.'

The boys laughed again. 'We'll miss that cheeky sense of humour of yours,' Tommy pressed the barrel against Sam's head. As Tommy was about to pull the trigger, he heard the wail of sirens and saw a blaze of headlights coming towards them.

'It's the fucking cops!' Robbie shouted looking in the direction of the security gate. He could see the outline of three police cars and a van coming down the wharf towards them. 'Who frigging told them?'

'No time for the why and fucking wherefores now, Robbie,' Tommy yelled as he dragged Sam to his feet.

The police vehicles screamed along the wharf.

'Why don't we jump in the boat and head out to sea?' Robbie cried above the growing crescendo of sirens.

'Too late,' Tommy bellowed. 'Let's go, Abo.' He took hold of Sam's arm and pulled him.

'Where are we going?' Robbie asked as he spun away from the impending storm.

'In the office. Sam is going to be our ticket out of here. Move, Robbie. Don't stand there like a stale bottle of piss!'

The two brothers bolted to the office, Tommy pushing Sam along. He tossed Sam through the doorway first. The brothers dived after him and fell to the floor. Tommy slammed the door shut and pushed a filing cabinet against it. Sam curled himself into a tight ball under the sink and prepared himself to meet his ancestors. Robbie pulled the faded curtains across the two narrow windows on either side of the small demountable.

'Stay on the floor, Robbie,' Tommy ordered. 'They'll plug us if we stand near the window.'

They heard the police vehicles screech to a halt in quick succession and the stamping of feet as the officers leapt out of the vehicles.

'Fucking flat feet,' Robbie cursed.

Tommy reached up with pistol in hand and peered through a hole in the curtain. The cars had stopped about two house lengths away from the office in a semi-circular formation. Tommy could see police crouched with weapons drawn behind their cars.

'How many?' Robbie asked.

'About twenty,' Tommy said quickly. 'Enough to do a lot of damage.'

'I don't want to die, Tommy,' Robbie sobbed.

'Shut up. I'm thinking.' Tommy continued to peer through the torn curtain. 'McCracken's running the show,' he observed. 'He's standing out there like John fucking Wayne.'

'Shoot the cunt,' Robbie cried. 'He's been nothing but trouble.'

'They'll open up on us with everything, you stupid prick.'

'The cunt must think it's Christmas,' Robbie commented as he crawled across the floor to peek out of the curtain. 'He's finally got the O'Learys.'

'Shut up. He's coming towards the office,' Tommy announced as he peered out.

'I'm shooting the bastard,' Robbie cried as he reached up to the window.

He aimed his pistol through the window but Tommy snatched it out of Robbie's hands. It crashed on the floor.

'Forget the shoot-out, Robbie. We have to use our fucking brains here,' Tommy stated as he smacked Robbie across the face.

'He's checking if Babs is still alive,' Tommy commented. 'She's dead as a maggot.'

'I don't want to die,' Robbie sobbed again and started to rock. 'I wish Mum and Dad were here.'

'Shut up,' Tommy growled. 'McCracken is saying something.' He strained to listen.

McCracken's voice blared over a loudspeaker. 'Tommy and Robbie O'Leary. It's Detective Senior Sergeant Dale McCracken here. Drop your weapons and come out peacefully. I promise no one will get hurt.'

'We have a hostage, McCracken,' Tommy shouted through the window. 'We'll shoot the Abo if you give us any trouble.'

'Show us that he's unharmed, then. Bring him to the doorway.'

Tommy motioned for Robbie to get Sam. Robbie crawled to Sam and shoved a pistol into the side of his head. Sam and Robbie slowly crawled to the closed door.

'Show us that he's safe,' McCracken announced.

Robbie motioned for Sam to stand. Sam got to his feet, while Tommy continued to watch the police through the window. Robbie gently pulled open the door and pushed Sam into the doorway while he stood to the side, holding a pistol against Sam's head. Sam stood in the doorway with his hands above his head.

'Are you hurt, Sam?' McCracken asked.

'I'm all right. Just need a drink of water.'

'Let him go,' McCracken stated. 'It's pointless continuing this. You're totally surrounded.'

'No. No fucking way,' Tommy shouted. 'Let us get on our cruiser and we won't kill Sam.'

'I don't negotiate with murderers, Tommy. You come peacefully and no one gets hurt. That's the option.'

'Fuck you, McCracken,' Robbie yelled and pushed Sam aside and slammed the door.

'Think about it, McCracken,' Tommy called through the window. 'We'll willing to wait. We've got food and water in here. Let us know when you're ready.'

McCracken walked back to the police cordon. Courtesy of their bargain, Peter and Dave were capturing the drama up close. The rest of the media were craning for glimpses, much further away.

'I wish I hadn't put Sam in this position,' Peter whispered. 'What's McCracken up to? Just give them what they want.'

'Looks like he wants to take the higher ground,' Dave replied. 'Maybe he thinks he'll be able to wear them down eventually.'

'He probably doesn't care if Sam gets killed in the crossfire.' Peter ran his hand through his hair.

'He's got the media watching him. It won't happen.'

'Better not,' he sighed. He inched closer to where McCracken was standing, sipping a cup of coffee he'd just been handed. A mountain of a police constable blocked him from getting any closer.

'Detective Senior Sergeant McCracken,' Peter managed to shout over the shoulder of the constable. 'How is the siege proceeding at present?'

'Get back to your designated location, Clancy, or I'll kick you out of here.'

'I think that can be recorded as "negotiations are tense at the moment"?' Peter told Dave, as they settled in for the duration.

***

Five hours had elapsed since McCracken had last spoken to the O'Leary brothers. From a light drizzle in the early morning, it was now blazing sunshine. It was a Mexican stand-off. Peter and Dave sat on the ground with their backs resting against the police van. Peter could see a police sniper slowly climbing the stairs to one of the cranes. The other officers appeared to be fused into crouching positions by the cars, their weapons trained on the office. McCracken was the only one who was animated, moving about and gesticulating.

Through the glare, Peter could see that the sniper had taken up position in the crane's cabin.

'We're in the impasse phase,' Dave observed. 'It's a matter of who'll give up first.'

'Ever been in a hostage situation?' Peter asked.

'No. I was a country cop, remember? Who takes hostages in a country town?'

'You know shit then?'

'Possibly.'

Another hour passed. Peter and Dave were still crouched behind the van when McCracken approached them.

'You're gracing us with your company, Dale,' Peter remarked as he stood up to stretch. 'Do you want to do an interview? I've got nothing else to do. Looks like you're not doing much either.'

'Shut the fuck up, Clancy,' McCracken hissed. 'Do you know where their mother might be living? You interviewed her once.'

'I went to their house in Clifton Hill just after the shooting and then I met up with her at Slugger Douglas's flat. I don't know anywhere else.'

'We've been there. We checked if she was at their holiday home in Portsea. We checked with her friends. They don't know where she is.

Fucking think, Clancy. Did she mention anywhere else?' McCracken barked.

Peter scratched his head as Dave muttered, 'You reckon she'd calm down the situation?'

'No. I'm very concerned that they may be missing their mummy right now,' McCracken said.

'Something comes to mind,' Peter broke his silence. 'No one knows this, but Ivy and Slugger were having an affair for many years. They used to meet at the Windsor Hotel for their trysts, Slugger told me one night. Could she be staying there?'

'Worth a try.' McCracken waved over two detectives.

'Windsor Hotel,' McCracken ordered. 'Ivy O'Leary could be staying there. If you find her, bring her here. Better be right, Clancy,' he added. 'It's our last chance.'

'What do you mean?'

'If she doesn't turn up, we're going in.'

What about Sam? Peter followed McCracken to the van. 'You can't let Sam die.'

'We're not going to negotiate with murderers.' McCracken stopped and spun around. 'It's likely they'll kill Sam. That's how the O'Learys operate. Tommy will be planning a way out of there, but Robbie's going to snap. I know him. A real psychopath.'

'You can't go in there like Rambo,' Peter said. 'Sam's going to walk out of there alive and in one piece. Remember the party snaps, Dale.'

'Photos or not,' McCracken said as he elbowed Peter away, 'I'll try to get Sam out alive but if these blokes crack I'm going to have to move fast. Hopefully Sam won't be in the crossfire. Remember, you're the one who put him in the situation.'

'Fuck you,' Peter groaned.

'You'd better hope we can find Mum O'Leary.'

Another two hours passed. Inside the office, the situation grew tenser. Sam remained huddled near the sink sipping water from a teacup, while Robbie and Tommy kept a careful watch near the windows. Robbie got more agitated.

'Why don't they leave?' Robbie shouted anxiously as he peered out of the curtain. 'Copper bastards!'

'Be careful doing that, 'Tommy snapped when he noticed Robbie looking out of the window. 'I'd say they have a sharpshooter somewhere nearby. Maybe in one of the cranes. Just hang on, Robbie. They'll come to their senses eventually.'

'I'm getting out of here now. I can't take it anymore,' Robbie ranted as he crawled back to where Sam was positioned and put his pistol to Sam's head. 'Get up, Abo.'

'What the fuck are you doing, Robbie?' Tommy rushed from the window. He grabbed Robbie from behind and wrapped his arm around his neck. 'Stupid bastard. You'll get us all killed,' he screeched as he tightened his grip.

Robbie reached up and smashed the butt of his pistol into the bridge of Tommy's nose. Tommy fell to the floor, writhing, a deep laceration to his head.

'I'm tired of doing everything your fucking way, Tommy,' Robbie raged as he pulled Sam to his feet. He pushed Sam to the window and tore the curtain down. 'Listen up, McCracken,' he yelled. 'Either you let us go now or I start cutting up the Abo.' Robbie tucked the pistol into his pants, grabbed Sam's arm and held it up. Then he reached inside his coat and produced a large hunting knife from a scabbard attached to his torso. He held up the hunting knife and pushed Sam's hand onto the ledge of the window. 'Do you see what I've got? I'm going to start with a finger for every fucking hour you don't let us go. If fingers don't work, I'm going for hands, starting now!'

Robbie raised the knife.

'Don't. Don't!' Peter screamed as he tried to push through the police. A burly detective tackled him and pushed him head down into the ground.

'I'm going to fucking do it, coppers! One, two...'

'All right, you made your point,' McCracken barked into the loudhailer.

'I'm not fucking around, McCracken.' Robbie raised the knife higher. 'Here we go.'

A police car with its siren blaring sped onto the wharf and parked behind the police cordon.

Robbie paused momentarily. 'What's going on, McCracken? I'm getting nervous. Bad things happen when I'm nervous.'

'Someone wants to talk to you, Robbie.' McCracken beckoned a bewildered Ivy O'Leary through the throng of police. McCracken gave her the loudhailer and flicked it on.

'What's my mother doing here?' Robbie barked as he lowered the knife and pushed Sam away. He pulled the pistol out of his pants.

'She's here to talk some sense to you, Robbie,' McCracken called. He nodded at Ivy.

'Don't let the cops push you around, Mum,' Robbie said as he waved the pistol around. 'The mongrels aren't taking us to jail.'

'Stop this madness, Robbie,' Ivy stammered softly into the loudhailer. McCracken urged her to speak louder. She wiped her eyes and continued. 'Is Tommy there? Where's Tommy?' Ivy said in a louder voice.

'He's okay,' Robbie replied. 'He hurt himself but he's okay. Why do you always worry about him?'

'I want to see him,' Ivy said.

McCracken whispered into Ivy's ear. 'And Sam. I want to see both of them.'

Robbie pushed Tommy and Sam to the window. Ivy dropped the loudspeaker when she saw Tommy. He was holding a blood-soaked tea towel against his forehead, unsteady on his feet. Ivy tried to dash towards the office but McCracken grabbed her by an arm.

'Tommy. You look hurt,' Ivy cried. 'Come out. You need help.'

'I'm all right, Mum,' Tommy grimaced as he wiped blood away from his face with the tea towel. 'See? Robbie and I had a disagreement.'

'Stop all this. Please give yourself up. You're not going to get away,' she pleaded.

'We're getting on the cruiser and pissing off, Mum,' Robbie added. 'You can come with us or stay. It's up to you.'

'You're acting stupid again, Robbie,' she screeched. 'Let Tommy talk. Tommy!'

'We're not going to jail, Mum,' Tommy said. 'We'll rot in there.'

'I'd rather have my sons in jail than in the ground. At least there I can see you.'

'We're not doing it, Mum,' Robbie added.

'You were always the hot-headed, stupid one, Robbie,' Ivy cried. 'Come on, Tommy, be sensible. Don't listen to your brother.'

'I'm sorry, Mum,' Tommy replied. 'We don't want to go to jail.'

'Please, Tommy. Please.' McCracken spoke into Ivy's ear. 'Are you all right, Sam?' she asked.

'Just tired, Missus,' Sam replied wearily.

'All these killings wouldn't have happened,' she raged, 'if you hadn't started selling that bloody heroin. I told Patrick not to get involved. All he thought about was money. Now he's dead and my other son is dead along with all those poor kids who've died from overdoses. If you have a conscience you'd give yourself up.'

'We're sorry, Mum,' yelped Tommy, 'we were just doing what Dad told us to do. We wanted to please him.'

'Pat only cared about himself.' She pursed her lips and reflected momentarily. 'He wasn't even your father, Tommy. I've always wanted to tell you but I never had the bloody guts.'

Tommy leaned against the windowsill.

'You're not Patrick's son, Tommy. You're Slugger's son.' With that Ivy crumpled to the ground. McCracken motioned to an ambulance officer.

A wounded animal howl came from the office. 'I killed him! I killed him! We thought he was dogging on us. Oh, God, I killed my own father!'

'Give it up, Tommy,' McCracken urged. 'This madness can't go on. Please.'

'I'm giving up, Mum,' Tommy yelled as he tore open the door and put his hands in the air. 'I love you, Mum. I'm so sorry.' He stepped out of the office dropping the blood-soaked towel in the process. The police raised their weapons. 'Don't shoot. I'm done with all this. I'm done. I'm coming, Mum.'

Tommy staggered towards his mother who was lying on her back, an oxygen mask on her face. She pulled away the mask and propped herself up on an elbow. 'Tommy.'

'Fucking dog, bastard,' Robbie shouted from the doorway. He pointed his pistol at Tommy and fired. Tommy fell face down with two bullet wounds to his back. Sam seized the moment to jump through the window. He dropped onto the ground and lay still.

'No! Not my Tommy!' Ivy screamed and tried to get up.

There was a crack from above as the sniper took a shot from the crane. Robbie froze. He dropped the pistol and slumped in the doorway. The shot had severed his pulmonary artery. Ivy managed to crawl to Tommy and was sobbing over his body with her ear pressed against his chest. Everyone else rushed forward.

'He's still alive,' Ivy cried. 'Our boy is still alive, Slugger.'

Peter and Dave scurried to where Sam was lying. Peter shook him while Dave checked his carotid pulse.

'You better be okay, Sam. I'll never forgive myself,' Peter yelled.

Suddenly Sam sat up and dusted the dirt off his body. 'I was just pretending to be dead,' he smiled. 'I do dead pretty well, don't I?'

'You bloody old bugger,' Peter said, as he grabbed him in an embrace.

***

Peter and Dave had nearly reached the Stag when they heard a familiar voice behind them.

'You forgot something, Clancy.'

He spun around to see an exhausted McCracken. 'You're looking old, Dale,' he observed. 'It must have been stressful not knowing how the siege would turn out. It's lucky you didn't have a dead hostage on your conscience.'

'I knew Sam wasn't in any danger.'

'Thanks to me,' Peter added. 'I'm the one who worked out where Ivy O'Leary might be.'

'Well you can crap on about what a hero you were in your column.'

'I suppose you want the photos?'

Peter pulled out his car keys, opened the passenger door and took the envelopes out of the glove box. He handed them to McCracken who tucked them inside his coat. 'That's it, then.'

'Don't ever try to cross me again, Clancy,' McCracken growled as he walked off.

'We'll catch up,' Peter laughed. 'Over lunch maybe?'

McCracken shook his head and kept walking.

'Can you shut up with the smartarse comments?' Dave grabbed his arm.

'He deserves it,' Peter fumed, pulling away. 'He's another Max Hillard. Thinks he's fucking king-dog. I can't stand them.'

Dave was still putting on his seat belt when Peter threw the Stag into first gear and sped away, tyres squealing. 'Front page,' he announced as he sped along the wharf. 'Two dead in hostage drama at docks. Killing of a hostage narrowly averted by the courageous mother of the O'Leary brothers, who broke the siege with her tearful pleas. Ivy O'Leary was located by investigative reporter, Peter Clancy during the tense standoff, which was nearly bungled by the actions of the police officer in charge, Detective Senior Sergeant Dale McCracken. How's that sound?'

'Are you crazy?' Dave said. 'McCracken is going to hate that.'

'He may think he's won this round but I haven't finished with Dale yet.'

Peter got to the hospital as quickly as he could after filing the story. He hadn't seen Bob in two days, but he had been extubated and was trying to talk. Peter was confident that Bob would come back to work and everything would get back to normal.

At least, that was what he thought until he left the lift and waited to be let into the intensive care unit. Dr Cross came through the door, hardly daring to look him in the eyes. Peter knew before she opened her mouth. He knew by her eyes. Bob was dead.

'Bob suffered a massive heart attack thirty minutes ago,' she explained. 'Unfortunately he did not survive it. We did everything we could to save him. I'm really terribly sorry.'

At least it was quick, he thought. 'I was working on an exclusive. I would have got here quicker.'

Dr Cross nodded. 'Don't punish yourself, you weren't to know. From what I've heard that's how it is with you journalists. The news has to get out there, no matter what. I'm sure he would have understood.'

Peter didn't know what more to say, but he knew one thing. Without Bob at the helm, Peter's life at *The Truth* would never be the same again.

WINDS OF CHANGE

28

'Well, mate,' Peter began softly, as he drifted past the coffin. 'The siege is over. Everyone's safe. The story's done and Dave took some great photos. It's a great story. The best the paper has done in a long time. I think we won't be just the sleaze rag anymore. I was all due to you, Bob. It's a pity you're not here to share the success. In a way I feel that you know about all this. We'll miss you, mate. Really will. The old *Truth* won't be the same without you.'

Another funeral. Saint Patrick's again. A bright, sunny day for a change. A good day for footy, as Bob would have remarked. Peter was beginning to feel like he had attended every funeral in Melbourne in the past month as he sat in one of the pews with Poppy, Dave, Shazza and Sam beside him. He'd asked Stella to join them but she'd declined politely, saying that she preferred to mourn Bob's death alone.

It was Peter's first public outing with Poppy, and Sam was supposed to still be in hospital but Sam being Sam, he had signed himself out that morning. Peter felt a lot better with Poppy beside him. He turned and looked at back at the numbers of mourners filing into the cathedral. It looked like hundreds were coming to pay their respects. Bob was a great man but Peter hadn't realised how many people had thought so. The Collingwood board members were there, along with legends and current players of the club, politicians, horse racing notables and celebrities. Probably all connected with the Collingwood Football Club.

Yes, this one was special. Even Ilmo was there to pay his respects. He nodded once at Peter as he filed past. The Owners of *The Truth* had come out of lofty isolation to attend. Bob would have wondered what all the fuss was about. He wasn't a footy legend so why the fucking fuss? That's what Bob would have thought. To Peter it was more than the death of a boss and mate; it was the death of an era. In a single moment everything, even Melbourne, had changed. He couldn't explain why, but it did.

Stella, Peter and his guests were given a privileged position right behind the coffin, and for the next hour they sat as the bishop said the mass and a select number of mourners gave humorous eulogies about Bob's life as a war correspondent in the Middle East, as a reporter at the *New York Post* and his long and tireless contribution to the Collingwood Football Club. Peter glanced at Stella when the mourner had spoken about New York. Her face was obscured by sunglasses and a veiled hat. They made an impenetrable barrier. Even in the midst of a crowd, she was still determined to mourn alone.

Suddenly Stella rose to deliver a heart-rending, tearful eulogy. She spoke about how she had been influenced by Bob, who had been her mentor in many aspects of her professional life. But there were also revelations. Bob had once lived, worked, married and divorced in London. He and Stella had been engaged to be married. Bob was like a house full of rooms that some people were allowed into and then there were the darkened, closed rooms where no one went. Now Peter felt like he hadn't really known Bob Connolly at all.

As he watched Stella come to the conclusion of her eulogy, Peter turned to his right. He could hear someone sobbing not far from him. It was Poppy. Strange.

'Are you all right?' Peter whispered as he took hold of her hand. Poppy pushed him away and stood up without replying. She brushed past him and walked briskly down the aisle before he could say any more. He left his seat and followed her as the bishop returned to the lectern.

Poppy was on the front steps, sobbing into her hands when Peter caught up with her. He sat down beside her and draped his arm around her.

'No. No. Please,' Poppy sniffed as she pulled away. 'I don't want to be touched. Please.'

'Sure,' Peter said as he dropped his arm limply back onto his lap. 'I'm here for you.'

'I know,' she attempted to smile as she dried her eyes with a tissue. 'I didn't want to make a scene in front of your friends.'

'I'm sure Bob didn't mind,' Peter chuckled. 'He was probably getting bored with the whole proceedings. Bob never liked fluff.'

They fell silent for a while. Poppy spoke first. 'When everyone spoke about how nice and great Bob was, it reminded me of everything my father wasn't.'

'Your father wasn't a nice man?'

'My father was a… Well, there's a word for what he was.' She stopped. 'I don't want to talk about it right now, Peter. Sorry.'

'Okay. When you're ready.'

'I'm going to go,' she leant across and pecked him on the cheek. 'I'll see you soon.' Poppy grabbed her handbag and stood up.

'Don't you want a lift back to work?'

'No. It's fine,' she replied, 'the walk will do me good.'

'We'll catch up soon?' Peter asked as Poppy walked down the steps.

'Soon. I'm going to make it up to you in a special way,' she smiled.

Peter watched her leave the cathedral grounds and continue down the street. He hadn't really known about Bob, and now he felt as if he knew nothing about Poppy. He was discovering that she, too, had darkened rooms in her house, and possibly ones she had boarded up long ago. He watched her disappear around a corner. He was still thinking about her as the coffin was carried out of the church, escorted by several current players from the club.

He excused himself from going to the cemetery, telling Sam and Dave he would catch up with them at Victoria Park for Bob's wake. Peter was getting tired of death. Death and crime investigation stories were so tightly intertwined that he didn't want to see another corpse, go to another funeral or visit a cemetery for a while. He wanted to lie in the sun and make love with Poppy and forget it all.

He decided to get to Victoria Park before everyone else. He was dying for a drink. As he drove east along Johnston Street and then north towards the Collingwood Social Club his thoughts drifted back to Poppy. How should he feel about her? There may have been a hint of uncertainty but he still had to see her. He wanted her regardless of her secret fetishes. *It's the 1980s, for heaven's sake. People are allowed to be kinky.* But occasionally, Peter just wanted to make old-fashioned love to her. What was wrong with missionary every now and again?

And what about a traditional relationship? Poppy was special. Yes, everything was changing.

Peter got to the function room behind the new Bob Rose Stand before anyone else had arrived. He sat near the large glass window overlooking Victoria Park; same spot where he and Bob used to watch a game and have a good piss up, win or lose. He remembered the first game of Aussie Rules he attended. Bob had taken him to a Collingwood versus North Melbourne game at VFL Park. Bob had told him to wear a Collingwood scarf while he'd worn a Collingwood beanie. His initiation to the game consisted of being hit over the head by a gang of umbrella-wielding grannies wearing North Melbourne duffel coats, who were sitting behind them. Bob had remarked that the old dears would run out of steam soon, which they did. Then he had remarked that being a Collingwood supporter was an honour but it came with a price: the most beloved Aussie Rules team was also the most hated. From then on, Peter was hooked.

Victoria Park, strangely enough, was one of the few places where, even in a crowd, Peter felt solitude and calm. He loved it all: the earthy scent of a muddy, clod-flinging game on a wet winter's day, the pungent smell of the Goanna oil. The players were supreme athletes, as well-muscled as the finest thoroughbred and as surefooted as an old stockhorse. He was happiest having a beer overlooking the ground, watching a game or watching training. *Sacred ground. Perfect. Except Bob's missing.* Peter had finished his second beer and was slaking his amber thirst with a third as the first guests arrived.

What a wake, Peter thought as he weaved and dodged his way to the bar for another refill. Three hours had passed already. *What the fuck? Free beer flowing. Why does free beer taste so good?* Then a couple of straight Jameson's for comic relief and Peter was heading to pissed kingdom on his boozy chariot. Bob's favourite music blared: Frank Sinatra, Irish music and Lou Reed. Everyone singing the club song: *Good old Collingwood forever. We know how to play the game...*

Club heavyweights and legends were in abundance. The beer and conversation was flowing. Bob would have loved to be here. *I'm going to have my wake before I kick the bucket.* Peter surveyed the crowd in an intoxicated haze. Was that a former prime minister and one of Australia's greatest female singers that he'd just had a deep and meaningful conversation with? What was the topic again? That's right, the strength of the Collingwood family. He was pissed. Definitely. Having silly and meaningless discussions with strangers was a sign he had crossed over to the dark side. Time to leave before the symptoms became any worse. Before it became terminal. Next stage was offering abiding love and friendship to total strangers, and possibly even charity. *Run now.* Peter swallowed his beer fast and headed for the exit before the attack could occur. Stella was standing between Peter and the exit, sipping a glass of wine.

'Are you going to be able to drive home, Peter?' she asked as he staggered past.

'I don't have to go far,' he slurred as he adjusted his jacket. 'The old Stag runs on auto pilot.'

'I could drop you home.'

'I'm going to be fine. Right as…pain. I mean rain.'

'I wanted to catch you before you left. I wanted to tell you how much you meant to Bob. He looked on you like a son.' She took a deep breath. 'He told me how much you reminded him of himself.'

'I'm honoured,' Peter returned. 'I wish I'd known more…About you and Bob.'

She drew breath. 'And in case you're wondering, I'm going home after this.'

'Aren't we all?'

'No. I'm going home. To New York. I can't see any reason to stay.'

'But the story?'

'I'll leave you my notes and my number. Call me if you need a hand.' She paused. 'You'll do just fine without me. I need to get out of here. I can't breathe now that Bob's…'

Peter was drunk enough to be inappropriate, but he wasn't quite drunk enough not to feel uncomfortable.

'I'm sorry,' Peter muttered as he placed a hand on Stella's shoulder.

Stella put down her glass. 'You should go home. Life's a drama isn't it, Peter? And it doesn't even make the papers.'

***

Peter lurched back to the Stag, which he vaguely recalled having parked in a laneway near the social club. *Not so drunk, see?* The Stag was exactly where he remembered. Forget the ten minutes that he had wasted going up and down Trenerry Crescent. He was hoping that any cops on tonight were Collingwood fans or he could be in a pickle. The Stag wouldn't let him down. Just drive via the back streets and don't drive like an old man. Look confident.

He leant against the car fumbling through his pockets for the keys. *Found them.* But before he was going anywhere he needed a piss. A well-earned one. He walked part way up the laneway, took a look around, took position near a brick wall and undid his fly. He immediately felt relaxed as his stream flowed and flowed. *Zen.*

Shit! The sting of a hand pushing his head into the wall. Peter's immediate reaction was to cover his exposed genitals. Then he realised. He was still pissing and he was pissing on his hands. He tried to move. A sharp punch to the lumbar region. He froze. A gloved hand pushed his face hard against the brick wall. The wall smelt musty and damp. Thankfully the peeing soon stopped.

'Don't move and don't talk,' a muffled growl came from behind him. Peter could hear boots scraping on the cobblestones. The voice was gruff, as if disguised. 'You really stuffed up,' the man continued. 'I gave those photos to Stella, then she leaves and you take over. A bloody pity. She knew what she was doing. You haven't got a clue.'

Peter tried to move his mouth to speak.

'I said don't talk, Clancy. You useless prick.'

Peter felt his head being pressed so hard against the wall that he thought he'd either crack the bricks or crack his skull. It was Stella's informant. It had to be.

'You gave those photos to McCracken. You stupid bastard! Don't you know McCracken and Donarto set up their own operation with an overseas crime boss? I thought you would have worked that out by now.'

Peter tried to give a muffled reply but he couldn't move his mouth.

'They wanted the O'Leary's turf and now they have it. But for you, it's getting personal. So pull your act together. You could be on the slab next.'

Peter attempted to turn his head.

'Don't turn around. I'll be in touch.'

The hand pulled away from his neck and heavy boots ran up the laneway to the street. Peter caught a quick glimpse of a man in the shadows. Tall and dressed in dark clothing. He couldn't improve on the description. Then the man was gone.

Peter looked down at his sodden pants and realised he would have to drive home like that or minus his pants and underwear. Peter chose the second option and prayed desperately that he wouldn't be pulled over.

***

At work, Peter was the cause célèbre. At least for a week. He was the journalist who took gonzo to the limit. Hunter S Thompson would have been proud. Television current affair programs and newspapers wanted to interview him. Only Ilmo remained unconvinced. He described Peter's approach to newsgathering as reckless and bordering on guerrilla tactics. Maybe Ilmo was sore that Peter had knocked him back for an exclusive interview. And a new term was coined. Guerrilla journalism. Blah, blah. Peter wasn't interested. If he could be nominated for a Walkley Award he'd be happy. If he could get a free season ticket for every Collingwood game, even better. Free drinks at the Tote for a day. Already done, my son.

The pub moved very quickly to honour one of its most famous patrons and biggest investors. Free drinks for Peter all day. He was found legless and curled up near the jukebox singing 'Black Night' at four o'clock in the afternoon. Ah, the heavy price of fame. Sam had been nominated for a bravery award, which he had promptly refused. Tommy O'Leary was going to live, albeit confined to a wheelchair and in one of Her Majesty's facilities. It could have been worse for Tommy. He might have been stuck in that same wheelchair in a nursing home stinking of urine with nothing but a bunch of old dears for company. And a sad end to the week; Babs had been buried with little fanfare or fuss. Sam had attended. Buddy Bell had been absent.

Peter tried to talk to Sam about Babs, but Sam shut him down straight away. He could see Sam was grieving in his own way, but that was how blackfellas were. Once someone had died, they were forbidden to speak of them again. They couldn't even say their names, Peter knew that. Meanwhile, Peter heard on the grapevine that Buddy had been released from custody and had promptly disappeared into the ether. Gone.

Not to be outdone, Concheetah and Ted had thrown a costume party at the Velour Lounge. Nothing too decadent, Peter had been warned. Sam and Dave went dressed as cowboys and Peter as a rock star. Very sedate. The other guests were far more innovative. Peter had expected a heavy element of Melbourne's quirky, underground community to attend and he was so very right.

Concheetah's party was a steroid-injected combination of Fellini movie, Village People video and Roman orgy. It was champagne, cocaine, feather boas and leather. Dave stood bug-eyed next to the door and Sam leaned against the wall, his hat pulled over his face. They lasted half an hour before ducking for the exit but Peter remained. He couldn't leave. He was the special guest. Peter made a mental note: if he woke up in Concheetah's bed then something had gone very wrong.

The night ebbed away in a boozy haze. Peter was called to the stage by Concheetah to cut a cake shaped like an erect penis. He swore he felt a pain in his groin as he sliced into it. Then he waltzed with Concheetah. Kissed unexpectedly on the mouth by Her Highness. And yes, it did still feel like being kissed by a man. Ted, dressed in lederhosen on the bar, tapped his drunken heart out to a Judy Garland song and feigned collapse at the end. After that it was all a blur. Again.

Peter woke in a bed that wasn't his own, an enormous portrait of Concheetah gazing seductively down on him. He quickly checked under the sheets. Fully clothed. He was on a fold-out bed in the lounge. *Thank God. I like you Concheetah, but you're a mate.* That thought still in his mind, Concheetah in full regalia was standing over him, pressing a cup of espresso into his shaky hand. Peter looked at her with a sense of wonderment. *Doesn't Concheetah ever just want to kick back, slip off the wig and make-up and wear a T-shirt and shorts? Become Colin every now and again?* Obviously not. He sipped his coffee as his head throbbed, while Concheetah reassured him that he hadn't done anything to disgrace himself. *Was that a wink?* He gulped his coffee, saying he had to be at the office in a hurry. All this fame was getting too much, he thought as he dashed down the stairs of Concheetah's apartment block. He had to reel it in fast. *The liver may collapse.* He had always longed to live the life of an English rocker but…He did actually hope to live longer than John Bonham. No, he didn't want to die by inhaling his own vomit. Yes, it did only take him a week to realise that.

Fame-week over, Peter was knuckling down at the word processor again. He had really missed it. Normality was underrated. Strong coffee on the desk, piles of growing papers, a half-eaten breakfast bagel sitting in the in tray, the smell of cigarette smoke in the air. Comfort. At least for a few minutes. He thought briefly about Stella and wondered how she was. Then he thought about Poppy.

Peter had rung Poppy's flat as well as her office several times over the last week. Probably too many. And no answer. He contemplated going to her flat after work but he didn't want to look like a love-struck stalker. He would just try to run into her again at that coffee shop. That was more his style. He assumed Poppy feared he would continue prying and he'd uncover all the masks she was wearing. *That's my job. Professional prier. I'll find all your secrets eventually.* No, he just wanted to be with her. And the sex. A week seemed like a very long time. Bugger it, he was going to her place tonight. *Just tell me where I stand, Pretty Poppy.*

Apart from the lustful itch emanating from his groin, Peter's other pain-in-the-arse was the bloke filling in for Bob. Bill Symes. *Nice bloke but such a dithering, vacillating fuck. I'm not upset about it. Okay. Possibly.* A tiny piece of Peter had relished the thought of being asked to step in temporarily as editor, but the Owner hadn't even approached him. Bill was trying to fill Bob's giant shoes with his tottering baby feet. According to the Owner's message, delivered from afar to Bill, the circulation figures had sharply increased since Peter's crime investigation column. It was Carry On Truth, of sorts. Via Bill the intermediary, the Owners said that they would like a bigger dose of sleaze added to Peter's stories. It was *The Truth*, after all. As if violent crime wasn't enough, Peter had to discover that that the violent crim was some sex romping, kinky killer. The kinky killer. *Actually, I could use that,* Peter thought as he scribbled it into his tattered notepad.

He glanced up from the processor to look down to the editor's office. Bob's name had been removed and replaced with Bill Symes's. *Sounds like an accountant.* Bill didn't even smoke or drink. How could he take over? Peter hadn't stepped into that office since Bob had died. He didn't know if he would be able to again. But Bob would have wanted him to carry on. He could feel Bob standing beside him, admonishing him for still fucking whingeing and telling him to stop dropping his bundle. There was a story to get out. *Thanks, Bobby boy. Over it.*

He flipped over a new page of his notepad and wrote down every word he could remember from the lane encounter with the dark stranger. Donarto, McCracken, overseas crime boss. *Yes, should have dug more there.* The colony of smelly rats was larger than he thought. And the other keyword: It's personal. What did the stranger mean? Personal? He was as far removed from being chummy with Donarto and McCracken as a rabbi was from a Nazi. Peter scribbled in large letters. *Dark stranger. Who would want to feed information to the media? Who would want to keep their identity a secret? Connecting the dots. Someone from another criminal organisation? No. They would just kill them. What if it's a whistle blower from within the police who's too afraid to go to their superiors? My God!* The O'Leary story was only part one. *This could spawn sequels, like Rocky. But where to from here?* Peter shut the notepad and leant back on his chair, staring at the ceiling. Connect the dots.

He was still mulling it over when the telephone rang. It was Sam. 'Dave and me, we're going to a stereo shop,' he announced.

'I didn't know you wanted a stereo,' Peter replied.

'I don't,' Sam continued.' But I want to go to a stereo shop.'

'Just browsing?'

'In a sense.'

'You're coming with us,' Sam said.

'Not this again,' Peter shook his head. 'Where are you?'

'In reception. Shazza said you didn't want visitors, so she let me use her phone. Come on. Stop mucking around,' Sam growled. 'Meet us outside in two minutes. We haven't got all day.'

Peter put down the receiver, grabbed his jacket and slowly complied.

Dave was standing by the reception desk. 'We're taking another car, by the way. Yours looks too obvious. We'll take Shazza's.'

＊＊＊

Dave pulled up a couple of shops short of the Sounds Alive Stereo Shop in Coburg, did a U-turn and parked Shazza's Ford on the other side of the road. Peter, in the rear seat, lay back and waited.

'That must be the most nondescript stereo shop I've ever seen. Looks dead rather than alive,' Peter remarked. The shop looked like it had been converted from something else. There were a couple of speakers on display, posters stuck to the window and nothing else. 'Looks like business isn't great. Are you sure you want to go in there? There would be better places selling stereos.'

'Here.' Sam handed Peter a leaflet.

Peter had a quick glance at it. 'This doesn't say anything. They don't advertise very well.'

'Babs mentioned a stereo shop we had to drive to in Coburg that night,' Sam explained, 'and I found this on the floor of her car.'

'Do you think this is where you had to deliver the heroin?' Peter frowned as he took a closer look at the shop. 'You're joking. I think Babs was having you on. Why would you want to run a drug organisation out of there?'

'We could go in and check it out,' Sam suggested as he opened his door. 'We're after a bargain, right, Dave?'

'I'll come along for a laugh,' Peter swung open his door.

'Stay here, young fella,' Sam ordered. 'We don't want to be recognised. Keep the engine running in case we need to get out in a hurry.'

Dave and Sam stepped through the front door of the shop and looked about cautiously. Stereo equipment of various kinds and in all stages of assembly lined the shelves. A large poster stuck on the back wall announced that the Sounds Alive Stereo Shop had the best prices in Melbourne. Beneath that was the counter, which had various stereo accessories inside its glass display. Disco music blared from a stereo unit that had flashing red and green lights on the speakers.

'Looks like there's no one around,' Sam commented as they continued to browse around the shop.

'Maybe out the back,' Dave said as he noticed a door with *No Entry* on it. 'Maybe they're up to other stuff.'

Sam was drawn to the disco unit with the lights that pulsated to the beat of the music. 'I like that,' he said as he turned the buttons. 'I wonder how it would play some country music?'

'It looks like a metal safe with buttons and dials.' Dave examined it up close. 'Strange writing. Russian or something?'

Sam turned the volume up to an ear splitting level until the shop was reverberating to the sound of Donna Summer.

'Sam,' Dave growled as he turned down the volume, 'you'll attract attention.'

'That's the idea.'

The back door opened and a man resembling an Eastern bloc wrestler squeezed through the doorway and lumbered towards Sam and Dave. He was attired entirely in black from his bulbous neck to his feet.

'You like?' the man grunted. His accent sounded like a slap in the face. 'If you like the disco beat, you'll go big time for this baby.'

Sam twisted around to see the man's face, as scarred and pitted as an old male cattle dog's. 'You're as big as Arnie Schwarzenegger. Sound like him, too.'

'No. I'm Russian,' the man puffed out his chest. 'He pussy. I'm Dimitry, former Soviet weight-lifter, now stereo salesman. I'm real Aussie, Aussie, Aussie.' He laughed like a bellowing bull in rut. 'Oi, oi, oi!'

Dave said, 'It's a solid unit,' as he patted the metal frame. 'That wouldn't break at a party.'

'We also have German stereo, but these better. Imported direct from Russia,' Dimitry replied. 'A factory in Moscow makes them. When they're not making tractors and trucks, they make stereo. Has tubes instead of transistors. Much better sound. You listen.' He pulled a CD from the side pocket of his leather jacket and slipped it into the stereo. He turned up the volume.

'You listen!'

A blood-curdling scream blasted out of the metal, light emitting speakers. Dimitry moved to the beat. Sam and Dave covered their ears as the whole shop seemed to shake.

'Deep Purple,' Dimitry bellowed as he nodded his huge head up and down. 'Greatest band on earth. I see them when they came here a few years ago. Best day of my life. Very popular in Russia.'

Even above the wall of sound, a male voice could be heard yelling in Russian from behind the counter. Dimitry quickly turned down the volume. A diminutive man with a shaved head stood with his hands on his hips. Content with the noise level, the man returned back through the curtain screen.

'My boss,' Dimitry said with a hangdog look. 'He like Donna Summer and Bee Gees. No like Deep Purple.'

'That's a shame,' Sam remarked as he removed his fingers from his ears. 'That music might be good for scaring away intruders.'

'Good,' Dimitry slapped Sam on the back. Sam grabbed hold of the display cabinet with one hand to stop himself falling. 'You understand me. Are you interested in buying?'

'Can we think about it?' Dave ventured. 'Just looking at the moment.'

'Can we let you know?' Sam added.

'We only open certain times,' Dimitry responded. 'We are very exclusive. You come back on Friday and ask for Dimitry. Okkie dokkie? I give you best price, mate.' Dimitry watched them leave the shop, a look of regret on this face.

'That was an…experience,' said Sam.' I think I'm deaf in my left ear.'

'It'll come back,' Dave replied. 'What do you think?'

Sam tilted his head to hear. 'Of the stereos?'

'No,' Dave said louder, 'of the whole setup?'

'Looks like they couldn't run a twenty-first in a brewery,' Sam remarked. 'What are Russians doing in Australia anyway?'

Dave shrugged. 'You'd probably find Eskimos selling ice-creams if you looked hard enough.'

'Let's have a look around the back.' Sam walked down a lane that connected the back of the shops to the side-street, Dave following close behind.

'Interesting,' Sam said, noticing the large metal shed attached to the back of the shop. 'Looks like a factory out here. They must stock a lot of Russian stereos.'

'Look at the fencing. That's razor wire running along the top of it. It would cut you to ribbons if you climbed over that. And the flood lights.'

'The Russians like their security,' Sam observed. 'Or they've got something to hide.'

'We have company.'

They had attracted the attention of two Rottweilers. One charged the fence, biting the wire mesh in its frustration. A voice yelled at the dogs, which spun around and galloped back to the shed.

'Let's go before the Russians come out,' said Dave.

'They must have good quality stereos,' Sam grinned as he took a final look at the security fence.

Peter was lying across the back seat snoozing when Sam and Dave returned to the car. He woke with a start when Sam slammed his door shut.

'Sorry to wake you, young fella,' Sam laughed. 'Is that woman of yours wearing you out?'

'Not really,' Peter yawned as he sat up. 'I haven't seen her since the funeral. What did you discover, Starsky and Hutch?'

'The Russians sell lousy stereos. We never had the chance to see the German ones,' Dave commented as he started the motor and slipped the car into first gear.

'Russians?'

'Yeah,' Dave replied. 'Vodka, caviar, stereos you could drive a tank over.'

'Do you think they could be selling the heroin?' Peter asked.

'Not too sure,' Sam said.

'The bloke reckons he's a former Soviet weight-lifter but he's not much of a salesman. You'd probably like him, though. The guy is a Deep Purple fan.'

'The man has excellent taste.'

'That's what you call it?' Sam added. 'Having your eardrums shattered is taste? Give me Tammy Wynette, Merle Haggard or Slim Dusty any day.'

'A few Russians have defected here over the years. Usually athletes. Nothing unusual,' Peter continued as he stretched out his arms. 'They'd have to sell a few stereos to pay the rent.'

'What about all the security?' Sam questioned. 'Razor wire, guard dogs, spotlights.'

'Not too sure about that,' said Dave. 'Looks excessive to me.'

Peter shrugged. 'There may be a lot of break-ins in the area.'

'You think we're wasting our time, don't you?' Sam asked.

'Babs wasn't actually credible. She sold marijuana off her front porch.'

'You didn't really know her,' Sam bristled. 'She just wanted a better start in life.'

'And pinching heroin and selling it to people was going to improve her life and better the lives of those she sold it to? Wake up, Sam.'

'You think this Poppy girl is the ant's pants,' Sam fumed. 'Big time lawyer. Good looking. I didn't think you liked those sort of girls.'

'I enjoy her company. She's different. I like that.'

'I've met her type before,' said Sam. 'You look at them and they're not what they seem. Thornydevils, I call them.'

'What the hell are you talking about? You hardly know her and when you've been around her you've always been rude to her. Thornydevils?'

'Yep. They camouflage themselves when necessary and they have spikes.'

'Is this some ancient Aboriginal ancestor story passed from the dreamtime?' Peter sat back again, shaking his head.

'Show some respect, young fella. Nothing to do with that,' Sam replied. 'I've been around a long time. I know a lot about cattle and I know a lot about people. I watch. I learn. And I'm not saying any more about it because now you're jumping up and down like when you were a kid. You bloody work it out. I'm done.'

'She's fine Sam,' Peter softened. 'She's just a little mixed up. Aren't we all?' He always found it difficult to be angry at Sam. Always. It was like arguing with your grandfather. 'She's a little mixed up but I really like her. I'm hoping she'll see me again. I'm big enough to work it out. And I'm sorry about insulting Babs.' He reached over the seat and patted Sam on the shoulder.

'It's all right. Family don't need to fight,' Sam said.

'That's good,' Dave sighed with relief. 'We have to all pull together. So what's next?'

'I forgot to tell you,' Peter said. 'After Bob's funeral, I had a visit from the bloke who gave Stella those photos.'

'I don't want to see any more crook photos. Please,' Sam begged. 'I thought doing it on a beach was daring.'

'You're lucky, Sam. He didn't give me any this time. No photographs, but he did give me some information. He reckons that Donarto and McCracken are involved in a heroin importation business.' He paused for a moment. 'I had a feeling that Donarto was dirty and McCracken was just enjoying the benefits, but it never occurred to me he had an active involvement.'

'Did he give you any evidence to prove his allegations?' Dave enquired.

'The O'Learys were the competition and now they're not. He said he would be in touch.'

'That's a bloody bugger,' Sam commented. 'You reckon he's legit?'

'Well, he mentioned Stella,' Peter continued, 'and he was really anxious about protecting his identity. 'I think he's an insider, a whistle-blower from within the police force. He doesn't trust anyone from within, and he's so desperate that he's come to us.'

'You couldn't identify him?' Dave asked.

'A tall man wearing a mask. He had heavy boots on and had an Australian accent.'

'If he is the only source, we play the waiting game,' said Dave.

'Have we got time to wait?' Sam sighed.

The waiting game. Ensconced in the Stag at six o'clock on a chilly Melbourne winter evening. *Here I am parked in front of Poppy's apartment block waiting like a lovesick schoolboy. And I've even bought flowers, albeit from a supermarket, but still flowers. Crazy.*

He toyed with buying a box of chocolates but family favourites probably wouldn't cut it in the romance department. *What's happening, Clancy? What's overpowered me? I've never waited for a woman, nor bought flowers before, not even for funerals.* He had to know where he stood. He grabbed a tattered picnic blanket from under the seat and wrapped himself in it. He wound back the car seat and went into waiting position.

Peter fell into a light sleep, only barely aware that the blanket smelt like stale food and spilt wine. Comforting smells, but he couldn't remember the last time he had spilt something on it. The only thing missing was the thermos of coffee. In his haste to get rid of Sam and Dave he hadn't prepared his hot drink.

He had slept in the Stag many times, casing out places, sleeping off a drinking bout, or after misplacing the keys to his flat. The leather seats were as comfortable as a bed. Maybe he should sleep in the Stag more often. If he could install a coffee machine and a small fridge he would be set. Peter was toying with that idea in his dreams when he was awoken by the grumble of Poppy's sports car easing into the driveway beside the Stag. He quickly threw off the blanket, pulled the seat up and leapt out of the car, hoping he looked nonchalant rather than desperate.

Poppy saw him and smiled. 'I've been looking for you,' she said as she rushed from her car and planted a kiss on his lips. They clung to each other, searching out each other's mouths over and over.

She was radiant, beautiful. She could have worn a hessian sack and still looked ravishing. 'Me too,' Peter replied, reluctantly breaking away. 'I've been ringing your office, hanging around that coffee shop. Now I'm parked like a stalker in front of your flat. You can call the police, but I had to see you. I didn't know what really happened the other day so I was worried. I've really missed you. Really have.'

'The funeral brought back some bad childhood memories,' she replied. 'It was silly of me. I'm sorry if I caused you any pain. Then I thought you'd think I'm crazy and you'd want to avoid me.'

Peter smiled. 'You don't have to ever feel embarrassed or crazy around me. That's what I love about you. You're beautifully different.'

'Love?' she smiled. 'You mentioned love?'

'I was just waiting for the right time to say it,' he admitted, 'and now it's arrived.'

'So what are we going to do about it? I was scared you might just hang around for the sex. I want more than that.'

'I love fucking you, of course,' he murmured, 'but I also want to be with you. I want to do everything with you. I want to go places with you. I want to cry and laugh with you.'

She seemed pleased. 'No one I've ever met has been as eloquent as you.' She looked at him. 'Those eyes of yours!' she shuddered. 'You remember how I said I was going to make it up to you?'

'Remember? I haven't been able to stop thinking about it.'

'I have a weekend retreat in the Yarra Valley. It's in the bush and very secluded,' she whispered into Peter's ear. 'Very few people know about it.'

'You never told me about a retreat.'

'I had to be certain you'd understand,' she traced his lips with her index finger. 'You grew up in the bush, didn't you? You're going to love it. No phones, no television, a fireplace, some cattle in the paddock you can play with. Total peace. And no interruptions. We can fuck all day and night. Eat, drink wine, pat the cattle and fuck,' she cooed.

'I've missed the bush, it's true. Getting back to nature,' Peter said as he ran his hands over her breasts.

'Control yourself, mister!' she laughed as she looked around. 'Let's not titillate the South Yarra set for free.'

'So, you'd prefer to go inside and get warm?' Peter suggested as he raised one eyebrow.

'Better than that,' Poppy replied. 'How about we go to the farm tonight?'

'Tonight? What about work tomorrow?' he asked.

'Bugger work. Where we're going, work doesn't exist.'

'All right,' he responded, 'on one proviso.'

'You want to pack clothes? I wouldn't be too worried about clothes.'

'We drop by my place so I can get my toothbrush, at least.'

'Done. You go home and I'll pack a few things.' She kissed Peter on the cheek. 'Then I'll come past your flat and we'll go in my car. You can fondle me all the way to the Yarra Valley.'

29

Dave stopped the Ford under a tree in the street adjacent to the lane behind the stereo shop. 'I hope you're right about this, Sam,' he remarked as he switched off the ignition and leaned across the back seat to grab his camera bag. 'I think we're wasting our time, myself.'

'Why do you guys always doubt my hunches?' Sam shook his head as he slipped off his seatbelt. 'I have a feeling about this. I feel it in my gut. Call me crazy, I don't care.' Sam gestured out of the window toward two men standing chatting near the shed while the guard dogs patrolled the security fence. 'They're working late.'

'As I said, they're big on security. Those German stereo units are worth a bundle.'

'Looks like they're settling in for the night,' Sam commented as he continued to observe the two men.

'I hope we're not,' Dave wrapped his arms around himself for warmth. 'It's bloody cold. Peter was right to leave work early. This is when I miss living up north.'

'Did he tell you where he was going?' Sam asked.

'He had an interview or something,' Dave shrugged. 'He doesn't tell me much.'

'I bet he was going to find Poppy.'

'Another hunch?' Dave joked as he lowered his seat.

'It's the secret Aboriginal ways. You wouldn't understand being a white fella,' Sam joked.

'Ever thought of becoming a private detective? You could solve crimes by hunches.'

'Yeah. You and I could become a team. Starsky and Hunch,' Sam laughed.

'Very funny, Sam, but it isn't making me any warmer.' Dave closed his eyes.

'Don't you go to sleep on me.'

'Never,' said Dave.

'Wake up!' Sam poked Dave a few minutes later.

'What now?' Dave asked.

Sam pointed to a truck that had pulled up to the security gate. One of the men ran to the gate and unlocked a chain to let the truck in.

Dave watched the truck reverse up to an open door of the shed. Then he lay back down again. 'So?' Dave yawned. 'That's a delivery truck. Delivering stereos I guess. That's how the business works. Stereos come in and they go out to the customers. It's called business.'

'Maybe I'm wrong,' Sam admitted. 'Maybe it's just a normal business.'

'We'll give it five more minutes then we're going,' Dave checked his wristwatch. He had just closed his eyes again when Sam shook him.

'Wake up! They're here.'

'Who? What?' Dave murmured. He inched up in his seat and moved his gaze towards the shed.

'It's them isn't it?'

'Possibly.'

Two men and a woman came out of the shed to watch the two security men remove cartons from the truck and carry them into the shed. They were clearly in a hurry.

Sam insisted, 'It's them.'

'I'll check.' Dave pushed his camera with zoom lens attached out of the open window and peered through it. He fiddled with the lens.

'Is it them?' Sam asked impatiently. 'Is it them?'

'You're right, Sam,' Dave replied as he lowered the camera. 'You're right. It's McCracken, Donarto and…' He paused. 'Poppy. They look pretty concerned about that shipment of stereos. But I think it's more than stereos.' He took a deep breath. 'What's Poppy doing there?'

'My hunch was right,' Sam smiled. 'We have to tell Peter right away. I knew that bloody girlfriend of his was crook.'

Dave held the camera up to his face again. 'I'll get a photo of them. I'll use a long exposure. Hope I won't need a flash,' Dave stated as he adjusted the camera. 'And there's that bald bloke from the shop who yelled at the salesman. He's come into the picture.'

'Get the photo,' urged Sam. 'We have to tell Peter right away.'

'Okay. Closer. Closer for the group photo. Gotcha!' Dave clicked off a series of shots then threw the camera into the back seat. 'Quick. The bald bloke might have noticed us. He's looking this way. Buckle up.'

Dave started the car and moved away slowly as the bald man kept watching. He didn't want to display any urgency.

'There doesn't seem to be anyone following us,' Sam commented as he turned around to look out of the rear window.

'Good,' Dave exhaled. 'We were lucky there.'

'We've got to get to Peter,' Sam said. 'He said something about missing Poppy. Do you know where she lives?'

'Not a clue,' Dave replied. 'All he's ever told me is that she lives in South Yarra.'

'Bloody great. We better get back to his flat. He could be home.'

'Yeah, all right. It's as good a place to start looking as anywhere, I suppose.' Dave was turning towards Bell Street when the Ford began to splutter. 'What the?' he muttered. The engine cut out and the Ford coasted to a stop.

'Sounds like maybe you ran out of petrol,' suggested Sam.

'No, the gauge shows three-quarters full.' Dave flicked it with his finger. It dropped to E and stayed there. 'Shit!'

'I saw a petrol station about a mile or so back,' said Sam. 'We'll have to walk there.'

'What about Peter?'

'He'll just have to be cautious until we find him. You think his life's in danger?' he asked.

'Peter's life is always in danger.'

It was an hour before Dave stopped the Ford in front of Peter's flat. Sam hurried to the laneway where Peter usually parked the Stag and was buoyed to see it in position. He signalled Dave to stay in the Ford while he checked the flat. He took the key from under the mat and went in. Peter wasn't there. Apart from a jumble of clothes on the bed, nothing had been touched.

'He's not home. Bloody hell,' Sam puffed as he got back into the Ford.

'We're stumped,' Dave stated. 'I don't know where else to turn.'

'Stupid bugger should have stuck to the sleaze stories. This sort of stuff can get you killed.'

'We could wait,' Dave suggested. 'Or go to the Tote? Or he might have popped out.' He was still thinking when the door to the Apollo Café slid open and Con emerged, wearing an apron and gloves, and approached the car. Sam wound down his window.

'You looking for Peter?' Con asked as he removed the gloves.

'Sure are.'

Con leaned against the car door. 'I was cleaning the shop when Peter's girlfriend, Popitsa, pull up.'

'You mean Poppy,' Dave corrected.

'Yes, her,' Con continued. 'She pull up here in a beautiful sport car and Peter come down. I come outside to look at the car. I say hello to Poppy and she say nothing, like she never seen me before. Anyway, Peter gets in her car. He carry a bag.'

'Did he say where they were going?' Dave asked urgently.

'He was very happy. He joke that he was going away to get filthy on the weekend, but I don't understand. Is not the weekend. He was happy to go away to work?'

'Did he say a dirty weekend, maybe?'

'Maybe.'

'Did he tell you where he was going? Any address?'

'He said they go away to Poppy's farm.'

'Yes, but where? Did he tell you where, Con?' asked Dave.

'No, I don't think so.'

Sam's face fell. He began to wind up the window.

'No, wait,' said Con. 'I remember. I remember now, because I go there once to buy some grapes to make my special wine. He said they go to the Yarra Valley.'

'That's it?' Dave asked.

'The Yarra Valley. Yes,' Con answered.

'What now?' Sam asked Dave.

'We're stumped again. Maybe it's in the phone book.'

'We can check.'

'Is everything okay?' Con asked, 'This filthy work, is dangerous?'

'This dirty weekend could be, Con.'

30

'This is the life of decadence,' Peter stretched his naked frame out on a rug between Poppy and a blazing log fire. He took a drink from the wine glass that he had perched on the coffee table. After returning it, he caressed Poppy's face. She lay on her back with her eyes closed.

'Drinking wine. Lying next to a beautiful woman on a rug. A fire to keep our naked bodies warm. I'm about to make love. Does life get any better than this?'

'Are you just going to talk about it or are you going to do something about it?' She took hold of Peter's neck with both hands and pulled him towards her. 'Or maybe you get off just writing about sleaze and sex.' She kissed him briefly on the mouth and felt for his erection. 'Practise what you preach, mister.' She began to stroke him.

'That's so nice. I really don't fucking know or care,' Peter moaned. 'So good with your hands.'

'Do you get that hard when you write your salacious stories?' She smiled as she continued to stroke him. 'Writing about sex all day must keep you aroused. Must be embarrassing to have an erection while you're working.'

'Only when I did a story about drug crazed prostitutes,' he joked, pulling away. 'They turn me on so much. I couldn't leave the typewriter alone for hours.'

'Sick, sick man,' Poppy playfully smacked Peter on the face. 'You talk too much. How about helping yourself to my body, you filthy man?' She lay back on the rug and parted her legs. 'Help yourself,' she whispered. 'I'm yours.'

'Don't you want to take charge and tie me down? I may lose control of myself.'

'I'm giving you permission,' Poppy said as she stroked herself. 'I want you to take me. I'm your present. Au naturel. You're in control now.'

'I want you so much it hurts.' He eased himself on top of Poppy and pushed her legs wider apart. She gasped as he entered her.

'Fuck me hard, Peter. Fuck me,' Poppy cried. 'Fuck me!'

Peter closed his eyes and slid slowly in and out of her, varying the pace and rhythm, conscious that he didn't want to orgasm or have Poppy orgasm for as long as possible. Poppy's cries grew louder, as if she was going to climax. *Not now. Let's come together. How intense will that be. Now that would be a petite mort.* 'You're so beautiful Poppy,' he murmured, elevated to another level of pleasure. 'I want you so much. I lo…' He looked into Poppy's face. Her eyes were wide open as she moaned and cried. She seemed to be looking in the distance, at something on the ceiling. She was somewhere else. 'You okay?' Peter asked as he slowed his thrusts.

'I was…I was…dreaming of doing this forever,' she stammered as she shut her eyes and held tightly onto his shoulders.

***

'So you want to report that your friend's in danger?' the police officer yawned as he leant across the counter at the Russell Street Police Headquarters to fix a closer gaze on Dave and then Sam. He was a grizzled, middle-aged man and had probably last looked concerned many years ago. They had finally got to see a police officer after waiting for sixty crucial minutes. It wasn't too long before they felt they were wasting their time. It was etched all over the face of Sergeant Hausler. There was a steady stream of characters, lowlife and oddballs in and out. Uniformed police and detectives rushed about, shuffling papers, looking busy, interviewing criminals and victims of crime at their desks. It looked like it operated on chaos theory.

'We think his life's in danger,' Dave exclaimed. 'He's missing.'

'Let me see if I've got it straight. The last time you heard anything about him was tonight when he was going away on a weekend with his girlfriend.'

'Yes.'

'Okay,' Sergeant Hausler straightened up and took a deep breath, 'this Peter Clancy went away with his girlfriend. How the bloody hell is he in danger? You know who he has gone with and you know roughly where's he's gone. So he hasn't gone missing. I wouldn't bloody mind going missing like that. The missus might get upset about it, though,' he chuckled.

'Peter Clancy is a journalist at *The Truth*,' Dave explained. 'He uncovered a drug importation business while doing one of his stories. There are some big players in it. He doesn't know it, but the girl he's been seeing, Poppy Reynolds, is involved. She could be taking him away to have him killed.'

'Peter Clancy,' Sergeant Hausler scratched his chin. 'I've heard of him. Sounds like one of those bloody journalists who can't keep his nose out of trouble.'

'His life is at risk,' Dave pleaded. 'You've got to believe us. I was a cop up in Queensland for ten years. I know what I'm talking about.'

'Not what I've heard,' Sergeant Hausler laughed. 'It sounds like the Keystone bloody Cops up there.'

'Can you do anything?' Sam asked. 'Or are we wasting our time?'

'Well, you can fill out a form.' Sergeant Hausler shoved a form in Sam's direction.' And if you haven't heard from Mister Clancy in a day or two, we'll go and have a look for him. How about that?'

'Great,' Dave grabbed the form. 'He could be lying cold in a shallow grave by then.'

'Well, the quicker you fill out the form the sooner we can look for him. Next.'

'Why even bloody bother,' Sam grumbled. 'Cops never listen.'

'We could get *The Truth* to print that Peter is missing,' Dave suggested. 'Someone might see it out there and ring the cops.'

'That won't happen until tomorrow.'

'I don't know what else to do.'

'Let's go home,' Sam said. 'We have to hope that he'll be all right and we've overreacted.'

They headed to the door dodging a young man with a torn, bloodied shirt, accompanied by his crying girlfriend. They burst through the door and rushed to the counter.

'Help,' the girl screamed as she held on to her boyfriend's arm, 'me boyfriend's been assaulted.'

'Take him to an emergency department, miss,' Sergeant Hausler said dryly from behind the counter. 'This isn't a hospital.'

'You've got to help him,' the girlfriend pleaded.

'You'll have to wait,' Hausler replied.

'Fuck this. Useless copper pricks,' the girlfriend yelled as she pulled her dazed boyfriend around and headed back through the exit door.

'Another happy customer?' Sam chuckled. They headed for the same door but stopped in their tracks when a familiar name was announced.

'Peter Clancy?' a deep, only barely female voice called behind them. Sam and Dave turned in near unison to see a tall, well-built woman. She appeared to be in her thirties.

'We're his friends, Sam Clancy and Dave Tindall. Do you know Peter?' Dave asked.

'I know all of you.' Dave looked startled. 'The docks? Who'd you reckon sorted out most of the paperwork? I'm Viv Jenner,' the woman said as she held up her badge. 'Detective Jenner.'

'You don't look like a copper,' Sam observed as he looked Jenner up and down. 'You don't look male enough.'

'Yeah? I hear that a lot,' Jenner grinned slightly. 'I may be able to help you with your friend Peter Clancy.'

'You can?' Dave said. 'We were ready to give up.'

'Follow me.' Jenner gestured for them to follow her out of the front door.

'Don't you want to talk to us in an interview room?' Dave queried as they walked up the road and turned into Mackenzie Street.

'More comfortable in my car,' Jenner replied as she walked briskly towards a Ford Falcon. She opened the driver's door, hopped in then unlocked the doors, telling the men to get in. She turned on the heater and rubbed her hands. 'Sorry about this,' she said. 'We'll be able to speak more freely out here. Hopefully this heater should kick in soon.'

'We're trying to find Peter. I don't know if we have a lot of time. He went away with his girlfriend, Poppy Reynolds, tonight,' Dave interjected. 'Maybe you've heard of her?'

'We think his life is in danger,' Sam added as he leaned between the bucket seats. 'Seems that Poppy Reynolds is involved in importing drugs with some crim blokes. Peter doesn't know it. Dave and I saw something fishy going on tonight at a stereo shop in Coburg.'

'You mean Sounds Alive?' said Jenner. Sam nodded.

Right,' she continued, picking her words carefully. 'I can't say very much, but I think you might have stumbled across something.' She turned down the heater. 'I have to be careful with what I tell you, but we've been watching the same shop.'

'I don't understand why this Poppy would get involved,' Sam pondered, 'She's got a good job and she's a looker.'

Jenner looked shrewdly at the pair. 'You asked me before if I'd heard of Poppy Reynolds. I know her. I know all about her. Poppy's pretty on the outside but she's all about reinvention. Pretty Poppy used to be a high-class hooker, straight out of a posh private school. Called herself Peach in those days. She was an escort, on the arm of whichever low-life, cashed-up hit man or minor celebrity was willing to pay a thousand for the night. Then suddenly she gave it all up to go to university and study law. Peter Clancy's a pretty boy, but I seriously doubt she'd be dating him for his looks.'

'Why haven't the police done anything about these people? They went all out to get the O'Learys,' Dave commented.

'Look, this is awkward, but I already know a bit about you two and I reckon I can trust you.' Jenner lowered her voice. 'How do I put this? There are police officers and prominent people like McCracken and Donarto involved in this and I've had to tread very carefully. I have been stalled at every turn…'

Dave frowned. 'Someone gave Stella and Peter some porno photographs, but ever since then we've been doing the heavy lifting.'

'That wasn't you,' Sam interrupted, 'who took those photos?'

'This isn't really the place or the time,' Jenner replied. 'I didn't join the police force to be a crook. All I'm prepared to say is that I'm a keen amateur photographer. Birds mostly. You get a lot of leatherheads, tits and boobys around here. If you know where to look, that is.'

Sam smiled. 'You'll help us? You'll help us find Peter?'

'I will. Do you know where Peter went with Poppy?'

'To a farm in the Yarra Valley. That's all we know,' Sam responded. 'Will that be hard to find?'

'The Yarra Valley is a pretty big area, but I think I know the place that she would go. Tony Donarto owns a weekender near Yarra Glen.'

'Well, can't you grab a few of your mates and head out there?' Sam asked.

'I'm a bit reluctant…We have to be careful.'

'We're going aren't we?' Dave enquired.

'Just us three.' Jenner turned on the ignition. She glanced at Sam's frown. 'Don't worry, if danger comes to us I'll call for reinforcements.'

'That's the plan?' Sam raised his eyebrows. 'I've been taken hostage and been shot at once already this month. Nothing against you, ma'am, but I'd prefer it didn't happen again.'

'We're wasting time. Seatbelts.' She slipped on her seat belt and reversed the car.

Dave put on his seatbelt. Sam was still fumbling to locate his. 'Hold on, mate,' said Dave. 'We'll find him, Sam.'

✳✳✳

'Let's try something different.' Poppy pushed Peter onto his back and straddled him.

'Isn't having sex in front of the fire enough?'

'That was just the entree.' She reached into her handbag.

'Not handcuffs again,' Peter pleaded, 'my wrists are still sore.'

'Not handcuffs.' She retrieved a piece of black leather, too small to be a bag too large to be a pair of gloves. 'Something better.'

He watched Poppy mould the leather with her hands to reveal its full shape. He remarked, 'Very fashionable. I saw someone wearing a leather mask like that recently. I think it was at Concheetah's party. Poor bastard could eat, no worries, but he couldn't see.'

'It's called a passion mask. A bit gothic, isn't it? It's my favourite out of my collection.'

'No doll collection for you then, hey?' Peter laughed. 'You going to put that thing on?'

'No,' Poppy replied as she stretched the mask out with her hands, 'you are. Sit still.'

She pulled it over Peter's head. It was then he noticed the lacing that ran behind the ear. Was it really at Concheetah's party? 'I don't think so, Poppy,' he said. 'I won't be able to see anything.'

'All the better for you,' Poppy teased as she continued to pull it over his head. 'Try it, you'll like it.' She did up the lacing and pulled the mask tighter. 'It heightens the other senses.'

'Not so tight,' he complained. 'I'm starting to feel like the man in the iron mask.'

'Hmm,' replied Poppy.

271

The leather mask was taut against his skin, simultaneously sensuous and scary. He tried to ignore the knot in his stomach. *A novel way to overcome claustrophobia,* he thought as he lay back on the rug. *Like at the river when I was a kid.*

Poppy lay on top on him kissing him on the mouth briefly before slithering slowly down his torso.

He started to breathe more heavily. 'Are you going to…?'

'Shush. You can never tell what I'm about to do next.'

Her fingers running gently over his penis aroused him. He tried to reach out for her as excruciating pleasure began to overwhelm him. She slapped his hands and pushed him down on his back again.

'Control yourself,' she commanded. 'You have to be patient.'

'I don't know how much more I can take,' Peter moaned. 'I can't see you. Shit, I can barely hear you. If you're going to suck my cock, do it soon. I'll explode all over the fucking lounge. It's exquisite torture. That's what it is.'

'Quiet!' she said, stroking his penis. 'You have to trust me. Trust me.'

'Oh God,' Peter whispered.

'You never stop talking do you?' she said before running her tongue up and down his penis. 'You need to be punished for talking too much. For knowing too much.'

'Yes,' Peter yelled, 'all right. Whatever you say. Punish me.' Suddenly, Poppy drew away from him. He reached for her. 'Where are you going? Don't stop. Keep going.'

'Be quiet,' she murmured. 'Calm down. Slow down all your senses. You don't want to orgasm too quickly, do you?'

'What? Come on,' he reached for her again and couldn't feel her anywhere. 'I am relaxed. I am…really.' He tried thinking of something else. Tried to slow everything down. *Thinking.* The mask was familiar. *Thinking.* He'd seen it before. *Thinking.* He lost his erection. *Oh, shit!* It wasn't at the party. *Not at Concheetah's. Fuck! It can't be! It can't be!* He knew exactly where he'd seen the mask before. In McCracken's photographs. *It must be! The girl in the photos. Poppy?*

'Poppy, don't!' Peter sat up and attempted to pull off the mask. 'Don't do this.'

No reply.

He tried to stand up, clawing at the mask. It was stuck hard on his face. He stumbled over the coffee table, shattering the wine glasses.

'Get this off me, Poppy!' He pulled himself up from the floor. 'Let's talk about this. Where are you?'

He was able to pull the mask up over his nose but it wouldn't go any further. He felt like he was drowning. Like at the river. He was going down. His hands flayed around in an effort to find a wall or piece of furniture to hold onto. He hit his head on a cupboard. He kept feeling his way around the room. He felt the heat of the fire across his bare skin. *I don't want to fall into the fucking fire. If I could get to the door. Escape. But how? Can't get this mask off. No car.*

'Poppy! Get this fucking mask off me,' Peter cried. 'Come on!' He propped himself against what felt like a post. He heard the front door opening. 'Poppy?' He held out his hands. 'Come over here. Help me. This isn't funny.'

'Not Poppy, you arsehole.' The voice was definitely not Poppy's. If Peter had to guess, he'd have placed it somewhere closer to Siberia. 'I am your nightmare.' The man grabbed Peter by one arm and flung him across the room. He felt excruciating pain in his head as it smashed against the edge of the stone fireplace. Darkness.

Peter was woken by the sound of cattle mooing. *I must be dead.* He'd always imagined that the Clancys would go to a cattle station afterlife. Peter was there. *I want to see Dad. If I'm dead, then I want Dad.* The afterlife didn't include that voice, did it? There it was again, growling in a language that he couldn't understand. Along with other voices. In Russian? He had watched the odd subtitled Russian movie during his misspent adulthood.

He had the sense that he was lying naked on wet concrete, somewhere outside. He felt for the mask and was relieved to find it gone. He slowly opened his eyes as he raised himself up onto his hands. The cattle yard was bathed in a dim glow coming from an artificial light source. A fog was drifting in, making the light even duller. A shed attached to the yard was the source of the light. Looking down he could see that he was stretched out in sloppy cow manure. *Yes, I'm really in the shit this time. Literally.*

Peter lifted himself up onto one knee, in an effort to stand. His head felt like it would explode with pain. He ran his hand over his head. He felt a large mat of dried blood congealed in his hair. He grabbed hold of the metal yard rails and pulled himself up. The metal was so cold that it stung his fingers. He surveyed the yard's construction. The top rail was at head height, which would make it difficult to climb over in a hurry. The gaps between the rails were a hand width apart. If he could summon all his strength, he might be able to climb the rails and piss off before anyone noticed.

He steadied himself enough to look around, his head still throbbing. He had to use all his willpower to stop himself from passing out from the pain shooting from temple to temple. He could hear faint noises, but the loudest sound he could hear was that of his teeth chattering. Apart from the pain in his head, he was starting to feel the bitter cold of the Yarra Valley.

Peter's naked body began to grow numb from the chill. If he didn't get something to cover himself with, he'd end up with hypothermia. The voices were coming from the shed in front of him. Now he could hear people speaking in English. Behind him were about twenty head of cattle of various ages, penned in a small yard, separated from the one he was in by a gate chained to a gnarled wooden post. He stumbled to the gate to see if he could loosen it. It was secured with a padlock. Trapped like a cow before slaughter, he thought. The cattle sniffed him with curiosity. He could smell their moist coats and feel their breath on his bare skin as he pulled at the chain. The cattle didn't shy as he continued his desperate efforts. *I love cattle. They remind me of the station.*

The chain was attached to a bolt jutting from the wooden post. He kept tugging at it and thanked God when the wood started to fracture around the bolt. He pulled hard at the chain and was able to rattle it loose. He might be able to pull the bolt straight out of the wooden post. A few more attempts. *Shit!* Peter tensed and let the chain drop from his hand. *Those Russian voices are coming. They're coming for me.*

They emerged from the shed to the yard where Peter was held, like spectres coming out of the fog. Two torchlights swayed towards him. In the gloom, he counted five figures striding towards him. *Too late to escape.* He pressed his back against the gate. *Give way. Give way.* The only way they were going to get him out of there was through the gate at the other end. Or they could just shoot him through the rails. That would be easy. *I've seen cattle killed like this. Shit, I don't want to die like a cow.*

'Peter Clancy,' a Russian voice said out of the fog. 'Welcome to my happy farm.'

The man now stood at the side of the rails and Peter was able to see him entirely. A short, squat, bald man with a face like a bulldog, he bore a slight resemblance to Khrushchev. Peter couldn't help but be mesmerised by the man's teeth. They were capped, the eye tooth in gold, and they seemed to shine through the fog. He was followed by a tall, lumbering man with features as ravaged as Keith Richards's. *This must be the man who tried to sell Sam and Dave a stereo*. Behind him stood Donarto and McCracken. And Poppy.

'You should be pleased, Peter Clancy,' the squat man continued. 'You are very popular man. All your friends are here, too. You know, if it wasn't for Poppy, you'd already be dead. So sentimental.'

'Not my fucking friends,' Peter's teeth chattered as he cupped both hands over his groin. 'If we're such good friends, how about letting me go?'

'Yes, I've heard you have big sense of humour. Unfortunately for you, freedom is not possible.' The squat man laughed. 'You see,' he continued, 'They all come to say farewell.'

'Well, then, I'd hate to disappoint them,' quipped Peter. He had no idea where to go to from here. His mind was reeling.

'Anticipation, I find, gives us the greatest pleasure in life. We are not in hurry. I will introduce myself—I'm Viktor Babikov. Russian businessman. How do you say it? Entrepreneur. And this is my associate Dimitry Zlobin. He was butcher before he became weight-lifter in Soviet Union.' Babikov patted Zlobin on the shoulder, who reached inside his jacket and produced a large meat cleaver. 'And of course, the others you know.'

'So why am I here?' Peter asked.

'Still asking the questions. You are a big journalist, but this interview, you will never print. So sad for you. So all right, you ask me and I will answer,' Babikov continued. 'You see, Peter Clancy, we were very happy for you to assist us in destroying the O'Learys. You should have stopped there. When you start looking around our business, you make us very upset.'

'You call killing people with drugs a business?'

'No, no. You don't understand,' Babikov smirked. 'We don't kill anybody. We don't put gun to head and say you must take these drugs. We only supply a market. These days, people want all sorts of drugs, not just heroin or cannabis. They want variety like alcohol, like food.

You want to go to restaurant and only see two meals on the menu? No. With your help, my business partners and I control all the Melbourne market. And soon we will own O'Leary's wharf. Then slowly, slowly, we own all of Australia.'

'Why bother telling me all this?' interrupted Peter.

Babikov frowned. 'You should know how pathetic and futile your life was before you die. You think you can make a difference to anything? You make big fuss and the O'Learys are out of business but not us, never us. Don't you know, Peter Clancy, we are connected with, how you say it, the Russian mafia? Money is no object. What we cannot buy, we destroy. It is the winning formula, Peter Clancy. You we bought with your dick, with our little Poppy. In little while, we will control the wharves, the airports, the police, the law, the politicians. We are unstoppable.'

'You're a crazy fucking bastard, Babikov,' Peter said.

'Not crazy, Peter Clancy. Russian.'

'And you've all done your deals with the devil, by the look of you,' Peter glared at Donarto, McCracken and Poppy.

'They had individual skills that could help our business. And in return, I have been very generous.'

'I can understand McCracken being handy, but Donarto? Fat piece of shit.'

'Let me kill him,' Donarto raged as he pushed his hands through the rails in an attempt to grab Peter. 'I'll cut your fucking balls off.'

'Let Dimitry do that. He will do a better job,' McCracken sniggered as he took hold of Donarto.

'What's the use of Donarto?' Peter asked.

Babikov sighed. 'You are disappointment, Peter Clancy. All it will take is a generous donation to his party to make him mayor of Melbourne. A mayor is a good thing to have in your pocket, don't you think? Your story about him with that girl—pfft—forgotten,' Babikov concluded with a clap of his hands.

'And you used Poppy to lure me here?'

'Poppy was very helpful babysitter for you. It was her suggestion to bring you here. She is very clever girl,' Babikov replied turning to Poppy.

Peter glared at her. 'Fraternising with your clients—that's not the Poppy I knew.'

'You never knew me,' she replied impassively, avoiding eye contact. 'Nor were you meant to. I was just doing business. And in business you have to destroy the opposition.'

'You cold, psycho bitch!' he cried. 'I had feelings for you. I even let you tie me up. You mad bitch. Wasn't I fucking crazy?' He ran at the rails thrusting his hands through in an attempt to grab one of them. Donarto and McCracken stood back and started to laugh. Poppy looked away.

'You're not a big man now, Clancy,' McCracken sneered.

'I'm going inside. I'm getting cold,' Poppy stated abruptly.

'We're staying,' said McCracken. 'Watching Clancy die will be the highlight of this whole bloody saga.'

Poppy looked bored. 'And one final thing, Peter. You asked me once which was my favourite Frederick Forsyth book.' She turned away and began walking back to the shed. 'It's *The Odessa File*.'

Fucking bitch, Peter thought.

'He is getting agitated,' Babikov pointed to Zlobin. 'And he is boring me. Do it now.'

Zlobin nodded slowly in agreement and lumbered towards the gate, brandishing his cleaver. Peter threw himself against the gate at the opposite end of the cattle yard, as Zlobin advanced. Peter detected that the cattle were getting uneasy.

'Why don't you just fucking shoot me, you big bastard?'

'Too quick,' Babikov sneered. 'Killing can be pleasurable. Like hunting. It can give you joy.'

Zlobin raised the cleaver as he approached Peter. Peter kept pressing hard against the gate. The cattle started to call out in panic and push up against each other.

'Stay still,' Babikov advised, 'and it won't hurt as much.'

'Fuck you, commo,' Peter yelled as he attempted to kick Zlobin in the groin. Like kicking a cement post. Then snap, a cracking sound, as the wood fractured. Peter felt himself falling backwards as the gate broke away. The cattle were bunched together but instead of trampling him, they jumped over, rushing towards Zlobin, who was attempting to push them away from him. One large steer slammed its head into Zlobin's abdomen and he dropped the cleaver. He was toppled to the ground by the impact still holding his abdomen, as the cattle trampled him. Babikov rushed to the gate and opened it to let out the cattle.

He jumped back as they charged towards freedom. McCracken and Donarto careered through the yard, dodging and weaving.

Peter rolled away. He remembered how, when he was a child, he had once drifted into a cattle yard and instead of being stomped to death, the cattle had parted as he wandered through the yard and hopped out the other side. Now he stood up and started to run with the cattle, towards the darkness. *Give me the night, give me the bush,* he thought. He could make out thick scrub a hundred metres away. *Safety.* He could hear Babikov, Donarto and McCracken stomping towards him. Peter dropped and hugged the ground as a torch shone in his direction. When it had passed over him he got up and kept running into the night, into the dense undergrowth. He fell against a tree, panting. Then he suddenly heard gunfire. Bullets were coming in his direction. One bullet struck the tree he was leaning against. *Keep going. Keep going.* He kept running, charging headfirst into low hanging limbs, sensing the stony ground under his feet, feeling the pain as his feet were ripped by sharp stones and twigs. *But run where? Can't see. Need help! Need help!* The bullets were still coming.

***

'I think we're lost,' Detective Jenner sighed as she backed up the police car back along the narrow dirt road. 'It looks different at night. Bugger!'

'Do you know where this farm is?' Dave asked.

'I know it's somewhere along here. I've just gone down the wrong track.' Jenner reversed back to the bitumen road and continued to slowly drive.

'Peter's in trouble,' Sam said anxiously. 'I know someone's trying to kill him. I can sense it.'

'How do you know that?' Jenner asked.

'Don't ask,' Dave interrupted. 'He has a sixth sense.'

'Can you sense where the farm is then?' Jenner asked.

'Can't help you on that one,' Sam said.

Just then, Jenner screeched the car to a halt and wound down her window. 'What the?'

Sam and Dave followed suit. 'That's gunfire,' said Dave.

'And not far away,' Sam added.

'I think we need back up,' Jenner said nervously. She lifted the handset of the radio transmitter from its holder and was about to speak into it.

'What's that?' Dave yelled.

A few metres ahead of them, a white silhouette flashed alongside the road, caught for a moment in the headlights. It was moving towards them.

'Bloody hell! I think it's Peter!' Sam added.

Jenner lifted up her head, dropping the handset as she caught sight of a naked, torn and bloodied Peter falling across the bonnet of the car.

31

Tullamarine International Airport. Two weeks later

'Are you sure you want to go to London?' Sam asked as he sat with Peter in the waiting lounge. 'Not running away again, are you?'

'Why do you want to go so far away? You could pick any job you want now. You cracked open a huge overseas drug ring. Because of you, McCracken, Donarto and Poppy, along with those Russians are going to jail for a long time. They reckon there's going to be a Royal Commission into police corruption. All of it is due to you,' Dave said. 'You were a big part of it. You know that.'

'Sorry, I just want to get away,' Peter explained. 'I've got some bad memories.'

'It's not about that bloody Poppy, is it?' Sam asked.

'I don't know. I'm not a good judge of women, I guess.'

'Don't run away, Peter,' he responded, 'just go for a holiday. Have a rest.'

'No. No,' Peter insisted. 'I've always had this ambition of working in London with the big boys. You'll take care of the Stag for me, Sam, won't you? While I'm away?'

'I said I would, didn't I? Got the keys right here, young fella.' He patted his trouser pocket.

'You know you've nothing to prove now,' Dave remarked.

'It's not that. I just don't want to get to forty and realise my life's slipped away. I've got to give it a go. What about yourselves? What are you going to do?'

'Melbourne's interesting all right, but it's not home. We're thinking of heading back to Queensland sooner or later,' Sam answered. 'Apparently Shazza might come with us.'

'Looking serious, Dave,' Peter smiled.

'Looks that way. Who knows, we may even get engaged,' Dave blushed.

'Congratulations,' Peter shook Dave's hand. 'You're not worried about seeing Max again?'

'Queensland's big enough for us to stay out of each other's way.'

Their laughter was interrupted by an announcement over the public address system.

Qantas Flight QF1 to London via Singapore is now ready for boarding through gate lounge thirty-seven.

'Young fella,' Sam said as he cleared his throat, 'there's something I want to tell you before you go.'

'Yeah,' Peter said impatiently as grabbed his carry-on bag, 'but you better make it quick.'

'You know how I said my real name is Samson Clancy?'

Peter was distracted by the farewells of others around them. 'Sorry, Sam, but can't it wait? Only my plane's boarding.' He leapt to his feet.

'No worries. Can't miss your plane. We'll catch up soon,' he grinned.

'In London? Melbourne's a country town compared to London.'

'The Queen lives there,' Sam joked. 'She'll look after me.'

'I'll be in touch,' Peter said as he shook Dave's and then Sam's hand.

'I just know it, young fella. Wherever you go,' Sam laughed, 'there's going to be bloody trouble. And I'm going to be the one who will have to get you out of it. I just know it.'

He was almost through the doors leading to customs before Dave noticed that Peter had left a book behind. Twenty-two hours and nothing to read seemed an awful prospect. He picked up the book and ran after him.

'Here, you almost forgot this,' he said, handing it to Peter. 'Good book?'

'Thanks, mate, it's an old favourite of mine. *The Odessa File.* You should read it someday.'

'Not a big reader, I'm afraid,' said Dave.

'Well then,' Peter declared with a grin, 'just in case you never get around to it, I'll tell you how it ends. The journalist wins. Remember that.'

Dave looked at him blankly. 'Have a great trip, mate.'

Peter tucked the book under his arm, and chuckled to himself. With a final wave goodbye to Sam, he farewelled marvellous, murderous Melbourne and disappeared through the automatic sliding doors.

THE END